A MENACING MEMORY

It was a newspaper clipping from twelve years ago. She stared at it for a long time. The face of a handsome young man, now long dead, stared back at her from the floor. The headline read COLLEGE STUDENT FOUND DEAD. Across the text of the article was written in black block letters, "HAVE YOU EVER DONE ANYTHING YOU'RE ASHAMED OF?"

Jess started to tremble. She crossed her arms tightly over her chest, but couldn't stop the shaking. She whispered, "No, *No* . . ."

She squeezed her eyes tightly shut, but her knees began to buckle. She sank slowly to the floor, hugging herself, shaking herself, trying hard not to cry. . . .

EXPOSURE

DONNA BALL

EXPOSURE

A SIGNET BOOK

SIGNET
Published by the Penguin Group
Penguin Books USA Inc., 375 Hudson Street,
New York, New York 10014, U.S.A.
Penguin Books Ltd, 27 Wrights Lane,
London W8 5TZ, England
Penguin Books Australia Ltd, Ringwood,
Victoria, Australia
Penguin Books Canada Ltd, 10 Alcorn Avenue,
Toronto, Ontario, Canada M4V 3B2
Penguin Books (N.Z.) Ltd, 182-190 Wairau Road,
Auckland 10, New Zealand

Penguin Books Ltd, Registered Offices:
Harmondsworth, Middlesex, England

First published by Signet, an imprint of Dutton Signet,
a division of Penguin Books USA Inc.

First Printing, April, 1996
10 9 8 7 6 5 4 3 2 1

 REGISTERED TRADEMARK—MARCA REGISTRADA

Printed in the United States of America

PUBLISHER'S NOTE
This is a work of fiction. Names, characters, places, and incidents either
are the product of the author's imagination or are used fictitiously,
and any resemblance to actual persons, living or dead, events, or locales
is entirely coincidental.

Chapter 1

On Jessamine Cray's thirty-second birthday two things happened. Her show, in syndication for only two years, was picked up in four more major markets, and she received her first threatening fan letter.

She did not understand the threat then, of course. No one did. All she saw was another piece of unsigned, unmarked, slightly weird fan mail. In her job she got a lot of that. This one was not as creepy as some, but it had its own peculiar charm. And for that reason she noticed it.

Twelve minutes before the show Jess had a lot on her mind, not the least of which was how to keep anyone from finding out it was her birthday. When one is in a job that prizes youth and beauty far above brains or skill, one does not advertise any birthdays past twenty-eight. She trusted the excitement over the new markets would act in her favor on that score, although Jess's ten years of television experience had taught her not to get excited about anything until it was in writing and signed by at least two network executives.

The studio was in chaos. The stage manager was screaming at the director, and the director was screaming back; the cameramen were playing poker; the producer was locked in the sound booth, meditating. Twelve minutes before the show, everyone dealt with the tension in his or her own way. Jess's cohost, for example, who liked to think of himself as a serious journalist, was no doubt studying his background material, preparing for his interviews, greeting the guests. Jess preferred to read fan mail.

She threaded her way through the jungle of cables, cameras, and dollies, making a point to smile at everyone she passed, whether or not they glanced in her direction. She didn't really think those smiles made a difference in how well she was liked—not that it even mattered whether or not the assistant script girl or the fill-in electrician liked her—but Jessamine Cray had been smiling since she was ten years old, and it was a hard habit to break. She reached her office through the buzz of activity in the bullpen—last-minute changes being jockeyed back and forth, research material being faxed in, telephones being manned—with ten minutes before air time. She closed the door.

Jess's office had glass half walls on three sides. She told herself she liked the sense of accessibility a glass office gave her, but the truth was that the *Speaking of Which* studio shared space with the local station, WSBN Philadelphia, and their office space had once been the newsroom in days when glass half walls had been in vogue. No one had ever offered to change it for her, and Jess had never asked.

Inside the office twelve square feet of the one solid wall was taken up by framed awards and certificates, mostly from local women's clubs, rotary clubs, and charities. Centered and prominently displayed were two framed magazine covers, both featuring the smiling face of Jessamine Cray. One was from *People* two years ago, and the other from *TV Guide* three months ago. The *TV Guide* cover featured Jess looking witty and creative in a pair of oversized reading glasses and a caption that read, "The girl with the incredible eyes . . ."

The wall did not contain covers from *Time* or *Newsweek,* an Emmy Award or a Pulitzer, nor was it likely to. There had been a lot of controversy among the staff about the *TV Guide* caption, which Jess shrugged off while contentedly framing and hanging the cover. She *did* have incredible eyes—aqua green rimmed with startling black—and she had been called worse things than "girl" by members of her own crew. Jessamine Cray was a mill worker's daughter from Jackson, Mississippi, and the first woman in her family ever to go to college. She knew how to make the best of what she had.

Every morning her secretary, Sylvia, opened and stacked the fan mail in time for Jess to look through it before the ten-thirty show. She never sorted or censored it; Jess wanted the negative feedback as well as the positive. She even had a little superstition in which she judged the success of the upcoming show by the number of positive fan letters she could read before the taping.

Today looked like a good one. The first three letters were raves. Someone loved the compassion with which she treated her guests. Someone else liked the way she wore her hair on April third. Yet another really liked the show about prison guards who fell in love with their wards and wanted to know where he could write one of the guests. That one was a little strange, but she put it in the positive stack anyway.

The next envelope was typed and addressed simply, "Jessamine Cray, Speaking of Which." That wasn't unusual, and she didn't glance at the envelope twice. Inside was a single sheet of folded white paper. In the center was the typed line:

Have you ever done anything you're ashamed of?

For a moment she just frowned at it, not understanding. She even started to crumple it and move on to the next one, then she hesitated.

Have you ever done anything you're ashamed of?

Creepy. Just a little.

That was when she noticed the envelope didn't have a return address. Or a stamp. She punched the intercom button. "Sylvia!"

When there was no answer, she tried again, then stood and looked through the glass wall. She could see her secretary was not at her desk. "Damn it," she muttered. Five minutes until air time. She shoved the letter into the oversized pocket of her jacket and left the office. She wasn't taking any more chances with fan mail. She didn't want to jinx the show.

Trish Siegel, producer of *Speaking of Which* for the past five years, met her halfway to the set.

"Did you read the book?" she demanded.

"What book?"

"The book whose author you're interviewing in the first segment. Jesus, they hate it when you don't read their books."

"I'm sure Dan read it. He always does."

"You're leading off the interview!"

"I read the cover." Jess thrust the folded paper at her. "What do you make of this?"

Trish unfolded the letter and squinted at it myopically, then grunted. "Honey, I haven't had *time* to do anything I'm ashamed of in the past twenty years." She returned the letter and pushed a hardbound book into Jess's hand. "At least hold it in your lap, will you? Maybe you'll look like you know what you're talking about."

Dan was waiting for them on the set. Dark haired, good-looking, not too tall. Star material.

"Well, if it isn't the girl with the incredible eyes," he drawled when he saw her. He didn't always know when to let a good thing go. "Morning, ladies."

Jess hoisted herself up into the high-back stool, arranging her skirt and accepting a few last-minute touches from the makeup girl. The letter was tucked back in her jacket pocket and by now almost forgotten. She flipped through the book. "The author of a book called *Dead Love* and the cop who caught the Silk Scarf Killer on the same show? Who thinks up these things, anyway?"

"Women," replied Dan, and the theme music began.

Jess smiled into Camera Two. "Welcome to another episode of *Speaking of Which*," she said. "I'm Jessamine Cray."

"And I'm Dan Webber. On today's show . . ."

It was a good show. Jess worked the audience while Dan interviewed the author in the first segment, and they reversed the procedure during the second. The author, whose book was about a serial killer not too different from the one responsible for the Silk Scarf murders—thus the tie-in—wasn't as dull as most and knew how to hold up his end of an interview. The policeman, Lyle Candler, was easygoing and articulate, which was also a surprise.

They brought him on during a commercial, an average-looking man in his mid-thirties who had probably spent more than he could afford on the blazer he wore for the television appearance. Jess never met guests before the show and tried to compensate by making them feel at home on the set.

She smiled as he was being anchored into his microphone. "Nervous?"

He glanced dubiously down at the microphone suspended by a network of wires from his lapel. "You better believe it."

She chuckled. "Me, too."

He looked surprised. "You do this every day. I've never been on television before."

"And I've never tracked down a serial killer before. Relax, Detective. You've already done the hard part."

That made him laugh, and when the countdown started, they were both ready for the cameras. "And now," Jess said into Camera One, "from fiction to fact . . ."

The Silk Scarf murders had made national headlines for weeks, not because of the nature of the crime, which was not particularly shocking by the standards of the day, but because of the location and, to some extent, the age of the victims. Six young women had been found strangled, naked and bound hand and foot with silk scarves—but not sexually assaulted—on various high-school campuses in the Philadelphia area, creating panic among parents, students, and school officials for almost half a school year. All had been blondes, and all but two had been cheerleaders.

It was a great interview, despite the author, who kept trying to draw attention back to himself with irrelevant questions about copycat killers and comments like "Of course, in my book . . ." Candler had an easy, down-to-earth manner that made the audience feel like a privileged part of a police investigation. The phone lines backed up with calls. Jess added another show to the case file she was mentally building to prove that a talk show did not have to be dirty or outrageous to be interesting.

After each show it was part of Jess's routine to thank each guest and the studio audience. Dan warmed them up; Jess saw them out. More often than not she had to stretch for nice things to say to the guests, but this time it was easy.

"You were great," she said to Candler, shaking his hand warmly. Then she glanced at the writer, whose name was already slipping from her memory. "Both of you, really. Thanks so much."

The writer looked disgruntled and mumbled something as he tried to disengage himself from his microphone. The stage manager came forward to help.

"Great show!" Trish announced, striding onto the set. "Gentlemen, thank you." She helped Candler off with his mike. To Jess she said, "You coming to the party?"

"What party?"

"The one celebrating the new markets, of course."

Jess groaned. "Do I have to? I hate those things."

"Five o'clock, on the set. Be there."

Dan shook Candler's hand. "It was a pleasure, Detective. You really hooked the audience." He glanced after the retreating writer and added wryly in a slightly lower tone, "To tell the truth, I think *you* should have written the book."

They all laughed, and Candler looked at Jess. "You made it easy."

"That's because I had a fascinating subject," she told him sincerely. "Dan is right; you really should write a book. You have a wonderful stage presence."

He chuckled. "I'm not sure what one thing has to do with the other, but maybe I'll think about it."

"I just wish we could have had more time," Jess said. "Every time you answered one question, I thought of two more, and I didn't get halfway through my list. Why are we all so intrigued by bizarre crimes and the people involved with them, I wonder?"

"Sounds like a topic for your next show." He smiled.

She lifted a finger of acknowledgment, eyes twinkling. "I'll bring it up at the story meeting."

It was time for her to move out into the audience, but he looked as though he had more to say. She hesitated, and he spoke.

"Uh, listen. If you would really like to talk some more . . ." He glanced at his watch. "Maybe we could have lunch."

Jess hated it when that happened. Men were always mistaking her friendly interest for something more, even when they must surely realize it was part of her job.

She found her most regretful smile. "I'm really sorry but . . ."

He was quicker than most. "Of course not. I understand. You can't go out with every guy that comes on the show." A faint haze of embarrassment tinged his cheeks, though she liked the way he tried to hide it with a grin. "I guess they all ask you, too, don't they?"

Jess smiled. "Not all."

Trish called. "Jess! Five o'clock. I mean it!"

Jess looked back at him and impulsively, perhaps because she liked the way he grinned through his embarrassment, she said, "Why don't you come back this afternoon for the party? It's just an informal thing here on the set."

He said, "Thanks, but I'm really more comfortable down at police headquarters than on a TV set. And that's where I should be right now." He shook her hand again. "Thanks again, Ms. Cray. It's been a real pleasure."

He nodded at Dan and followed the stage manager's guidance out of the studio.

Dan draped a solicitous arm around her shoulders. "Yet another heart shattered on the altar of the girl with the incredible eyes."

She scowled at him. "Go work on your tan."

"On my way."

"Dan."

When he looked back, she reached into her pocket and drew out the note. "What do you think of this?"

He read the note. "You taking a poll?"

"It was in with my fan mail this morning."

He clicked his tongue against his teeth, raising an eyebrow at her. "Have you been naughty?"

"What do you think it means?"

He returned the paper to her. "Nothing. The first rule of being a celebrity is 'Don't Read Unsigned Fan Mail.' Hasn't anybody ever told your secretary to screen out this crap?"

"I want to read the crap." She folded the paper back into her pocket. "How else will I know when to start looking for another job?"

He shrugged. "Suit yourself. But I'd think a big-name talk-show hostess like you would have better things to do with her time."

"Are you coming to the party?"

"Hell no, I've got a golf game. Public relations is your job, remember?"

"And what's yours?"

He grinned and tapped his head. "Everything else."

She glared after him for a moment, then walked into the audience, smiling and offering her hand, first to one and then to another. "You've been just great . . . thanks so much for coming . . . it was an exciting show, wasn't it? . . . You're so kind . . . thank you . . ."

Jess was frequently amazed by the number of people who thought her workday ended at eleven-thirty in the morning, as soon as the show finished taping. The truth was that between staff meetings and planning meetings and preparing for the next day's show—not to mention the numerous public appearances that frequently wrecked her schedule—she was often in the office until after eight o'clock. That day was more hectic than usual because she had aerobics and a final fitting on her summer wardrobe—both essential parts of the job—and she had barely settled down at her desk with the file on tomorrow's show when Sylvia buzzed her. "It's five o'clock," she said. "Trish said to remind you about the party before I left."

Again Jess stifled a groan. "She's going to have photographers there, isn't she? Why else would she keep bugging me to be there?"

"She didn't say."

Jess sighed and closed the file. "All right. I'm on my way as soon as I fix my makeup."

"Good night then, Ms. Cray."

She completely forgot to ask Sylvia if she knew anything about the note, and it wasn't until she put on her jacket and slipped her hands into empty pockets that she even thought about it. Somewhere between aerobics and wardrobe fittings the piece of paper had been lost or thrown away.

She made her way down to the set, but could tell at a distance it was dark and empty. Ladders and scaffolding crouched like skeletons in the shadows; coils of cables snaked across the floor. There was nothing quite so eerie as a deserted soundstage, and Jessamine hated the dark.

She called out, just in case she was in the right place at the wrong time, then swore under her breath as she snagged her stocking on a hidden equipment box. She started to turn back, then thought she heard something ahead. She moved forward and stepped into a pit of absolute blackness.

She knew where she was. She knew the set was less than ten feet to her right, with its familiar rose-

and-blue sofa, its high upholstered stools, its cozy coffee table ... at home with Jessamine and Dan, warm and comfortable. She knew the camera stands and booms and dollies and ladders were just out of her range of vision, the trappings of high technology and civilization at its most refined. She knew that she had simply moved into one of those odd pools of shadow where no ambient light reached, and she knew if she waited only another moment, her eyes would adjust and she would see all those things that were just outside the pool. But in those few heart-stopping seconds that she stood there, blind and frozen, logic was wiped away and emotions more primitive took over; she might have been in the heart of the darkest jungle or at the bottom of the deepest sea, and anything could have been lurking in the shadows, ready to snare her.

Only children were afraid of the dark. She wasn't a child.

She clenched her fists tightly at her sides. She made herself call out. "Trish?" Her voice sounded tiny and was quickly swallowed up by the dark. "Hey, who's there?"

Nothing.

It was stupid, she knew, but her heart was pounding. The darkness was inky. Anything could be out there. Anything.

The lights suddenly came on, and the entire staff and crew shouted, "Surprise!" They were gathered around a huge cake with "Happy Birthday, Jess" written on it in pink icing. Jess took a startled step backward, and her hands flew to her face to hide a gasp, but the gasp turned into laughter and the pounding of her heartbeat into delight. Everybody started singing "Happy Birthday." Sylvia thrust a glass of champagne into her hand. Trish threw an arm around her shoulders and pulled her forward. Dan Webber winked at her and lifted his glass in salute.

Jess thought she had a pretty good life.

Jess arrived home about eleven, a little drunk, smiling to herself, very content. It had been a good party—a good day.

Jess lived in a town-house condo with its own enclosed courtyard garden and a view of the pool. It had white plush carpet and an emerald green curved leather sofa. Her mother had never even dreamed of a time when she might have white carpeting on her floors.

There were glass tables and recessed lighting and a large painting of a peacock over the sofa. She kept a fully stocked bar, though she rarely drank anything stronger than wine. She had a gourmet kitchen, though most of her meals were from the microwave, and she had all her dinner parties catered. Twice a month someone came in to feed, water, and maintain the potted plants and trees that cast such artistic shadows on the wall. Sometimes she felt as though she were living in a hotel, but she liked that feeling. It was all part of the lifestyle, and she had worked hard for it.

She had just kicked off her shoes and put down her briefcase—she had brought home the file on tomorrow's show—when the phone rang. She smiled as she answered it.

"Hello, Mama." Her mother hadn't missed calling on Jess's birthday since she had left home.

But the voice on the other end was not her mother's. It was hoarse, raspy, obviously disguised, and almost undistinguishable. It said, "Have you ever done anything you're ashamed of? Have you, Jess? *Have you?*"

Chapter 2

Dan Webber figured he was about half in love with Jessamine Cray, which put him on par with every other man who had ever worked with her, met her, or even nodded to her on the street. She had that kind of face, voice, smile, eyes, look, manner. . . . She was the kind of woman who could sometimes, unexpectedly, and for no good reason at all, make a man's knees go weak just by glancing in his direction.

She was attractive, but not classically beautiful. Her face was too square for current fashion, her forehead too broad, her mouth not quite lush enough. Her eyes were, as others before him had noted, her most remarkable feature. Second would have to be her smile. Her hair was dark, which was unusual in an industry that preferred blondes, and she wore it smooth and shiny, just skimming her shoulders. She was fairly tall for a woman in television and worked hard at keeping her figure, which as far as Dan could tell needed very little work at all.

They had been together for five years, and in that time they had developed their own work rhythms, sensitivities, and patterns. When Jess was in over her head with an interview, Dan knew how to rescue her. When he came in with a hangover, head-ache, or bad attitude, she knew instinctively how to get him back on track. And even if he had not been half in love with her, he would have known something was wrong with her the next afternoon.

Staying trim was not the only thing at which Jess worked hard. Although few would guess it, she worked hard at her job. She didn't always read the books, do the research, and study the background, but she listened, made notes, and spent every minute of every working day formulating her own unique approach to the subject of the upcoming show. So when Dan watched her spend an entire story meeting shredding a bran muffin and staring at the plate, he knew something was wrong.

He walked her back to her office. She was wearing a pair of stovepipe jeans, heels, and a belted white shirt whose tails did not quite cover the rear beneath. He let himself fall behind a step or two to appreciate the view.

When he caught up with her again, he said casually, "So what's up, kiddo?"

She barely glanced at him. "What do you mean?"

"You weren't exactly with us back there."

She gave an irritated little shrug of her shoulders, still not meeting his eyes. "UFO abductees—it's a stupid show."

"Come on, you love that shit."

"Everybody's done it. How many times have we done it this year?"

"Hey, you gotta keep up."

"I hate it when we have those weirdos on."

"They're all weirdos."

She said, "I think I'm being stalked."

He let a beat pass in silence.

"It happens." Now she looked at him, and there was real worry in her eyes. "David Letterman, Michael J. Fox, Jodie Foster . . ."

"Now you've hit the big time."

She pushed open the door of her office and he followed her inside. "So what happened? More fan mail?"

She gave him a look that was so sharp and suspicious that he automatically put up his hands in self-defense. "Sorry."

She made her shoulders relax and went behind the desk. "You're right, it's stupid. I should just ignore it."

"I never said that."

He sat on the edge of her desk, consciously aware of striking a pose for the benefit of everyone in the bullpen who happened to glance in their direction. He had a theory about Jess and her glass walls—that she ensured her privacy by making sure she never had any. Nothing untoward ever happened behind Jessamine Cray's closed door, no secrets were ever hidden there. Office gossip was defused before it ever started because everything was out in the open.

"Come on, now I'm curious. What's going on?"

She opened a file drawer and took out a bulging brown folder. UFO clips, no doubt.

"Someone called me last night, late. I think it was the same person who sent that note yesterday."

Dan frowned a little. "Not good."

She sat down behind the desk, but didn't open the file. "He said the same thing—'Have you ever done anything you're ashamed of?' He was disguis-

ing his voice. It was . . ." The shudder she suppressed was not entirely exaggerated. "Creepy."

Dan said, "Get an unlisted number."

She looked up at him. "I already have one."

For a moment he didn't know what to say. She
slid open her top drawer and took out a thin white
envelope, then held it in her hand for a moment as
though deciding whether or not to trust him with
its contents.

She said, "This came in the morning's mail."

Dan reached for the envelope, but still she held
onto it for another second, uncertain. When she
finally released it, Dan didn't know what to expect.

He scanned the single sheet of paper, front and
back, twice before finally admitting, "I don't get it."
He looked up. "It's a job application."

Jess swallowed. Her hands were clasped together
tightly on the desk, the skin drawn white and
smooth over the delicate shape of her knuckles. "It's
my application, for the first job I ever had in television. It's ten years old."

He turned the paper back over, confirming what
he'd already seen. "So where did it come from?"

"That's just it. I don't know."

Dan looked at the envelope again. There was no
return address, and the postmark was from the
downtown post office. "Strange," he admitted, "but
I don't see the point. Everybody knows you got your
break as the hometown weather girl. It's part of
your legend."

Jess said, "That's just it. I got my break because
of that job, and I got that job because . . ." Her
hands tightened. "I lied on the application."

"Oh, yeah?" Dan scanned the paper again.

"Where? Name, age, sex . . . you've gotta be damn good to fake that . . ."

"Education," she interrupted shortly, and though her tone was terse, her hands relaxed, almost as though she were relieved to have it out in the open. "See, he highlighted it with yellow."

Again Dan turned the paper over, checking. "So?"

"It says there I graduated from the University of Georgia. I didn't."

"Where did you graduate?"

"Nowhere. I left school in the middle of my junior year. I never finished."

Dan made a noncommittal sound and looked back at the paper. "I still don't get it."

"You wouldn't." Jess leaned forward and snatched the paper from him.

"You're not telling me you're *embarrassed* because you didn't finish college?"

"You don't think there's something just a little bit strange about somebody who'd go to all the trouble to dig up a ten-year-old job application and send it to me through the mail?"

"Weird, definitely. Threatening, hardly."

"Who would do such a thing?"

"Who cares?" He got to his feet. "This is definitely small potatoes. Let me know when you start getting dead roses through the mail. Better yet, dead decapitated roses."

"Real funny, Webber. I can't tell you what a comfort you are."

"Come on, Jess, what are you afraid of? That Trish will fire you if she finds out you didn't finish college?"

"Do you think you could keep this to yourself?"

"Not a chance." He turned for the door, then paused to assure her, "They won't fire you, you know. College education or not, you've still got the cutest ass on television."

Jess watched him leave the room, expressionless. She even watched him stop by Sylvia's desk and dispense what he considered the requisite amount of charm to the office staff.

When he was gone, she opened the file folder and pretended to peruse its contents. What she was really looking at was the ten-year-old job application she had surreptitiously placed on top. And she was trying, very hard, not to remember what had happened her junior year of college.

Damn it all, anyway, she thought, and before she could stop herself, her hand tightened convulsively on the paper, crumpling the job application into a ball. *"Damn* it," she whispered out loud.

She glanced around quickly to make certain no one had observed her outburst, mild though it was. Then she tossed the paper into the trash can under her desk and turned her attention back to the file folder, really reading it this time.

She told herself she felt better, but she didn't. She told herself to forget it, but she couldn't. And she told herself it was over, but she knew it wasn't.

Jeremy Styles turned off the television set and resumed his seat in front of the blank screen, pulling the tab on another beer. He didn't usually drink during the day—it was bad for discipline—but he had had four in the past hour. The first had been in celebration. The last had been an anesthetic.

Jessamine Cray, he decided with the calm rationality of one well over the edge of inebriation, was an idiot. Jessamine Cray of the short, sassy skirts and teacup tits, so delectable on the outside, was an intellectual midget, an imbecile, a cretinous boor with all the taste and discernment of a third-world illiterate, cotton dust and cobwebs on the inside. And despite all that, or perhaps because of it, she had somehow managed to make him look like a fool.

That he couldn't allow. That was completely unacceptable.

He had taped the show. He would watch it again later tonight. And he would watch it again after that, and again. He was not the first to observe that there was a singular and undeniable relationship between hatred and obsession.

He was a man of reason, not physicality. Miss Jessamine Cray had made it perfectly clear what kind of man she preferred, and it was equally clear he could not compete in that arena. But she had to be shown a thing or two. She might be a mental deficient, but she wasn't incapable of learning.

And it would be such a pleasure to teach her.

He reached for the phone and dialed the number he knew by heart. When the line was answered, he requested his extension and waited for his party to come on the line.

"Roz," he said warmly, for he wasn't so drunk he couldn't make himself sound perfectly sober with minimal effort. "Jeremy Styles. Just wanted to thank you for that last package . . . yeah, it was great. Just what I needed. Listen, I've got kind of a challenge for you. What if I wanted to find out everything I could about Jessamine Cray? . . . Yeah, that's right. Where would I start?"

He listened for a while, nodding and making an occasional note on the pad he always kept by the phone. Then he smiled, thanked the voice on the other end, and hung up. He sat back, satisfied, and reached for another beer. This was going to be easier than he'd thought.

Research, after all, was his specialty.

Chapter 3

At five-thirty that afternoon the door to Jess's office was flung open and Trish strode in. "Happy hour," she announced. "Let's go."

Jess switched off the microcassette recorder into which she had been dictating replies to fan letters. She glanced up a little distractedly. "Oh, Trish. Sorry, I can't. I promised Sylvia I'd have these ready to be typed in the morning, and I'm not even halfway through."

Trish gave a disgusted shake of her head, which sent her long silver earrings to jangling. "You've got a few things to learn about television, young lady. The first is, when the boss asks you out for drinks, you go. The second is, don't let your secretary push you around. Come on." She took Jess's purse from the coatrack near the door; then handed it to her. "Pack it in. Let's get to Charlie's before all the good ones get away."

Charlie's Tavern was across the street from the studio, a popular hangout for lawyers, stockbrokers, and up-and-coming politicians, as well as newsroom personnel. Jess always felt a little self-conscious going in there, but Trish was right—you didn't turn down the boss.

She transferred the unanswered letters and cassette recorder into her briefcase. "My birthday was yesterday."

"So?"

"So what's the occasion?"

"Does there have to be an occasion?"

"You don't ask me out for drinks every day."

"Yeah, well I just didn't want people to think we were lovers. I'd watch that birthday talk if I were you, by the way. In this business it doesn't pay to advertise your age."

Jess swung the straps of her briefcase and her purse over her shoulder. "I don't suppose you'd consider going to Aubergine would you?"

Again the earrings jangled. "They water down the drinks with fruit juice. I'm buying, I pick the saloon."

Jess lifted an eyebrow. "You're buying? I'm impressed."

Trish Siegel was somewhere between thirty-five and fifty years old—following her own advice, she never let it slip—rail thin, hyperkinetic, and abrasive. She wore her brown hair blunt-cut above the ears. Her work uniform was jeans and combat boots, her only decoration a variety of outrageous earrings. She was a chain smoker and lit a cigarette as soon as they were on the street.

"So what is this crap about your receiving threatening mail?" she demanded.

Jess stifled a groan. "Good God. Dan Webber gossips like an old woman."

"On behalf of women everywhere, I object to that remark. He didn't tell me; as a matter of fact, Sylvia did."

"It's nothing, it's stupid. Try to keep a secret in this place."

"Sweetheart, we're not in the secret-keeping business."

The light changed and they crossed the street with the surge of the crowd. Jess liked crowds, she always had. The feeling of being part of the mass, swept along with the tide, lost in the herd—it felt safe to her somehow. Jess doubted she would ever be comfortable living in a small town again.

"Do you know what you need?" Trish demanded as she pushed open the door of the bar.

"A vacation."

Charlie's was dark and noisy. The local news was on television. The bar was crowded with men in shirtsleeves and ties. More than one head turned to observe their entry.

Trish gestured expansively. "Take your pick."

"You ought to be ashamed of yourself. Men aren't the solution to every problem. I read that somewhere."

They moved toward a vacant booth.

"You're right. They're the cause of most of them. But they have been known to be an excellent anti-dote to depression. *I* read that somewhere."

"I'm not depressed."

Jess slid into the booth, placing her briefcase and purse on the seat beside her. Trish took the opposite side, trailing cigarette smoke, and leaned across the table. "The world is full of assholes, Jess," she said. "The trick is not to let them ruin your day." She gave an elaborate shrug and stubbed out her ciga-rette. "It's part of the job. What can I tell you?"

Jess was growing uncomfortable. "I told you, it's

nothing. How did a couple of letters get to be such a big deal?"

"You're the talent," Trish replied around another cigarette. She struck a match. "Of course it's a big deal."

A dark-haired, sloe-eyed waiter hovered over them. "Jack Daniels," Trish told him. "And something fruity for the lady."

"Wine spritzer," Jess said.

Trish watched him go, turning in her seat a little. "Not bad," she observed.

"He's gay," said Jess.

"God, what a cliché."

Jess edged away unobtrusively from the stream of smoke, which was another reason she hated coming to Charlie's. She would have to wash her hair before going to bed to get the smell out, and the blouse would have to be dry-cleaned. Aubergine had a non-smokers section . . . not, of course, that that would have stopped Trish.

A man at the bar was staring at Jess. When she caught his eye, he quickly looked away. That made Jess want to sink down a little further in her seat.

Trish muttered, "Shit."

"What?"

"Smile. Your best friend is homing in."

Jess twisted around to see Casey Darnell waving as she made her way toward her. Jess had made the mistake of getting the flu for eight days last year. Since the show had just gone into syndication and the schedule was tight, Trish had had to bring in a replacement. Casey Darnell was that replacement, and the audience had loved her—so much that she had been back three times since. Casey was twenty-four years old, blond, perky, and she wanted Jess's job with undisguised avarice. Jess thought sourly that she wouldn't put it past Casey to have made that phone call last night in an attempt to upset Jess enough to miss a show.

"Hi, Jess; hi, Trish." Casey swooped down on Jess and enveloped her in a cloud of flowery perfume, kissing the air beside her cheek. She knew Trish would never stand for that kind of behavior. "How's everything with the *Speaking of Which* crowd? God, I miss you guys. Doing that show is the most fun I've ever had."

Jess smiled weakly, and Trish took another drag on her cigarette.

Casey scanned their table. "Having dinner?"

"Yes," said Jess.

"No," Trish said.

Casey waited a moment expectantly. No one invited her to sit down. Jess avoided her eyes and felt small and foolish. But she didn't speak up.

"Well," Casey said brightly, "I'm just on my way out. Say hello to Dan, will you?" And she winked. "Tell him to give me a call sometime."

Trish said, "Nice seeing you, Casey."

And Jess added, " 'Bye, Casey."

When she was gone, Trish pretended to shudder. "Casey and Dan? Now there's a picture I don't need floating around in my head."

"We were rude."

"I might have to work with her now and then, but I don't have to like her. And rule number three in television—you're allowed to be rude to someone who's after your job."

The waiter brought their drinks. Trish looked after him soulfully.

Jess said, "Do me a favor."

"If it's about making this the Jess and Dan show," Trish said with an adamant shake of her head, "no can do. You two already have a better deal than I do, and to be frank, the powers that be just aren't ready to build this show around personalities yet. I mean, hell, you know what the competition is. Forget fifteen minutes of fame—the day will come when everyone in America will have his own talk show, and it's starting to look to me as though that day might be next week. So we're keeping it loose for now, more chance to grow. Don't let it bother you, though; you and Dan made this show, and we all know it. You can still call the shots when push comes to shove."

Jess almost smiled. She had heard the speech before, and she knew the only reason Trish felt compelled to repeat it now was because of the new markets. The more markets they got, the more power the stars were likely to grab. But Jess wasn't ready to make that kind of noise yet.

She said, "Actually, I was going to ask you to turn around and look at that guy at the bar. The one with the red hair. Do you know him?"

Trish looked annoyed at her own faux pas, but she did as she was asked. "No," she replied, snuffing out her cigarette. "Cute pecs though."

Jess sipped her drink. "He keeps staring at me."

"You could do worse."

Jess shook her head. Her stomach muscles were tense, and she found herself consciously trying to avoid looking at the bar—which was directly in her line of vision. "It's not that kind of staring," she said lowly. "It's . . . weird. Sneaky."

Trish lit another cigarette, looking at Jess for a moment. "You're in tens of thousands of living rooms every morning," she said. "You're also a fairly attractive woman. When you go out, people are going to stare. Men are going to stare. Surprise."

Jess took a breath. "You're right. He's probably just trying to hit on me. God, I hate this." And she still couldn't make herself look at the bar.

Trish said seriously, "It's a control thing, you know. These letter-writing terrorists, these telephone highwaymen—most of the time they're twisted little men with quarter-inch dicks who get their jollies by fantasizing about the rich and famous. They don't have a life of their own, so they try to be part of yours—in whatever sick, deviant way they can."

Jess took a larger swallow of her drink. "I can't tell you how much better that makes me feel."

"He only has as much power as you give him," Trish said.

Jess glanced at the bar. He was looking at her. He didn't look friendly. He didn't look like someone who recognized a celebrity or was thinking about trying to pick up a woman. His stare was flat and gray, and this time he didn't look away first. Jess quickly broke eye contact and shrank further against the wall, trying to block his line of sight.

Trish waved at the cloud of smoke that was drifting Jess's way. "Does this bother you? Why didn't you say something? Jesus, you're such a wimp."

She stubbed out the cigarette. Jess started to protest, then thought better of it. She said, focusing on her drink again, "I thought about it all night. 'Have you ever done anything you're ashamed of.' What an oddball thing to say. A person could go crazy thinking about it."

"Probably the point." Trish lit another cigarette. It wasn't until she spoke again that Jess realized she seemed nervous, even for Trish, and that she was smoking more than usual.

"There's something else," Trish said.

Jess tensed.

Trish looked at the tip of her cigarette, flipped some ashes in the general direction of the ashtray, and took another draw. She said, "Dan's been offered his own show."

Jess stared at her.

"He hasn't decided yet. We've got a lot on our side. The new deal is a little sweeter, but it's risky and he knows it. The market is overcrowded, blah blah, he's got a sure thing here. We've got a good chance of keeping him. But I thought you ought to know."

Jess said, "And I was having such a good day." She took a long swallow of her drink, forcing her voice to remain calm, her expression even. "He couldn't have told me himself?"

Trish replied briefly, "He wouldn't. Not until he was sure."

A surge of anger tightened every muscle in Jess's body. Anger at Dan, who thought nothing of betraying a five-year partnership, who couldn't even face her like a man, who held her entire career in the palm of his hand and didn't bother to mention that he might be tossing it out the window any day now. Anger at Trish, who was obviously so well-rehearsed at that "no can do" speech because she had just given it to Dan, she who was going behind Dan's back to confide in Jess with the obvious hope of playing both ends against the middle while she pretended to be a friend to both of them. And anger at herself because she was so damn gullible, and she knew she wouldn't confront either one of them about taking advantage of that.

She said, still calmly, "When?"

"I think they came to him a couple of days ago."

Jess said, watching her carefully, "Should I call my agent?"

Trish smiled. "Let's wait a few days, see what happens. I'll keep you informed."

Right, Jess thought, *about everything but what kind of deal you end up cutting Dan in order to keep him* . . . And then she was ashamed of herself. Trish was a producer, she couldn't be faulted for acting like one. Dan had a right to do whatever was necessary to get ahead. After all, she hadn't gotten this far herself without cutting a few deals along the way. She was still angry, but she tried to push it aside. It was no one's fault.

The uncomfortable silence went on a few minutes longer, then Trish said, "So, how's your sex life?"

Jess tried to relax. "Back to that again."

Trish shrugged. "I'm running out of material. Besides, I'm curious. I've known you five years and don't remember you being in what is popularly called a relationship once."

Jess thought about Brett. Eyes so blue that, the first time she had seen them, they had taken her breath away. God, it was so long ago. And only yesterday.

"It could lead to a suspect, you know."

Jess was startled. "What?"

"Old boyfriends, old grudges . . . ?"

"Oh." Jess leaned back in the booth, wriggling a little further from the bar. She could still see the redhead, though, and his head was turned in her direction. God, she hated this. "I can't tell you how relieved I am to hear that. I was beginning to think all this interest you're showing in my social life was leading up to a proposition."

"I didn't think beauty queens from Mississippi knew about things like that."

"And I didn't think television producers knew about tracking down suspects."

"Hey, you produce this show long enough and you get to be an expert on just about everything."

Jess lifted her glass again. "Well, the answer is no. No boyfriends, no recent exes, not even any bad dates, lately."

"That's pathetic. Why don't you go out and have yourself a wild fling, get written up in the tabloids, maybe have a few indiscreet photos published—it'd be great for the show and sure as hell wouldn't do you any harm to have a little fun."

"Thank you, I have enough problems."

"You know what they say about all work and no play. Maybe I should call that redhead over."

She turned as though to do so, and Jess looked up. He was gone. For some reason that made Jess's heart pound with brief alarm.

Trish looked back with a shrug. "Not in the cards. But come on now, think hard. Isn't there someone you're just the least bit interested in?"

Jess's heartbeat settled down, and she was embarrassed over her reaction. The poor guy had probably been nothing more than a curious fan, and if she had had her way, she would have had him arrested. This had to stop. She couldn't let herself be manipulated this way.

She said, deliberately forcing herself to relax, "Well, there's this guy who lives across the courtyard from me. He's an artist or a photographer, I think. Sometimes he works out in front of his picture window."

"In the buff?"

Jess returned a steady look. "You're a very strange woman, Trish."

Trish shrugged. "I say go for him. An artist is better than nothing."

Jess said, "Do you want to order something to eat?"

"Can't." Trish glanced at her watch. "I've got a dinner at eight. Little black dress time. Can't tell you how I'm looking forward to that."

They were silent for a time, Trish finishing her cigarette, gazing absently around the bar. Occasionally she'd spot a familiar face and nod a greeting. Jess saw quite a few of those faces, too—familiar, but not quite recognizable, studio people, prop people, news people, people she saw every day but didn't really know. It should have been comforting to be surrounded by so many commonplace faces, but these weren't friendly strangers to her, they were just strangers. And she hated what she was thinking: Any one of them could have sent the note. Any one of them could have tracked down an old job application and made a phone call. . . .

Trish said, "So have you?"

Jess took another swallow of her drink, finishing it off. "Have I what?"

"Ever done anything you're ashamed of?"

Jess took a long slow breath that was shakier than she expected it to be. "Jesus. Haven't you?"

Trish looked at her long and steadily. Then she abruptly tossed down the last of her drink and stubbed out her cigarette. "Hell, no. I'm perfect. Ready to go?"

On the way out Jess spotted the redheaded man. He was having dinner with a woman and another man at one of the tables near the window. On impulse she left Trish's side and made her way over to them.

He looked up when she stood beside them. Dull gray eyes. Too pale skin.

"Hello," she said and extended her hand. "I'm Jessamine Cray."

He stood up, holding his napkin. His handshake was surprisingly hot. "Rick Baker," he said, and he smiled. "I know who you are, Miss Cray."

When he smiled, Jess knew she had made a mistake. When he smiled, he looked like an average guy greeting a woman in bar. She said, "Do I know you?"

"Actually, yes. My firm handles some of the legal work for the show. I sat in on a discussion about protecting the identity of a juvenile last year, remember? The kid who claimed he'd watched the murder of his family?"

Jess *did* remember. She felt like an idiot and hoped it didn't show. "Yes," she said. "I thought I recognized you."

He gave a little shake of his head. "I was just

thinking about that case. There are some weird people in this world, aren't there?"

"Yes," Jess agreed, a little more weakly. "Well, it was nice seeing you again."

"A pleasure, Miss Cray."

Jess returned to Trish. Trish looped her arm through Jess's. "You are something else," she said.

Chapter 4

Saturday. Jess slept till eight, jogged three miles, ate an orange, and did her laundry. The life of a glamour queen.

She had yogurt for lunch and watched the man across the courtyard work out in front of his patio door. He was wearing red shorts and a shiny layer of sweat and nothing else. Jess figured he was twenty-six or -seven, not all that much younger than she. His body belonged in a Nautilus commercial.

Her breakfast nook faced his patio door across a small expanse of grass. As she sat there, licking the spoon and watching, it occurred to her that if she could see him, he could see her. Almost as if on cue, he stood and began doing a slow series of waist stretches. Their eyes met. He smiled.

Jess felt heat creep into her cheeks. She knew she should move away or draw the curtain, but she just sat there, watching him smile at her, until he finished his stretches, looped a towel around his neck, and sauntered away.

Have you ever done anything you're ashamed of? Little things, big things, nothing very important . . .

Damn it. She had promised herself she'd forget about that. But it was too late now. If the trick was not to let them ruin your day, she had already failed the first test.

She opened her briefcase and shuffled through the papers inside until she found it. She smoothed the wrinkles out of the job application and gazed at it thoughtfully for a long time. Maybe she should have left it in the trash. Maybe it meant nothing. Maybe it was just someone's bizarre idea of a joke, or maybe it was a mistake. But she couldn't ignore it. Because she hadn't shown Dan the note that had been attached to the job application.

She took the note from the pocket of her briefcase and unfolded it, placing it atop the wrinkled sheet of paper. *Have you ever done anything you're ashamed of?*

"But what?" she muttered out loud. Her hands tightened on the papers. "What?"

Jess called her mother.

"Thanks for leaving the birthday message, Mama. I know how you hate talking to the machine."

"I thought you might call me back." Just a trace of accusation in her tone. It didn't take much.

"I got in real late. The folks on the show gave me a party."

"Well, that was nice, wasn't it? You coming home for Mother's Day?"

Jess hadn't been home for Mother's Day in eight years. She didn't know where her mother got these ideas.

"Gosh, Mama, I don't know. We're behind schedule and nobody's taking any time off . . . it would be real hard."

Jess's mother lived in a nice brick ranch house

on two acres outside Jackson, three bedrooms, full
basement, and every square inch of it was crowded
with junk. Jess's mother saved everything. Old toilet
paper rolls—"You can make things out of them"—
mismatched buttons, boxes, clothing cut into neat
quilting squares—her mother had never learned
how to quilt—catalogs, magazines, newspapers,
shopping bags, oatmeal boxes, appliances. There
were at least three televisions in every room; most
of the time one of them was turned on. A radio her
father had started taking apart before he died five
years before was still scattered over the kitchen
table. In an effort to get organized, her mother had
started collecting those brightly colored plastic
boxes and filling them with tools and cast-off pieces
of broken china and knotted spools of thread and
faded silk flowers, with the result that one entire
bedroom was now crammed with colored boxes that
had contents no one could identify. When Jess came
to visit, she had to squeeze down a hallway lined
with discarded furniture to get to her bedroom, then
remove all the winter coats from her bed in order
to sleep in it. And Jess did not know what disturbed
her most: the way her mother lived, or the fact that,
until only a few years ago, Jess had not seen anything odd about it.

She felt bad about lying, but she didn't like to
go home.

She said, before her mother could pursue the
subject of Mother's Day, "Mama . . . I've been thinking about Brett lately." She sat down on the sofa,
drawing up her knees and cradling the phone between her shoulder and her ear. "Silly things. His
eyes. The way his laugh sounded. Remember that

time you came down to visit and he took us to the zoo? That was fun, wasn't it?"

There was a poignant silence, then her mother said gruffly, "It was hot. I thought you'd gotten over that."

And without giving Jess a chance to reply, she went on, "Mildred wanted me to speak to you about those freaks you had on last Thursday. I mean, I never. I thought I was embarrassed when you had those lesbian cops on last month, but this . . ."

Jess repressed a sigh. Until six months ago, she would have said that the thing for which she was most grateful was that *Speaking of Which* was not carried in Jackson, Mississippi. But then her mother's next-door neighbor, Mildred, had gotten a satellite dish, and whatever peace Jess might once have enjoyed came to an end.

"Mama," she explained patiently, "I've told you before, I don't have anything to do with who's on the show."

"It's your show, isn't it? You ought to have some say."

"I don't even know who was on last Thursday. The show is taped, remember?"

"Well, I guess I know that. But how you could forget men who would cut their own things off . . ."

It went on. Jess watched the clock, and when half an hour had passed, she told her mother someone was at the door. She promised to try to come home for Mother's Day. Another lie. She told her mother she loved her, which was true. And she was glad to hang up.

She folded the note and job application into the

top drawer of her desk, then changed into her swimsuit and went down to the pool.

The weather had been unseasonably warm, and
the pool was crowded, but her neighbors were polite
and never intruded on Jess's privacy. She found a
chaise set back from the water's edge with partial
shade and opened a book on her lap. She gazed at
the pages for a long time, trying to clear her mind
with only partial success. After a time she climbed
into the water and swam a few laps. When she got
out, the photographer across the courtyard was
there, wearing black swim briefs and watching her
behind dark glasses.

Jessamine squeezed the water out of the ends of
her hair, tugged down the back of her swimsuit, and
returned to her chair. His chair was across the pool
from hers. He poured suntan oil into his palm, massaged it into the ball of his shoulder, and watched
her. Jess put on her own sunglasses. She blotted
the ends of her dripping hair with a towel and lay
back in the chaise. He stroked oil over his throat
and chest muscles. The hair on his chest glistened
copper in the sunlight. Jess watched him. It was
amazing how much security a pair of dark glasses
could give.

Her little patch of shade grew smaller, and Jess
baked in the sun. There was a pleasant breeze, and
she would have been content to stay the rest of the
afternoon, but she couldn't afford to get burned.
Gretchen in makeup was temperamental about
things like that.

She tied a sarong skirt around her waist and put

on her sandals, and when she looked up, he was standing over her.

"Hi," he said. He had a nice smile. "My name is Steve Lobell. I live across the courtyard from you."

Jess, still shielded by the dark glasses, said, "I know. I'm Jessamine Cray."

The smile turned into a grin. "I know."

Jess's heart beat a little faster. The old boy-girl thing, mixed with a good measure of embarrassment. He knew she'd been watching him. She knew he'd been showing off for her. They were both old enough to know better.

He said, "I was just going in for something cold to drink. Can I bring you one?"

Jess's eyes were on a level with his crotch. He smelled like coconut oil and sun sweat. She picked up her book and towel and swung her feet to the ground. "Actually, I was starting to get too much sun. I'm on my way in."

"Oh." He stepped back as she stood up. Then he said, "I make a mean daiquiri. And it's shady on my patio."

Jess hesitated. She could tell he didn't expect her to say yes. She smiled. "Sure. Why not?"

He didn't invite her in, at least not formally. Jess liked that. They reached his condo through the courtyard, and he left the sliding glass door open to the kitchen while he mixed the drinks. Jess had an impression of dark brick and copper and had a whiff of temperature-controlled air that smelled of furniture polish, but she did not follow him inside. His patio had a half wall around it and redwood furniture. It was shaded by a couple of ornamental trees on the west side of the wall and tropical plants strategically arranged inside it.

Jess started to sit down on one of the redwood chairs, then changed her mind. She thought, *this is crazy*. She glanced across the courtyard in the direction of her own patio. She should leave. She had things to do. This *was* crazy.

From inside the kitchen he said, "I've been meaning to introduce myself before. I see you around sometimes, you know. But I didn't want to intrude, with you being a celebrity and all."

Jess decided to stay.

She heard the whir of the blender, and after a moment he came out with two frosty glasses in his hands. He had pulled on a shirt over his swim briefs, but hadn't buttoned it. White on black. Very sexy.

He said, "I guess you get that a lot. Strange men just coming up to you and wanting to introduce themselves."

Jess smiled as she took her drink. He seemed nice. She hadn't expected that. "Not really," she said. "Not as often as you'd think."

He nodded gravely and sat down across from her. "They're probably shy—like me."

That made her laugh.

He did make a good daiquiri. They sat and talked while the afternoon faded, and Jess did not think about unsettling notes or phone calls once. He made another pitcher of daiquiris and told her he was a commercial photographer. They talked about his work a lot, and her work a little. His hobby was gardening, and he talked knowledgeably about the plants on his patio. Jess thought that was sweet.

After a while he mentioned he had some steaks in the fridge and suggested firing up the barbecue. Jess said that sounded nice.

The evening grew cool, and he draped a light cotton jacket over her shoulders. His fingers lingered against her skin, but not too long. She thought about having sex with him, about those strong athletic limbs entwined with hers, and the daiquiris were just strong enough to make such a thing seem possible. It had been a long time since she had had a real date. And he was such a nice young man.

He lit citronella candles in the soft blue twilight and served steak and salad at the patio table. He offered a very nice Cabernet—wine was another one of his hobbies—but they both decided daiquiris were more in keeping with the picnic atmosphere. It was all very romantic and carefree, and Jess was having fun for the first time in months, perhaps longer.

She smiled at him across the table. "This is really nice. Thank you."

"Glad you like it."

"I don't mean just the meal." She gestured. "The afternoon, the conversation, the atmosphere. It's nice."

He smiled. It was the kind of smile that, though innocent and sincere, promised heavy moves were coming up. Jess didn't mind. She would have been disappointed had he not made at least one genuine pass at her before the evening was over.

He said, "I'll make coffee if you like."

"Maybe later."

She rested her chin on one hand, gazing at him.

"You remind me of someone I used to know," she said, realizing it suddenly.

He lifted an eyebrow. "That doesn't sound good."

"It is," she assured him. She swallowed hard. "He was . . . my first love."

He got up and came around to her side of the table, taking her hands. "It's getting cold," he said, tugging her to her feet. "Let's go inside."

She glanced at the table. "The dishes."

"I'll get them later."

Heavy moves, she thought, and her heart beat a little faster. She settled into his embrace as he slipped an arm around her shoulders. "Do you like jazz?"

She murmured, "Brett liked jazz."

"Who's that?"

"The guy you remind me of." Young, energetic, good looking . . . and Jess had spent the past month or so watching him flex his muscles before the patio door without even realizing why she found him so fascinating.

Suddenly, she wasn't quite so comfortable with Steve as she had been a moment ago. The magic was fading from the night.

He turned her in his arms. Their thighs and pelvises touched. His hands skimmed her swimsuit from just beneath her breasts to the knot of the sarong tied low on her hip. The caress should have been arousing. A moment ago it would have been. Jess tried to recapture that state.

Steve said softly, "I hope this guy isn't going to be a problem."

His eyes were brown, not blue.

Jess shook her head, trying to concentrate on the here and now, on him, not Brett. "He's dead."

Steve grinned. "You didn't kill him, did you?"

A chill seized Jess's spine. She stepped away from him. His jacket slid from her shoulders onto the ground. For a moment she just stared at him.

She said hoarsely, "I have to go."

Confusion flashed across his face. "Hey, what . . ."

She pushed past him.

"Come on, I was only kidding! What's the matter with you?"

She walked quickly, almost running, and didn't stop until she was safe behind her own closed door. Then, because she could feel him standing there in the dark, scowling across the courtyard at her, she closed all the drapes before she turned on the lights.

"Shit," she whispered tightly and pressed her fingers to her cold cheeks.

She felt foolish, embarrassed, and stupid. Her hands were shaking. She was dismayed by her own behavior. What was the matter with her, indeed?

Steve would think she was crazy. She should apologize. But she couldn't face him tonight. She turned toward the telephone, wondering whether he was listed in the directory, and then her eyes fell on the envelope that had been pushed under her front door.

She had entered through the patio door, so the envelope might have been left there any time during the day. It was a manila envelope, sealed, with no writing or postmark on the outside. Jess picked it up carefully, her heart thudding. She ripped it open with her thumbnail.

At first she thought it was empty, and a little

thread of relief whispered through her. She shook the envelope halfheartedly, and an oddly-shaped piece of paper floated to the floor.

It was a newspaper clipping from twelve years ago. She stared at it for a long time. The face of a handsome young man, now long dead, stared back at her from the floor. The headline read, "College Student Found Dead." Across the text of the article was written in black letters, "Have you ever done anything you're ashamed of?"

Jess started to tremble. She crossed her arms tightly over her chest, but couldn't stop the shaking. She whispered, "No. *No* . . ."

She squeezed her eyes tightly shut, but her knees began to buckle. She sank slowly to the floor, hugging herself, shaking, trying hard not to cry.

Chapter 5

Dan said, "I locked my keys in the car, had to hike two miles in the rain to a telephone, got mugged *and* missed Philly's home opener—and from the way you look, I still had a better weekend than you did."

Jess mumbled, "Thanks a lot," and edged past him toward her office.

Sylvia, overhearing, exclaimed, "Mugged? Were you really?"

And someone else said, "Were you hurt?"

"What did they get?"

"American Express and thirty-two fifty. And my driver's license, which some convicted felon is probably using at this moment to get a fake passport."

"Jesus, how awful."

"What a world we live in, huh?"

"You're telling me."

Jess took advantage of the hubbub to slip into her office, but she could feel Dan watching her, and she didn't bother to close the door. After a moment he followed her, and he closed the door.

Jess said, "I'm sorry you were mugged. Were you hurt?"

"Only my pride. There's something very emasculating about meekly turning over everything you own to some punk with a knife. It goes against the grain somehow."

Jess unpacked her briefcase. "You don't argue with these guys."

"So they tell me." He sprawled in the chair across from her desk, watching her alertly. "So how was your weekend?"

Jess snapped the briefcase closed and began organizing the papers on her desk. "You're lucky they didn't get much."

"This isn't the first time for me. I used to work the crime beat in Miami, remember? I learned not to carry anything on my person I can't afford to lose. Now what the hell is going on with you? You look like shit, I'm not kidding."

"UFOs," she muttered, not looking up from the files she was rearranging. "You know what the twist is, don't you? Now they're kidnapping fetuses. Aliens, that is. I mean, for Chrissakes, *fetuses*."

"Yeah, it's caused me a lot of sleepless nights."

"Why can't we do a cooking show? Remember when we used to do that? A plain old-fashioned cooking show, with guest chefs and kitchen fires—"

"Who, us? We never did anything like that. You must be thinking of some other show you were the star of."

Her lips tightened. "Joan Lunden does cooking shoes. Kathie Lee does cooking shows. Oprah does cooking shows, for God's sake. Why can't we do one stinking cooking show, is that too much to ask?"

Dan watched her carefully. "I'll see what I can do."

And then he added casually, "So. How's the fan mail today?"

Jess looked up at him abruptly. Her eyes were bloodshot and pocketed, stripped by fatigue of all animation or expression. And yet Dan thought he detected the faintest trace of emotion there. Could it be anger?

She said, "What about you, Dan? Have you ever done anything you're ashamed of?"

He started to smile, but it was easy to see she wasn't kidding. "I take it the fan mail is not running so great."

"So answer the question." Her voice was clipped, her expression cold. "Have you?"

Dan looked at her for a moment, then got to his feet. He said, "Funny how a question like that can make you lose your sense of humor." His voice was flat. "See you, Jess."

When he was gone, Jess propped her elbows on her desk and allowed herself the brief indulgence of resting her face in her hands, despite knowing everyone was watching her through the glass walls. "Great," she muttered. "Perfect."

Dan was mad at her, and they were taping in front of a live audience in less than an hour. Dan had never been mad at her before. If this kept up, she would methodically manage to alienate every friend she had or hoped to have. And it infuriated her to think that a perfect stranger could have that much control over her life.

Sylvia tapped on her door and then opened it without waiting for a reply. "Here's the mail," she said. "Fan mail's on top."

She placed the bundle on Jess's desk as she had been accustomed to doing for the past three years and turned to leave.

Jess said, "Wait."

Sylvia looked surprised.

Jess picked up the top stack of mail—separated from the others by a rubber band—and held it out to her secretary. "From now on I want you to go through the fan mail and separate it. Three stacks: positive, critical and . . ."

Jess found herself momentarily at a loss for words, and Sylvia provided deftly, "Weird."

Jess did not know how she was surprised that Sylvia should know about the strange mail she had received. There were no secrets on this set.

"That's right," she said. She sat back in her chair, trying to relax a little as Sylvia took the mail from her.

"Should I do anything special to the weird ones?" Sylvia inquired. "Like put them in plastic bags or something for the police?"

That made Jess smile. "No, that won't be necessary. But . . ." And the smile left her. "Save the envelopes, will you?"

She didn't know what good it would do, but it was a start. And she felt marginally better having done something, however small, to regain control of her life.

The show wasn't too bad. Dan was a consummate professional and not a bad actor, and if he was still annoyed with Jess, he didn't let it show. One of their guests was a university professor who actually had some convincing evidence for the case of alien abductions. Another was a former Secret Service agent who claimed inside information on the White House cover-up of UFO landings. By the time they stirred in the mix of actual abductees, it made for a lively debate.

Jess had a list of prepared questions that she carried in case of emergency—if her mind went blank or the panel discussion got out of control or, most dreaded of all, if there was dead air—and she had to refer to it only twice. Once she was distracted and asked a follow-up question that was a complete non sequitur, but Dan rescued her gracefully. All in all it wasn't a bad show.

She tried not to think too much about the guests. The woman who went to bed one night six months pregnant and woke up the next morning not pregnant at all. The man who had watched naked, large-headed humanoids perform abdominal surgery on his wife. The university professor who seemed so credible . . . but was he? And the special agent whose time in the Secret Service had probably lasted a little longer than Jess's . . . there were a lot of crazy people in the world. And any of them, for any reason at all, could become fixated on a celebrity.

On the other hand, the only fan mail Sylvia had been able to put into the "weird" stack was a badly typed letter from a man in Des Moines who wanted to know what size bra Jess wore. Maybe it was over.

Maybe it was. But the damage was already done, and she was not sure if she could ever look at anyone again without wondering if he or she might be the one.

She didn't spend as much time with the audience as usual; she hoped no one noticed. Dan was waiting for her outside the studio.

"Do you want to walk down to Servo's for lunch?" he asked.

Jess hadn't planned to eat lunch, but she could hardly refuse the overture after the way she had treated Dan earlier. She said, "Sure. Just let me change my shoes."

Like any wise city-dweller she kept a pair of Reeboks in her desk drawer for broken downtown sidewalks and uneven pavement. She told Sylvia as she passed her desk, "I'm going out to lunch."

"Oh." Sylvia looked disappointed. She was accustomed to going to lunch first and staying as long as she liked. Then she said, "They delivered your wardrobe. Part of it anyway."

Jess saw the garment bag folded over the chair as she sat down to replace her shoes. She wondered which piece it was and why Evangelyne's hadn't waited until the entire set was ready to deliver. She tied her shoes and hurried back out. "I'm just going to Servo's," she told Sylvia. "Can I bring you anything?"

"No, thanks. I'm dieting." With a wan expression she held up a paper bag that looked as though it couldn't possibly hold anything more substantial than an apple and a few carrot sticks.

Sylvia was always dieting and always remained about thirty pounds overweight. That might have been because, in addition to the apple and carrot sticks, she invariably stopped by Servo's herself for a sandwich and a bag of chips. Otherwise, she wouldn't have been so conscientious about her lunch break or stayed away so long. An apple and carrot sticks she could eat at her desk.

"Back in about twenty minutes then."

Jess was smiling to herself over her own powers of deduction as she left the office, and Dan caught her at it.

"Whatever you're thinking," he said, "keep thinking it. It's a definite improvement from this morning."

Her expression twisted ruefully, and she lifted her shoulders. "I was just wondering if I'm so smart, how come I let myself get so rattled about such a stupid thing. I'm sorry I was short with you."

"Forget it."

They took the elevator to the ground floor. This close to the noon broadcast the people from the news were bustling through the corridors on last-minute errands and urgent business, but none of them was in too much of a hurry to raise a hand to Dan or respond to his greeting.

"How's it going, man?"

"Saw the show Friday—pretty high-class stuff!"

"We're on for tomorrow night, right?"

Jess did not know any of those people. But they all, it occurred to her uneasily, knew her.

"So how come you're on such friendly terms with the news staff?" she asked as they pushed through the revolving door.

He waited until they were outside to answer. "Why shouldn't I be?"

"I don't know. It's just that I see them every day, too, and I'm not going out with any of them tomorrow night."

He grinned. "Let's face it, hon. You're a bit of a snob."

She was genuinely astonished. "I am not!"

"All right, not a snob. But a little standoffish.

People are intimidated by you. You're hard to get to know."

Jess had truly never realized that about herself before. She worked so hard to make people feel at ease, at being nice to people, at making sure everyone *liked* her. It was a bit of a shock to realize her efforts were for nothing.

She said a little stiffly, "I don't mean to be."

"I know." Dan's tone was unconcerned. He touched her shoulder protectively as they reached the curb, then crossed the street with the crowd.

The day was grim and overcast, and the city looked weary. The heat wave of the weekend had moderated into stale stickiness that crept underneath her collar and clung to her underclothes. Jess wished she had skipped lunch as she had originally planned.

Dan said, "I've been playing your game."

"What game?"

Dan walked with his hands in his pockets, handsome profile tilted back, not looking at her. "The 'What are you most ashamed of' game."

Jess tensed.

He said, still without looking at her, "I was fifteen. I had only a learner's permit, I wasn't allowed to drive without an adult, and I certainly wasn't allowed to borrow my dad's car . . . but I didn't let that stop me. There was this party I wanted to go to. I sneaked out of the house after my parents were asleep, helped myself to the keys, and picked up five or six of my friends for the party. I had a few beers, had a really great time, and on the way back something ran out in front of me—a dog or something—and I drove the car up a tree. Totaled it. I wasn't about to be caught out after curfew, drunk, having wrecked my dad's car . . . so I walked home. Went to bed, got up in the morning for school, never said a word. I let them think the car had been stolen and why not? It had been. They even arrested some guy, and I never said a word."

It took a moment for Jess to realize the story was over. "Did he go to jail?"

Still Dan didn't look at her. "Turns out he had been operating a car-theft ring in the county for over a year. They didn't have the evidence to convict him for my dad's car, but he went to jail on the other counts. There's a moral there somewhere, I guess."

Jess didn't know what to say.

A bell chimed as he pushed open the glass door of Servo's Deli. The air was thick with the smell of spices and old wood, sausages and fried food. There were three people in line ahead of them.

Jess said, "I made a real ass of myself this weekend with a date."

"I didn't know you did. Date, that is."

"It didn't start out that way. That's the worst part—he's a neighbor. I have to see him again."

"Bad strategy. Never make a fool of yourself with anyone you work with or live next door to."

"I'll remember that next time."

Dan ordered a Greek salad with no dressing. Jess ordered a yogurt.

"It's crazy to come to a place like this for rabbit food," Jess commented.

"I do it for the smells."

That made Jess smile.

Dan paid for her yogurt, and she let him. He took

the sack containing their order and shouldered open the door. He gestured to a group of three canopied tables arranged on a scrap of side yard next to the building. "Do you want to sit?"

It was too muggy to be sitting outside, and the air smelled of garbage and exhaust. Sylvia was expecting her back. Her desk was piled with work, and they had a production meeting at two.

She said, "Sure. Why not?"

Dan discarded the paper sack and handed her the yogurt and plastic spoon. He sat on the curved cement half bench across from her and took the plastic wrap off his salad. He said, "So what did you do?"

Jess popped the lid on her yogurt and shrugged uncomfortably. "It was stupid. He said something and it just set me off."

"What? Something dirty?"

"Something perfectly innocent. This whole business is making me insane. I know you don't think I'm being stalked—"

"I never said that."

She looked at him sharply, but his expression was bland. He speared an olive with his plastic fork, waiting for her to continue.

She sighed. She dropped her eyes to her yogurt cup, stirred the contents a few times, then abandoned the spoon in the center of the container.

"My junior year in college, I fell in love with a boy. His name was Brett—a philosophy major. He was . . ." Her expression softened with remembrance. ". . . wild and sweet and crazy and smart, and to a girl from Jackson, Mississippi, he was about as exotic as a shooting star fallen to earth. He dazzled me, he pampered me, he made me feel—and this is the truth—he was the first person who made me believe I could be something more than a beauty queen. God, I adored him. Eventually, we got a little apartment together off campus, and that's a big step when your tuition is being paid for out of scholarship funds and you never know where living expenses are coming from month to month. I was terrified my mother would find out and try to make me come home . . . I told her I was sharing with a girlfriend, and I took a part-time job at a pizza parlor to make up the difference in rent."

She tried not to get swept up by the memories, but she was fighting a losing battle. The apartment had bright yellow walls, she remembered, and they both had groaned at the color. The first day they moved in they stayed up into the early hours of the morning, drinking a liter of Chianti and painting a huge white daisy on the living-room wall. Then they'd made love till dawn. Youth. Innocence. Faith. Were there any better words to describe first love?

"There was only one problem," she said. "He was graduating that year. And of course we didn't see it as a problem. He was going to take a year off before graduate school and teach. 'Life experience', he called it. When I graduated, I was going to get a job while he went on to graduate school and . . . well, you know how it goes.

"Then he got accepted to Cornell. I mean, from the University of Georgia to Cornell—do you know how often that happens? Of course it was an honor. Of course he couldn't turn it down. The only thing was, I didn't know he had even applied. I thought our plans were all set. I should have been happy for him, but I was furious. We had a horrible fight. I stormed out of the apartment. He threw my things after me.

"I was a wreck. It was all over the campus, how he had thrown me out or I'd thrown him out, depending on which version you heard, and there was nowhere I could go to get away from it. Not that I wanted to. I wallowed in it, I think, the way you do when you're young—the drama, the self-pity, the certainty that this is the worst thing that will ever happen to you in your whole life.

"He tried to make up. He was a philosophy major, and I guess that signifies some sort of maturity. I moved back into the dorm with my old roommates, and after about three days he started calling, trying to arrange a meeting with me. But I was so hurt and angry I wouldn't even talk to him. I just wanted to hurt him back, so what did I do but go out with another guy? A football player. I made sure Brett knew about it. I even . . ." After all this time, she was embarrassed to remember. ". . . spent the night with him. God, I don't even remember his name. Isn't that awful? I thought I was doing it to get even with Brett, but the only person I really hurt was myself. The next morning I felt so awful, so dirty and cheap, that I went straight to Brett to confess.

"I found him at the desk in front of the window where we used to study. There was a hole in the side of his head, and blood was everywhere—on the walls and smeared on the window and congealed in drops, like stalactites, from the edge of the desk. He had killed himself with my .38—the gun my dad insisted I take with me when I went away to college. We always had guns in the South. I had put it away somewhere and never even thought about it. But he did."

She picked up the spoon again, stared at it with absent absorption for a moment, then let it drop back into the yogurt. She said, "Later, I found out that his mother had died a few days earlier. He went home for the funeral, then came back and shot himself. All that time he was trying to reach me I thought he just wanted to make up. But he really needed me."

Dan was silent. Jess didn't look up. Then Dan said quietly, "You know you can't blame yourself, Jess. The guy was unstable. It was his choice."

Jess toyed with the spoon. "It was my first dead body. My only dead body. I never thought it would be so . . . bloody."

She pushed the yogurt aside and said, "Anyway, all this garbage—the notes, the phone calls—it's brought it all back. I guess you never really get over something like that."

Dan was frowning thoughtfully. Jess could see his old reporter's instincts kicking in, and that annoyed her vaguely.

He said, "Do you think there's a connection?"

"What?"

"Between the notes and the boyfriend. Do you think it's related somehow?"

She shrugged. "How could it be?" And she tried not to let disappointment show in her tone. She was not sure why she had told Dan about Brett, but she had not intended for him to launch an investigation.

"Look," she explained, "it's just that you asked why this is getting to me so badly, and I told you.

Everyone has something they're ashamed of. Some things are worse than others, that's all."

She stuffed the plastic top into the untouched container of yogurt and looked around for a trash can.

Dan said seriously, "You have nothing to be ashamed of in Brett's death, Jess. It wasn't your fault."

"Maybe. Maybe not. But I'll always feel guilty about it."

Dan had barely touched his salad; the lunchtime conversation had hardly been conducive to digestion. Jess glanced at her watch.

"Look, I shouldn't stay," she said. "You finish your lunch. I'll start back."

"That's okay." Dan crumpled up his paper napkin and recapped the salad. "I'll walk with you."

Something about the way he said that made Jess wonder if he was uneasy about her walking alone the short distance to the office. He had never expressed such a concern before.

They tossed away the remnants of their lunches and started back down the street. Dan said, "I wonder how hard it would be to get hold of a ten-year-old personnel file."

She was tired of talking about it. This time her annoyance showed. "What?"

"The job application. That's what kicked it all off, isn't it?"

"There was a note before that." She walked a little faster.

"Yes, but there's the connection between what happened in college and your stalker. He underlined your college information."

"But the college information was wrong—falsified."

"And he had to *know* it was wrong."

"You're giving me a headache."

"You think it was just a coincidence?"

"I don't think it matters. I think the important thing—the thing that worries me most—is how the creep got my unlisted phone number."

"Oh, that's easy. You put your phone number on a dozen pieces of paper every day that you don't even think about. Canceled checks, bills, credit card orders, call-back messages . . . all an enterprising stalker needs to do is go through your trash."

"I guess that's how he got my address, too."

Dan looked at her sharply. "He knows where you live?"

Jess told him about the note that had been slipped under her door Saturday afternoon. Dan frowned again.

"Well, that certainly complicates matters, doesn't it? Of course getting an address is almost easier than getting a phone number. There are probably a dozen ways to get your address from the studio alone. And once he had it, all he had to do was walk in your house and help himself to anything else he wanted to know about you."

The very thought gave her a chill. "It's a security complex," she said shortly. "Don't be ridiculous."

"Strangers are pushing notes under your door. How secure can it be?" Then he cast her a sideways glance. "Then again, maybe it's someone you know. Maybe it's a neighbor."

"Thank you, Dan Webber, for another sleepless night." She increased her pace again, both from anger and a figurative, if not literal, need to put distance between herself and what he was saying.

Dan kept up with her effortlessly. "I thought you wanted me to take you seriously." He stopped then and looked at her. "And I'll tell you the truth, Jess. If somebody's out there who gets his jollies from digging into your personal life and sending you suggestive notes—and if that person knows where you live—that's getting pretty close to serious from where I stand. Maybe *you're* the one who should start taking it seriously."

Jess met his gaze for another moment, and she didn't like what she saw there. She started walking again. He said nothing more.

The moment Jess rounded the corner Sylvia started shutting down her computer and packing away her notepad. By the time Jess reached her desk, Sylvia had her purse and lunch bag in hand. Any other day Jess would have told her to have a good lunch and let her go. But maybe fear was an empowering emotion—as much as Jess hated to think of herself as afraid.

"Before you go," she said, "I want you to find me a locksmith. Make an appointment to have my locks changed at home."

Sylvia's reluctance was predictable. She glanced at her watch. "They're probably all at lunch."

Jess continued toward her office. "I seriously doubt that every locksmith in the city of Philadelphia goes to lunch at the same time. It's not a union rule, you know."

"I'll need to know how many locks you have and what kind." Sylvia was determined to make this as difficult as possible. "I'll also need to know what kind you want."

Jess turned, her mouth set against exasperation. "Just get me someone on the phone, will you do that, please?"

"Yes, ma'am."

Jess left the door open, anticipating Sylvia's announcement that she couldn't get anyone on the phone. In most ways Sylvia was the perfect secretary, but she could be intractable at times. And maybe Trish was right; Jess *did* let Sylvia boss her around.

She started to hang her purse on its usual hook by the door, then she thought about what Dan had said regarding all the different ways a perfect stranger could get her phone number or her address. One of them could certainly be by simply walking into her office and opening her purse.

Uneasily, she took her purse to her desk and started to put it in the bottom drawer, then stopped herself. "No, damn it," she muttered. There had to be a limit to how much she would let this one nameless, gutless terrorist run her life.

Besides, the damage was already done.

Defiantly, she hung her purse on the hook by the door, and that was when she noticed the garment bag still folded over the chair beside the credenza. She picked the bag up and slid the garment out of its plastic covering.

She saw immediately there had been a mistake. The gown was some kind of evening dress, and she hadn't ordered anything like that. In fact, it was more like a bridesmaid's dress, or a prom dress, made of pale pink organza with a full skirt and sequined bodice and oversized pink fabric roses instead of a bow in back. It took her a moment to realize that her smile was reminiscent because the more she looked at the dress, the more familiar it became. In fact, it was *very* similar to a dress she had worn to a junior-senior prom in high school.

She turned the gown around and felt herself go cold.

"Miss Cray, I have Security Lock and Key on line one."

Jess whirled to face Sylvia. "Where did this come from?" she demanded hoarsely.

"It was delivered this morning." She made a moue of distaste and gestured to the stain that covered most of the front of the gown from bodice to hem. "The dry cleaner wasn't able to do much with it, was he? What *is* that on the front anyway?"

Jess said as steadily as she could manage, "What does it look like to you?"

Sylvia came forward to examine the stain. She touched the fabric gingerly. "It looks like . . ." She looked up at Jess, her expression shadowed with disgust and concern. "Blood."

Chapter 6

It took Dan three phone calls to find out exactly how hard it was to pull a ten-year-old personnel file. *Not bad for an ex-newshound*, he thought, but when his final call was put through he was disappointed.

"Excuse me, sir, what year did you say?"

Dan repeated his request.

"Oh, well, we don't keep any records that old." The personnel manager of WTLB in Jackson seemed relieved not to have to go digging through the dusty boxes and files.

"Are you sure? Perhaps you made an exception in this case. It's Jessamine Cray."

"Oh, sure, I know her. I know of her that is. She has some kind of talk show. My goodness, did she used to work here?"

Dan closed his eyes and repeated patiently. "In the news department. She did the weather."

"Well, imagine that." She sounded delighted. "And what was it you wanted again?"

"I'm doing a book on talk show hosts and how they got their starts." It was just bizarre enough to sound plausible. "And I was wondering whether, if I came down say, next Tuesday, I might be able to look at Miss Cray's file, maybe talk to some people who knew her."

"Well, as I told you, we don't keep records that long. We're a small station, and a lot of people come and go. We generally keep employment records on file for five years, which is about as far back as people ever phone for references, then they're destroyed. Of course," she added helpfully, "if this were a tax matter, her W-4 is probably still on file somewhere. It would take me a few days to check. But then, that's not the case, is it?"

"No, it's not."

"Tell me something." The note of suspicion underlying her pleasant tone made Dan wonder if she was not just a little smarter than she seemed. "Are you having much luck with this approach? Asking for old personnel files on celebrities? Because I must say, even if I *did* have the file, it would be against company policy to release it to you without authorization from the party involved."

"Oh, I have authorization," he assured her. "And yes, actually. People have been very cooperative."

"Well, I'm sorry we couldn't help you then."

That had a note of finality to it, and Dan interjected quickly, "Just one more thing."

"Yes?"

"I wonder if you recall anyone else making the same kind of request for Miss Cray's file in . . . oh, say, the last year or so." He chuckled in what he hoped was an ingratiating manner. "I'm worried about competition."

"No. I'm sure I would remember, and if anyone had asked for a ten-year-old file, I would have told him the same thing I told you—it's not possible."

"All right. Thank you for your time."

He hung up the phone, drumming the point of

his pencil on his desk blotter thoughtfully. "That," he murmured aloud, "is what some people might call a dead end."

And he had just wasted twenty minutes. He glanced at his watch and saw he was late for the production meeting. Shrugging into his jacket, he told his secretary where he was going and left the office.

He knew something was wrong before he passed Jess's office. The writers and secretaries had a tense, uneasy look about them, and they kept glancing toward the glass walls of Jess's office. When Dan did the same, he saw that Trish was inside, and so was a security officer. He went quickly to the door.

"What's going on?"

Trish exclaimed, in response to nothing in particular and without looking around, "Son of a bitch!"

Sylvia murmured, "It's disgusting. God, can you imagine?" Her voice had a graveside tone, the kind one might use at the sight of a particularly gruesome accident.

They were all hovering over something in the corner of the room, but Dan could not tell what. It was Jess who answered his question, beckoning him inside.

"Just a mix-up at the dry cleaner's," she said. Although her voice was conversational and her expression perfectly calm, the dark rings under her eyes were even more pronounced than they had been that morning. There were fine lines around the corners of her mouth that Dan had never noticed before.

When he got closer, Dan could see the cause of all the excitement was an ugly pink dress with a huge brown stain on the front. The security officer, whose nameplate identified him as Mike, was examining it.

"It could be blood," he said. "You'd have to have a lab analyze it to be sure."

Dan looked at Trish with a question in his raised eyebrows. She thrust a scrap of paper at him. "This was pinned to the dress," she said. "Now what do you suppose it means?"

It was an ordinary sheet of white paper, the kind that could be found in any office anywhere. In bold black marker, written in block letters, were the words "HAVE YOU EVER DONE ANYTHING YOU'RE ASHAMED OF?"

Dan glanced at Jess. "This guy knows only one song, doesn't he?"

Trish looked sharply at Jess. "What do you mean? Have you gotten more of these since the one you showed me?"

Jess said, "Look, I think we're all getting a little too excited about this. All I wanted to do is find out whether or not anybody knew who'd delivered this." She picked up the dress and dropped the white plastic bag over it, hiding the gruesome stain from view. The bag was unmarked, the kind used by half a dozen department stores in the area.

Sylvia said defensively, "He was wearing a brown uniform, that's all I remember. He looked like any other delivery man who's ever been here, and I figured they wouldn't have let him up if he wasn't okay."

Mike said, "No one gets to the elevator without signing in. But there's no record of any delivery to this office this morning. All I can figure is he must have given us a phony destination. It'll take us a while to track it down."

Jess folded the garment bag neatly in half and placed it on the floor between the chair and the filing cabinet, out of sight. The package made a crisp crinkling sound as she did so. "There's no need for that," she said. "No harm was done, and it's not important."

Trish threw up her hands in exasperation. "I'd like to know what you *do* find important! A guy sends you threatening notes, follows up with something like this—"

Jess turned on her. Her face was composed, her voice reasonable, but the tension in her body was so strong her muscles seemed to strain with it. She said, "You didn't seem to think it was important when I showed you the first note last week." Her gaze moved around the room; it wasn't accusing, but it seemed to be. "None of you did. And now I think you're right. This is just some sick creep's idea of a joke, and I'm not going to let it interfere with my life."

She looked at her secretary. "Sylvia, why don't you go to lunch? Mike, thanks for coming up."

Mike hesitated and looked at Trish for dismissal. Trish said, "From now on nothing comes to Miss Cray's office without being inspected first."

And when Jess drew an impatient breath, Trish said sharply, "Do you want it to be a bomb next time?"

"Oh, for heaven's sake, Trish, scare the man to death, will you? Are you trying to say it's better if the bomb goes off in Security than up here?"

As she spoke, she gave Mike one of her enchanting smiles, but Trish remained unmoved. "That's what they get paid for," she snapped.

Mike said, "We'll take care of it, Ms. Siegel."

When Sylvia and Mike were gone, Dan went over to the corner and picked up the dress. "What are you going to do with this?"

"I don't know. Throw it away." She wouldn't meet his eyes.

"The police might want it."

"There, you see!" Trish threw open her hands. "She won't call the police," she said to Dan. To Jess she insisted, "Did I tell you to call the police? Was I right?"

Jess rolled her eyes at her. "And tell them what? Someone's been delivering the wrong laundry?"

"And calling your unlisted number and coming to your house," Dan said.

Trish stared at her.

Jess looked uncomfortable. "I really don't want to deal with this now."

That was obvious. Dan said, "So what's the significance of the dress? Why the stain on front? And why would anyone send it to you?"

She managed a shrug that was too elaborate not to be forced. "To tell the truth, I don't know. It looks a little like one I wore to a prom—actually, I didn't even go to the prom. I got stood up."

"You?" Trish snorted, patting her pockets for cigarettes. "Unbelievable."

"Other than that," Jess continued, sounding almost relieved, "it means nothing to me. The stain is probably coffee."

Dan had seen coffee stains and he had seen bloodstains. He didn't think the stain on the gown was coffee. But he would be very surprised if it was human blood.

He said, "Do you want me to get rid of this for you?"

She cast him a relieved look. "Thanks. Now." She pressed her hands together and tried to look ready for business. "I thought we had a meeting."

The first report arrived on Jeremy Styles's computer early Monday morning. It was absurdly easy. Jessamine Cray's life, had she but known it, was an open book.

Jeremy Styles prided himself on the accuracy of his research and took full advantage of everything the information superhighway offered. He looked with disdain on writers who used their computers as nothing more than glorified typewriters. His was fully equipped with a CD-ROM and full multimedia capabilities—video, audio, and over one thousand volumes of the world's greatest literature and reference material available to him at the touch of a button. He was linked by modem to all the major on-line services and local networks. When Roz, his friend at the library research desk, had located Jessamines Cray's date and place of birth for him, the rest had been a simple matter of time.

What he had before him now was her credit report. She spent far too much money at Victoria's Secret. Somehow that didn't surprise him. She owed $160,000 on her condo and $15,000 on a BMW. That did surprise him. He would have figured her for the Corvette type.

In addition to the credit report he had her employment history, her telephone records for the past six months, her college transcript, her high-school record. None of it had taken more than a few keystroke commands to obtain. A little harder to come by, but well worth the effort, was her last month's bank statement. To actually access an account was well beyond his skill, though he knew people online who claimed they could do it. But a bank statement could be obtained through normal electronic banking procedures, and as long as one had the right Social Security number and code, how was the bank's computer to tell one person from the other?

Sometimes he thought about going into the private investigation business.

What he was going to do with the information he wasn't at all sure. Maybe he'd write an exposé. Maybe he'd send it all to her in a neat, anonymous little bundle, just to show her there were people out there who were smarter than her, faster than her, even more intimidating than her. Maybe it was enough just to have the information—to savor the power it represented.

He shifted the pages, scanning the list of deposits and canceled checks. The woman made an obscene amount of money for doing nothing. A flame of resentment kindled for that, and he let it grow. And then he sat forward, frowning, as his attention was caught by something he hadn't expected.

After a moment he turned to the telephone and dialed Information. He copied down the number he received on request, and then dialed it.

When his call was answered, he sat back in his chair, smiling and relaxed, in his element now. "Yes," he said, "I'd like some information on a patient, please."

Jessamine Cray, it was beginning to appear, had a secret or two. And he could tell already that uncovering those secrets was going to prove very interesting indeed.

"It's insanity, that's what it is. The whole fucking world is so screwed up you can't even joke about it anymore."

Trish Siegel paced tensely back and forth in front of the window of her fourth-floor office, an unlit cigarette in her hand. The building had been smoke-free for the past three years, which to Trish meant going up to the roof twelve or fifteen times a day, where the other exiles gathered, rain or shine, to satisfy their habit. When the roof was not convenient—during meetings or telephone conversations, for example—she compromised by using a smokeless ashtray or by carrying around an unlit cigarette like a talisman. The effectiveness of these compromises was evident in the stale-smoke smell that clung to the room day and night and the yellow film, detectable only by non-smokers, that stained her windows.

Dan, an ex-smoker himself, watched Trish's growing agitation and gave her another three minutes before she gave in and lit the cigarette. He agreed mildly, "Yep. Going to hell in a handbasket."

She stopped pacing long enough to shoot him a sharp, accusatory look. "And just how much did *you* know about this, anyway? How far were you going to let it go before you mentioned it to somebody?"

Trish had a big office, as befitted her station, with a sitting area decorated with bright blue club chairs, a low round table, and a television set that was always on, volume on mute. In the center of the table was a fruit and cheese tray and a selection of mineral waters, to which Dan had been helping himself liberally in lieu of his missed lunch. He sat comfortably back in one of the club chairs, his ankle resting on one knee, sipping Evian and enjoying the break from the routine. But now he shifted uncomfortably, the moment of false peace gone.

"Come on, Trish, I'm not Jess's keeper—and neither are you for that matter. Besides, it's not like it was bloody underwear or something. It was just an evening dress. Why are you making such a big deal out of this?"

Trish stared at him. "That has got to be one of the most perverse sexist remarks I've heard come out of your mouth this year. *Underwear?* Jesus! Maybe I should have Security start checking *your* briefcase every morning!"

He leaned forward and started building a sandwich of Havarti and party rye. "I'm serious. You're taking this harder than Jess is. What's set you off?"

"I just don't like things going on in my office I don't know about. I don't like to think any creep off the street can get to my people. Anonymous notes are one thing—we get them all the time. But when they start walking in here . . ."

Dan lost the bet with himself when Trish swung back to her desk, picked up a lighter, and lit the cigarette two minutes early. A pungent film of blue smoke drifted his way, but Dan didn't mind. His own smoking days were in the far too recent past, and he liked the smell.

Trish took another harsh drag on the cigarette and folded her arms tightly in front of her. "I was attacked last year," she said abruptly. "In the parking garage across the street. He didn't hurt me—well, I skinned my knee when I tried to run away—but that was only because a car pulled out just then and scared him off. I carry a gun in my purse now."

Dan put the sandwich down, untasted. He tried not to stare at her, but he couldn't help it. He said softly, "Jesus, Trish."

She drew again on the cigarette and exhaled a quick, thin stream. She stood in profile to him. "It's a screwed-up world," she said. "I hate it, but I'm not going to be a victim to it." Now she turned on him, her eyes angry. "And neither are any of my people. Why didn't you tell me she'd gotten more than one note?"

"I thought Jess would have told you herself if she wanted you to know. She probably didn't want to upset you, and she would have been right. None of it should concern you."

She glared at him. "I've got a show with two stars, one of whom is getting ready to defect. That makes the one who's left very, very important, do you get that? And when something threatens her, it had damn well better concern me."

Dan's jaw tightened, but there was no other visible reaction to her words. He reached forward again and picked up the sandwich he had abandoned, saying casually, "I don't think that kind of abuse is in my contract."

Trish exhaled another stream of smoke and ran her fingers through her hair, leaving it in spikes. "Damn it," she said, "who could be doing this? Where do those wackos come from, anyway?"

"You're kidding, right?" Dan twisted off the cap

of a fruit-flavored water. "You just finished doing a show featuring people whose babies have been kidnapped by aliens from another planet, and you're asking me where the weirdos come from?"

Trish turned alert eyes on him, the cigarette hovering in the air midway to her lips. "You think it might be someone from our show?"

Dan shrugged, leaning back in the chair. "In the past year alone we've interviewed vampires, serial killers, child molesters, people who abuse their grandparents, people who were abused *by* their grandparents . . . and that's not even the top of the list. Yeah, now that I think about it, if you're looking for perverts and psychopaths, our guest list might be a good place to start."

Trish's expression clouded with worry. Ashes dropped on the carpet, and she absently scrubbed them out with the toe of her boot. She said, "I don't want this to get out of hand, Dan. Someone should talk to Jess."

"I've talked to her. You've talked to her. Who else did you have in mind, a therapist? Why don't you let the woman manage her own life?"

She drew on the cigarette, but it had burned to the filter. Angrily, she stabbed it into the ashtray. "I can't afford to have her flake out on me now, she's too valuable. Someone should do something."

Dan glanced at his watch and stood, taking the bottled water with him. "What are you looking at me for?" he said. "You're the one with a gun in your purse. I've got to get back to work or my costar— the important one—might actually know more about tomorrow's show than I do, and that would be a first in television history."

"Dan, damn it . . ."

But he was already gone, and she was swearing at a closed door.

Dan allowed himself to hold a grudge for approximately four minutes, the time it took him to walk back to his office. But he couldn't really blame Trish; it was part of her job to make him feel like a rat when he was considering another offer. He had to admit he didn't know anything about how it felt to be a woman and vulnerable—he was certain of it, because they had done a show early in the year on that very subject—and he supposed it was only natural that Trish should identify with Jess and take it out on him.

He stopped by his secretary's desk on the way to his own office. "Women," he commented, "are going to rule the world."

Bethany looked up from her computer and replied pleasantly, "I certainly hope so. Is there something I can do for you?"

Dan realized he was sitting on the corner of her desk, and he stood up. He had known Bethany for two years and didn't think she would misinterpret a friendly gesture, but with all the rules and regs about harassment, one could never be sure. Most of the time Dan couldn't even remember what the rules were.

He said, "That detective who was on the show last week—what was his name?"

Bethany exited the program she was in and called up another. "Which day?"

"I don't remember."

There was no expression on her face as she

tapped on the keyboard, but Dan had the distinct impression that the limited intellect of television talk show hosts would be a hot topic of conversation around the lounge at coffee break time.

In less than a half a minute she said, "Candler? Lieutenant Lyle Candler?"

"Yes, that's the one. Do we have a number on him?"

"Work or home?"

"Work."

She pulled a notepad close, copied down the number, and said, "Shall I dial?"

He didn't know why that should irritate him, a reasonable offer by the perfect secretary. He held out his hand for the note. "Thank you. I do know how to operate a telephone. Sometimes I do it for hours on end."

Her eyebrow twitched slightly as she tore off the page and handed it to him. Dan wanted to apologize, but he couldn't come up with anything witty enough. It had been a trying day.

He closed the door of his office and sat down behind the desk, looking at the page with the telephone number and extension on it. Candler had seemed like a nice enough guy. It wouldn't hurt to call and talk to him in a purely nonprofessional way, to get his take on the situation.

Jess wouldn't do it. Though in almost every other way Jess was a strong, ambitious, independent woman, she was quirky about drawing attention to herself, or having people inconvenience themselves for her. It had something to with having grown up in the South, Dan thought. She would consider asking Candler's advice an unladylike intrusion. Dan was neither a Southerner nor a lady, and he had no such scruples. He dialed the number.

Candler wasn't in. When asked if he wanted to be transferred to his voice mail, Dan hesitated for just a minute. He was interfering. Jess wouldn't like it, and hadn't he just finished telling Trish to let the woman manage her own life? He glanced at the plastic bag–covered bundle hanging on his coatrack, and he thought, *What the hell*.

He said, "Yes, please. Transfer me."

When he got the detective's voice mail, he said, "Lieutenant Candler, this is Dan Webber from *Speaking of Which*. I hope I'm not out of line, but I have a personal matter I'd like to ask your advice about. Give me a call at your convenience. You can reach me here at the office in the afternoons, or if you're out this way sometime, stop by. I'll buy you a drink. Thanks." He left his number and hung up, pleased with the sound of it. Not too urgent, not too mysterious, not making more of it than he should. He was glad he had called. It was the right thing to do.

The next day's show featured a panel of young men who had been falsely imprisoned—so they claimed—in foreign countries. It was the kind of show Dan liked, with subject matter that was anchored more or less in solid news, and it required a lot of research. He spent the rest of the afternoon buried in background, and once he became immersed, he didn't think of Candler—or Jess—again at all.

Chapter 7

Jess was behind on almost everything. She had a speech to write for an appearance at a journalism class later in the week, the fan mail was stacking up, and she knew almost nothing about tomorrow's show. She hated the kinds of shows she couldn't bluff her way through, and it was hard to concentrate.

She wished she hadn't told Dan about Brett. She felt as though she had given away a part of herself to someone who might not value it, and she had done it impulsively, without thought. Something like that was private; the sharing of it left her exposed and vulnerable, and that was a feeling she did not like.

As her tormentor no doubt knew.

Have you ever done anything you're ashamed of? The list was growing longer by the day. Running out on poor Steve the way she had done Saturday night. Would she ever be able to face him again? Evading her mother about coming home for the weekend. Now making that embarrassing confession to Dan. She had no right to burden him with her guilts and nightmares; never mind that he had started it with his own confession. He was curious, and that was understandable, but he hadn't bargained for what she had given him.

They were co-workers and casual friends, and as such had shared large portions of their lives with one another over the years. But there were limits as to what their relationship could endure, and Jess was constantly juggling to stay on the proper side of the line that separated them.

And then there was that stupid dress. In a way she was relieved because this time the threat—or reminder, or whatever it was—seemed less personal. There was no picture, no application form completed in Jess's own handwriting, nothing to indicate the kind of invasion of privacy she was accustomed to expect from him. But that she couldn't relate to this message was even more disturbing.

The dress was not that unusual. Just because it reminded her of a prom dress she might once have worn didn't mean it *was* the dress. And she was certain she had never had a stain like that on anything she had ever owned. But the dress, and the stain, meant something to *him*. Now he had a secret, something he knew that Jess didn't, and that frightened her.

Just as he had intended.

At six o'clock Sylvia left, and the only progress Jess had made with the fan mail was in the form of three letters that Sylvia had already typed and placed on her desk for signature. Three letters. The speech had yet to be written. And the file folder on one of the boys who was to be on tomorrow's show—one who supposedly spent eighteen months in jail for littering in Malaysia—lay open on her desk. She couldn't remember the last time she turned a page.

What the hell, she thought, and closed the file with a snap. *Let Dan carry it. He loves this stuff. Besides, he's the one who's bailing out. He ought to have to work for a living as long as he's here.*

On the other hand, if she let Dan carry too many shows, it might become obvious to those who mattered that *he* was the talent and *she* was expendable. What was to stop the guys upstairs from making this *The Dan Webber Show*? If Dan wanted his own show, maybe Trish's idea of a sweet deal would be to give it to him. . . .

"Damn!" she muttered out loud and picked up the folder again. As if she didn't have enough problems without worrying about Dan and his career options.

With a ferocious effort she managed to focus on the material at hand for the time it took to jot down two legal-sized pages worth of questions and comments, far more than she would ever use. At eight o'clock she looked up and congratulated herself smugly. She would have a surprise or two for Dan Webber tomorrow morning.

The satisfaction of a job well done, along with the skipped lunch, had a positive effect on her appetite, and she wondered if there was anyone left in the building with whom to have dinner. The bullpen was empty, the lights already turned down so low that most of the desks were in shadows. She dialed Trish's office, but got no answer. Dan might still be working, but she doubted it. He wasn't one to put in long hours at the office, although she knew he often took work home. Besides, Dan was not even on her top-ten list of dinner companions tonight.

Her muscles were stiff from sitting at her desk for so long, and her eyes ached. She still had a speech to write and more than a dozen letters to answer, and she hated to leave her desk cluttered with unfinished work. She could take the letters home, of course, and dictate replies over a glass of cold wine and a plate of cheese. It sounded like heaven. But if she didn't get that speech done before she left, she would obsess about it all night. And she wasn't sure she could face another hour, or even two, at her desk.

Stretching, she decided to kill two birds with one stone. The first-floor gym was never very busy this time of night; she could use the time on the treadmill to dictate her speech. Then home to the glass of wine and the unanswered fan mail. After the chaos this day had been, it was good to have a plan.

She kept a gym bag in the bottom drawer of her file cabinet. As she went for it, her phone rang. She picked it up, expecting the familiar voice of Dan or Trish or even someone on the production staff with a last-minute change in tomorrow's line-up. She decided if it was Dan she would have dinner with him after all.

"Hi, this is Jess."

Nothing.

"Hello?"

There was no voice, but the distinct sound of breathing on the other end of the line. Heavy, deliberate breathing.

Jess slammed the receiver down, as infuriated by the prank as by the predictable effect it had on her. Her pulse was racing.

"Damn," she said, trying to reassure herself with

the sound of her own voice. But her voice was too
shaky to reassure anyone. She felt foolish for over-
reacting. No one did the heavy breathing bit anymore. It had probably just been someone with a bad
cold, a wrong number, or a speech impediment, and
she had hung up without giving the person a chance
to explain.

She cleared her throat self-consciously and murmured, "Oh, well. If it's important, they'll call back."

But she wouldn't answer the phone. She grabbed
her gym bag and her briefcase and left the office.

She noticed on the way to the elevators that she
was still wearing the sneakers she had put on at
lunch, and she was annoyed. That meant her street
shoes were still in the desk drawer, and she would
have to go back for them before she left. She didn't
want to turn into one of those women who had
more pairs of shoes at the office than they did at
home.

She punched the button for the elevator, and
when it was slow in coming, pushed it again. She
couldn't imagine what was holding it up this time
of night. A minute passed, then two. Then three.

There was obviously something wrong with the
elevator. She never waited this long, even at the
height of the business day. She tried the button
one more time, and when there was no response,
muttered, "Great" and turned for the stairwell. It
was only four floors down, and this would save wear
and tear on the stair-stepping machine.

The door clanged behind her and echoed down
the stairwell, muffling her steps as she took them
at a brisk, bouncing pace. She slowed at the half-
floor landing, and that was when she heard the dis-

tinctive, echoing *click* of metal on metal. The door above her had closed, not with the raucous clang of someone in a hurry, but carefully, stealthily, almost muffled.

Jess waited, listening for footsteps. When they didn't come, she thought she must have been mistaken about the sound, or that whoever had opened the door had closed it without entering. She continued down the steps again, and then she heard it— the quick tap-tap of shoes on metal, someone coming down the steps toward her.

She stopped again and turned, looking up, waiting for the figure to appear around the bend that preceded the third-floor landing. The footsteps stopped.

Her pulse began to pound too fast, too heavy. She called. "Hello? Is someone there?"

Nothing. Her skin prickled.

She tried to remember how many footsteps she had heard, how close he might be. There was no door between her and the top of the stairs; whoever had entered the staircase must still be there. Then why had he stopped? Why didn't he answer when she called?

And then she heard it again. One step, a tap on metal. Echoing. Another. Slow. Stealthily.

She called again, sharply. "Who's there? Answer me, please!"

The footsteps stopped. A chill went down Jess's spine. She could picture him there, just above her— how close?—poised, waiting to spring. She could almost hear him breathing.

And then a voice floated down to her. A husky, sibilant whisper, echoing and disembodied. "Jess . . ."

It was close. Too close. "Aren't you ashamed of yourself, Jess? Aren't you?"

She may have cried out, but the sound was drowned in the clatter of her own footsteps and the roaring of her heartbeat as she flung herself down the steps. The briefcase bounced against her thigh, and the strap of the gym bag swung off her shoulder and slid down her arm. She stumbled over the bag and saved herself from a fall by grabbing the handrail, letting the bag drop. Momentum carried her down a few more steps before she could pull herself to a stop with a wrenching pain in her shoulder. She bit back another cry, blood and breath rushing in her ears as she strained for some sound from above, and tried to still her heart, tried to listen. . . .

And there. A step. Clear, clanging, deliberate. She couldn't tell how far away. Her heart wouldn't stop thundering, her breath hissing and trembling through her nostrils. She pressed her fingers tightly against her lips, holding back gasps. Another step. He was in no hurry. He was coming.

"Jess . . ."

The voice again, echoing, distorted, more of a whisper than a shout. But it reverberated off the walls, tumbled down the stairs, rose up to surround her. The sound of it caused Jess to shrink back against the wall, squeezing her eyes closed as though the voice itself had eyes, as though it could follow her.

"Wait for me, Jess. I have something for you."

The steps again. *Clang, clang* . . . Slow and steady. Coming for her.

A wave of sheer, paralyzing terror washed over her, and Jess was almost persuaded in that moment to obey the voice, to wait, to just stay where she was and wait until he appeared and then she would know. At least she would know the face of her tormentor, at least she wouldn't have to be afraid anymore. . . .

Her eyes snapped open, and she pushed away from the wall in a single movement. She started to resume her frantic headlong flight down the stairs, but then she hesitated. She could hear him coming closer. She could hear him, but he couldn't hear her, not if she was careful. If she ran for it, he would be on her in an instant. He was too close. She had let him get too close. She couldn't outrun him now.

Clang, clang. In no hurry.

He thought she was too afraid to run. He thought she was trapped. She looked down at her rubber-soled Reeboks and tested the sound on the step below her. Nothing. Another step behind her. She clutched her briefcase close to her body to minimize the sound of it scraping against her clothes, and, holding on to the handrail, she moved quickly and silently down the stairs.

Her lungs were bursting from the effort to silence the sound of her breathing, and her heartbeat thundered and roared in her ears by the time she reached the next landing. The door there was marked with a large numeral 2. She couldn't even hear his footsteps anymore, though she knew he was close. Too close.

Abandoning stealth, she rushed to the door and pushed the bar with all her might. It made a banging, clanking sound that was so loud she thought surely everyone in the building must hear it . . . but the door did not open. She pushed again, stifling a cry, but nothing happened. She was trapped.

She turned wildly and looked back up the staircase just in time to see something coming at her from above. She screamed as it struck her face—*No*—wrapped itself around her, blinding her. She clawed at it, gasping, dragging the material away from her face, her hair.

From above the voice was caressing. "They smell like you."

Jess stared at the fabric in her hands, her vision shaking with each pounding beat of her heart, blurring so badly she almost didn't recognize what she held. A pair of tights. Her tights. From her gym bag.

She shrank back instinctively, shielding her face as something else dropped toward her. Her leotard. He was standing on the half landing just above her, emptying the contents of her gym bag.

Jess flung the tights aside and looked up. He was there. The bend of the staircase allowed her to see his shoes, but nothing more. Men's shoes. Brown leather oxfords with perforations on the uppers. He was there.

Suddenly, terror turned to rage, and she screamed at him, "I can see you, you bastard! Why are you doing this?"

The shoes stepped back, out of sight. Jess felt a surge of triumph. *She* had alarmed him. She had the power now. He wasn't invincible.

She pushed away from the door, shouting, "Who are you? Why are you—"

There was a crashing sound, and the stairway went dark.

For a single, heart-stopping moment Jess couldn't

move. She stood pinned in a pool of black with a maniac only a few steps above her, and she couldn't move. The darkness was a living thing, grabbing at her ankles, wrapping itself around her knees, closing on her thighs. It filled her lungs, she couldn't breathe. It burned her eyes. It got inside her skin, turning her blood to ice.

And then she heard the footsteps again. *Clang-clang-clang-clang*, purposeful and sure, and she realized there was light coming from above, faint and filtering, lighting his way but leaving her in blackness. She flung herself away from the door, groping for the handrail, missed, overbalanced, and fell hard against a step. *Clang-clang-clang* . . . Closer? Or farther away?

Dragging in gasps of breath that sounded like sobs, she inched along the surface of the step until her hand met the concrete wall. It was entirely dark now. As the light from above drifted down and her eyes adjusted, she could see shapes. She swept her hand up the wall until she felt the handrail and then pulled herself up. Footsteps above her. Gripping the handrail with both hands, she plunged downward into the darkness, around a sharp bend, and light spilled upward from the landing below. Above her a banging metal sound, echoing . . . a door crashed closed just as she reached the first-floor landing. She threw her weight against the bar and stumbled into the lobby.

A Security officer in a crisp blue uniform stood staring at her. Jess burst into tears.

Chapter 8

Dan had just rounded the corner to the elevator when a voice called his name from the left. He turned, and for an instant drew a complete blank on the man who was coming toward him. He had a razor sharp memory for facts, but when it came to names, Jess could outshine him every time.

"I was just on my way to your office. I know it's late, but I thought I'd take a chance you were still in."

"Lieutenant Candler." Recognition came to him just in time, and Dan accepted the other man's handshake as he reached him. "I hope you didn't make a special trip."

"It's on my way home," the detective assured him. "And I've got to admit, your message made me curious."

"Well. That's great. I didn't expect such a quick response. It's not an emergency or anything."

Dan hoped he sounded more enthusiastic than he felt. He was tired and he wanted to go home. Whatever quixotic impulse had prompted him to intervene on Jess's behalf this afternoon was gone now, and he already regretted it.

Apparently, he wasn't very good at disguising his

feelings after all, because the detective said, "Look, if you'd rather do this another time. . . ."

"No, not at all." He was in it now, and he might as well see it through. He had promised the man a drink after all. "There's a bar across the street, if you've got time."

Candler shrugged acquiescence. "I'm off duty."

Dan gestured toward the elevators. "Actually, it's a little awkward. I probably shouldn't have called you at all, and I'd appreciate your keeping this off the record for the time being."

The detective's interest sharpened. "I'll try."

"It's nothing criminal," Dan hastened to assure him. "That is to say, my co-worker, Jessamine Cray, has been—"

The elevator door opened just as they reached it, and a rather harried young man in a Security uniform stepped out. It was not the same one Dan had met that afternoon.

"Excuse me, Mr. Webber." He came toward Dan at a rush. "We're looking for someone who may have entered this floor within the last five minutes from the stairs. Did you see anyone?"

Dan answered, frowning, "Just a janitor. What's going on?"

"Which way?"

Dan gestured. "Back toward the bullpen. What—?"

The young man was already running down the hall.

Dan stared after him for a moment then glanced back at Candler. Urgency sharpened his voice more than he had intended. "I'll have to give you a rain check on that drink," he said. "Something's wrong. I need to check in with Security."

"Mind if I tag along?"

Dan said, "Come on," and he caught the elevator before it left the floor.

Jess was not hurt. She had glass in her hair and a few bleeding scratches, one on her leg and several on her hands, from the broken light fixture. There was a bruise on her shin and her shoulder was sore, but she wasn't hurt. They took her into the Security office and tried to force coffee and iodine on her, and she tried not to lose patience.

"I'm okay," she said for what must have been the tenth time. She was shaken and embarrassed and terrified. She wanted to go home. "Really. I didn't mean to break down like that. I just—I don't do well with dark places."

Dan paced the small cubicle like a caged lion. "I don't understand why the elevators weren't working. They were working fine a minute ago."

"I explained that to Miss Cray." Hanson was the night shift Security supervisor, a sixtyish man with a quiet manner and sharp eyes. "The cleaning service shuts down the elevators every night between eight and eight-thirty for dusting and vacuuming. Takes about five minutes."

Dan glared at him. "And you think that's all right? A lot of women work in this building. You think it's acceptable to make them take the stairs alone at night just to avoid inconveniencing the cleaning service?"

Jess found his concern touching—and irritating. "It was just bad timing, Dan. I could have waited for the elevator, but I didn't."

She dabbed at a scratch on her palm with a tissue, and when she saw Dan watching, she balled up the tissue in her hand. She was still shaking, and he noticed it.

"Now you tell me," she demanded, taking the offensive before he could, "what Lieutenant Candler is doing here. I certainly hope you haven't taken it upon yourself—"

Dan made a brusque, dismissing gesture with his hand. "We were having drinks, that's all. And damn lucky for you he was here."

"How?" she demanded a little shrilly. "How was it lucky for me? Damn it, Dan, I didn't ask you to interfere—"

She became aware of Hanson's interested gaze, and she broke off abruptly, embarrassed. The silence weighed heavy for three or four long beats, and then the door to the Security office opened.

A young Security officer entered, escorting a man in a green uniform with "Professional Cleaning Service" scrolled in yellow on the pocket. Behind him was Lieutenant Candler.

"Miss Cray, this is Gerardo Montez." The Security officer tried to sound composed, but couldn't quite control the note of excitement in his voice. "Is this the man you saw on the stairway?"

A tightness started in Jess's spine and went through every muscle in her body as she slowly raised her eyes to the man. Her stomach, her chest, her throat, all knotted in sequence, and she was afraid to draw a deep breath. He had dark skin, Latin features, long black hair, and sullen eyes. She made herself meet those eyes. He was thin and wiry, but probably strong. He looked like the type who would see nothing wrong with slapping his girlfriend around every once in a while. She wanted it to be him. And she didn't.

Her eyes moved to his feet, and the relief she felt confused her. "No," she said. "It's not him."

The Security man frowned. "You're sure?"

And without giving her a chance to dispute his own assumption, he turned to Montez and demanded, "You were on the stairway tonight, weren't you? Just a little while ago."

Montez nodded once, his eyes burning with contempt and fixed on Jess.

"What were you doing there?"

"My job to sweep the stairs. You think they get clean with nobody sweeping them? Light was out. I went to get a new bulb." He shrugged elaborately, finishing his story.

Jess shook her head impatiently, gesturing to Montez's dusty black canvas shoes. "It's not him. He's wearing sneakers. The man who followed me was wearing regular shoes—brown leather oxfords."

"What about the voice, Miss Cray? You said the man spoke to you on the stairwell. Could it have been this man's voice?"

"No. I mean, it was disguised but—no." Her tone was decisive. "It's not the same."

The young Security officer looked inconvenienced and uncertain. He insisted to Montez, a little pompously now, "Well, did you see anybody when you left the stairwell? Anybody in the hall?"

Montez's eyes went slowly to Dan and rested there. "Him," he said.

Dan sat on the corner of Hanson's desk, swinging his foot. His shoes were brown, with laces.

Hanson said, "Okay, Mr. Montez, you can go."

He pointedly did not apologize for the mistake. The younger officer didn't even wait for the door to close behind Montez before he said, "I think we ought to double-check his background. There's something slippery there. I think he's hiding something."

Hanson said, "The guy scrubs toilets for minimum wage. He probably doesn't even have his green card. You were expecting maybe Billy Graham?"

Candler stood at the threshold until Montez left, then he entered the room. He smiled sympathetically at Jess. He had her gym bag and a black umbrella in his hand. "Feeling better?"

She took a breath. "Feeling foolish. I didn't mean to cause all this excitement."

Dan said irritably, "For God's sake, Jess, stop apologizing for being a victim!"

Candler handed her the gym bag. "This is yours, then? Some of the things were spilled."

She was loath to take it, to touch what *he* had touched. "He, um, took my clothes out and . . . threw them down the stairs at me."

The young Security man was listening intently. Candler glanced at Hanson, who said, "Jim, why don't you go back up and rewalk the floors? See if anybody else was on the fourth floor tonight."

Jess made herself take the bag. She set it on the floor beside her chair. Unconsciously, she wiped her hands with the balled-up tissue as soon as she put the bag down.

Candler indicated the umbrella. "It looks like he used this to knock out the light on the landing."

"It's mine," Jess said. "It was in my gym bag."

Candler returned it to her. Once again, Jess wiped her hands when she had put it away.

Dan said, "Aren't you going to take fingerprints or anything?"

Candler pointed out, "There really hasn't been a crime. And even so, it would be hard to match prints at this point. We don't even have a starting list of suspects." And he looked at Jess inquisitively. "Do we?"

Jess managed a weak smile. "I thought you said there hadn't been a crime."

His expression was sober. "Not technically, maybe. But I do advise you file a report. In cases like this, documentation is everything."

Dan said alertly, "What do you mean, cases like this?"

Jess said, "I don't want to file a report." Her voice was tight. She could feel it winding through her body again, the piano wire of tension. "Not tonight. I can't do it tonight. Do I have to do it tonight?"

"The morning is soon enough," Candler assured her. "Can you come down to the station first thing?"

Dan said, demanding an answer to his question, "Lieutenant?"

Candler glanced at Jess, looked uncomfortable, and replied, "Domestic violence, stalking . . . the laws exist, but they're hard to enforce. The longer the paper trail, the better chance we have of protecting the victim. I know it sounds crazy, but there's your court system for you."

Jess took a long breath, then released it. "Maybe it was just an . . . isolated incident. Somebody with a twisted sense of humor."

Dan shot her an incredulous, disgusted look. "For God's sake, Jess."

He turned to Candler. "What are the chances of catching this creep tonight?"

Candler looked at Hanson, a gesture of professional courtesy more than anything. "Unless your Security sweep turns up someone without authorization to be in the building, I'd say none. If it was an intruder, he's long gone. If it was someone who works here . . ." A small lift of his shoulder spoke volumes about the chances of proving anything.

"In that case . . ." Dan picked up Jess's gym bag and briefcase with a proprietorial air. "Let's get out of here."

Jess didn't particularly like the way he took over, but the truth was she wanted to go home. She wanted to get out of this awful little office that smelled of Brüt and stale coffee and reminded her, not of security, but of danger. She wanted to put this night behind her. She wanted a hot bath and a very large glass of wine and she wanted to forget.

She stood. "Thanks, Mr. Hanson. I'm sorry for the trouble."

He got to his feet. "We'll let you know what we find, Miss Cray. Don't you worry about anything." He looked at Chandler with a cool professional nod. "Lieutenant."

Their steps echoed loudly in the marble-tiled lobby. The building had an eerie night quiet; machines were shut down, voices were absent, elevators were still. In the newsroom upstairs, business proceeded as usual. Phones rang, keyboards clacked, fax machines whined, and televisions chattered. But here all was still, and nighttime was draped over the plate glass windows like a shroud.

Candler said, "This isn't really my beat, you know. But if you'd like to tell me what's been going on, I'll be glad to listen."

Jess glanced at him gratefully. He was a nice man. And she could strangle Dan for bringing him into this.

"I'm afraid that would be overkill, wouldn't it?" she said, trying to make her voice light—or as light as possible under the circumstances. "I mean, you're the guy who solved the Silk Scarf killings, and all I've got is one little man with a twisted sense of humor."

"And a handful of notes and a phone call and a few very strange presents," Dan put in sharply.

Candler said, "What makes you think it's a man?"

Jess was startled. She actually slowed her steps. "What?"

"Do you have anything that's gender-specific?"

Jess said slowly, "No . . . The voice—it's always a whisper, disguised somehow. So I guess, no. Not really."

"Then let's keep an open mind. What about these notes?"

Jess didn't want to talk about it. The last thing she wanted to do was talk about it. Dan, however, had no such scruples. He gave the detective a concise replay of everything Jess had told him, from the first note to the phone call and the envelope under her door over the weekend, to the prom dress delivered today. Not for the first time Jess had cause to resent his close-to-photographic memory.

Candler refused to draw any conclusions. He

pushed open the door and held it for Jess, saying only, "You should put all of this in your report tomorrow."

"Jess didn't want to involve the police," Dan said.

They were out on the street, illuminated by the cool wash of streetlights and headlights and the white fluorescent backlight of the building. The day's warmth had left the air, and Jess shivered.

"The notes haven't threatened anything," Candler agreed, "and neither did the phone call. It would be hard to get anything on this guy even if we could find him. Tonight was a little different. It might substantiate a restraining order."

Jess echoed, "Restraining order?"

And Dan said, "Perfect. Why don't we just put an ad in the paper, advising all psychopaths to please not come within a hundred yards of Jessamine Cray?"

Candler's smile was apologetic. "It's not a perfect world, Mr. Webber."

"So the bottom line is we should just wait until this creep hurts her before we bother to call the police? *Then* you might do something?" His tone held that same note of suppressed outrage he used when confronting an uncooperative guest on the show.

Candler glanced at Jess, and Dan looked embarrassed—and annoyed, although whether the annoyance was with himself or with Candler was not evident.

Candler said, "I don't think it will get to that point. By confronting Miss Cray in the staircase tonight, he almost tipped his hand. He ran away when you said you could see him, right? My guess is he's either too scared to try anything else, or getting too careless to stay hidden much longer."

He addressed Jess sympathetically. "I know tonight was an ordeal, but in a way it was the best thing that could have happened. You did get a look at him, and you confronted him with that."

"Just his shoes," Jess said. She tried not to shiver as she remembered. "All I saw was his shoes."

"But he doesn't know that."

Jess knew he meant the words to be reassuring, but they could be interpreted another way. Up until now, the stalker had been secure in his anonymity. What would be his reaction if he thought Jess could be a threat to him?

In the heavy night silence the thought might as well have been shouted. It was implicit in the look the two men shared, in the way they glanced quickly away from Jess when they saw she, too, understood.

Candler took a card out of his pocket and handed it to Jess. "Try not to worry," he said gently. "Don't let him win. And come by the station first thing in the morning," he reminded her. "It's on Eleventh and—"

"Yes, I know." She took the card, swallowing hard, and when she raised her eyes to his, she knew she had just made a promise she didn't want to keep, but couldn't break. "I'll be there."

"Good night then."

Candler's eyes lingered for a moment, imparting strength and reassurance. Jess supposed he had plenty of opportunity to practice that look in his line of work.

He turned to Dan, offering his hand. "You still owe me a drink."

"I won't forget. Thanks for coming."

"Drive carefully going home." That was for Jess.

Candler glanced again at Dan, and another one of those male signals passed. He said, "Good night," and walked toward the corner of the building, where a gray sedan was parked.

Dan said, "Are you in the garage across the street?"

Jess nodded.

"So am I. I'll walk you to your car."

He checked the traffic, then pressed her shoulder, ushering her across the street.

Like any other woman who worked in a big city and sometimes found herself walking alone to her car at night, Jess considered herself alert to danger and as prepared for it as anyone could reasonably be. She had taken a one-day seminar in personal protection that had included some street-fighting moves. She carried her purse close to her body and her keys in her hand. She had a spray canister of tear gas in the outside pocket of her briefcase. Until now all those measures had seemed perfectly adequate.

Now, although she would never have told him so, she was glad to have Dan walk her to her car.

When they reached the opposite curb, Dan said, "All right, go ahead. Let me have it."

"What?"

"The lecture."

"You shouldn't have interfered. You wasted the man's time and made me feel like an idiot."

"For what?" Again his tone was incredulous. "For being terrorized in a stairwell by a maniac?"

"For having such a pathetic story. A few notes. A

dirty prom dress. It wouldn't even make a good movie-of-the-week."

Now, away from the building and everything that reminded her of it, she could make her tone almost cavalier. Dan was neither impressed, nor amused.

"The truth is, I'm almost ready to agree with you. Not about your story, but about calling Chandler. He wasn't very helpful. What level are you on?"

"Two. And I think he was trying not to scare me," she added pointedly. "It was considerate."

"They probably teach that in detective school."

When she turned for the elevator, he caught her arm. "I'm down this aisle. I'll drive you up."

She stared at him in exasperation.

"Don't give me that look. You're getting a free ride. Come on."

"Oh, for heaven's sake."

But when he tugged on her arm, she didn't pull away. The echo of their footsteps on the concrete was eerie, and she didn't really want to get in the elevator by herself.

Dan unlocked his silver Lexus, passenger side first, and handed Jess her briefcase and gym bag when she was seated. His car smelled like leather and luxury. She let herself relax briefly against the headrest when he closed the door; and realized this was the first time she had felt safe all day.

She asked, "Did you get your license back?"

For a moment he looked blank, then he said, "Damn. I was supposed to go by the DMV. I forgot all about it." He inserted the key into the ignition and the dashboard lit up in Christmas colors. "One advantage of dealing with someone else's troubles, I guess. You forget about your own."

Jess said firmly, "I really don't want you dealing with my troubles, Dan."

He backed out of the parking space with a careless glance in the side mirror and turned the car toward the second story. "Don't worry. This is about as far as my sense of chivalry goes."

"Good."

Jess leaned her head back again. Her muscles ached from being knotted, but when she tried to relax them, they trembled. She clenched and unclenched her fists, trying to stop it.

Dan said, "I didn't throw away that dress, by the way. I think it should go to the police. If you don't want to turn it over to them, I will."

Jess said slowly, "Roger. Roger . . . something."

"What?"

She sat up straight. "The guy I went to the prom with. Isn't that funny? The name just popped into my head. Roger . . . something to do with food. A funny name. God, I can't remember."

He glanced at her. "I thought you said you didn't go to the prom."

She sank back against the seat, frowning as she tried to remember. "I didn't. At least, not that year . . . there were two proms, you know. My junior year and my senior year. One year something happened, and I didn't get to wear the dress. . . ." She pressed her fingertips to her forehead and closed her eyes. "I don't know. High school was a long time ago."

"This morning was a long time ago," Dan agreed.

He pulled up behind her white BMW. Jess gathered her belongings.

"I'm following you home," he said.

She looked at him for a moment, knowing she

didn't have the energy to argue. Knowing she didn't want to.

"I suppose I should be grateful you're letting me drive my own car."

"Just say thank you and get out."

"Thank you." She opened the door.

"Hey, Jess."

She looked back. He was leaning toward her, frowning a little. "You must have gone to the prom," he said. "Otherwise how would anyone know what kind of dress you wore?"

She thought about that all the way home. And all the way home, Dan's headlights were never out of her rearview mirror.

He parked in the guest spot beside hers and stood beside her car while she got out.

"You don't have to see me to the door," she said wearily.

He took the gym bag and briefcase from her again. "Indulge me."

"You're making me paranoid."

"Under the circumstances it might not be a bad idea if you were a little paranoid."

The parking area was brightly lit and the walk to Jess's front door less than twenty feet. Motion-sensor lights came on over her building, filling the shadows with light, when she was midway down the walk. Dan noted all this silently, but stood with her until she unlocked the door anyway.

She turned to take her bags from him, but he held them out of reach. He reached inside and turned on the light, then preceded her in.

Jess removed her mail from the mailbox and stood just inside the door, watching him indulgently as he went from room to room, opening closets and checking behind doors. "Cute, Webber," she said. "You've been watching too many low-budget TV shows."

"I'll have you know I learned this from the very best of Robert Parker." He checked the lock on the sliding glass door.

"Do you want me to make coffee or something?"

"No, I've got to be up early in the morning." He tugged at the movable portion of the front window and found it locked. "So do you." He looked back at her. "You're not going to forget your appointment at the police station, are you?"

She said wearily, "I won't forget. Dan, this is really sweet of you, but . . ."

He noticed the mail she held in her hand. "Do you want me to look through that for you?"

She hesitated, glancing down at the envelopes. Until he pointed it out, she had not been consciously aware that she was avoiding looking at them.

Her mouth was dry as she flipped through them once, too fast, and then more carefully. She looked up at him in relief. "Just bills."

He smiled. "I wish I could look that happy when I said that." He paused. "You okay?"

She tried to give him an honest answer. She wasn't sure she knew the truth. "I think so. I will be."

"Do you want me to stay?"

He looked serious. Jess smiled. "Good night, Dan."

He smiled, too. "Good night, sweetie." He took

her chin in his fingers and kissed her lightly on the lips. "Lock up."

"I will."

She could see his shadow through the sidelight, waiting until he heard the click of the deadbolt, the slide of the chain. She listened to his footsteps retreating on the walk and smiled to herself as she turned back into the room, touching her lips lightly. He had never kissed her before. She hadn't expected it.

And then she remembered that, with everything else that had happened that day, she had never talked to the locksmith about changing her locks.

She was suddenly too tired to eat and too nervous to undress for a bath. She drank half a bottle of wine, but it didn't help. She slept with the light on for the first time since she was a child.

Chapter 9

Freddie Glanbury disliked Lyle Candler intensely. In turn, Freddie was disliked by three-quarters of the police force—the other one-fourth were merely indifferent—most of his colleagues, and everyone he had ever interviewed. Freddie was generally oblivious to other people's opinions of him. In his view he was just a working stiff trying to get by the best he could and everyone else in the world was just trying to make sure he didn't. The only opinions that mattered, therefore, were his own.

Freddie made his living with a camera and a notebook, telephoto lenses and hidden tape recorders. His press credentials were kept active by a weekly tabloid, but he sold his stories to anyone who would buy them. More and more, he liked to brag, those sales were going to so-called mainstream news organizations: local television, daily papers. He was a reporter. He had credibility.

The only thing that stood between Freddie Glanbury and the big story was luck. Being in the right place at the right time, knowing the right questions to ask, the right people to ask them of. Lieutenant Lyle Candler could be his ticket. Freddie knew star power when he saw it, and Candler's star was definitely on the ascendant. He had been on talk shows. He was being interviewed for a book—a book Freddie should have written, but some big name asshole had beaten him to it. Before anybody knew it, Candler's name would be in front of the "played by" billing on the Sunday Night Movie credits.

The thing was—the most frustrating, irritating, maddening thing was—Freddie had known Candler before he was famous. The precinct had been one of his favorite haunts long before the Silk Scarf business, and all he had ever gotten out of it was a few small time political scandals—Councilman Caught in Topless Bar—and a photograph of a football star brought in for DWI.

Freddie had missed the break in the Silk Scarf killings by a matter of mere days. He had been in the wrong place at the wrong time. He wasn't going to let that happen again. Candler would start to get the big cases, the celebrity cases, the unsolvable, sensationalistic, photographic cases; it was inevitable. And Freddie would be there.

Knowing that was enough to risk getting caught in a misdemeanor. Or was searching a police detective's desk without permission a felony? It probably didn't matter, because if Lyle Candler caught him, Freddie had a feeling he wouldn't retain enough of his teeth to protest his innocence in either case. The words "police brutality" meant nothing to bigshots like Candler.

So he was careful to keep the door to the squad room in his peripheral vision and his hearing tuned to the sound of footsteps, and with the heightened senses of an experienced second-story man he knew Candler was coming before he rounded the corner.

He was furtive and he was good, and though there were half a dozen officers in the room and all of them did him the honor of a suspicious glance or two, none of them were able to catch him at anything. And by the time Candler came into the room, Freddie was sitting on the edge of his desk, an innocent citizen waiting for the detective to show up for work. He hadn't found anything.

Candler's expression was implacable as he reached him, his tone conversational. "Get your ass off my desk, Glanbury, and your sleazebag face out of my sight."

"Hey, you can't talk to me like that." But he stood up anyway.

"I just did." Candler's eyes were cold. "And if I find so much as a paper clip missing from my desk, you're going to spend the next couple of nights as prime-time entertainment for the boys downstairs, and that's a goddamn promise."

Downstairs were the jail cells, some of them filled with hard-timers awaiting shipment to state or federal prisons. Freddie said, "Your paper clips are just fine."

Candler filled a Styrofoam cup with coffee from the drip machine nearby. One of the perks of being a celebrity cop, Freddie thought—a desk closer to the coffee machine.

Freddie said, "What do you know about that woman they found in the river last night?"

"Nothing." Candler elbowed past him and sat down at his desk.

"Is it true both her feet were missing?"

"Yeah, and you know what else? She had fins and

a tail and green scales up to her ass. Get out of here, Freddie."

A dull flush suffused Freddie's skin. "You know what, Lieutenant? Cops like you are the reason this country's turning into a nation of criminals. The people have a right to know. You can't—"

And suddenly he stopped, his eyes narrowing as his attention was caught by something far more interesting. He was a good reporter. He always had an eye out for news. "Say, isn't that that girl—what's her name? From the talk show?"

Candler followed the direction of his gaze. Jessamine Cray had just entered the squad room, looking beautiful, confused, and out of place in a powder pink linen suit and long gold chain around her neck, hair as glossy as raven's wings, eyes like something in a Renaissance painting. Heads turned. Three detectives scrambled to their feet and moved forward to help her. It wasn't that she was that drop-dead gorgeous, observed Candler from his own safe distance behind his desk. It was that she had class. Twenty-four-karat gold. The best clothes, the most expensive hairdresser, makeup experts fussing over her twice a day. Style. Confidence. Presence. The whole package. A woman like that walked into a room, people noticed.

Scanning the room, she saw him and smiled nervously. He returned her smile and pushed away from his desk.

Freddie's eyes narrowed speculatively. "Friend of yours now, is she? You must've made quite an impression on her show. You want to talk about it, or should I just draw my own conclusions?"

Candler ignored him, picking up his coffee cup.

As he moved past him, his hand jostled, then tipped, and Freddie Glanbury yelped and jumped back as the steaming contents of the cup splashed on the front of his shirt and jeans.

"Goddamn you, Candler, you did that on purpose! I ought to sue you! I'll have your goddamn badge! Jesus!"

Fury gave way to agony as he tried to pluck the hot material away from his thighs and stomach, shaking one foot and then the other in an effort to alleviate the discomfort.

Candler looked at him sympathetically. "Gee, I'm sorry, Freddie. Guess you shouldn't have been standing so close, huh?"

Then he leaned forward and advised confidentially, "I'd go change if I were you. It kind of looks like you wet yourself."

"You son of a bitch! You think you can just get away with this shit, don't you?"

Candler walked away.

Bob Wexford had won the joust for Jess's attention and was gesturing her toward his desk. But Jess looked relieved when she saw Candler, and Bob looked resigned.

Candler said, "I'll take care of this one, Bob."

Bob muttered, "Yeah, I figured you might." Apparently, Jess had mentioned his name.

"I didn't know if I should bother you," Jess explained apologetically as Bob went back to his desk. "I know you're busy and this isn't really your department."

Candler smiled and gestured her through the maze of desks toward an open interview room. "Things are a little slow in the serial killer business these days," he replied. "I think I can spare a minute."

Freddie Glanbury gave Candler a malevolent look as he brushed by, and Jess noticed. She could not have missed the incident earlier.

"Not a fan of yours, I presume."

"A boil on the face of humanity—Freddie Glanbury. He calls himself a reporter, but what he is is the worst kind of parasite. He's not even a very good one—most of the time. But last year he happened to stumble on a witness we were protecting—cost us the case, almost cost a good cop his life. First Amendment says we can't kick him out, but no law says we have to be nice to him."

He opened the door of the interview room and flicked on an overhead light. "Can I get you a cup of coffee?" And he grinned. "I promise to be careful with it."

The room was small and dreary, painted the color of a rainy morning. A table, three chairs, a two-way mirror. Jess wished she hadn't come.

She said, looking quickly back at Candler, "Um, no thanks."

"I'll bet you drink tea, right? Do you want me to see if I can scrounge up a bag?"

She started to shake her head, then changed her mind. Obviously, it was important to him to make her feel comfortable. "If it's not too much trouble."

He gestured toward one of the chairs that were drawn up to the table. "It's not much, but try to make yourself comfortable. I'll be back in a minute."

He closed the door behind him, which Jess thought was considerate. She didn't enjoy the prospect of being stared at by a roomful of police officers, not to mention their suspects. But after a few moments alone in the room, she began to wonder if it would not have been preferable to be able to see what was going on outside instead of just imagining it. A woman shrieked and burst into a string of profanity. She sounded drunk or high. Another woman's voice spoke sternly to her. A man's voice, yelling, demanding justice. Another man telling him to calm down. Jess blew out a breath through her teeth and sat down gingerly on the edge of a chair. She placed her hands atop the table, then in her lap. The wooden tabletop was sticky. She wondered who was watching through the two-way mirror.

Candler returned, holding two Styrofoam cups by the inside rims and balancing a yellow legal pad under his arm while he opened the door. Jess hurried to help him, taking the cup with the string from the tea bag protruding while he closed the door on the noise from the outside. "Sorry," he apologized, indicating the outer room. "It gets a little crazy sometimes."

The door muffled, but did not completely close out, the clatter and commotion. Still, it seemed calmer. At least the screaming had stopped.

Jess said, "This must be your busiest time of day. I'll try not to take too long."

Candler removed a handful of sugar and sugar-substitute packets from his pocket and placed them on the table. "Not really," he said. "These little storm cycles come and go, you never can predict when. Except during the full moon, of course, then it all goes wild."

"Do you specialize in serial killings?" Jess asked, curious.

Candler smiled and shook his head, sitting in the chair nearest her. That created an informal atmosphere, not like a policeman taking a statement but like two friends chatting. Jess was aware of the gesture and appreciated it.

"There aren't enough of them to keep a detective busy full time, thank God," he said. "I'm assigned to Major Crimes, but I get mostly homicides. And contrary to what you see on TV, the life of a homicide cop is pretty much routine. We get a call, most of the time we nail the perp within seventy-two hours—it's the boyfriend, the uncle, the brother, the partner, and he's left a trail a blind man couldn't miss. Killers are not very smart as a general rule, and the mistake they make is in thinking we're not very smart either. Sometimes they don't even try to run away. Eighty-seven percent of all killers know their victims, which is another thing that makes them easy to track down. It's when strangers start killing strangers that cops get worried. That's when society really starts to break down."

Then he grimaced and broke open a packet of sugar into his coffee. "Sorry. That was from a speech I gave last year at a junior college. I didn't mean to get carried away."

Jess dunked her tea bag, smiling at him. "Must be the same class I'm speaking to Thursday. Career day, right?"

He chuckled. "The secret to being a good educator—a well-stocked Rolodex."

Gradually, Jess began to think it might not have been such a bad idea to come here after all. She said, "You have a good interrogatory manner. If I were the victim of a crime, I'd want you on my case. You make people feel at ease."

He gave a slightly self-conscious lift of his shoulder. "It comes with practice."

"I don't think so. I think you probably either have it or you don't."

"That's nice of you to say. You're the expert, after all, and I've got to admit, I'm a little nervous."

"I think you just lost points for putting me at ease. The person in charge should never be nervous."

"Aren't you, before a show?"

"All the time."

She smiled, and he smiled. The moment was almost comfortable.

Then he took out a ballpoint pen and placed it atop the yellow pad. He said, "I'm not interrogating you, Miss Cray, and I know this isn't a show. You start whenever you're ready; tell it in any order you like. I'll take notes, and ask you questions, but I'll try not to be too much of a pain in the ass. The more we can get on the record, the more we'll be able to give the judge to work with if we ever get close enough to nail the creep. First, just let me ask you—has anything like this ever happened to you before?"

Jess shook her head. "I think everyone in the public eye gets spooky fan mail now and then—once someone even sent me a pair of underwear they wanted autographed—but never anything as . . . systematic as this. I have some of the notes, if you want to see them."

She reached into her purse and took out the folded manila envelope in which she had stored the souvenirs. She handed it over a little nervously. "I threw away the first one," she said. "But all the others are there. They're in order."

He opened the envelope and took out the contents. He went through the entire collection once, then started from the beginning and studied each piece of paper. Behind the silence the background ebb and flow of outer noise continued—voices raised, voices murmured, slamming doors, squeaky drawers. Laughter—obscenely inappropriate yet oddly reassuring. Jess dunked the tea bag a few more times, then, lacking a spoon, used her fingers to wind the string around the bag and squeeze out the moisture. She carefully transferred the bag to a purple tin ashtray, spilling only a few drops on the table.

Candler held up a paper, face toward her. "What's this?"

Jess cleared her throat. "It's a photocopy of the application for the first job I ever had in television. The highlighted part, under education—he did that. I didn't really graduate from the university, I just said I did. I dropped out in my junior year. It was like—the note, 'Have you ever done anything you're ashamed of?'—and the job application was the answer to that question. That I should have been ashamed of lying."

He just nodded, his expression revealing nothing. "How many people know you didn't graduate?"

Jess had to think about that for a while. "Well . . . it was never really a secret. I stayed in town a while, worked as a waitress . . . everyone I worked with knew. My mother knew. All her friends and neighbors, I guess. They could have told anyone. My classmates. Anyone who went to the trouble to call the registrar's office ..." And she shook her head. "A lot of people, I guess. Why?"

"Have you mentioned it to anyone lately? Within the last year or so?"

"I don't think so. Why would I?"

"A boyfriend? Someone you work with? Maybe you were just making casual conversation at a party. You might not have actually said in so many words that you lied on a job application, but you might have been talking about college days and said something that might have implied you didn't finish."

"I might have," Jess admitted dubiously. "I meet so many people, I have so many conversations ... I really can't remember. And to tell you the truth, I'd forgotten about that application. It was years ago."

"But it was the job that gave you your start in television."

"Yes," she agreed uncertainly. "But I really don't see ..."

For the first time a faint frown appeared between his brows. Jess didn't know him well enough to determine whether the frown was one of concentration or concern. He sipped his coffee, his eyes on the photocopy before him. "Someone went to a certain amount of trouble to get this application form. Notes are one thing, but this is personal."

He moved aside the application form and held up the newspaper clipping. COLLEGE STUDENT FOUND DEAD "So is this." His tone was grave, but not unkind. "Do you want to tell me about it?"

In a halting, sometimes unsteady voice, Jess told him about Brett. He listened with eyes that were gentle and alert. Then he picked up his pen.

"Do you know if he had any family?"

"His parents, an older brother."

"You wouldn't happen to know where they are?"

"They were from Florida. Clearwater. Why? You surely don't think—"

"It's a place to start, Miss Cray. This is not profiling like an obsessed fan. It seems fairly obvious someone has a personal ax to grind with you, and we have two references here to that incident in college. The chances are strong this is all related."

Jess pressed her hands together tightly in her lap. "It was," she said, "the worst thing that's ever happened to me. I think—I've never gotten over it. I don't think I ever will."

He nodded, understanding. "No one should have to confront death that young. And he was your first love."

She whispered, "Yes."

The moment of silence that passed was just long enough to be respectful, not so long as to become maudlin. He moved through the papers again.

"Aside from the one note you threw away, was there anything else? Something you haven't told me yet?"

"The phone call." She sipped her tea, pretending to be calm. It was hot and bitter. "Saturday night, after I found the envelope with the newspaper clipping under my door. The voice was kind of low and whispery. It sounded like the one on the stairwell last night, but I can't be sure. It could have been anyone."

He was writing on the pad.

"And the dress," she added.

He looked up. "What?"

"Yesterday someone delivered a dress to my office. It looked a little like a dress I bought for a prom in high school . . . a lot like it, actually. Only the front of it had a dark stain. It looked like blood, but I guess we were all just a little excited. It probably wasn't."

He didn't stop frowning. "Do you still have it?"

"Dan does. He said he was going to turn it over to you guys. To the police."

"I'll send someone around for it today if you think it's still at the office."

"He didn't take it home last night. I suppose it is."

And then she set the teacup down, her eyes widening with slow realization. "Wait a minute," she said. "That blows your theory about this whole thing being related to Brett and college, doesn't it? That dress isn't related to anything that I know of, not in my life."

He nodded thoughtfully, the tip of his pen tapping against the legal pad. "What about the stain on the front? Does it remind you of anything? Can you think of any reason it should be there?"

She shook her head. "I'm not even sure I ever wore the dress. I certainly didn't get a stain like that on it." She looked down at her cup, hunching her shoulders uncomfortably. "As for what it reminds me of . . . this is going to sound awful." She raised her eyes again. "That pink suit Jackie Kennedy wore, the day of the assassination, all wrapped up in tissue paper and put away somewhere. That's what it reminds me of."

His face reflected no change of expression. The pen continued tapping. "You're right, though," he

said. "This is a change of pattern. And it complicates things."

He leaned back in his chair and scribbled a few
notes. Jess tried to read them, but the angle of the
pad was wrong.

"Let's go over what happened last night again.
From the beginning. Why were you in the building
so late?"

She told the story over again, in every tedious
detail. She answered every question, retraced every
step. She couldn't stop herself from glancing surreptitiously at her watch once or twice. She had already
been there over an hour.

"And so all you really saw of him was his shoes,
right? Do you know anyone who wears shoes like
that?"

She smiled tiredly. "You mean besides the detective I spoke to when I came in this morning? And
the parking attendant who took my car? And about
half a dozen lawyers I passed on the street?"

"I know," he agreed. "It's not much to go on. Let
me ask you this. Can you think of anyone who dis-
likes you enough to want to punish you, or scare
you? Maybe an old boyfriend, a jealous co-worker,
someone you've had a confrontation with in the
past—I don't know, a lawsuit or something?"

Jess swallowed hard, remembering what he had
said earlier about the victims of crimes knowing the
perpetrator. "So you really don't think this is just a
crazed fan. You think . . . it's someone I know."

"We're not ruling anything out. But at this point
. . . yes. I think it almost definitely has to be someone you know."

The very thought that anyone hated her that much made Jess feel sick inside.

Candler must have seen it on her face because his own expression softened. He said, "We all have secrets, things we wish we hadn't done, things we wish we had done differently . . . I think what has happened here is that someone has locked onto one of your secrets and is trying to use it against you. So if we're going to have any chance at all of solving this, Miss Cray, you've got to tell me: What *have* you done that you're ashamed of?"

Jess looked at him for a long time, then she replied simply, "A lot."

The interview didn't last much longer. Lieutenant Candler told her to call if anything else happened, but he evinced no opinion as to whom he thought might be responsible or why, or if she was in any real danger at all.

As she left, he put his hand on her shoulder and told her, "I know I probably haven't been very encouraging, but you've taken the first step, and you're not alone anymore. We can handle this."

That was something, she supposed.

But she spent the entire drive back to the office watching her rearview mirror, and she tipped the parking attendant five dollars to park her car in a spot near the booth. And it wasn't her imagination that the Security officer on duty stared at her oddly when she passed, and she saw him turn to his partner and tell him something under his breath when he thought she wasn't looking. Then the other man stared at her. It wasn't hard to figure out what they had been talking about.

Jess stabbed the elevator button, her jaw knotted. The elevator arrived within thirty seconds.

Sylvia was waiting for her when she came in. "You're late," she informed her. "We were worried. Trish has been calling every ten minutes."

"I had an appointment."

Jess tried to get by toward her office. Sylvia circled her like a sheepdog, pink message slips in one hand, mail in the other. "Your summer wardrobe arrived—the real thing, I made the delivery man wait while I checked off every piece. Trish's idea," she added. "And it wasn't the same man who was here yesterday. I made sure of that."

"Thanks." Jess wondered if Sylvia knew about the incident on the stairwell. She wondered if Trish did.

She tried to move around Sylvia, but was blocked again. "Messages," she said, presenting them. "And mail. I sorted it like you said."

She waited expectantly.

Jess said nothing, staring at the other woman's feet.

Sylvia asked, "Something wrong?"

Jess cleared her throat. "Cute shoes."

"Oh." Sylvia held out one foot for examination. It was clad in a brown oxford shoe, men's style, with perforations around the toe seams. "Thanks."

Jess hated herself. She frowned, flipping through the message slips. "What's this?" She held up one.

Sylvia peered at it. "Jeremy Styles. Wasn't he on the show last week?"

Jess's voice was impatient. "I know he was on the show. What did he want?"

"He didn't say. But he called twice."

Jess returned the messages to her. "These will

have to wait. I've got to be in makeup in ten minutes."

"What about the mail?"

Jess glanced at the envelopes in her hand. "Oh. I'll read them while Gretchen's doing my face, I guess."

"Aren't you going to ask me?"

"Ask you what?"

"If there was anything weird."

Jess had almost made it to her door. Now she stopped, dread draining through her. She made herself turn around, made herself ask. "Was there?"

"Only this." Almost triumphantly, Sylvia pulled a legal-sized white envelope from her pocket.

Jess took it slowly. It was stamped, not metered. The postmark was clearly Philadelphia. A part of her mind observed objectively that the detective would want to see it and she should be careful how she handled it. The address was in black marker: Jessamine Cray, Speaking of Which, Philadelphia. Sylvia had already slit it neatly with a letter opener.

Jess pried open the envelope and took out the contents. Her throat ached with the cold fear that gripped her there, and she could actually feel her heart throbbing hollowly in her stomach. Nothing but a sick, almost manic curiosity compelled her to keep going.

She unfolded the paper. Sylvia crowded close, reading over her shoulder, although she had already seen it.

"Was I right?" she demanded in hushed tones. "Is it weird or what? What do you think it means?"

On the single sheet of white paper a photograph had been glued—a small picture, perhaps one inch by two, in black-and-white, of a young man sixteen or seventeen years old. Printing below the picture identified him and his affiliations with various clubs, organizations, and athletic teams.

"Roger Dill," Jess whispered. "That was his name."

"Who?"

Jess's eyes were fixed on the page, unable to pull away. The paper shook with a fine high tremble, like a leaf in the wind.

The eyes had been neatly scissored out of the photograph, and across the page, in huge block letters that partially obscured the photograph was written the single word: SHAME.

Jess jerked her eyes away, and swallowed hard. Her hand convulsed on the paper, crumpling it at the bottom, but otherwise she kept her calm.

She said, "Call the airlines, get me on the first flight to Jackson Saturday morning. I'm going home."

Chapter 10

From the airport gift shop Jess purchased an absurdly expensive beaded sweater and a Mother's Day card with a soft-focus photograph of roses on it and a quote from the Bible. When her mother unwrapped the sweater, she gave an obligatory smile and remarked, "Isn't that pretty?" then carefully refolded the tissue paper around the sweater, closed up the box, and put it away in a closet with her other treasures. She put the card on display on top of the television set, alongside photographs in cheap metal frames, colorful postcards that were propped up against the frames, and old copies of *Guideposts*.

They went to church services at Nazareth Baptist, a sprawling tan brick building located on the highway four miles from the Cray house. On three separate occasions Jess's mother pointed out what a lovely corsage Rosalind Gerber had gotten from her daughter for Mother's Day. Jess smiled absently and agreed that yes, it was lovely.

She kept waiting to feel how wonderful it was to be home, but she never did. There was nothing wonderful about the boxy brick house furnished by Sears and crowded with stack after stack of junk that any serious trash-picker would have rejected.

There was nothing nostalgic about the Sunday morning routine or the too big church with its beige-curtained baptistry and knotty pine walls. She didn't feel at home when women in polyester dresses and flowered hats came up to her and told her how pretty she looked and how well she was doing, and how much they all loved her mama. What she did feel was a jolt of surprise, every now and then, that she had actually come from this place, had once been a part of these people. It occurred to Jess for the first time that she had not had a happy childhood.

What was good about being home was that for two days and one night she did not have to cringe every time the phone rang, or look over her shoulder whenever she left the house, or jump when her name was called. No one knew she was here. That alone was worth the trip.

Her mother insisted upon putting a roast in the oven even though Jess offered to take her downtown for a real Mother's Day out. Jess's mother was an excellent country cook, but roast beef, buttermilk biscuits, mashed potatoes, and gravy were exactly the kinds of things the camera no longer allowed Jess to eat. She could not, of course, make her mother understand that without hurting her feelings, so she ate.

Mothers and daughters.

After dinner Jess's mother sat on the front porch in her Sunday clothes and house slippers, watching the traffic go by. Jess stood in the center of a narrow hallway piled high with boxes, bookshelves, and clear plastic containers, despairing of ever finding her high-school yearbooks. They were located at last underneath the bed in her old room—which had now been converted to a combination sewing room, guest room, and storage room—along with several other photo albums from her youth. She took them all out to the front porch and sat in the big wooden rocker beside her mother.

She didn't open the yearbooks right away. Instead, she flipped through plastic-coated pages of family vacations and birthdays, smiling occasionally and turning the book to share some memory with her mother. Jess at age three with chocolate cake all over her face. Jess and the beagle puppy who had been hit by a car when she was eight. Jess at the lake with Daddy, her face scrunched up as he held her poised over his head, preparing to toss her into the water. She didn't look very happy in that one.

Her mother rocked and fanned herself with a church bulletin, smiling and nodding in a disinterested way whenever Jess showed her a picture, carrying on a mostly one-sided conversation about her neighbor Mildred's new Chrysler. It had red leather seats and a cellular phone, which Mildred couldn't figure out how to use.

Then Jess saw a photograph that did not make her smile. She looked at it for a long time; so long in fact that her mother stopped talking and glanced over at her. Jess closed the photograph album.

"Mama," she said impulsively, "why don't you come back with me for a visit? We could drive out to Shepherd's Village one afternoon. It's been a long time since you've seen him."

Her mother's face went like stone. She fanned a little faster, rocked a little slower, but her voice was flat, as devoid of emotion as she could make it. "I don't like to get on an airplane at my age."

"We could drive."

"With my back? I couldn't sit that long."

"Mama, you ought to go him see once in a while."

"It was your idea to move him up to that fancy place so far away from home. You go see him."

Jess was silent for a time. When she spoke, her tone was subdued. "He's your son, Mama."

Her mother rocked and fanned, gazing at the highway. "He don't know if I come or not. He don't care. He don't even know who I am. Or you either."

She stopped rocking and sat forward in her chair. "Well, I'll be. That looks like Sylvie Byrd's car. Wonder what she's doing out this way, and couldn't even be bothered to come to church."

Jess went into the house for a glass of iced tea. Her flight was at six o'clock and she would have to start packing soon. She came back out onto the porch and opened the first of the yearbooks.

1981. It seemed like yesterday. It *was* yesterday, in someone else's lifetime. Someone with a dark spiral perm and a big cheerleader's smile. Someone who was president of her sophomore class and vice president of FBLA and secretary of the French Club and why shouldn't she be all that and more? Miss Junior Miss. Miss Watts County Farm Association. Miss Castlebury Junior High. Miss High Water. Miss Teenage Mississippi. Homecoming Queen? Of course. Head cheerleader? Certainly. She was Frank and Mary Ann Cray's girl, and nothing she achieved was ever unexpected. Nothing she did was ever quite enough.

She made herself look through the class photos

of every book. She was in all of them, of course,
usually in several places. In her junior and senior
years she had color photos, one in her white gown
with the gold sash and crown, carrying a spray of
pink roses, Homecoming Queen. In the other she
was at the top of the cheerleader's pyramid, front
inside cover. Roger Dill was there every year, a class
ahead of hers, but it was his senior-class picture she
was looking for.

The last time she had seen that photograph the
eyes had been cut out.

It was coming back to her in scraps and broken
pieces, but it was still foggy. He had been a senior,
football quarterback, any girl would have died to
have gone to the prom with him. She had bought a
new dress . . . no, that wasn't right. She couldn't
have a dress because she had just spent a lot of
money on the pink evening gown for the Miss Newbury High competition. She had been first runner-
up. She was furious, not because she'd lost the competition, but because everyone had already seen her
in the pink dress, and now she would have to wear
it again to the prom. She was almost relieved when
Roger pulled a hamstring at practice the afternoon
before the prom, leaving her without a date.

"Wait a minute," she murmured out loud.

Her mother, who had been commenting on the
state of her Audrey Hepburn rose, gave Jess an annoyed look. Jess flipped quickly back through the
pages of the yearbook.

There. It was just as she had thought. Her picture
had been taken, in color, as a member of the Miss
Newbury High's court. She was wearing the pink
dress.

And it was very, very similar to the one that had been delivered to her office, covered in stains only last week.

She hadn't gone to the prom that year, just as she had thought. First runner-up in the Miss Newbury High pageant, captain of the cheerleading squad, easily the most popular girl in the junior class, if not the school . . . it had been quite a blow.

She *hadn't* worn the dress to the prom, but she had had her picture taken in it. What did it mean? And what did any of it have to do with the class picture of Roger Dill, eyes slashed out and the word "Shame" scrawled across the top?

She turned to the back of the book again, gazing thoughtfully at the photograph of the boy she barely remembered. It might be interesting to give him a call.

She said, "Mama, do you happen to know if the Dills are still in town? They had a son named Roger. He used to play football in high school, and I dated him for a while."

Her mother nodded, rocking. "Of course I remember him. Who wouldn't? But his folks left town not long after the accident, you remember that. Took a big loss on their house, I understand. I heard he left his job—you remember he was some kind of big shot over at the power plant—and went to work for a cable company. Good money in it, I guess."

Jess's mother had always had a remarkable ability to answer any question with far more information than anyone wanted to know—while somehow managing to leave out the most important facts. Jess said, "What accident?"

Her mother stopped rocking and stared at her.

"Good heavens, don't tell me you've forgotten that!" Then she frowned and sat back. "Well, maybe you were off at college when it happened, but I know I told you about it. I knew you'd be interested, him being an old classmate and all."

"He was a year ahead of me," Jess pointed out. But her heart was beating hard, and her stomach was tight.

"Well, I know I told you about it." She started rocking again. "He was home on break from Ole Miss, winter time it had to be because there was ice on the roads, but not Christmas. Maybe it was just a weekend. Anyway, he had a blowout on Henderson Road—you know that big noisy car he always drove—and skidded right into a light pole."

Jess's throat was dry. She was surprised to be able to form the words. "He was killed?"

She nodded. "Closed casket ceremony."

It was a question she didn't want to ask, but had to . . . even though she thought she already knew the answer. "Why?"

"It was the steering column, I think. Went right through his face. They say his eyes were completely gone."

Dan could tell before he entered Jess's office that the trip home had not done her any good at all. He stood outside the glass wall and wondered if she, who was always so concerned about her outward image, had any idea how she looked.

It wasn't that she was less than impeccably groomed. It was an hour before show time, and her sleek dark hair had already benefited from the attention of the on-site salon. Except for the slight disarray caused by one or two passes of her fingers through her hair, the coiffure was perfect. Her makeup was flawless—except that her lipstick had been chewed off and the exposed lips were pale and cracked. The bright red suit she wore was almost too cheerful with its sassy short skirt and yellow-and-black striped tie. The tie was slightly crooked, and the makeup tissues around her collar detracted from the effect, but there was nothing she couldn't easily rectify in two minutes or less.

What struck Dan as he stood outside her office— what anyone would notice when they glanced her way—was not how Jess looked, but how she acted. Jess, who was always on, always ready with a smile, a nod, a pleasant expression, always excruciatingly aware of her highly visable position, sat hunched over her desk, one hand clutching her throat while the other pressed the telephone to her ear, frowning. Scared, vulnerable, in distress. Dan felt an unexplained flash of anger to see her like that. He wasn't sure what he was angry with—the sick bastard who had reduced her to this, himself for being unable to prevent it, or Jess for letting him see it.

He moved toward her door with strides that were a little too energetic, tossing an absent greeting toward Jess's secretary. Then he paused. He kept his voice low as he inquired, "How's the mail today?"

"Nothing today," Sylvia admitted. But the glitter in her eyes seemed almost avaricious. "But did you hear about the one we got last week?"

"I heard."

Dan looked at the secretary for a moment. Plain, overweight, perhaps enjoying the tribulations of her glamorous boss a little too much? He said, "Are you happy working for Miss Cray, Sylvia? Does she treat you all right?"

She looked surprised. "Yeah, sure. I mean, I guess. She's okay. Why, are you looking for somebody?"

Was she a little too eager on the uptake? Or was she behaving exactly like a normal office employee, leaping to perfectly normal conclusions, and flattered to think she was valuable enough to be stolen away from one star by another?

Dan gave a small shake of his head, annoyed with himself, and tried not to imagine the wildfire of office gossip that would be spreading along the grapevine within the hour. He would probably end up spending the entire afternoon reassuring Bethany that he did *not* intend to fire her.

"Never mind," he said. He gestured toward Jess's door. "I'll just go in."

Jess was off the phone when he opened the door, but she sat staring at the instrument bleakly as though it held all the responsibility for and all the answers to her woes. Dan dreaded the upcoming show if this was any indicator of her mood.

As he closed the door behind him, he said, "So how was your mom?"

She glanced up at him and smiled briefly. Her eyes were haunted. "She made me go to church and eat pot roast."

He pretended to wince. "A lethal combination. Did you get a chance to go over the notes I left you on Leon Marsh?"

She looked blank.

The show today was on child prodigies, of whom Leon Marsh, an eight-year-old black boy who had written a credible opera, was the most animated and therefore the most likely to make a good interview. Jess had missed Friday's production meeting and couldn't know that. Dan had put together a quick profile for her because he didn't like to think he would be responsible for carrying the show by himself—and because, if truth be told, he wanted to help her out. The realization that his efforts on her behalf had been wasted irritated him, as did the certainty that he would be carrying the show after all. But he wasn't as irritated as he was worried—and scared.

"Goddamn it, Jess, why do you even bother to come to work at all?"

Her eyes flashed, as he hoped they would, but too briefly. Anger gave way to weariness in less than an instant, and she pressed two fingers to her temples. "Don't start with me, Dan."

He was aware, as always, of the transparent walls and the watching eyes. He dropped to a chair and crossed one ankle over his knee, keeping his voice and his demeanor deliberately casual. "So tell me about the weekend. What happened? Good God." And sudden alarm made him sit up straight. "The bastard didn't follow you there, did he?"

She shook her head. "No. Nothing happened. I mean . . . it's just so weird. That picture—the one with the eyes cut out. It turns out the boy died in a traffic accident not long after high school, and his eyes were gouged out."

Dan frowned. "That is weird. Did you tell Candler?"

She gave a nod toward the phone. "I left a message. He's going to call back. And you know what else? I finally figured out about that pink dress. I didn't wear it to the prom, though I had planned to until Roger—the boy in the photograph—stood me up. But I *did* wear it in a beauty pageant that same year—and I had my picture taken for the yearbook in it." Once against she rubbed her temples wearily. "I don't know what any of it means."

Then she looked at him. "I'll tell you what I hate most, though, about this whole business. Not being scared, not the sense of invasion, not the vulnerability—but the time it takes. The time I have to think about it, and worry about it, and try to figure it out . . . I'm so tired of it all."

And before he could respond, she briskly pushed back from the desk, squared her shoulders, and reached for the stack of papers in her In basket. "But that's all the time I'm going to spend on it this morning. Don't worry about the show. I'll read your notes and be ready." She gave him a smile that was almost rueful. "After all, I've got plenty of time now that I no longer read fan mail."

Dan was standing to leave when Sylvia buzzed. Jess's eyes darted quickly toward the phone, but she didn't pause in her search through the papers. She found the show file with Dan's notes neatly clipped on top, and she held it up triumphantly. "I'll read it," she promised.

He looked doubtful, then came over to her. With a deft touch, he plucked the tissues from the collar of her blouse and tossed them in the trash. "See you on the set," he said.

Jess's hand went quickly and self-consciously to her collar. Dan winked at her. She smiled and sank back into her chair as he closed the door behind him. Then she reached for the phone.

"Yes, Sylvia."

"Jeremy Styles is on two."

She frowned a little. "Who?"

"You remember, he called all last week, must have left a half dozen messages. He said it was important."

"Oh." It came back to her. "That writer. Did you tell him I don't have anything to do with scheduling the guests or formatting the show? What can he want?"

"I don't know. I tried to transfer him to production, but he wants to talk only to you. He said it was personal."

Jess stifled a groan, but she had dealt with difficult guests—and ex-guests—before. She said, resigned, "All right, I'll take it. But I'm expecting a call from Detective Candler so—"

"I'll buzz you," Sylvia promised.

Jess took a breath, sat back, and punched the button for line two. She put on her warm and professional voice as she greeted him, "Mr. Styles. This is Jessamine Cray. What can I do for you?"

"Miss Cray." His voice, too, was pleasant and professional. That surprised her. "I wasn't sure you'd remember me."

Jess waited politely. She had become an expert over the years at not giving too much encouragement.

He filled in the silence before it became embarrassing. "Actually, I think there's something I can do for you. I have some material here I think you'll find very interesting."

"That's thoughtful of you, Mr. Styles, but my secretary should have told you I don't have anything to do with scheduling topics for the show. However, if you—"

The intercom buzzed. Line one was blinking.

"—would like to send the material to the production department here at the studio, I'm sure someone will get back to you," she finished in a rush. Her finger was already poised over line one. He tried to interrupt, but she talked over him. "I'm afraid I have someone on the other line, so I must go. But thank you so much for calling."

She pushed the button for line one. "Detective Candler?"

"I got your message." The power of reassurance he carried in his voice was nothing short of amazing. Jess felt all her muscles relax in a soothing ripple as soon as he began to speak. "Has something happened?"

Briefly, she explained to him the events of the weekend. They did not sound quite so dramatic when laid out for him in sequence, nor did they make any more sense to her now, with this telling, than they had at any one of the two dozen times she had gone over and over them in her head.

"I know there's a connection," she said. "That stupid pink dress. Roger Dill, the prom, the car accident . . . there has to be a connection, doesn't there? I just don't know what it is."

"And you say the family, the Dills, moved out of Jackson after their son's accident?" Candler sounded distracted, and Jess realized it was because he had been writing down everything she'd said. "Any idea where they went?"

"No. My mother would've told me if she knew,

believe me. She said he went to work for one of the cable television companies."

"Shouldn't be too hard to trace. The Castoses turned out to be a dead end, by the way."

For a moment she was nonplussed. "You . . . talked to Brett's family?"

For a moment she was so overwhelmed with memories, with fuzzy, tangled emotions that she almost missed his reply. The picture Brett carried of his parents in his wallet. Not many boys did that, and she had thought it was proof at the time of what a very special person he was. She couldn't remember what the photograph looked like, but she carried a very clear picture of Brett's father in her head the first and only time she had ever seen him, at the funeral. Gray and bowed, a face sagging with age lines, eyes too stunned to even reflect the accusation Jess was sure he had been feeling for her. In a matter of days he had lost both son and wife, and he was a man barely alive himself.

Candler was saying, "Greg Castos, the boy's father, died three years ago. Cancer. The surviving son, Paul, lives in Iowa, owns a liquor store, a Bronco, and a vacation house on a lake. Married fifteen years, three kids. I don't think he could be involved in any way. The postmark on the letters was local, and Castos hasn't been back east since his father's funeral. As far as we can tell he's never been to Philadelphia."

Jess felt momentary unease for the invasion of privacy represented by this dry recital of facts, which she tried to brush away. This was police work; it was necessary. And what about her privacy, which had been so brutally invaded? No, she refused to feel guilty about Paul Castos, on top of everything else.

Candler said, "We tested the stains on the dress. They were bloodstains all right—cow blood."

Jess repeated stupidly, "Cow?"

"The kind that comes from any cut of fresh beef. The guy probably smeared the drip pan from his steak over the dress before he tossed his dinner on the barbecue. Not very imaginative, huh?"

Jess released a shaky breath, resisting a hysterical urge to giggle. It did present a bizarre picture. "I guess not," she murmured.

"I'll need to see that last picture and the note," Candler said. "I can send a detective by for them this morning."

"Oh."

Her startled tone must have alarmed him because he said, "You *did* keep it, didn't you?"

"Oh, yes. Yes, of course. It's just—not here. I took it home and left it there over the weekend."

He was silent for a moment. "I get off at six. I could stop by and pick it up on my way home."

"I don't like to ask you to do that."

"It's my job."

She smiled into the receiver. "Not when you're off duty."

He chuckled. "Don't kid yourself. I'm never off duty. Will you be home after six?"

"Yes. Thank you. And . . . I don't know what the etiquette is on thanking a public servant for doing his job, but—I feel a lot better, just knowing you're taking this seriously."

She could almost see his smile, gentle and self-mocking, drifting down across the telephone line. "That's part of the job, too."

"Still . . . thanks."

"You're welcome. And Jess."

Something in his tone made her stop smiling. "I'm not doing you any favors. This is the kind of thing everyone should take seriously—including you."

Chapter 11

Freddie Glanbury got a seat in the audience for the taping of *Speaking of Which* that day, which wasn't hard to do. Unlike many of the larger syndicated shows, *Speaking of Which* didn't advertise for an audience and was hardly ever sold out. All he had to do was stop at the desk on the first floor an hour before taping, ask for ticket, and he was handed a neatly printed card—"Admit One."

The show itself was boring, but watching Jessamine Cray was very enlightening, indeed. Twice she misread a cue, once she called a guest by the wrong name, and once she treated the television watchers of America to five full seconds of dead air—which would of course be edited out, along with most if not all of her other flubs that day. That was precisely why they taped shows like this, and why Freddie had wanted to see it live.

Because it wasn't the mistakes Jessamine made in front of the cameras that were telling, but the way she reacted to them. It was the way she reacted to everything. Her co-host, Webber, moved easily across the stage and up and down the aisles, and when he screwed up a name or mispronounced a word he apologized warmly or joked it away. Jessamine Cray's movements were stiff and wary, her smile as phony as a painted doll's. There was no humor in her at all. Her voice was mechanical and often distracted; she spent a lot of time shuffling through note cards and then appeared to have forgotten what she was looking for. A couple of times, when she realized she had made a mistake or missed a cue, the look in her eyes was one of absolute panic.

Any disinterested observer could see that this was a woman on the verge of falling apart. And Freddie was not a disinterested observer.

When the show was winding down, he edged out of the studio and into the corridor, where there were the usual number of entry-level staff members waiting to do their jobs as soon as taping was finished—whether it be deliver a message, drive a guest somewhere, or break down the set. He nodded at one of them, a young man in white shirt and tie who was carrying a clipboard, and spoke in a quiet, friendly tone.

"Freddie Glanbury, United Press," he said. Sometimes he lied. "How're you doing?"

The young man looked surprised to have been singled out by a member of the press—or perhaps to find a member of the press here at all. "Fine, I guess. I mean, okay." He looked suddenly suspicious. "Are you supposed to be here?"

Freddie grinned and showed him his ticket. "Listen," he continued, keeping his voice confidential, "I'm doing a follow-up on that business with Miss Cray. Any new developments?"

The young man looked so confused that for a moment Freddie thought he'd struck a dry well, then the expression cleared. "Oh, you mean that guy on the stairwell. No, as far as I know they never caught anybody."

"Yeah," Freddie murmured. "The guy on the stairwell. Some pervert, I guess. The city's full of them."

"So they say."

"So how's she holding up? She seemed a little shaky to me today."

The kid shrugged. "Listen, you really need to ask somebody who knows. I'm just a gofher around here. Excuse me."

As the final round of applause signaled the end of the show, he shouldered into the room and toward the stage. Freddie stared thoughtfully after him, eyes narrowed.

He asked a few questions, got a few answers, and already the headlines were beginning to form in his mind. On his way down in the elevator he happened to run into Jeff Denaro, one of the newswriters for Channel 6, whose offices were on the second floor. Jeff nodded to him, but deliberately didn't invite conversation. Freddie was used to such treatment, and it didn't bother him at all.

Freddie said, "So what are you guys running on the Jessamine Cray situation?"

Jeff looked more surprised than annoyed, which meant Freddie's gamble had paid off. The local news service didn't have it yet.

"What are you talking about?"

Freddie smiled smugly. "That's what I get paid to tell you."

"Not by me you don't." The other man's voice was crisp. Then, with slightly more patience he said,

"Look, Glanbury, we don't do a gossip segment. We're hard news."

"So is this."

And possibly because he remembered the time Freddie had bought him a drink for no particular reason at all—Freddie made it a point to do that with all the hard news people in town at least every three months or so—he added, "Look, check with the entertainment editor. But I can guarantee we won't use it."

The door opened and Jeff got off. Freddie watched him go, smiling. "We'll see about that," he said.

Silk Scarf Cop Called in to Save Life of Celebrity Talk-Show Host. Headlines.

This time next week, Jeff Denaro—and everyone else like him in this town—would be begging to buy Freddie Glanbury drinks. And it was about damn time.

"That," declared Trish in a tone that was low and dark with menace, "was a fiasco second only to the opening of Al Capone's secret tunnel on live TV. For God's sake, Jess, you were humiliated by an eight-year-old! What's wrong with you?"

She flung up a hand before Jess could answer and corrected herself with a sharp breath. "All right, bad question. The fact is, it doesn't *matter* what's wrong with you. You can't let it affect the show." She looked at Jess with anger and stubbornness warring with apology in her eyes for just a moment, then jerked her eyes away and lit a cigarette.

"You know that as well as I do," she added in a mumble.

Jess answered, "Yes. I do."

They were in Trish's office, and the only thing that kept Jess from feeling like a schoolgirl brought before the principal was the cigarette in Trish's hand and the chains that dangled on her boots as she stalked back and forth. *Dominatrix is in for spring,* thought Jess, but couldn't even make herself smile.

Trish swung on her, one arm crossed beneath her breasts and the opposite elbow resting on it while she drew on the cigarette. "Do you need a vacation?" she demanded. "Christ, I thought you just had a vacation! Didn't you go home this weekend?"

Jess swallowed hard. "Look, I know I've let you down. I'm letting everybody down, including myself. But I think things are coming under control now. The police are investigating—"

Her eyes sharpened. "Anything?"

Jess shook her head. "But they're making progress. And it makes me feel better to know someone else is in charge."

"Well, all I know is that you'd better start feeling a whole lot better than you did today." And she fixed Jess with a meaningful look. "This is not a good time, you know. If ratings start to drop, if Dan leaves . . . well, there are only about six dozen talk shows waiting to take the place of this one, aren't there?"

As if on cue, Dan opened the door and strolled in. He glanced from woman to woman, lifted an eyebrow, and said, "Am I interrupting something?"

Trish gave an angry shake of her head and stubbed out her cigarette. "You're late, Webber. Sit down. We've got a show to plan."

*   *   *

For the next two hours Jess concentrated exclusively on her job. And when the meeting broke up, she started thinking about what she would do without this job. Start canvassing local news shows for an anchor position? Hope for an opening on one of the television tabloids? Go back to reading the weather or maybe end up in radio? The thought left a cold clamminess in her stomach. She was thirty-two years old, and she had a right to expect some security after all these years. But how much longer could she expect her looks to carry her? God, it wasn't fair. And the most unfair thing about it was that she was doing this to herself.

Dan dropped a companionable arm around her shoulders, and she jumped involuntarily. He gave her shoulders a friendly squeeze. "Come on, we're not all bad guys. Do you want to have dinner tonight?"

She shrugged irritably from his touch. "I told you, don't start with me."

"Who's starting? I just want to eat."

Jess turned the corner that lead to her office. He kept pace.

"Look," he said, "why don't you go home, have a bubble bath, put on a pretty dress, some sparkly jewelry, high heels, and I'll pick you up at eight. Bet we can get into Regine's if I call now."

She turned on him angrily. "Damn it, I don't need your pity! Why are you doing this?"

He was unsurprised by her outburst, but his expression was perfectly serious—something she didn't notice until it was too late.

"Come on, Jess," he said quietly, "I just wanted to do something nice for you, that's all."

"If you wanted to do something nice," she snapped back, "why didn't you tell me you were leaving the show?"

She turned on her heel and stalked off, leaving him. She closed the door of her office firmly, but she made the mistake of glancing up and saw him through the glass wall, watching her with a look of puzzlement and concern. And she felt like a jerk.

She almost went back to apologize. He just wanted to do something nice for her, and that was sweet. Then it occurred to her that his invitation had sounded something like a date—a lot like a date, as a matter of fact—and she wondered if he had intended it that way. The possibility made her feel odd—excited and embarrassed and then chagrined at the way she had responded. She actually moved toward the door to call him in, but he had already gone.

It was just as well. She was in no mood to make light dinner conversation by candlelight at Regine's. And he had lied to her by omission about leaving the show. She had far too much to worry about to be concerned with Dan's feelings anyway . . . and she felt like a heel.

Have you ever done anything you're ashamed of?

Chapter 12

It was quarter to six when Jess got home, and she was physically and emotionally exhausted. She had gotten in so late the night before that she hadn't even unpacked, and she was looking forward to that bubble bath Dan had suggested, a very large glass of wine, and a quiet evening with nothing to do but laundry. Nothing would keep her awake tonight.

She was locking her car when she happened to glance up and see a familiar lanky figure unfold itself from the interior of a low red Corvette four spaces down. Their eyes met, and there was no way to pretend she hadn't seen him. Jess lifted her hand and smiled weakly. Then, because she liked to believe she had *some* character after all, she walked across the parking lot toward him.

"Hi, Steve."

He took a grocery sack out of the trunk. She saw cheese, broccoli, and a bottle of wine. His face was carefully expressionless. "Hello."

She stood there for a moment awkwardly while he closed the trunk. "So. How've you been?" *Stupid,* she chided herself miserably. She had done better with the eight-year-old, and he had made her sound like an idiot.

"Okay." His manner was polite, but there was wariness in his eyes.

She blurted out, "Look, about the other night—"

"It's okay, really."

"No, I wanted to explain—"

"No need, I understand. We just didn't hit it off, okay?"

"But it was nothing personal, it's just that—"

"Look, it's okay. Really."

She stopped, drew a breath, and managed a smile. "Good then. I just didn't want you to think . . . that is, no hard feelings, okay?"

"Okay."

Another few moments passed in awkward silence, then he gestured with his elbow toward the path that led to his condo. "Well, I gotta be going."

"Me, too." Then she said impulsively, "Listen, if you'd like—we could give it another try sometime. I'm not much of a cook, but I could probably put together some eggs or something."

He looked uncomfortable. "Yeah. Well. Listen, I've got to go. I've, uh, got someone waiting for me."

"Oh. Sure." Jess stepped back as though she had been physically pushed. She could feel heat creeping out of her collar and hoped the fading light of day disguised it. "Well, see you around sometime."

"Right."

She hurried quickly up her own path and wondered if there could possibly be a more thoroughly miserable ending to a perfectly miserable day. Humiliated from the top of her head to the tips of her toes. Turned down by a man who got his kicks by working out in front of an open window. Made a fool of herself not just once, but more times than

she could count in a single twelve-hour period. There had to be a limit to just how much damage a person could inflict upon herself before some inner instinct for self-preservation took over, but if there was, Jess had not found it yet.

She was just turning the key in the deadbolt when a voice behind her said, "Miss Cray?"

She spun around with a gasp and pressed herself against the door.

A small balding man with a shy, ingratiating smile stepped out of the shadows of the overhang. He said, "I didn't mean to startle you. I thought you saw me when you walked up."

She stared at him, trying to get her heart back to a normal rhythm. He had a legal-sized manila envelope in his hand, and the first thing she thought—because she had been sued four times in the past two years, for nothing more than being a celebrity—was that he was a process server. At the same time he looked familiar to her. A neighbor? Noting her wariness, he prompted, "Jeremy Styles. I was a guest on your show a couple of weeks ago. I wrote *Dead Love*."

"Oh." Of course. The face came back to her now, and she had talked to him only that morning. What in the world could he want with her now? Jess didn't know whether to be relieved or angry. "How did you find out where I live?" she demanded suspiciously.

His smile was ingratiating. "It wasn't very hard. I don't mean to bother you, Miss Cray, but if you could give me just a few minutes of your time I'd appreciate it."

She turned back to the door. The gesture was rude and her voice was cool, but she didn't care. "I really wish you hadn't come here, Mr. Styles. I told you this morning I have nothing to do with scheduling the show, and I certainly don't conduct business from my home. Good evening."

"Oh, this has nothing to do with the show," he was quick to assure her. "It's personal."

He took a small, ingratiating step forward as she turned the handle of the door, removing her keys. He held out the envelope to her. "I knew you'd want to see this. I'd like to explain it to you if I might."

Jess took the envelope hesitantly. It seemed to contain nothing more menacing than papers. "What is it?"

He hesitated, looking uncomfortable. "Well, that's what I'd like to explain."

It was probably a movie script or the outline of a new book he wanted her to read. Jess really couldn't deal with this tonight. She offered it back to him. "Really, Mr. Styles, I don't have time right now. If you'd make an appointment with my secretary . . ."

His shoulders slumped, his head bowed, and the animation went out of his eyes. He seemed to shrink under her rejection like an inflatable doll slowly losing air. He mumbled without looking at her, "Yeah, I understand. Keep the envelope though. My card's inside. You can call if you have any questions."

She opened her mouth to say something—what, she had no idea, but he was already turning away. She tucked the envelope under her arm and opened the door.

He was as smooth as an acrobat. With no warning whatsoever he braced his foot inside the threshold, caught the door in his other hand, and he followed her inside. Jess was so outraged she forgot to be afraid as she whirled on him.

"What the hell do you think you're doing?" she demanded furiously. "Get out of here!"

He closed the door and leaned against it, barring exit. His breathing was quick and his eyes had a fevered gleam, but his voice was polite. "I'm sorry, Miss Cray. But it's a little hard to get an appointment with you. And believe me, you want to hear what I've got to say."

It was then that the needle of fear stabbed, as cold as steel. The little man with the shiny head and round glasses, soft-spoken, ineffectual, so easy to overlook . . . but now he wasn't ineffectual. Now he wasn't being overlooked. Jess's heart thudded like hammer strikes in her chest.

She demanded hoarsely, "What do you want?"

He looked around the room, and the expression in his eyes grew interested and appreciative. "So this is how the rich and famous live," he said. "Not bad. Not my taste, but not bad."

He pushed away from the door and looked at her with a supercilious, patronizing smile. "I'm not one of your fans, Miss Cray. That's the first thing you should know. Nonetheless, I've gone to a great deal of trouble on your behalf." He gestured to the envelope in her hand. "The least you could do is read it. Is there anything to drink?"

Jess's head reeled with confusion—what she didn't want to believe, what she had to believe. This mild-spoken man, this respected author, this perfectly legitimate member of society and former guest on her show had not just forced his way into her apartment and blocked her exit. He was not in one moment eyeing her with subtle threats and in the next requesting a drink with all the politeness of an invited guest.

He was eccentric, ill-mannered, socially inept, that was all. He didn't mean her any harm. But, he was angry and menacing, and the gleam in his eyes was dangerous. He had forced his way in. How could he *not* mean her harm?

She decided to take no chances. She said, very steadily, "What would you like?"

He seemed a little surprised that she was so easily subdued. "Scotch will be fine."

"Excuse me."

She put the envelope on the glass-topped dining table and turned the corner to the kitchen. Her hands were slippery with sweat as she grabbed the telephone receiver, her pulse jerking erratically. What if she was wrong? What if he was just a harmless crackpot? What if he wasn't?

She had just punched out the first number when he came up behind her and snatched the receiver out of her hand. "Don't do that." He sounded more impatient than alarmed. "Who were you calling, anyway, your boyfriend? Forget that. This is one on one, just you and me. Now, sit down!"

He grabbed her arm and pushed her the few steps back into the dining area, then shoved her into a chair at the table. Jess didn't dare try to fight him. She sat there, her mouth dry, breathing hard, and tried to pretend this wasn't happening. Not this way. Not now, not to her, not like this. She had never expected it to be like this.

His eyes narrowed behind the glasses as he looked down at her. "That surprised you, didn't it? You're not used to being pushed around. Prissy little pussycats like you never are, that's the problem."

Jess darted her eyes to the front door, but it was too far away, and he could catch her a dozen times before she made it. The patio door was secured with a burglar bar and an interior keyed lock; it was only a few steps away, but she could never undo both locks before he was upon her. He might have a weapon. Even if he didn't, he was only steps away from the kitchen and a half dozen razor-sharp knives. Frantically, she debated her own chances of reaching the knives before he did, but she knew they were nil. He was blocking her way, but even if she got past him, would she really be able to use a knife on a man?

Yes, damn it, yes . . .

But she knew the gap between the will and the reality was large, and she hated herself for being a coward and a fool.

Jess's lips felt numb. He towered over her, this small man with the fierce scowl, and she was small and helpless. She managed, "Why are you doing this?"

Her voice was tiny, tremulous. The sound of it horrified her, but it seemed to excite him into a new fever of contempt.

"Because you're stupid, that's why." He practically spat out the words, shoving his hands deep into his pockets as he paced back and forth before her in short, angry strides. "You're so goddamn stupid you don't even know how stupid you are, and the worst part of it is you don't have to know! Miss Cotton Queen, Miss Castlebury Junior High, Miss Cute-as-a-goddamn-button, all you have to do is twitch your ass and bat those great big eyelashes and the world falls down at your feet, right?"

Jess felt a chill, slow and prickling, and with it the odd sensation of time having stopped, hovering suspended in shock between one moment and the next. Miss Castlebury Junior High. How had he known that? Until this weekend, until the bloody pink dress, she hadn't thought of that title in years. But he had known. Could it be just a coincidence? *How had he known that?*

And then, as though flung from a slingshot, time resumed. Jeremy Styles continued pacing back and forth in front of her, his eyes shooting venom, his lips flecked with spittle as his vitriol increased. "It's people like you who give the whole business a bad name, do you know that? Do you bother to research your subject? Why should you, when all you have to do is smile at the camera and the world believes every word you say? Do you bother to find out the difference between the truth and what makes ratings? Does it matter? Hell, no. And if it did, you'd choose ratings, wouldn't you? Jesus, you people make me sick!"

And with that hissing pronouncement he thrust his fingers against his balding scalp as though to physically press down frustration—or perhaps to pull out what few remaining strands of hair he had. His face was splotched with violent spots of anger, his lips thin and white. Jess dared not speak. She dared not move. She thought desperately if she sat very still and made herself very small he might forget about her entirely.

Abruptly, he drew in a breath and let it out again, forcing his arms to his sides. He looked down at

Jess. The exaggerated calm in his voice and the cold little quirk of a smile was terrifying.

"Well," he said, "now you know my pet peeve. So here's the difference between you and me, Miss Cray. I'm interested in the truth. I research my subjects. Every book I write is based on truth, did you know that? No, of course not. You thought I wrote novels. You thought *Dead Love* was just another piece of fiction. While if you had even bothered to read the book, you would have *known* it was based on fact, you would have seen the parallels, you would have known what questions to ask instead of virtually ignoring me, making me look like a tongue-tied fool, while you fawned all over that asshole cop—"

Again a sharp breath. A silence. Jess thought disjointedly, *That's it? He's mad at me because I made him look bad on the show? How funny, the same thing happened to me only today. Only it was an eight-year-old making me look bad. . . .* It was hysterical sub-chatter, background noise to block out the fear that tightened like a spring in her belly. She had to get out of here, but she didn't know how. She had to get help but she didn't know where. How could this be happening to her? *How?*

He flashed her another cold, tight smile. "But I digress. You wanted to know what was in the envelope. I'll tell you. It's notes for a new book. A book based on you, Miss Cray."

He looked at her so expectantly that she was afraid to remain silent. *Humor him, keep him calm, whatever you do, don't make him angry. . . .*

She said, "I . . . I'm flattered."

He gave a short, satisfied nod. "You should be.

I'm good. I'm one of the best. I think I'll call it *Princess*. Do you like that?"

Jess swallowed hard. "Yes. I do. Of course."

He looked smug. "I thought you would. That's what you've always been, isn't it? Daddy's little princess."

He leaned over her, one hand planted on the table beside her, effectively trapping her in her chair, while the other caressed her cheek. Jess tried not to shrink back, but she couldn't help it. He saw her terror and fed off it.

He chuckled and straightened up. "Of course, I wouldn't be doing my job if I didn't expose the truth behind the fairy tale. That's what we're here for, right? So go ahead." Abruptly, he pulled out the chair next to Jess's and flung himself into it. He gestured to the envelope that still lay on the table in front of Jess. "Read. After all, it's customary to get the subject's approval before writing a book, isn't it? Customary," he added with a smirk, "but not necessary."

Jess said, almost steadily, "I'm sure . . . that whatever you do will be perfect, Mr. Styles. You don't . . . need my permission.

"I know that, bitch!" The anger in his tone made her jump. "Now, read!"

Her hands were shaking as she reached for the envelope, and the clasp flap tore. Papers spilled out onto the table, and she stared at them dumbly. She couldn't make herself pick them up. She couldn't, though her life depended on it, make the typed lines focus into words.

She looked up at him helplessly. "Why are you doing this?" she pleaded.

"Because people need to know," he snapped back. "They need to know what's behind that million-dollar smile and that empty-headed drivel of yours. They need to know what kind of person they're letting into their living rooms every day, what kind of person they're letting fill their heads with idiocy, and maybe you do, too, did you ever think of that? Maybe it's time somebody pointed out to you just exactly what kind of person you are. Maybe then you wouldn't be so goddamn high and mighty!"

She said in a small, high voice, "Look, Mr. Styles, I don't know what I've done—"

"Nothing, that's what!" he shouted. He slapped his fist against the table with a crack that caused the crystal vase of silk daylilies at its center to rattle. "You haven't done one single damn thing to deserve what you've got! Hell, you didn't even finish college!"

Jess's heart stopped.

"You lied about it, too, didn't you?" he sneered. "All this time, the precious weather girl turned star has been climbing her way to the top by stepping on lies."

Seeing her stricken look, he gave a short, ugly laugh. "Got you on that one, didn't I? I'm the first one to call you on it, right? Well, it's all there."

He shoved at the papers with his index finger, eyes glittering maliciously. "Like that boyfriend you killed back in Georgia. Some people get away with murder, don't they, Princess? People are going to love reading about that."

Jess's hand gripped the arms of the chair so hard that her fingers throbbed. The pulse that pounded in her throat was cold. She whispered, "Stop it. Stop . . ."

"And what about that poor idiot brother you've got locked away in the loony bin? Twenty-eight years old and still peeing his pants. You tried real hard to keep *him* a secret, didn't you? God forbid that you should be embarrassed by anything as inconvenient as a retarded relative. But you've been ashamed of him all your life, haven't you? Maybe that's because you feel guilty about him just the way you do about that poor kid in college, and God knows how many others you've mowed down in your wake. You don't have a hell of a lot of luck with men, now do you, Miss Cray?"

She wanted to scream at him; she wanted to launch herself at his throat, to beat him with her fists until he took back everything he said; she wanted to run from him and knew she had to get away from him even if it meant flinging herself through the patio door, even if it meant going for the kitchen knives. He was insane. He was insane, and his only purpose was to torment her, to keep on tormenting her until there was nothing left. . . .

Suddenly, a sound tore through the apartment, harsh and raucous, startling them both. Again time froze, but this time only for a split second. An instant of his surprised eyes and slightly slack expression, an instant of his turning away in curiosity, and then Jess identified the sound—the door buzzer.

She sprang from her chair and launched herself across to the front door. He was just distracted enough, and her movement was just unexpected enough, for her to get past him. But if he followed her, if he tried to stop her . . . She wanted to scream for help, but didn't have the breath. All she could manage were hoarse rasping sobs as she threw herself on the door, fumbling with the locks, grabbing at the handle.

The handle wouldn't twist. The door wouldn't open. She cried out loud and banged her fist against the door. The locks. She tried again, turning them the other way. The door flew open when she tugged.

Detective Lyle Candler stood there.

"Oh, God!" she cried. "It's him! Help me, please . . . it's him!"

Chapter 13

Jess would forever remember those next few moments in three-dimensional detail. Parts of the evening that followed would later become blurred or missing altogether, but those first few moments were imprinted forever in crisp color and stereo sound.

Styles, rising slowly from the table, looking angry and confused. Candler stepping calmly inside, the click of the door behind him. Jess clutching at his coat. The sound of the dry sobs that were backed up in her throat.

"He . . . he broke in here," she gasped. "He had . . . those papers, he tried to make me read them . . . God, he knew about everything! The pink dress, college, Brett . . . oh God, he knows about Evan!" Her voice rose sharply there and started to break into something as shrill as a scream. "Nobody knows about Evan!"

Styles stared at her, gripping the back of the chair, the expression on his face bewildered. "What are you talking about, lady?" he demanded. "What's wrong with you?"

Candler touched her arm lightly, indicating that she should stay where she was. He reached into his inside pocket and pulled out his identification wallet, holding it up to Styles as he crossed toward him.

"I'm Lieutenant Lyle Candler with the Philadelphia Police Department. Do you remember me?"

His voice was friendly and his movements easy—too friendly and too easy as far as Jess was concerned. She wrapped her arms around herself to stop the trembling, and she wanted to scream at him to do something, to stop this maniac, to get him away from her, to make this madness stop. . . . And then she had to stop her own rampaging hysteria, to draw in a deep breath and try to focus on what was happening.

Candler went on, "We were on Miss Cray's show together. Your name is Styles, isn't it? You wrote the book."

The little man did not look so menacing now. "That's right," he answered and darted a quick glance at Jess. "What is this?"

"That was all about the same time Miss Cray started having her troubles, wasn't it?"

"What troubles? Listen I don't know what's going on here, but—"

"Did Miss Cray invite you here, Mr. Styles?"

"I'm here, aren't I?" Belligerently. "What are you implying?"

Jess said, "I didn't; I told him to go away. I just opened the door, and he pushed his way in." She meant for it to be an angry accusation, but it came out as little more than a tremulous complaint.

Candler tucked is ID back into his pocket. His pleasant, conversational tone didn't alter. "Are you carrying a weapon, Mr. Styles?"

Now Styles looked incredulous—and for the first

time, genuinely alarmed. "Are you kidding? Hey, what is this?"

"Will you please turn and put your hands on the wall? Stand with your feet well apart."

Jess watched as Candler patted the other man down for a weapon. "He has it all written down." The words came out in a rush, tumbling over each other, and she hardly recognized the voice as her own. "College, the jobs, high school, the beauty pageant, Brett, he has it all written down!"

Styles cast her a look over his shoulder, and Jess shrank back.

Candler said, "Miss Cray has been receiving threatening notes and phone calls with veiled references to her past. You wouldn't know anything about that, would you Mr. Styles?"

"What?" There was no more bravado in Styles's voice now, just genuine fear. "No! No, I don't know what you're talking about! What is this?"

Candler said, "Did he touch you, Jess?"

"He . . . he grabbed my arm," she answered weakly. "He wouldn't let me call 911. He pushed me into the chair."

"What are you talking about?" Styles demanded shrilly. "Are you crazy? What are you saying?"

Candler said, "All right, Mr. Styles, you can move away from the wall. Please put your hands behind your back."

As he did so, Candler snapped a pair of handcuffs around his wrists. He said, "You have the right to remain silent. You have the right to an attorney. If you want to talk to an attorney and cannot afford one . . ."

That was when everything started to blur for Jess.

She whispered, "Excuse me." She pushed away from the wall and ran for the bathroom. She barely got the door closed before she collapsed on the floor and began to retch violently.

She came out with a damp washcloth clutched in her hand, not because she needed it, but because she had forgotten she was carrying it. A blue light pulsed in the room, and she realized, after a very long time, that it was coming from the patrol car outside her window. She thought, irrelevantly, *Oh, God, the neighbors,* and then she heard a familiar voice and turned to see Dan forcing his way past the clutch of people at her front door—some of them in uniforms, some of them not.

"Jess! Jess, are you all right?" He spotted her and made his way toward her quickly, his face stamped with alarm. "For God's sake, what happened? What's going on?"

Jess wondered if someone had called him. "Dan," she said stupidly, "what are you doing here?"

A patrolman escorted Jeremy Styles, handcuffed and white-faced with outrage, past the door. "I want my lawyer, do you understand that?" Styles demanded. "I'll have the badges of every one of you wind-up robocops before I'm finished, by God. As for you—"

He twisted around to face Jess, his eyes churning with venom. Jess shrank back a little, but there was nowhere to hide. The patrolman gave an especially forceful tug on Styles' arm, and Jess never got to hear the remainder of his threat.

Dan stared after him. "I know that man," he said. Then, catching both of Jess's arms, he demanded,

"Are you hurt? You're white as a sheet. What did he do to you?"

Jess shook her head, pulling away from him. She felt a little foolish now that Styles was gone and the excitement was dying down.

"No, I'm fine," she insisted. "Who called you? You shouldn't have come."

"Nobody called me," Dan replied impatiently. "I was just passing by and saw the commotion."

"You live halfway across town." Candler's voice surprised them both. It was pleasant as always, but his eyes were not particularly friendly. "You were just passing by?"

Dan scowled, looking from Candler to Jess. He said to Jess, "All right. I came by to see if I could talk you into reconsidering dinner. Imagine my surprise when I saw your house surrounded by squad cars and your door blocked by cops. For Christ's sakes, Jess, I thought that maniac had gotten to you! Will you please tell me what's going on?"

Candler turned to hand an envelope—the one Styles had given her—to another man, murmuring a few quiet words of instruction to him. When he left, only the three of them remained.

Jess released a shaky breath. "It was him," she told Dan. "Styles. He's the one who . . . was behind everything."

Dan's frown sharpened for a minute and he repeated, "Styles?" His brow cleared. "Wait a minute, I do know him. He was on the show with Candler— and that was the day you got the first note, wasn't it?"

It was a question that required no response as he

looked sharply at Candler. "Are you kidding me? It was him all the time? That wimpy little guy?"

Jess said weakly, "He didn't seem so wimpy a while ago."

Candler's reply was careful. "There's some evidence to suggest he might be the man we're looking for, yes." He looked at Jess soberly. "I've got to be honest with you. We've got a weak forceful entry charge and an even weaker physical assault. It might be enough to get me a search warrant, in which case we can hope to turn up some stronger evidence. In the meantime, though, I'd like to ask you a few more questions."

Jess's hand convulsed suddenly around the washcloth, squeezing droplets of water onto the carpet. "Do you mean . . . he might get out?"

"Not if we can help it," he was quick to assure her. "Don't worry. Now, I know it's been a hard night, but I need to take a statement from you while it's still fresh in your mind. Could we sit down?"

"Are you going to question him tonight?" Jess insisted anxiously. "Are you going to find out why he did this?"

"Just as soon as I'm finished here." He gestured toward the sofa, inviting her to sit.

Jess looked at the wet cloth in her hand and for a moment couldn't remember how it had gotten there. Then she balled it up and dropped it carelessly onto a side table. She rubbed her arms to ward off a chill and walked to the sofa.

Candler sat next to her, taking out a small black notebook. Dan dropped into a chair opposite the sofa and sat forward with his elbows resting on his knees, regarding them with the alert intensity of a network anchor at the interview of a lifetime.

Candler said gently, "Just start from the beginning. What time did you get home?"

The words came haltingly at first, and then more quickly, with an almost cathartic ease. She told about her encounter with Steve, and how Styles came up behind her as she opened her door. How she had told him to make an appointment, how he had looked so hangdog and started to turn away. How he had pushed his way inside.

"God, I should have known," she said softly, suppressing a shudder. "I must have had half a dozen message slips from him last week, and then this morning, when I talked to him—"

"You talked to him?" Candler questioned.

Jess related what she remembered of the conversation.

"I just thought he was trying to promote himself," Jess explained, "or line up another spot on the show. People do that sometimes. They get the talk show syndrome, and they just can't let go. So I guess I was pretty short with him." She swallowed hard. "I must have made him mad. So he decided to come here and have it out."

"What happened once he was inside?"

Jess related the aborted attempt at the phone call, the way he had dragged her over to the dining table and made her sit down. Now the story became more difficult to tell, as her throat started to tighten.

"I finally . . . figured out that he thought he had been treated badly on the show. He said I had made him look stupid, that I'd asked the wrong questions, spent more time on . . . my other guest than on him." She cleared her throat, but the tightness remained. "I guess he was right. I remember—" She glanced hesitantly at Candler. "One of the few things I remember about that show is that you came off as a much better interview subject than he did. It happens that way, sometimes."

Dan nodded in thoughtful agreement, his full attention on Jess. Candler scribbled in the notebook.

"And then he gave you those papers to read?"

Jess nodded. "He said he was writing a book about me. He went on and on about how much research he put into his books. He was very angry. He swore at me a few times, said people like me gave journalism a bad name. And then he called me . . ." Her own choked-off breath surprised her. "Miss Castlebury Junior High. I think that's when I began to suspect . . . that the knew more about my life than anyone had a right to."

She was silent for a moment, remembering, and remembering made her temporarily distrustful of her voice. She hugged her arms so hard she could feel the bones against her fingers.

She dragged in another breath and looked up. "Then he said something about my not having finished college, and I knew it had to be him. It all started with that job application and the lie about college. And he knew about Brett, and my brother Evan—"

Candler looked up. "Your brother?"

Peripherally, Jess sensed Dan's surprise, but she didn't look at him. "Yes. He's in an extended care facility for the mentally disabled. Shepherd's Village. I moved him here from the county home in Jackson about three years ago."

"And no one else knows about him?"

"No." Jess's tone was flat. She looked straight ahead, clasping her hands together tightly in her lap. It was stupid, to still feel so uncomfortable with the subject. And it wasn't that she was uncomfortable about Evan; it was just that talking about him to strangers seemed . . . disrespectful somehow.

She said, in a slightly more relaxed tone, "You've got to understand. Where I come from—in my family—a child like Evan was an embarrassment. Almost like a curse. And it was twenty years ago; people weren't as open about things like that as they are today. My parents were . . . well, ashamed of Evan. They never talked about him. I don't think some of their best friends even knew about him. And my mother never goes to see him." She couldn't quite keep the bitterness out of her tone, which fell almost immediately as she added, "Not that I'm any better. He's only twenty-five miles away, and I haven't been out there in over a year."

She took another breath and met Dan's eyes directly across from her. "So when he mentioned Evan, I knew. I mean, the whole thing was about things I was ashamed of, right? And Evan was the next logical step."

Candler asked a few more questions, relating mostly to whether or not she could make a positive identification of the voice on the telephone or the man on the stairs—which, in all honesty, she could not. He asked for the last note she had gotten, and the yearbook photograph. It was with an odd sensation of destiny narrowly averted that she remembered this was why he had come in the first place, why he had happened to be at her door at the most crucial moment.

Candler put away his notebook and the envelope containing the last message, and stood. "All right. I'll go see what Mr. Styles has to say for himself."

"I thought you were off duty," Jess suddenly remembered.

He smiled wryly. "I was."

She took his hand and held it tightly for a moment. "Thank you," she said simply.

He smiled gently. "Get some sleep tonight," he advised and squeezed her fingers. "The worst is over."

The worst is over. The words were like music as they rolled through her head.

Dan murmured absently, "Good night, Lieutenant." But he did not get up, and he still had that intensely thoughtful, Dan Rather look on his face.

Candler nodded to him on his way to the door. "I'll call tomorrow, Jess," he said. "Meantime, relax. This one had a happy ending."

She smiled at him, and it felt like the first real smile she had experienced in weeks.

When he was gone, she turned back to Dan. He roused himself from his own deep thoughts to give her a sympathetic, comradely look. "Well," he commented, "I guess you never can tell, can you?"

She moved toward the liquor cabinet. "Do you want something to drink? I need something to drink."

"About Styles, I mean. Who could have guessed he was more than your ordinary irritating egocentric know-it-all?"

"Yeah, they should make them wear signs." Jess

stared at the bewildering display of cut-glass decanters and amber-colored liquors that she often served but rarely tasted. "What should I drink? What's good for a nervous breakdown?"

Dan got up and came over to her. "Nothing." He closed the doors of the cabinet and put his hands on her shoulders, gently turning her to face him. "You shouldn't have anything to drink. Do you want me to call someone to come stay with you tonight?"

The chill seized Jess again, fiercely and unexpectedly. She clutched her arms and took a few short, tense steps away from him. When she spoke, her voice was low and tight.

"Do you know what the worst part was? His anger. You could feel it, like something sharp and dangerous in the air. My father used to yell like that, and you can't imagine how terrifying that is when you're small, how tiny and helpless it makes you feel. You just want to curl up and disappear, you're so scared." Her voice dropped another notch; her fingers dug into her arms. "He made me feel like that all over again. God, I hated that. And I hated myself for being such a goddamn coward."

She shot Dan a quick, harsh look over her shoulder. "But you wouldn't understand that. You couldn't understand it if you've never been a little girl who was raised to never stand up against the bullies—especially when the biggest bully of all was her own father."

Dan said shortly, "You're right, I wouldn't understand. But I'm not going to apologize anymore for being a man."

Then his tone gentled as he added, "But I didn't know about your father. I'm sorry."

She shrugged uncomfortably. "Just another one of those ugly little secrets you don't talk about. My father liked to terrorize his wife and daughter so he could feel like a big man. My mother ignored her own son because he was defective and he embarrassed her—and she taught me to be embarrassed, too. I'm where I am today because I've spent my life trying to get away from them, but God, the baggage we all take with us into adulthood. I don't think I ever realized that until all this started."

She pushed a hand through her hair and blew out another unsteady breath. "And I guess," she added, trying hard to inject humor into the bitterness of her tone, "that's something else I have to thank the son of a bitch for. I could have gone the rest of my life without knowing how neurotic I am if he hadn't brought it all to the surface."

Dan smiled and caught her hand. "As you said, we all have baggage. Yours is no worse than anyone else's."

He closed the distance between them a step, taking her other hand and holding it close to the other against his chest. "Your hands are like ice. Do you want me to make you some tea or something?"

She couldn't help smiling at that. "How domestic of you."

"I have a lot of surprising talents." For a moment the gentle light in his eyes was tempting, and she almost succumbed to it. But then the memory of the evening returned to her like a miasma, and she couldn't maintain her smile. He noticed and squeezed her hands.

"Listen," he said, "I know you well enough to realize that sometime in the middle of the night you're going to wake up worrying about what's going to be in the paper tomorrow. Don't. If anybody asks, you had to call the police to escort an over-enthusiastic fan off the premises. Simple enough?"

She looked at him gratefully. "Thanks."

"Are you going to be okay alone? We could sent out for Chinese."

She almost said yes. She *didn't* want to be alone. But Dan couldn't stay forever, and she had to learn to deal with the aftermath of trauma in her own way. Besides, there was nothing to be afraid of. Not now.

She shook her head. "But thanks—for everything. Especially . . ." And this was hard to say. She made herself hold his gaze. "For not asking. About Evan, I mean."

He didn't have to respond to that. The understanding was in his eyes.

"Good night, sweetie." He leaned forward and kissed her forehead. "Make yourself some dinner, go to bed early. As the man said, get some rest. It's over."

Over. She kept repeating the word to herself like a mantra until finally, sometime in the early dark hours of the morning, she fell asleep.

Chapter 14

It was a classic case of being in the right place at the right time. Freddie Glanbury couldn't believe his luck when he followed Lyle Candler—an off-duty Candler, he knew because he'd checked—straight to Jessica Cray's front door. Headlines began to rewrite themselves in his head: Romance on the Air or Silk Scarf Cop Seeks Comfort in the Arms of Talk-Show Hostess. Not exactly prize-winning material, but it would move a few papers through supermarket checkouts. And Freddie still had to bring home a paycheck.

He set up across the street, hoping for a few candid shots through a slit in a window curtain—it was amazing what you could do with a second-hand telephoto lense and a little ingenuity—when he got what he was convinced might very well be the break of his life.

He knew better than to come on like gangbusters, flashing his press card and demanding answers. That was the short route to nowhere when your name was Freddie Glanbury and real news was involved. So he took his photos from across the street with high-speed, light-sensitive film, and when the crowd of neighbors and curiosity seekers started to gather on the front lawn, he mingled with them, keeping his eyes and ears open and watching for his break. He thought it might come when Dan Webber himself pushed through the crowd and ran up the walk to the front door, but the door opened and closed behind him so fast Freddie barely had a glimpse inside. He decided to try a different tack.

"Anybody hurt?" he asked in a concerned tone of the woman standing next to him.

She glanced at him, her expression worried. "I thought I heard someone say something about a rapist."

Freddie thought exultantly, *Jesus!*

"No, that's not it," came a man's bored tone next to her. "Some guy tried to break in, that's all. The police got him, though."

"I heard it was a fight with her boyfriend," said someone else. "She got pissed and called the cops."

Any one of which, of course, would make a great story. All Freddie had to do was pick one. *Sources close to Ms. Cray are quoted as saying . . .* That, with the photos he had, was all he needed.

Pleased with the night's work, he turned to go when Jessamine Cray's door opened and two uniforms escorted a handcuffed man out. Escorted was not perhaps the most accurate word. Hustled, maybe. The handcuffed man was furious.

"Candler, you arrogant son of a bitch! You'll be sorry for this night's work! I'll sue you and your whole department! Not one of you will ever work in this town again!" When one of the officers tried to take his arm and guide him toward the waiting patrol car, he jerked away furiously. "Keep your hands

off me. Every move you make from now on is going
to be reported to my lawyer."

Freddie was intrigued. The little guy didn't look
like your average burglar—or rapist, either. But it
was the mention of Candler's name that did it. He
decided the story could use a little fleshing out.

He waited until the police cars pulled away and
the crowd of neighbors drifted back toward their
individual evening pursuits—most of them complaining loudly about the state of security in their
community—then Freddie wandered nonchalantly
toward the green sedan parked at the curb in front
of Jess's building. The car wasn't Cray's, and it
wasn't Candler's or Webber's—Freddie had seen
both of them arrive. So it had to belong to the suspect, whoever he might be.

Freddie could only assume the charges must not
be very serious, or the police would have secured
his car. Of course, the trouble with the police was
that they would need a search warrant. Freddie op-
erated under no such constraints.

He causally put his hand on the driver's-side handle. No alarm. He lifted. He was unlocked. Jesus,
the guy must be a real idiot—or else he'd been in a
hell of a hurry. Freddie opened the door and slipped
inside, just as though he belonged there.

There was a briefcase on the floor. It wasn't
locked, either, which wasn't surprising. There was
nothing inside to interest the average thief—a few
unmailed bills with the return address headed "Jeremy Styles," a legal pad with some phone numbers
and Jessamine Cray's home address, and an unmarked file folder. Freddie glanced through the
folder quickly, scanning the hand-scrawled notes by

streetlight. Dates, places, a few photocopied documents and fax sheets—it looked like research on a book of some kind.

Then he caught the name "Jessamine Cray," and he began to read more carefully. That was when he realized he had stumbled onto a gold mine.

Chapter 15

Most people complained about the graveyard shift, but Emmalou Richman liked it. There were a lot of good shows on between eleven P.M. and seven A.M., folks just didn't realize. Good shows, too, not that crap they passed off on prime time. *Sci-Fi Theater* and *I Love Lucy* and *M*A*S*H* and *Highway Patrol* and *Dragnet*, great movies like *Jaws* and *The Mark of Zorro* and *The Bride of Frankenstein*. And then there was Rush Limbaugh at one—she never missed Rush—and Jerry Springer at four, when she took her dinner break. The night passed quickly.

Emmalou was an R.N.—policy required that an R.N. be on duty at all times—but there wasn't much happening on the graveyard shift that required the skills of a registered nurse. Shepherd's Village was a psychiatric facility, but the patients admitted there were carefully selected. They were tactfully referred to as "mentally disadvantaged," and their conditions ranged from mild autism to coma. No violent, schizophrenic or delusional patients were accepted; Emmalou wouldn't have put up with that. Mostly they were sweet things, great big grown-up babies with round faces and drooling smiles, and they hardly ever bothered her during her shows.

When she came on duty, she checked the med
sheet, dispensed what sleeping pills and tranqs were
ordered, and made a quick round of the patients,
just to make sure they were all tucked in tight and
no one had wet the bed. If one of them was sick—
which hardly ever happened; Shepherd's Village was
an *excellent* facility—she took vitals every two
hours. Otherwise, she had the night to herself.

Sometimes she chatted with Rosa, whose name-
tag called her a Nursing Assistant but who was really just a cleaning lady in a uniform, or Pete
Simpson, the security guard whom she suspected
of having a tiny crush on her. Security was not a
particularly demanding job at Shepherd's Village, especially at this time of night with all the patients—
or residents, as the latest memo from Administra-
tion said they were to be called—asleep. Emmalou
didn't mind keeping Pete company, as long as he
didn't pester her during Rush. And sometimes she
even packed an extra brownie or two in her lunch
sack for him.

In fact, they had just finished sharing a Tupper-
ware box of those brownies and watching an episode
of Perry Mason—a good one, in black and white—
and Pete had returned to his desk in the front lobby
when Emmalou heard the first cry. It wasn't even a
cry, really, more of a moan or a whimper. It was
five o'clock in the morning, and the theme music
from *I Dream of Jeannie* was beginning to play.

Emmalou turn down the volume on the set and
listened intently. She never had it loud, and she
always kept one ear cocked in case one of them had
nightmares, or got up and started wandering around
in the middle of the night. She was a good nurse.

She glanced over her shoulders through the glass partition that separated the nurse's station from the patient rooms, half expecting to see some pajama-clad resident stumbling down the hall, rubbing his or her eyes sleepily and whining with disorientation. Maybe the Rinshaw girl, who had seemed a little restless early on, or Ricky Jarvison, who had just gotten back on schedule after having his days and nights mixed up for three weeks. But the corridor, softly illuminated by night lighting that tracked the walls just above the carpet level, was empty.

Then she heard it again, not a whimper this time, but a genuine cry, a terrified, breathless cry, and then a crash, as if glass was breaking. The sound propelled Emmalou out of her chair and sent her flying out into the hallway.

Her heart was pounding so hard she thought the combination of fear, exertion, and forty extra pounds might fell her right there of a heart attack as she stood, listening intently, desperately scanning the closed doors that lined the corridor. And then the pounding in her ears eased enough for her to hear the sobs, weaker now, the gurgling gasps for breath, and she whirled to her right, following the sounds.

Emmalou pushed open the door to Room 12 and slapped the light switch. She said, "Evan? Sweetie?"

It took a moment for her eyes to adjust to the sudden illumination. It took yet another moment for her to draw in a breath. Then she began to scream.

But she didn't scream for long.

"You're wearing that pink shirt again," Jess said. "I hate that shirt."

"It looks great on me," Dan responded. "Brings out the color of my eyes."

"It makes you look like a wuss."

"That's a sexist remark."

They were on the set, five minutes before taping, the eye of the storm surrounded by chaos. Electricians were stringing cable, cameramen setting up shots, floor men removing dust covers from the set furniture and placing microphones. For once, Jess was on the set in time for a sound check. The audience was in place and murmuring excitedly, for the energy level was contagious.

Jess called out to the floor director, "Tell me the truth, Harry, would any self-respecting man be caught in public wearing a shirt like this?"

Harry grinned and made a circle of his thumb and forefinger. He had his headset on and probably hadn't heard what she said, but her good spirits and friendly banter were a welcome change from what they'd all had to put up with the past few weeks. Things were back to normal on the set of *Speaking of Which*, and as far as the crew was concerned, it was about damn time.

Jess turned her appeal to the audience, "Audience, help me out here. A round of applause if you think Dan should change his shirt."

Beneath the spattering of cheers and a few boos, Dan shared a grin with her, slipping into his jacket and microphone pack. He said under cover of the audience response, "Welcome back, sweetie."

She made a playful face at him. "You only say that because you'd be lost without me."

She picked up the portable microphone and

turned toward the booth. "All right, are we ready? I'm ready. Are you ready, audience?"

Roaring applause now.

"Okay! Let's bring on some expert guests, let's get those cameras rolling. But . . ." And she pretended to cover the microphone with her hand as she said to the nearest cameraman, "Don't show Dan from the neck down. That shirt might do serious damage to someone's television set."

The audience loved it. When the theme music started to play and the cameras were rolling, the rhythm was already there, the flow was perfect. "Hello, America, I'm Jessamine Cray . . ."

"And I'm Dan Webber, and this is *Speaking of Which*. Today we're speaking about the high-tech world of electronic surveillance. Microphones the size of a peanut"—he held up an example "—that can pick up conversations half a block away. Video cameras that can be mounted almost anywhere—without your ever knowing it. Sound like something out of James Bond? Think nobody but high-level government spies would have access to this kind of technology?"

"Think again," Jess said. "Most of these devices are available at your local Radio Shack, and you are going to be absolutely amazed at who's using them—and what they're using them for. When we come back, we'll find out who's watching you."

"All *right*," Trish exclaimed with firm satisfaction. "That's what I call a show. We're on track now! Great job, guys."

Jess grinned at her as she shook hands with the last of the departing audience members. There was nothing better than this feeling, the adrenaline glow, the satisfaction of a job well done. It had been too long since she had had that feeling. The show had flowed, the audience had been lively, the pick-ups timely. It was a talk-show truism that the show reflected the personality of its host; never had that been portrayed more accurately than today.

Gathering up the papers on which he had jotted his notes, Dan said, "It's amazing what putting a stalker behind bars will do for the morale of a show."

Trish shook her head in amazement, as she had done more than once since she had learned of the events of the Friday before. "Jesus, I can't believe it. You were right all along."

Dan looked startled. "About what?"

"About its being a guest from the show. To think that creep sat right here in that chair."

Jess joined them on the set, examining the props that were left on the table—long distance transmitters and receivers, telephone bugs hardly larger than a dust mite, tape recorders and video viewers disguised as all sorts of clever household items. "Do you know what I love about you, Trish? That you're *not* going to suggest we have him back on the show to discuss why he did it."

Trish pretended to be intrigued. " 'Celebrity Stalkers'," she murmured. "Talk show hostess confronts the man who terrorized her . . . imagine the ratings."

Jess suppressed a shudder. "Not even in jest."

Trish slipped her arm through Jess's solicitously. "Sorry, kiddo, I know it's not a laughing matter. You've been through hell, and I want you to know that, even though I might not have always shown it, I was pulling for you all the way."

Jess smiled, a little embarrassed by the sincerity. To cover it, she picked up a miniature tape recorder disguised as an Art Deco broach and held it against her lapel. "Pretty cute, huh? Say, do we get to keep these?"

"I want the cuff links," Dan said. "I'll fascinate and amaze my dates."

"I don't even want you to explain that," Jess said, pinning on the broach.

"They're yours." Trish slipped an arm through each of theirs. "Now what do you say? Lunch at Paulo's to celebrate?"

Dan said, "Do you know what one serving of their lobster quiche has in it? Six hundred and fifty calories and forty-three grams of fat."

Trish said, "Jesus, what do you do, keep a list?"

"I read it in *Philadelphia* magazine."

"We should do a show," Jess said.

Dan winked at her and she thought, *I love this job. I really do.*

Sylvia came bustling through the door just as they reached it, flushed faced and out of breath, a pink message slip in her hand. "Sorry," she panted, handing the slip to Jess. "I would have been here sooner, but I got tied up on the phone."

At the top of the slip was scrawled "Urgent." The message was "Hammond Rutger, Administrator, Shepherd's Village Convalescent Center." The Please Call Back box was checked.

Jess felt dread drain through her, numbing her for a brief and merciful moment. She looked from the message slip to Sylvia. "This came in at 10:05," she said.

Sylvia looked defensive. "You know we're not allowed to interrupt you during a show."

It was then that the full impact of a horrible premonition struck her. First a maniac had threatened her with knowledge about her brother at Shepherd's Village. Now she received a message at work from the administrator of Shepherd's Village. God, it couldn't be a coincidence. Could it?

Jess said hoarsely, looking at neither Dan nor Trish, "Excuse me. Um—go to lunch. I have to . . . excuse me."

She pushed passed Sylvia and turned toward her office. Halfway there, she started to run.

"An incident," Jess repeated tightly into the phone. "What the hell do you mean, an *incident*?"

"I assure you, Miss Cray, your brother is unharmed. However, since the police will undoubtedly want to talk to you about this, I thought it best that—"

"Police?" She gripped the edge of her desk to stop a sudden weakness in her legs. "What are you talking about? What happened? Tell me!"

She had been vaguely aware of a presence behind her, just as she was aware of the curious eyes of the entire bullpen full of people who had grown accustomed to following the soap opera that was her life. Now Dan came closer, moving in front of her so that he could see her eyes. His face was sharp with concern. She wanted to reach for him, just to feel the comfort of another human being, but she was afraid if she let go of the desk her legs would betray her.

"Your brother, Evan, is perfectly okay," Hammond Rutger assured her again. "He was understandably upset, but is resting comfortably now. Physically, he should have no long-term effects whatsoever."

It was hard to keep from screaming into the phone. "Tell me what happened!"

A pause. She thought her chest would break with the force of her heartbeat slamming against it.

Rutger said, "We had a break-in last night. I'm afraid one of our nurses was . . . well, she was killed. The incident happened in your brother's room."

Jess didn't remember much of what followed. She didn't remember hanging up the phone. She didn't remember picking up her purse. She did remember Dan taking her car keys from her and saying flatly, "I'm driving."

She supposed she had told him what happened. She didn't remember doing so. All she was really aware of was the gripping terror, the roiling anger, the crushing horror, and the outrage that twisted and spiraled inside her until she could hardly breathe for the pressure of it; she certainly couldn't think.

She strode through the bullpen and down the corridor, trying not to run, trying not to break down. Dan was beside her, as quiet as a ghost, as persistent as a shadow. When he pushed the elevator button for her, Jess threw up her hands tensely, pushing at the air between them as though the gesture could somehow make him disappear. "Will you stop hovering?" she demanded. Her voice was shrill, though she worked at keeping her tone low. "What are you doing? Can't you leave me alone?"

"No." Dan's voice was low, his face tight. When she drew a breath for a sharp, possibly hysterical, reply, he gripped her arm hard above the elbow and stood very close. "And if you're going to make a scene, do it in the elevator."

She was vaguely aware of the looks they were getting, curious and intense, from the passersby in the hall, the faces behind half-open office doors. She could not think of anything that mattered less at that moment than whether or not she made a scene or who saw her. She tugged furiously against Dan's hold on her arm.

"Let me go, damn you! This is none of your business; it has nothing to do with you!"

But Dan's fingers only dug tighter into her upper arm, and he wouldn't let her go. His eyes were deep indigo with shock and distress, and there were fine white lines around his mouth. He said very quietly, "You can't do this alone, Jess. You know that."

And she did know that. She couldn't even think about it alone; she couldn't even imagine it. How could she deal with it?

The fury that had sustained her this far became mitigated with pinpoints of confusion, and she couldn't hold Dan's gaze. "I have to call my mother," she said. Her voice sounded small. "I wonder if they called my mother."

Dan said, "Let's wait until we know more."

The elevator arrived, and they were the only ones making the ride down. It was then that Jess started to tremble.

"It's my fault this happened to him," she said.

She pressed back against the wall and locked her
knees, trying to keep her voice steady. "He did nothing to deserve this. He's as harmless as a puppy. He
was fine, he was safe, he was comfortable . . . and
then I did this to him."

Dan said, "It's not your fault. We don't know what
happened yet. Don't jump to any conclusions."

He put his arm around her shoulders, and she
was glad to lean on him.

Hammond Rutger was a small man with a Van-
dyke beard who managed to project the kind of con-
fident authority that put one in mind of European
royalty, despite his size. He was waiting for them in
the lobby, pacing back and forth, and the shell of
calm competence with which he generally surrounded himself was beginning to show a few
cracks.

He tried to take Jess's hand in one of those two-
handed grasps that seemed to be particularly popular with psychiatrists and clergymen, exclaiming
softly, "Miss Cray, on behalf of everyone here—"

Jess pushed past him. "I want to see my brother."

"Of course, of course."

As he led the way down a series of hallways, all
decorated in soothing Santa Fe tones of sandstone
and blue, Dan introduced himself. He then suggested without preamble, "It would help if you could
tell us more about what happened."

Rutger glanced uncertainly from him to Jess, then
said, "I don't have all the details of course, but I'll
tell you what I know. Apparently the . . . incident
. . . happened somewhere close to five A.M. this
morning. From what we—that is the police—have

been able to piece together, the night nurse, Ms. Richman, went to check on your brother around that time. She may have heard something, or seen something. We . . ." He cleared his throat a little, more out of awkwardness, it seemed, than embarrassment. "Well, I suppose we'll never know, will we?

"Apparently, she startled the intruder in your brother's room. There was some, er, damage to the room, but your brother was fine," he hastened to assure Jess again, "just fine. No harm to him at all, we made certain of that."

Jess walked faster.

Dan said, "Then what was the intruder doing there?"

Rutger sounded uncomfortable. "There's some evidence to suggest the intruder had intended to harm Evan. An overturned water glass and—a pillow on the floor, but—"

Jess stopped and turned, standing in front of him, blocking his way. Her face was ice white, her eyes enormous and dark. She said, very carefully, "You're telling me that someone walked in here at five o'clock in the morning without anyone noticing, went to my brother's room, and tried to smother him with a pillow—"

"That's not what I said—"

"Then what *would* you say, Mr. Rutger?" Her voice was shaking, her eyes on fire.

"He's all right, perfectly all right. He wasn't harmed—"

Jess turned sharply and started walking again.

"Miss Cray, please . . ." He reached out a hand

to stop her, and she whirled on him. He said gently, "We moved him to another room. It's this way."

They took the right-hand corridor he indicated, and Dan said, prompting him to resume his story, "The nurse interrupted him?"

He nodded heavily. "He shot her, then fled by the back door. She, um, well, she was shot point-blank in the face and died before she reached the hospital."

There was a slight, unsteady catch in Jess's step. Rutger said quietly, "It's here, Miss Cray. Room 242."

She pushed open the door and stepped inside, uncertain, her eyes sweeping the institution-standard room once. Blue walls, white metal furniture. A small cactus on the dresser, and beside it the teddy bear Jess had sent Evan for Christmas last year, its red plaid bow looking a little frayed around the edges. Where, she wondered, were all the other Christmas and birthday presents she had sent him? The television was on and tuned to a soap opera, volume low. Evan liked the television on all the time, even when he slept.

He was lying in bed, wearing a clean yellow T-shirt with a big rainbow on it and blue pajama bottoms. A thin white coverlet was over his knees. He stared at the television with vacant absorption.

Jess went over to the bed and sat on its edge gingerly. Dan and Rutger remained standing at the door. "Hi, sweetheart," she said softly. "It's me, Jess, remember me? Your sister. I'm here, baby."

His eyes did not flicker; his soft round face did not change. She touched his cheek lightly. Her hand was trembling.

"I guess you had a scary time, huh? But it's okay now. I'm here."

There wasn't a mark on him. The attendants had taken extra care to keep his hair neat and his clothes clean. He smelled like baby powder and shampoo. He didn't know Jess was there. He had never known.

Jess cleared her throat, trying to think of something to say to him. She couldn't. She couldn't think of one single thing.

"I know I haven't been to see you in a while . . ."

Have you ever done anything you're ashamed of?

"But I just want you know . . . I love you, baby. And . . . I'm so sorry."

She bent down and kissed his forehead. He didn't blink.

After a moment she stood and faced Hammond Rutger again. She said, "I want to see where it happened."

He seemed flustered. "Well, I really don't think that's appropriate. I mean, it is a crime scene and—"

Jess's tone, and her eyes, were hard. "Show me," she said.

After a moment Rutger led the way.

Dan questioned quietly as they walked, "Do the police anticipate making a quick arrest?"

"It's difficult to say, really." He sounded nervous. "They've just left, but I told them you'd be coming down. The card of the deputy you should talk with is in my office. To answer your question, though, I'm afraid I'm not very well informed. There was no sign of the killer when our guard discovered the body, though he looked, of course. So did the police. From what I gathered, they didn't have a great deal to go on. . . ."

He paused in front of a door that was barricaded with crime tape in an X shape across the door frame. He said, still very nervous, "You must be careful not to touch anything, of course. I'm not at all sure I should be letting you . . ."

Jess simply reached through the tape and pushed the door open. The doors had no locks, of course.

Jess had thought she was prepared. She wasn't.

She sensed the others come up behind her. Dan put a hand on her shoulder. She stared.

It was a spartan room, like the other, plain and easy to keep. The floor was linoleum, the walls glossy blue latex. There were no windows, and a single overhead fluorescent light fixture. There was a dark, wet-looking stain on the taupe carpet where the body had lain.

The bedclothes were twisted, and the door on the nightstand beside the bed was ajar. The pillow would have been taken as evidence, along with the broken glass.

And on the wall above the bed, written in red letters five inches high, was a single word: SHAME.

Chapter 16

At six-thirty that morning a jogger had discovered the body of a twelve-year-old girl, raped and strangled, behind a stone bench in Waterfront Park. Candler got the case. He was tired and sickened and discouraged when he returned to the office at two o'clock to rough out a preliminary report. It looked as though the perpetrator was the girl's fourteen-year-old stepbrother; he had the kid under surveillance and the crime lab rushing through its report. The case was solved. Sometimes it went like that.

Then he got a phone call from a sheriff's deputy in some small town half an hour away, who told him Dan Webber had asked him to call. He took out his notebook and started making notes.

He hadn't been off the phone ten minutes when the door to the squad room burst open and Jessamine Cray strode in.

She was wearing a navy-and-red suit with a short pleated skirt and a crisp white blouse, but she looked smudged and windblown. Her face and eyes were painted with television makeup that clung to her skin like a mask, but her lips were white and pressed into a tight, thin line. She was half a dozen feet away when he realized the hard glitter in her eyes was fury.

She stopped at his desk, gripping the edge of it with tight, white-knuckled fingers. "You let him go, you son of a bitch," she said. Her voice was low and shaking with the kind of thick rage that was almost palpable. *"You let him go."*

With his peripheral vision Candler saw Webber come up behind her, but he stood well aside and said nothing. Candler kept his focus on Jess.

He said calmly, "He wasn't the one, Jess."

"Damn you!" Her voice broke hoarsely, and she swept her fist out across the desk. A coffee mug crashed; heads turned. She didn't notice. "How dare you! I trusted you! You let him go, and do you know what happened? Do you?"

Dan Webber took a step toward her; she made an angry gesture as though to push him away.

Candler said, "It wasn't Styles, Jess. He was in jail until ten o'clock this morning."

For a moment it was as though she didn't hear him. Her eyes churned, and her nostrils flared with quick angry breaths. The moment she understood the significance of his words was as clear as a signpost on her face. She went still; the color drained from her face as the fury went out in her eyes, leaving them looking muddied and confused. She said, "What?"

Candler got up and pulled a chair beside the desk. She sank into it, staring at him. He didn't offer Webber a seat, and Webber didn't look as though he expected him to.

Candler picked up the pieces of the broken coffee mug and tossed them into the trash, but he didn't resume his seat behind the desk. He sat on the edge of the desk closest to Jess, and he spoke quietly to her. "I'm sorry about your brother. I just got off the phone with Deputy Lawrence, and I'm on my way out there now. We'll find who did this, Jess, but it wasn't Jeremy Styles."

He glanced at Webber because he could sense the challenge implicit in the other man's stare. He returned his attention to Jess and added, "It wasn't Styles who was stalking you, Jess, not unless there's more than one crazy out there with the same M.O. On the night you were trapped in the staircase, Styles was giving a speech to seventy-five members of the Friends of the Library in Allentown."

As he spoke, Jess shrunk into her chair. He could see the muscles of her throat work as she swallowed. She said, after a long time and with effort, "My God."

Her voice was small. Candler wanted to pat her hand, give her a reassuring squeeze on the shoulder, even put his arm around her—something to let her know it was going to be okay, to give her courage. He didn't touch her, of course. He might have, if Webber hadn't been there.

Dan said, "Can we take that to mean your department has upgraded the case from 'harmless crackpot' to 'serious threat'?"

Candler felt his muscles stiffen. It was an instinctive reaction to a primitive emotion, and because of it, he was careful to keep his tone and his manner polite. "I assure you, Mr. Webber, the department has always taken this case seriously. If you're asking whether the case has taken on more urgency now that the subject has shown a capacity for violence, the answer is of course."

Jess stood abruptly. "Excuse me. Is there a ladies' room?"

"Out the door you just came in and to the left. Do you need someone to walk with you?"

He had started to signal to Kelly, two desks down, but Jess shook her head quickly and even managed a faint smile. "No, I'm fine. Excuse me."

She didn't look fine, and both men watched her with concern until she was out the door.

Candler walked around his desk and started to stack the papers there. He didn't sit down. "You knew it wasn't Styles, didn't you?" he said.

There was wariness in Webber's posture, but his response was easy, and without any particular hesitation. "It didn't seem likely. But Jess was convinced it was him, and I guess I can see why. I wish she'd been right."

Now Candler sat down. He pulled out one of the forms and picked up a pen. "What's your relationship with Miss Cray?"

Dan's eyes narrowed a fraction. "What do you mean?"

"Just that you always seem to be with her. Why?"

His tone grew impatient. "The woman is in trouble. She needs a friend. I'm supposed to pretend I don't notice?"

"So that's it? Friends?"

Dan shoved his hands deep into his pockets. He said mildly, "What the hell are you getting at, Lieutenant?"

"Did Jess ever tell you about her brother?"

He hesitated. "Before last Friday, you mean? No."

Candler sat back in his chair. "Where were you this morning between four and five o'clock?"

Dan's eyes widened briefly with shock, then went hard. A muscle tightened in his jaw. "Sleeping. Where were you?"

"Alone?"

He scowled. "Yes, goddammit. What is this?"

"This," replied Candler, "is the department taking this case seriously."

Webber looked at him for another moment, then said, "I'll wait for Jess outside."

"You don't get it, do you?"

Webber had turned toward the door, but now looked back.

Candler said, "Jessamine Cray went to a lot of trouble to keep her brother a secret. She succeeded—until last Friday. Two days later, he was attacked. As far as I can tell, the people who knew that Jessamine Cray had a brother, much less where he was, make a very short list. So I ask you again: Where were you during the time in question?"

Dan turned and walked out the door.

Dan drove Jess home—not to her home, but to his. He had pulled into the parking garage before she noticed.

"Wait a minute, why are we here? I thought you were taking me home. What are you doing?"

"First," replied Dan, "I'm feeding you. Then I'm giving you a place to stay for the night. And if you need a shoulder to cry on, I can supply that, too."

She began shaking her head before he finished the first sentence. "I can't. I have too much to do. I have to call my mother. I've got to find another place for Evan. I should really go back to the hospital and sit with him. And I have a place to stay—my own place. Take me home, please."

Dan pulled into his parking space and turned off the ignition. "Jess," he said, and the expression on his face was inarguable. "There's a maniac out there who knows where you live. You're not going home tonight. Period."

She stared at him. "So what am I supposed to do—hide out forever?"

He pushed the button that unlocked the doors. "Not forever. Just until we get you some security over there."

"I don't need security!"

He didn't bother to answer as he got out. They both knew she could have used some security last night, and now Jeremy Styles was out of jail, maybe looking for her. . . .

But it wasn't Styles she had to be afraid of; it never had been. There was someone else, and this person used a gun to attack the innocent and the helpless.

Dan was right. She couldn't go through this alone. Not now, anyway.

She offered no more arguments as they got into the elevator for the ride to the tenth floor.

Jess had been to Dan's place only once before, for a party his girlfriend of the moment had persuaded him to give. She had been a decorator, Jess recalled, and had redone his entire apartment in an Egyptian motif just for the party—or perhaps as a flattering backdrop to her own exotic beauty. Jess almost did not recognize the place without its draped canopies and murals of the Nile and statues of obscure goddesses.

He said, "Do you remember the layout? Bathroom to your right, kitchen straight ahead. You can have the sofa bed in the study tonight, and if you want to make your phone calls in privacy, it's the first door on the left down that hall."

She said, "I'm not staying the night." But she spoke absently, looking around.

Dan's apartment was spacious and expensively furnished, as befitted a man of his income bracket, but its most attractive feature was the French doors surrounded by floor-to-ceiling windows that led to a small balcony overlooking the Delaware. Jess remembered the view as being spectacular with all those lights glittering from the waterfront, and the balcony a cool and soothing refuge from the clamor and clutter of the party inside. Now, however, the French doors were double-locked, and the view was of nothing but drop cloths and rubble. Gesturing, she said, "What's all that?"

"Wormwood or wood rot or something. They're taking down the wood railings on this side of the building and putting up stone walls, I think. Or at least that was the intention. They've been working on it since March."

He approached her with two wineglasses in his hand as he spoke. She accepted one and caught the scent of a rich Merlot. She gestured with her free hand. "Is it all right if we open the doors?"

He shrugged. "I guess. It might be a little chilly."

Jess released the twist lock and the deadbolt and pushed back the doors. The breeze was cool and, this high up, relatively untainted by gasoline fumes.

The sounds of traffic and river horns and construction far below were oddly soothing. Jess leaned against the door frame and sipped her wine, looking out over the cityscape, though seeing nothing, for a time. Dan stood beside her, respecting her silence.

Then she said, "I put the wrong man in jail." Fatigue weighed down her words, the kind of emotional overload that is reached when the mind is simply unable to absorb another surprise. "I was so sure. It made such perfect sense. The evidence was *there*. But I was wrong."

Dan took a sip of his wine. "Styles was a creep. He deserved to spend a night or two in jail."

"I should apologize to him."

"You should stay away from him."

She glanced at him, touched and vaguely amused by his sudden display of concern. She smiled tiredly and made an effort to brace her shoulders for what was ahead. "I've got to call my mother."

The first thing her mother said was, "Is he dead?"

The way she said it sent a chill down Jess's spine. "No, Mama. He's going to be fine. But I'm going to have to find a new place for him. And I think you should come see him."

Her mother was silent for a time. Then she said, "That's a shame."

Jess's hand gripped the receiver so hard it hurt. She wasn't sure whether her mother meant that it was a shame Evan had been attacked, or a shame he had lived through it. Or maybe she simply meant it was a shame Jess had to go to the trouble of finding a new nursing home for him.

She kept seeing that word drawn in letters as red as blood over the bed.

She said, "Mama, will you come?"

"No," the other woman answered slowly. "I don't guess I will. Not much I can do, anyhow."

Jess bit down hard on the words she should have said. Even thinking them exhausted her.

She said at length, "All right then, Mama." Her voice sounded drained and old. As old as she felt.

Her mother said, "Thank you for calling me, though."

Jess thought, without much emotion at all, *Damn you, old woman.* She said, "Good-bye, Mama. I'll talk to you soon."

She hung up the phone and leaned back in Dan's desk chair, cradling her wineglass against her chest. She didn't even have the energy it took to stand up and walk into the other room. So she just sat there and sipped her wine and thought about nothing at all.

The room was cozy and quiet, a comfortable retreat. The walls were deep green enamel, the trim russet. There was a free-standing fireplace and shelves with colorfully bound books. They were the kinds of books that were actually read, too, not the leather-bound volumes designed for show. Mysteries and true crime, biographies and histories. She didn't know why that surprised her; Dan liked to read. He had read Styles's book. Jess hadn't.

She shivered and took another large sip of wine.

His chair was leather, and comfortable. There was a computer on the desk and a crystal globe that looked like the kind of thing someone might have given him for Christmas, otherwise the surface was clear. Dan was neat at the office, too. Absently, she tugged at the top drawer of his desk. It was locked. She wondered what he kept in there.

The sofa had a muted paisley print, and the chairs were leather. The accent pieces were brass and dark wood; none of the lamps matched. Jess had a feeling that his decorator girlfriend hadn't made it to this room, and the decor benefited. It was a good, comfortable room—masculine without being overwhelming, very much like Dan. She felt safe here.

Dan stood at the doorway. "Everything okay?"

She took a breath, then released it with a wry grimace. "Sure. Perfect."

She dropped her eyes to her glass and took another sip. "I never realized how screwed-up my family was until all this started. And that's stupid, isn't it? I mean, how could I not? We practically specialize in screwed-up families on the show. Dysfunctional is the byword of the nineties, isn't it?"

She gave a quick sharp shake of her head and drank some more wine. Still she didn't look at Dan, and it really didn't matter whether or not he was listening. She talked because silence was not an option.

"It's just that I never thought of myself as part of a dysfunctional family. I thought I was perfect. I was raised to be perfect. I see now that the more perfect my parents could make me, the less bad they had to feel about Evan . . . or something like that. That probably had a lot to do with why my dad was so hard on us, too. Nothing was ever good enough for him. No matter how well I did, he always found a way to make me feel I'd let him down. To this day I sometimes wake up in the middle of the night with this horrible sense of guilt, as though I've done something shameful or forgotten to do something important or made an unforgivable mistake . . . He used to make me feel like that all the time. I wonder if it wasn't because he used to wake up in the middle of the night with exactly the same feeling, because of Evan."

She was silent for a moment, thinking about that. Then she drained her wine. "I should never have put him in that place. Something else I get to feel guilty about."

Dan said, "Come on out, I'll give you some more wine. I'm making pasta."

She followed him into his bright, copper and butcher-block kitchen and drank another glass of wine while he filled the room with the smells of olive oil and sautéed garlic. He had his shirtsleeves rolled up and his collar unbuttoned, and it occurred to Jess that she had known him for five years, but had never seen him like this, relaxed in his own environment.

"I didn't know you could cook," she said, perching on the edge of a counter with her wineglass.

He grinned. "I know only one dish. But I do it very well."

He took big ripe tomatoes and yellow onions from a hanging basket over the work island. His voice remained casual as he took a chopping knife down from its magnetic clip. "Jess, the police aren't going to be able to give you round-the-clock protection. Can you afford a private service?"

"Do you mean . . . like a bodyguard?" She shook her head. "No. I can't live my life with someone watching my every move. Not an option."

She could tell he wanted to argue, but concentrated instead on mincing an onion with a smooth sawing motion of the knife. "Are you up to talking about this?" he glanced at her. "The attack, the stalker, the whole thing. Because we can let it go for tonight, but what happened to your brother changed everything. And sooner or later you've got to think about that."

Jess took a big swallow of wine. "I'm having trouble thinking about anything else. Is there something I can do?"

While she shredded lettuce for salad, Dan said, "I think we've been looking at it the wrong way. We thought it was an obsessed fan, because that's the way people like us are conditioned to think. I mean, the first thing you said to me about the whole thing was Michael J. Fox and Jodie Foster, right?"

Jess said, "Do you want onions in the salad?"

He raked a portion of chopped onions from the cutting board into the salad bowl. "But I think it's something more personal than that. This guy, whoever he is, he knows what buttons to push. Jess, what if it's someone you know?"

Jess had begun to slice mushrooms; she stopped because she didn't trust herself to hold the knife steady. She did not know why the idea should shock her. Surely, somewhere in the back of her mind, she had allowed for the possibility. When she had spent the weekend poring over old high-school yearbooks, hadn't she been wondering whether or not one of those faces might look familiar to her . . . ?

Dan said, "These are pretty personal details he's coming up with from your past, but that's not what makes me think he's more than just a casual observer. Jess, you are the most guilt-ridden person I know, the most easily embarrassed, the most ... I don't know, perfectionistic. There's got to be a psychological term for what you are, and I know, it probably has something to do with being a woman in the nineties. But don't you see, this guy has got your number. *Shame.* What are you ashamed of? True, everyone's got something to be ashamed of, but you take the question personally. You've got a hundred different answers. You obsess on it. He knew exactly how to get under your skin."

"Or she," Jess murmured.

Dan tossed a handful of tomatoes into the sauté pan and stood back from the steam, giving her a puzzled glance.

"Lieutenant Candler said it could be a woman." Jess took another gulp of wine and felt steady enough to pick up the knife again. "Anyone could have found out those things about my past, you know. Styles did."

"It wasn't a woman," Dan said matter-of-factly. "Women don't shoot people in the face; it's too messy. Remember that criminal psychologist we had on who said if men had to clean up the messes they made, there'd be a lot less violent crime?"

"I don't remember."

"Jess, how many people knew where your brother was?"

She continued to slice mushrooms into neat one-eighth inch pieces, concentrating on keeping them uniform. "Not many," she answered in a moment. "My mother. She may have told some people, but I doubt it. She doesn't like to think about Evan, much less talk about him. The people at Shepherd's Village, of course. Some of them watch the show; they knew who I was. Trish."

Dan looked surprised. "Trish?"

Jess nodded. "We were talking once, and it came up. I don't know if she remembers. I don't know if she mentioned it to anyone, or if anyone overhead. I don't know who Jeremy Styles told. And if he could find out, anybody could, so you see your theory about it being someone I know doesn't necessarily hold up."

"All right, let's take it from another vantage point." Dan dropped angel hair pasta into boiling water. "What do all the notes have in common? The job application, the party dress, the yearbook photograph? Those events have got to mean something in particular to someone."

Jess was thoughtful for a moment. The knife was still. "Only to me," she said. "They were all meaningful events to me. But more important, I think, they made me start to *think* about things that were even more significant. The job application made me think about college, and Brett. The party dress made think about the one prom I was stood up for. And poor Roger . . . God, I hadn't thought about him in ages. And now he's dead."

Dan looked at her for a moment, but he wasn't really looking at her. He had that thoughtful, absent expression on his face he sometimes got when deep into the process of interviewing—formulating the probing questions, peeling away the defensive replies to get to the heart of the answer. He observed, more to himself than to her, "A lot of people die around you."

And then he glanced at her quickly. "Sorry. Poor taste."

Jess transferred the last of the salad ingredients into the bowl. The wine was having its desired effect, and she was neither disturbed nor impressed by the remark. "That's true," she agreed slowly. "I never thought about it before." And she still could not see any significance in the fact.

She cocked her head toward him then in muted curiosity. "Why all the interest, Dan? This isn't your problem, you know."

"Of course it is. You're my partner, we depend on each other. What happens to you, happens to me. You don't think I could carry the show by myself, do you?"

He spoke so casually, so matter-of-factly, that Jess was caught off guard. For a moment she didn't know what to say, surprised as much by the words as by the warm feeling of contentment that spread through her when he said them.

After a moment she replied, "Actually—yes, I do."

He tossed her a playfully smug smile as he transferred the steaming pasta into the sauté pan with the vegetables. "That's just my star personality coming through. That's what you're supposed to think."

She frowned a little. "What about your other offer? I thought—"

"Ah, come on, Jess, you don't really listen to Trish when she starts that trash, do you? I don't get any more offers than you do, and I don't take them any more seriously. Trish just uses the rumors to keep us in line."

Jess said, "That bitch." But there was no real venom in her tone. She was too relieved, and in a very strange way, happy deep down inside. So much of her security had been ripped away these past weeks. It was good to know one thing, at least, was unthreatened.

Jess wanted to dine on the patio. The decorative table Dan kept out there was shoved into a corner, blocked by bags of concrete mix and stacks of stone and covered with a drop cloth. However, they brought a small table to the open doors and settled it across the threshold, dining half in and half out of the room. Ðan lit a candle and covered it with a glass globe, and they watched the sunlight fade from the river.

Jess ate a little and drank a good deal more wine. She was beginning to feel fuzzy-headed, tingly. She thought Dan had planned it that way and was grateful.

After a time she said, "You're really too smart for our show, you know. I guess that's what makes me so insecure about losing you. Trish, too."

When she was tired, relaxed, or off guard, her Southern accent became pronounced. She knew that amused Dan and expected his teasing smile. "I'm glad to know you worry about losing me." He lifted his glass in a small salute before drinking.

"I don't lose sleep over it or anything." She was thoughtful for a moment, watching him in the candlelight. "So, is this it for you? The limit of your ambition?"

"I've got my own nationally syndicated—or semi-national, anyway—talk show. Who could ask for more?"

"You could," she answered immediately. "You're

good enough to go almost anywhere. I always wondered how you ended up in Philadelphia anyway."

He shrugged. "Somebody made me an offer I couldn't refuse, just as they did you." He sipped his wine, relaxing back in his chair. "I don't know. Sometimes I think about doing another kind of show—more hard news. Sometimes I wish I had more editorial input. Otherwise, I'm pretty satisfied with where my career is right now."

Jess said, "You could be an anchor. Maybe even network."

"Maybe someday, when the time is right. But I'm not much of a risk-taker, and it would have to be a pretty sure thing before I'd think about jumping ship. What about you? Is this what you want to be when you grow up?"

Jess smiled wanly. "Right now, my only ambition is to get through another day. But hey, maybe Trish was right." She tried to force lightness into her tone. "Maybe there's some way we can get some ratings out of this mess. That would make my ambition happy."

Dan reached across the table to take her hand. "Look Jess," he said quietly, "I know it's hard to believe, but the worst has got to be over now. Before today, the police didn't have anything to go on but a few notes, a couple of phone calls. They couldn't have held Styles even if he had been guilty, not on anything substantial. But now . . . well, as rotten as it sounds to say, now they've got a case. And chances are good they'll be able to solve it before too much longer."

She swallowed hard, but couldn't quite clear her throat of the lump that had formed there. She drained her wine. She focused on the darkening cityscape beyond the sheer drop of the balcony and let the vastness soothe her. "I feel safe up here," she murmured. "As though whatever is down there can't find me."

Dan's fingers tightened on hers, and he looked for a moment as though he wanted to say something, but the light was too poor and Jess's perception too confused for her to be able to read what that might be. And in the end he simply smiled and said, "It's getting chilly. Come on inside."

Jess let him pull her to her feet, and, coming around the table, she stood close to him. His face was softened by the lamplight inside the room, his eyes very blue. *Anchor man blue*, she thought fuzzily, looking into them.

She said, "Why are you being so nice to me, Dan?"

He hesitated, and his expression turned lightly wry. "I don't think you're drunk enough to hear the answer to that."

Jess replied, "I'm pretty drunk. Thank you by the way."

"You're welcome."

He smiled down at her. She leaned close. They kissed, and warmth spread through her, inching out the chill of the breeze from the open doors, the even deeper chill that had settled around her heart. She rested her cheek against his chest. "I think I'll stay the night," she murmured.

He held her. She listened to the beat of his heart. Then his lips brushed the top of her hair, and he took her shoulders and stepped away. "I'll make up the sofa bed," he said.

Chapter 17

Freddie's luck was changing. He could feel it in the air like the first winds of autumn or raindrops on a hot still day. It wasn't just the story he'd sold to the *Spectator*. That was nothing and he knew it—a three-paragraph insert on page 12 that had come in too late to even be indexed on the front page; he'd be surprised if more than a couple of hundred people had even read it. But they'd be reading it tomorrow. They'd be scrambling for that three-paragraph story on Monday. And that was only the beginning.

He was in the middle of a breaking story. That had never happened to him before. And all he'd had to do was play his hunches and follow his leads and—*pow*—it had fallen right into his lap.

Of course, it would have made a better story if the kid at the mental home had been killed instead of just scared, but still—who could've guessed? Today *Talk-Show Hostess Hides Bitter Secret*; tomorrow *Murderous Stalker Turns on Celebrity's Brother*. And if they thought he'd be turning over that story to the *Spectator* for salary, they had another thought coming. This time the news boys were calling *him*. Hell, he'd be negotiating with the networks before too long. He grinned as he started up the steps of his building. He might even make it as a guest on *Speaking of Which* before it was all over.

Freddie lived in a once middle-class neighborhood that was gradually being taken over by weeds and drugs. While he could still be reasonably sure of finding the hubcaps intact on his '78 Chevy if he parked it in the street at night, it wasn't the kind of place where he personally would want to be walking the streets after midnight unarmed. His apartment building housed six other units and smelled of disinfectant and sweat. He could hear a television from another floor. He took the inside stairs to his own second-floor apartment two at a time, whistling tunelessly under his breath and grinning to himself as he spun out fantasies of the future that would be his.

It wasn't just the breaking story. Oh no, that was just the stepping-stone. He had known that the minute he looked through Styles's file. With the information Styles had gathered on Jessamine Cray and the profile Freddie had started on Lieutenant Lyle Candler, he had a book. Not just a book—a blockbuster best-seller. And it was a story no one would believe.

Of course, it all depended on his beating Styles to the draw. He had heard that in really sensationalistic cases book contracts were sometimes presented at the scene of the murder, and the book itself was turned out in less than a week, on the shelves a week after that. Freddie didn't know that he could match that record, but he could damn sure try. Today Jessamine Cray was hot. In two weeks she could be yesterday's news.

He had a bagful of Mexican takeout in one arm

and a twelve-pack of beer under the other as he juggled his keys into the lock. But the door wasn't locked. It wasn't even closed. It hung propped on a splintered frame, arranged to look normal to the passing gaze. But it had been kicked in.

Freddie swore out loud as he pushed the door open and stepped inside. He realized a moment later how stupid that was, but right then he was too surprised to think anything at all. The light from a street lamp illuminated the room clearly, and the intruder made no effort to hide. Freddie had time to say, "You!"

Then the gun came up, and the bullet fired at close range went through his throat, killing him instantly.

Jess's answering machine picked up after four rings. *Hi, this is Jess. I'm sorry I missed you, but please leave a message at the sound of the tone.*

The tone sounded in the dark. The voice began to whisper.

"Shame on you, Jess. You should have been here. This one was for you."

Jess spent the next afternoon in New Jersey, inspecting convalescent centers that specialized in disabilities such as Evan's, and Dan insisted on coming with her. She had resisted at first, not because she didn't want his company, but because she didn't understand why he wanted to inconvenience himself in such a way, and because she was uncomfortable with allowing him into that very private part of her life. Still, she was glad he insisted. It was good to have someone else along, tempering her judge-

ment with perceptive questions and opinions of his
own, taking some of the burden off her shoulders,
distracting her when the reason all this was necessary threatened to overwhelm her. She began to understand the appeal of being part of a couple.

She found herself talking about Evan, freely and
without constraint. She had never done that before.
She wasn't even sure she had ever allowed herself
to think about him without restraint before.

"He was always . . . I don't know, like my baby
doll. He never cried. I used to rock him and hold
him and feed him just as I would my dolls. I guess
my parents knew even then something was wrong,
but he lived with us until he was two. Of course, it
didn't seem like he was two. He never learned to
walk or talk or smile. He just grew bigger and
sweeter. When they took him away from me, I
thought my heart would break. They didn't even
tell me."

Her voice grew tight with remembered resentment. "They treated the whole situation as though
it were a puppy who'd gotten run over by a car. One
day I came home from school and he was gone.
God, he could have been dead for all I knew. They
just said was that Evan had to 'go away.' Eventually,
of course, they took me to see him—Christmas, I
think it was. I don't think they meant to be cruel,
they just didn't think I was old enough to understand. Maybe *they* weren't old enough to understand. Anyway, it's just always seemed as though I
was the one responsible for him. Maybe the only
one who cared about him."

She glanced at Dan apologetically. "You probably
don't want to hear this. I'm sorry for running on."

It was nearing sunset, and he was driving—which was another advantage to being part of a couple, Jess mused absently. She was exhausted, emotionally and physically, and it was good to have someone else take the wheel.

Dan said, "Actually, I do want to hear it. You probably don't realize how little you talk about yourself. I've known you for five years, and I don't know anything about you at all."

Jess shrugged uncomfortably. "Another legacy from my family, I guess. We're masters at secrecy." And then she added, "Of course, aside from what's in the bio, I don't know a whole lot about you either."

"You never asked."

She sighed. "No. I guess I didn't. For a talk-show hostess, I'm not a very good listener, I'm afraid."

Dan pulled into the parking space in front of Jess's condo, applied the parking brake, and turned off the ignition. He reached a hand across the seat and massaged the back of Jess's neck briefly.

"I know it's hard to believe," he said, "but one day this is all going to be over. When it is, I'll tell you all my secrets. Maybe you'll tell me a few more of yours. Until then, let's just concentrate on getting through this."

She smiled at him gratefully. It was barely twilight, and he looked good in jeans and a sweater, his hair windblown, the last glow of the sun bringing out the gold of his tan. She said, "And to think I always thought you were just another pretty face."

Dan gave the back of her neck a last brief squeeze. "You should've paid closer attention."

"I will," she promised him, "in the future."

For a moment they sat there while the sunlight leaked out of the sky, not talking, feeling comfortable with one another. Then Jess turned to him and said, a little apologetically, "I'd ask you in, but I'm really beat."

Dan smiled at her. "No problem."

He handed her keys to her, and they got out, parting at Dan's car. Jess waved to him as she started up the walk.

It was that shadowy gray time of evening, not dark enough for the security lights to come on, not light enough to see really well without them. Jess's eyes were on her feet because there was a loose flagstone somewhere along the walk that she hadn't had a chance to report yet, but her keys were threaded tightly through her fingers in a defense posture, and she was alert to the tall shrubs and deep shadows that lined the walk.

Suddenly, she heard a sound from those shadows, then saw a movement in those shrubs. She stopped, her heart flying to her throat, her fingers clenching convulsively around her keys. She was less than ten feet from her front door. She would never make it. No one else was around. There was no place to run.

All of this went through her head in less than a second. And then she saw with her peripheral vision the form of a man detach itself from the shadows and step into her path.

She screamed, "*Dan!*" and whirled, running down the path the way she had come.

He caught her arm, she felt his fingers close on her jacket and skin, but she jerked away, *tore* away from his grip, running, and he was right behind her, reaching for her again. She saw Dan, running toward her, and she cried out again, then the loose flagstone caught her heel and she tripped. Dan caught her against him, hard.

He was glaring at something over her head. "What's the meaning of this, Candler?" he demanded.

Gasping, holding on to Dan's shirtfront like a heroine in a gothic novel, Jess turned. Lieutenant Lyle Candler stood there, frowning.

"Shit," Jess whispered, shaking. She closed her eyes, trying to draw a deep breath. *"Shit."*

"I'm sorry I scared you, Jess," Candler said when they were inside. "I'd been waiting for you a long time."

Dan said grimly, "Under the circumstances, don't you think lying in wait for Jess in the bushes is a little ill-advised?"

Candler barely glanced at him. He said to Jess, "I tried to reach you at the office. They didn't know where you were."

Jess hung up her coat and her purse. She still felt foolish and shaky. "We were out looking at convalescent homes. Perhaps you've heard? Recent events have forced me to relocate my brother."

Candler took a small notebook from his pocket. "How long did that take?"

Jess stared at him. What was the notebook for? And how odd that the mere sight of it could make her feel defensive.

"It took from the time we left the studio until now," Dan put in sharply, "what do you think? And what's with the notebook?"

Then Candler glanced at him, but only briefly.

He reached into his inside pocket again and took out a folded tabloid.

"I wonder if either of you have seen this."

Jess took the paper from him curiously. It was open to an inside page, to stories with headlines like *Zoo Makes Bizarre Discovery* and *Space Debris Blamed for Deadly Winter* and *Talk-Show Hostess Hides Bitter Secret.* . . .

She couldn't read the whole article. She scanned her name and Evan's, Shepherd's Village Convalescent Center and words like "tragic," "vegetative," and "neglected" until she felt her gorge rise. She handed the paper to Dan. It was a moment before she could speak.

"When . . ." She had to clear her throat, closing her fists. "When did this come out?"

Candler responded, "Two days ago. The day before the incident with your brother."

Dan finished reading and returned the paper to Candler. The look he gave the detective was long and meaningful. "Well," he said, "it looks like your short list got a little longer."

Jess sank to the sofa, focusing with great, determined effort. Two days ago. Someone had written this article for any maniac in the world to read, and then some maniac did read it and walked into Evan's room and . . .

Dan demanded, "Who wrote the story? Styles?"

"A man named Freddie Glanbury. He used to hang out at the precinct, digging for dirt. My guess is that's how he came upon this."

Dan said lowly, "Son of a bitch. He ought to be strung up by his balls."

Candler glanced at him. "It's a little late for that.

He was murdered last night. A thirty-eight through the throat, close range. A neighbor heard the shot, but no one reported it until late this morning when somebody happened to be going past his door and saw the body."

Jess just stared at him. Even Dan looked shocked.

Candler sat down in the chair opposite Jess, his elbows resting on his knees, and leaned forward. "I'm sorry Jess," he said, "but I have to ask. Where were you between eleven and eleven-thirty last night?"

Dan exclaimed, "For Christ's sake!"

It took a moment for Jess to understand. "You don't think that I . . . I didn't know him! I mean, I did, but . . ."

Dan looked at her sharply, and she turned back to Candler, explaining quickly, "I saw him at your office that time, remember? It's not as though . . . My God."

She stood abruptly and paced a few steps away, as though to put physical distance between herself and the accusation. Hugging her arms, she said, "I was asleep. I had—a little too much to drink I guess, and I went to bed early. I don't know what time. I can't believe you're asking me this."

And Dan put in impatiently, "It was before ten o'clock. And the reason I know is because I was there. I didn't want her coming back here alone after what happened with Evan, so she stayed at my place. All night. So have you got that? She was with me from show time yesterday morning until now. I was with her. We are each other's alibi. Satisfactory?"

Something flickered over Candler's eyes that was

a little too fast and a little too unexpected for Jess to read. He jotted a few things down in his notebook, and when he looked up at her again, his expression was perfectly bland. "Is that right, Jess?"

"Yes," she said. "I was upset. We had dinner and . . . a lot of wine. I slept on the sofa bed in Dan's study. You don't really think . . ."

He said, "Is there anyone else who can verify where the two of you were last night?"

Dan exclaimed, "Oh, for Christ's sake!"

Jess shook her head mutely.

Candler finished writing in the book and looked up. He said soberly, "No, I really don't think you killed Freddie Glanbury. But that's just my opinion, and my opinion is not going to make or break this case. I have to investigate."

Jess swallowed and nodded and, after a moment, she returned to her seat on the sofa. Dan came and stood behind her, his hand resting protectively on her shoulder.

Candler said, "The truth is, Glanbury's death might not have anything to do with you. The man was a sleaze, and he made a lot of enemies. But right before he died, the only thing he was working on was your story. Apparently, he'd picked up the story the town paper printed about the nurse who was murdered in your brother's room and was hawking it all over the city. He'd spoken to all the papers and television stations. Somehow he'd tied it into the stalker angle, and from what we can tell, was trying to turn it into some kind of major story— a newspaper series or maybe his big break on television, I don't know."

As he spoke, Jess felt herself sinking deeper into

despair. This was a never-ending nightmare. Just when she thought it was over, it got worse; just when she thought it couldn't get worse, it did. Dan's fingers squeezed her shoulder reassuringly.

"Just for your information," Candler added, "most of the news editors weren't interested in dealing with Freddie. But he put them on the trail, so you can expect to start seeing your name in print a little more often than you're used to. We're going to have to ask you to be careful in what you say to the press. The more information that's released, the muddier the waters get for us. I know publicity is part of your business, but the fewer details you give out on this case, the better chance we have of solving it."

Jess's eyes widened. "Wait a minute. First I'm a murder suspect, now I'm a publicity hound? The last time I checked I was the victim here!"

Candler said nothing for a moment. Then, "I never said you were a murder suspect, Jess."

Dan muttered, "Thanks for small favors. You can't catch the stalker, you can't keep Jess or her family safe, you can't keep the media from turning her life into a zoo . . . but at least you're not accusing her of murder."

Candler looked at the two of them for a minute, then he said, "As a matter of fact, I have a theory, if you'd care to hear it."

Dan did not look particularly interested, but Jess released a short tense breath pushing her fingers through her hair. "Anything," she said. "This can't go on."

Candler looked at Dan, then at her. He began slowly, "What we've seen so far are not necessarily the acts of a person who means you harm. On the staircase, for example, if he had wanted to hurt you, he could have. You had nowhere to run, you were trapped. And the notes—they refer to events in your past—but not to events that threaten you personally."

Jess's brow furrowed, and she leaned forward a little, trying to follow his logic. Dan looked impatient.

"The notes—what are you ashamed of—that would imply that the stalker is trying to torment you by reminding you of things you're ashamed of, or should be—like the lie on the job application. But what if he's not? What if he's trying to protect you?"

Jess said incredulously, "Protect me? How? By terrorizing me, invading my privacy, attacking my brother, then killing the nurse who tried to stop him—"

Candler held up a hand. Dan looking interested now, sitting on the arm of the sofa beside Jess.

"Think about it." Candler's face was very, very sober. "The things that have embarrassed— *shamed*—you most in your life. Being stood up for the junior-senior prom. The boy who stood you up is dead now. Being dumped by your first lover. He's dead, too. An institutionalized brother—"

Jess whispered, "Oh God!" She pressed her hands to her cheeks, and they were ice-cold. She could feel the physical process of blood draining from her head to her feet, the slow wave of cold, the tingling extremities, the spots before her eyes. And Candler's still, solemn face throughout it all.

Dan said, "But that's crazy! You're talking about things that happened fifteen years ago! Are you telling me that this . . . this maniac has been stalking

Jess since she was in high school? And those deaths—one was a suicide and the other an accident. They had nothing to do with Jess."

Candler said, looking at Jess, "As I said, it's just a theory. But you should know that Roger Dill's accident on those icy roads that winter weekend was due to a blowout in the right rear tire—one that could have been cause by a bullet."

Jess could feel her pupils dilate; a stab of pain went through her brain. She whispered, "Jesus."

Dan said, "Fifteen years. That's insane."

But he didn't sound nearly as convinced as he had a moment before.

Candler said, "Maybe. But when you throw Glanbury into the mix . . . This guy's trying to protect you, right? To get rid of the things that hurt you or embarrass you. He tried to get rid of your brother, but he was interrupted. He had to kill the nurse so he could get away. But he still hadn't done anything to help you . . . so he went to Glanbury, the person who wrote about your secrets—your shame, if you will—and he got rid of him for you. It was an act of love, in a way."

Jess shivered. "That's the most twisted thing I've ever heard." She felt sick. She had to get up again and walk away.

Dan's eyes were narrowed in thought. "You said Glanbury was poking around all over town, trying to make a story out of Jess and the stalker. Maybe he found out something he shouldn't. Maybe he was killed because he knew who the stalker was, couldn't it be as simple as that?"

"It could," agreed Candler.

But Jess could tell he didn't think so.

She said abruptly, "He's getting more violent."

Candler said nothing. Dan looked at her.

"At first he was just . . . suggestive. Now he's getting personal. He's killed twice. If he had succeeded with Evan, it would have been three times. He's like an animal with the taste of blood."

Candler said carefully, "That doesn't necessarily mean—"

"*Damn* it!" Jess said with sudden ferocity. Shoving her fingers into the pockets of her jeans, she walked a few feet away from Candler, then turned sharply. "I'm tired of this," she said. "That's the trouble with our whole society, don't you know that? We're afraid to order a pizza because the delivery boy might have a gun. The delivery boy is afraid to deliver the pizza because he might be shot instead of paid. We're afraid to go to the movies or drive our cars or walk home after a show or use the ATM, and damn it, I'm tired of it! I'm not going to be afraid anymore." Her eyes narrowed on Candler. "I want to nail the son of a bitch. I don't care what it takes. Do it."

Dan added, "You might start by getting her some protection. There's a maniac out there who knows how to use a gun, and the security in this complex is a joke; Styles proved that. Why don't you put a man on—"

Candler replied calmly but firmly, "I can't do that."

"Why the hell not?"

Candler looked at Jess. "I'm sorry, Jess," he said. "It's not right, but that's the way it is. No one has made a direct threat against you. Not even the letters can be considered threatening. We don't have any evidence whatsoever to lead us to believe you're in any danger. There's no way I can get protection approved for you."

Jess felt her throat go dry. Dan said bitterly, "Shit."

Candler glanced at Dan, then at Jess. He looked genuinely regretful. He said, "Look, I'll see what I can do. For now, let's start by talking about who you know who might want to do you harm."

They talked for half an hour, and names came up that Jess would never in a million years believe capable of terrorizing her, much less attacking Evan or killing Freddie Glanbury. Dan supplied most of them. And all of them went on the list. She kept thinking about high school, about the possibility that someone could have been following her, watching her every move, since then. About Evan. Poor Evan who had never done anything at all except embarrass her family . . . and maybe even embarrass her, just the faintest bit. She had never told anyone about him. Didn't that mean she was ashamed?

God, what had she done?

Candler gave her instructions about handling any further mail she might receive at home or in her office, and told her he would send someone around to take a series of elimination fingerprints from everyone who might have reason to handle her mail. She tried to pay attention. She tried to remember it all.

"From now on," Candler told her, "record every incoming call. You can do it with your answering machine. Just be sure to tell people you're recording them, or whatever we get will be inadmissible in court."

Dan said, "You don't really think the stalker is going to just let himself be recorded, do you?"

Candler shrugged. "You never can tell. Sometimes it's an ego trip for these guys, thinking they can outsmart technology."

When he stood to leave, Jess stood too. She swallowed hard, watching Candler's face. "This . . . person, whoever did this . . . whoever attacked Evan and maybe killed that reporter . . . you said he was trying to protect me. But maybe he's not. I need to know. Do you think I'm in danger?"

He didn't answer immediately. Then he said, "I'll be consulting with a criminal psychologist on the case, but from what I understand there's a pattern. First it's adoration, almost hero worship—in your case, a desire on the part of the perpetrator to protect you from unpleasantness or embarrassment— but eventually reality sets in. You'll do something to disappoint your protector, or he'll realize that nothing he can do will make you accessible to him . . . and then the scenario changes."

Jess demanded hoarsely, "How?"

Again he considered his answer. And the answer he gave was not really an answer at all. He said, "Do you own a gun?"

Jess was taken aback. "Why—no. Should I?"

Dan took a step closer, watching Candler.

Candler's reply was carefully worded. "It would be outside my duty as an officer of the law to advise a private citizen to arm herself. But do you know how to use a handgun?"

"I . . ." Again Jess swallowed and nodded. "Yes. My father taught me."

His eyes held hers and said something his words

did not. "Because in the wrong hands, a handgun can be a dangerous thing."

And Dan added quietly, "Or even in the right ones."

Candler glanced at him, then back to Jess. "Good night, then. I'll be in touch."

Dan left not long after that. It wasn't until she was alone, having double-checked all the locks, that she noticed the light on her answering machine blinking.

She thought, *I've got to call my mother. God, if this business about the stalker starts making the news, or even the tabloids . . .*

She pushed the button, and the tape rewound. The tone sounded, and the voice came, hoarse and husky, the androgynous half whisper that, even with the first syllable, had the power to chill Jess's blood.

"Shame on you, Jess. You should have been here. This one was for you."

Before the caller finished speaking, Jess was on her knees, her arms wrapped tightly around her middle, biting down hard on her lower lip to control the shaking. But she couldn't control the tears, or the words, high and thin, that bubbled up like a prayer, "No . . . please, no . . ."

Chapter 18

Excerpts from interrogation reports Case #1002386; Investigating Officer Lieutenant Lyle Candler, Philadelphia PD, Major Crimes Division:

Subject: Steven Lobell, neighbor

I hardly knew her. We only went out once. Hell, we didn't even go out; we just had dinner here at my house. I threw a couple of steaks on the barbecue and—hey, am I in some sort of trouble? That bitch didn't make a complaint, did she? Because if she did, she's lying.

Investigator's Note: See complaint #27846, simple battery, filed by Cynthia Kramer against Steven Lobell 8-06-92, charges dropped; complaint #34869, sexual harassment, filed by Amanda Remke, photographer's model, 3-30-94, pending. Subject appears to have a history of sexual intimidation and violence toward women.

[*cont*] If you ask me, she was the one that was weird. She used to watch me work out from her window. Never said anything, just watched. And then that night we got together she was all friendly, coming on to me like

crazy, if you want to know the truth, and then all of a sudden she freaked. Hell, I didn't even get to kiss her. Barely touched her. And she went streaking out of here like a cat with its tail on fire. . . .

No, I never sent her any letters. Why should I?

No, I never called her. Tried to look up her number once, when I realized it was her living across the courtyard, but it's unlisted.

May eight? Hey, that's easy. I was on a shoot in New York, Fresh 'n Sweet grapefruit juice.

No, I didn't know she had a brother. We didn't exactly talk about her family life. . . . No, I don't read the papers unless they're running my work. . . . Last Friday? Yeah, someone can confirm my whereabouts. I had a date sleeping over. Why? What is this anyway?

Investigator's Comments: Although the subject fits the personality profile established by the FBI for cases of this type, his alibi checks out for May 8 (the night the victim confronted the stalker in the stairwell of the WSBN building) and most probably checks out for the night of the attack on Evan Cray. The girlfriend (see attached form SR803) admits she was sleeping between three and five A.M., but confirms that the subject was in bed beside her when she awoke at 6:00 A.M. Conclusion: Unlikely suspect, but not impossible.

Subject: Patricia Siegel, producer, *Speaking of Which*

Yeah, I've known Jess five years. We're all

part of the original team here. Dan, Jess, me—
we all started together. We're pretty close, all
of us. I mean, we used to go out and get drunk
and sit up to all hours in the early days. Of
course, you can't do that anymore or some reporter will be calling your stars substance
abusers—which, come to think of it, is not
such a bad idea at that. Any publicity is good
publicity.

I guess I know more about Jess than anybody else in the world . . . which is not to say
I know a lot. She guards her privacy, which is
not always the smartest thing to do when
you're in the public eye. Yeah, she told me the
story about lying on her first job application
once—one of those all-nighters I told you
about. I thought it was pretty funny—except
for one little lie she might not be where she
is today, that kind of thing. No, I never knew
about her brother. That was one of those
things she'd want to keep "private." Pisses me
off in a way. Like she didn't trust me.

Freddie Glanbury? Never heard of him.
Until Jess told us he was dead, that is, and
that he's the one who wrote the article in the
Spectator that tipped off the real press as to
what was going on here—and may have gotten
her brother attacked. . . . I hope you're not
implying that any of us are enjoying this. This
place has been a madhouse for the last couple
of days. We produce an hour-show each and
every day, and it's hard enough to do without
fending off reporters every time we turn
around, not to mention the toll it's taking on

my star. . . . Yeah, I won't deny that the public-ity's good for the show, in the long run. In the short run, it's hell.

Investigator's Comments: Subject has no alibi for either of times in question. She lives alone, often works late alone. During the interview she seemed tense and agitated, chain-smoked. Her job and future advancement are closely aligned with the success of this show. Since the coverage of the stalking of Jessamine Cray began, she estimates viewership has increased by 25 percent.

Interesting aside: In 1992 *Speaking of Which* broadcast a show in which one of the guests became physically violent and attacked a mem-ber of the audience. The audience member was later revealed to be a plant, and the entire episode a publicity stunt engineered by the producer—with the full knowledge and cooper-ation, it is assumed, of her stars. As a result *Speaking of Which* doubled its market share.

Subject: Sylvia Graham, secretary to Ms. Cray

Sure, I like my job okay. I mean, Miss Cray is nice enough. A little snobby, but she always comes through at Christmas. Last year it was a Fendi purse and a three-hundred-dollar bonus. But that phony smile of hers, and that sweet-as-sugar accent—I mean really, sometimes it just makes my skin crawl. No, I wouldn't say she's easy to work for. I haven't had a full lunch hour in I-don't-know-when. People seem to like her, though. I mean, she gets tons of fan mail . . . well, I guess you know about that.

Sure, I have access to her personnel file. I can get it right through my computer. Was there something you wanted me to look up for you?

Well, I can't say I knew about that brother she tried so hard to keep secret—I mean, really, that's so stupid, isn't it?—but I figured there was something like that going on. After all, I'm the one who wrote the check every month to Shepherd's Village.

Investigator's Comments: Ms. Graham lives alone and has no alibi for any of the events in question. Co-workers describe her as stand-offish and "weird." Warrants further investigation.

Subject: Dan Webber

Yes, I've met Jess's mother. A couple of times when she's been in town. She always comes to the set, and I usually take her out to lunch afterward. The three of us do dinner. Jess doesn't get along all that well with her mother, a lot of daughters don't. I try to take the pressure off. She returns the favor when my folks are in town.

Of course, she talks about Jess's past, she's proud of her. Who wouldn't be? No, she never mentioned the brother. Neither did Jess.

No, Jess never talked about college, not until the notes started coming. High school either.

No, I don't know anyone who knew Jess before she got into television. No, she never talked much about her past. Yes, I'd say we're close, everyone on the show is, but you've got to understand about Jess. She's very, very good at her job—and her job is to get people to talk about themselves. You don't do that when you're talking about yourself, do you understand what I'm saying? She doesn't focus on herself. She listens. It would never have occurred to her to tell me those things about her past. Why should she?

Yes, my contract is up this year. So is Jess's. I get a lot of offers. I don't take all of them.

You seem awfully interested in my relationship with her. This has got to be the third time you've asked about it. We're friends, okay? On and off the show. Do you really think we could pull it off as well as we do in front of the cameras if we didn't at least like one another? No, we're not lovers, but do me a favor, will you? Start the rumor. It'll be great for the show's ratings.

I'm aware that I haven't been far away every time a crisis occurred with this stalker business. What surprises me is that *you're* surprised. We work together fourteen hours a day. We live less than fifteen minutes from one another. We're required by contract to make fifty percent of our outside public appearances together. What would be unusual is if I weren't around when something happened to her. Then you'd have reason to start questioning my whereabouts.

No, I never heard of Glanbury before he was killed. Wait a minute, I may have heard the

name or seen it on a byline—we go through a
lot of tabloids, looking for material for the
show—but I never met him. And I sure as hell
hope you're not going to ask me if I own a gun.

No, I don't.

I already told you, I was alone the night
Evan was attacked. As for the night Jess was
cornered in the stairwell—I have the best alibi
of all, don't I? I was with you.

Did I mention I resent this line of
questioning?

Investigator's Comments: Webber is also very
good at his job. He asked more questions than
he answered.

Jess said tensely, "I have to tell you, I'm not comfortable with the way you've been questioning my
co-workers and friends, as though . . . as though
they were suspects in the case. I've gotten some
complaints, and that does not make for a very pleasant work environment, let me assure you."

They were in her office, and Candler felt as
though the entire world was watching them through
the glass walls. He wondered what kind of personality it took to be comfortable working in a fishbowl
. . . and then he realized that, to a great extent, that
was the way Jessamine Cray lived. She sat back in
one of the chairs across from her desk; she paced
back and forth in front of it, the kick pleat of her
short black skirt flaring every time she did. It was
nine o'clock in the morning.

He said, "In a case like this, it's important that I
talk to everyone who knows you, whether they're
close personal friends or casual acquaintances. One

of them just might have the information I need to catch this guy, and they probably don't even know it. But I didn't mean to make anyone feel like a suspect."

Her relief was visible. She unclasped her hands and leaned back, resting her hands on the desk behind her. "God, am I glad to hear that. You don't know what it's like, thinking that someone you know, someone you work with or see every day could be terrorizing you . . . could be a murderer."

Candler said gravely, "I didn't say that none of the people I've interviewed is a suspect. The truth of the matter is, I've been able to eliminate only one or two of them positively. And you've got to come to terms with the possibility that the odds are it *is* someone you know. Even someone you know well."

Jess shook her head adamantly. Her raven's-wing hair caught and bounced the light, then settled into place in alignment with the curve of her chin as though it had been trained to grow that way. She said, "No. No, I can't believe that. No one I know—not personally—no one I know could have done that to Evan, much less murdered that poor reporter for no reason at all."

"No one," said Candler, "murders for no reason at all. Sometimes the reason may not make sense to anyone except the killer, but there's always a reason."

Jess released another long breath. "You still think . . . it's someone trying to protect me."

"It's not so hard to understand. A woman like you naturally triggers the protective instinct in a lot of men."

"What about the answering-machine tape?"

"We had an audio analyst go over it. Some of the background noises led us to the area around Glanbury's apartment. We think the killer called you from that area, maybe even Glanbury's apartment itself, after he killed him."

Jess touched her throat nervously and turned away. "This is insane," she said. Her voice was high and tight. "God, how did I ever get here?"

Candler wasn't sure how to respond. He finally decided the best response was none at all, and he said, "Look, Jess, I know it's not much comfort, but this guy made his big mistake when he killed Glanbury. When he killed that nurse, for that matter, because the sheriff's department down there is working in full cooperation with us. Murderers leave evidence, and our solve rate in cases like this is extremely high."

She smiled weakly. "I know. I haven't forgotten that I'm talking to the man who solved the Silk Scarf killings."

"Then believe me, we know what we're doing. We've got a real chance at solving this thing."

He gave her a moment to digest this and thought she might have looked fractionally reassured. Or perhaps it was just his imagination. Then he went on, "Look, the reason I came by was to talk to you about that theory I had. That whoever is doing this might be someone from your past, and that this might not be the first time he's—well, made himself known, so to speak."

The shadow was back in her eyes; her shoulders hunched as she took more of her weight on the hands that were braced against her desk. "It seems impossible," she said. But the doubt in her voice was more for her own conviction than his. "I mean, how could anyone hold a pattern for that long without showing himself? And if you're right, then it's not just Evan and Freddie Glanbury this guy has tried to kill, but . . ."

He could see the horror forming in her eyes, and he did not feel it would be helpful to anyone to let her dwell on the possibilities. He stepped quickly into the breach. "What I need you to do, Jess, is try to think of anyone who might be a link between now and then. Do you keep up with anyone that you went to high school with, or even college?"

She hesitated. "I still send Christmas cards to my sorority sisters," she said doubtfully at last.

"I'll need a list."

"And there are some people from my hometown, teachers and Sunday School counselors and such, that I send an annual letter to. Beauty pageant coaches. My agent, she's known me since my first job, and that wasn't long after college. God, I know so many people. In a job like mine I guess you do. But no one I could really say has been with me the whole time, since high school."

Candler said thoughtfully, "You may have just put your finger on it, you know."

"What?"

"A girl like you, cheerleader, beauty pageant winner, homecoming queen . . . you've really been a celebrity all your life, haven't you?"

Jess frowned a little. "I'm not sure I know what you mean."

"Just this." He sat forward a little on his chair, subduing the intensity he felt. "People who are in the spotlight don't know a fraction of the people who know them. This person we're looking for—you wouldn't necessarily know him if you met him on the street. Although, undoubtedly, he'd *expect* you to—which is what this whole thing has been about, getting your attention. But it could be anyone— someone who went to school with you, or rode the same bus you did, or simply read about you in the paper. The most obvious place to start is with the personnel records of everyone associated with the show, but I don't really expect them to be conclusive. The most helpful thing you can do is try to recall if anyone in your life now could have possibly had an association with your past. Your mail man, your yard boy, your car mechanic . . ."

Jess continued to frown. "But I already told you—"

Candler shook his head impatiently. "This wouldn't be someone you knew well, either then or now. It would be someone on the periphery of your life, someone you barely noticed . . ."

Jess said helplessly, "Then how can I be expected to recognize him now?"

They both looked up as the door to Jess's office opened without a knock. Sylvia stood there, looking vaguely ill and at the same time perversely excited. She was wearing the latex gloves Candler had suggested she use while opening the mail, and she held a legal-sized manila envelope in her hand.

"Um, Lieutenant," she said. Her voice was squeaky with self-importance. "I think I have something."

Chapter 19

Local Personality Stalked

What began as ordinary fan mail for local talk-show hostess Jessamine Cray has taken a tragic turn, resulting in the death of a nurse who was caring for her brother, Evan Cray. Evan Cray was a resident at a Lancaster County convalescent home for the mentally and emotionally disabled at the time.

Police say that certain evidence found at the scene provides a definite link between the threats made against Ms. Cray and the attack upon the nurse.

Jessamine Cray, with cohost Dan Webber, is the star of Speaking of Which, *seen locally on WSBN. According to police, Cray first filed a complaint May 9, after an incident in which she was terrorized late at night in the WSBN television building, where* Speaking of Which *is produced. She had apparently been receiving threatening mail and telephone calls for several weeks prior to that.*

Author Jeremy Styles, a former guest on Speaking of Which, *was questioned in connection with the case, then later released.*

Dan said into the telephone, "You have got to be kidding. You want *me* to give *you* an interview over this garbage?" He thumped the open newspaper with his thumb and forefinger dismissively, as though the man on the other end of line could see his action and the disgust it implied.

That particular newspaper was only one of several, and the article it contained was neither more or less accurate or informative than any of the others. It did, however, mention the show three times, and Dan's name once, which couldn't be all bad. Only a few of the papers had the connection between Freddie Glanbury and Jess, which was why Jim Brockett, news director for WSBN was calling Dan.

"Come on, Dan, you've got to see how embarrassing this is for us," Jim said. He did not do a very good wheedling tone. "We're neighbors, for God's sake, practically family, and we have nothing on this story. Less than nothing."

"That hasn't stopped you from mentioning it at noon and six for the past three days."

"All right, not an interview," Jim conceded. "An interview would be too much. How about a statement? One newsman to another, just professional courtesy."

Dan replied pleasantly, "And just which one of us is the professional here?"

Jim's tone grew chilled. "Shall I take that as the official position of the show?"

Dan said, "Take it anyway you want." Then he released an exasperated breath and added, "Look, did it ever occur to you that the reason you don't have anything on this story is because there *is* no story? Just take a look at everything that's been printed over the past week, and you'll see what a great job the media is doing of keeping the public informed about absolutely nothing."

"Won't wash, Webber." Jim's tone was dry. "Not if Freddie Glanbury's murder is involved, and that's what they're saying out there."

"Oh, yeah? Who's saying?"

"Stop with the games already. It just may interest you to know that Freddie himself gave me his working file, and it's just chock-full of all kinds of interesting stuff. Of course, Freddie's research methods were—shall we say—questionable at best, so I'd really like to have confirmation on some of this before I run it. However, if I can't get any cooperation . . ."

Dan sat up straighter. "What are you talking about? What kind of stuff?"

"Oh, background and whatnot." Jim was deliberately vague. "He said he was writing a book."

Dan frowned. That particular aspiration seemed to be extremely popular all of a sudden. "About Jess?"

"More or less."

"Listen, if you have any of Glanbury's personal papers, they could be evidence. You should turn them over to the police, you should know that."

"Of course I know that. And what I have are copies, not originals. So what do you say? Want a look?"

"Why waste my time?"

"Professional courtesy."

Dan hesitated. It probably *was* a waste of his time, but . . . "Oh, all right, send them up. I'll look them over and get back to you."

"An interview, right?"

"I'll see what I can do. But not today, we're filming promos for the new markets all afternoon. And not tomorrow, either—"

"Come on Webber, don't jerk me around."

"All right, I'll try to clear lunch on Friday."

"Do you want me to go with what I have?"

"What you have is nothing," Dan said impatiently. He noticed the light on line two was blinking. "You know it, I know it."

"Then toss me a crumb. Something to put on at noon. One quote."

The truth was that Dan had no intention of turning down a chance to have the show's name mentioned on the noon news, and he suspected Jim knew as much. But he had to make the other man work for it, or he wouldn't be taken seriously.

He said, "All right, here it is, and I'm a highly placed source. Security has increased on the set. Jess is cooperating fully with the police, but does not intend to allow her personal problems to interfere with the show."

"What about the Glanbury? What about her brother?"

"See you Friday."

Dan punched the second line. "Dan Webber."

"Mr. Webber." A slight pause, as though the speaker expected him to recognize his voice. "This is Jeremy Styles."

Dan sat forward, surprised. He picked up a pen, not because he expected to write anything down, but because it was a long ingrained newsman's habit.

"Mr. Styles." He kept his tone neutral despite the flowing adrenaline that had sharpened his senses. "I didn't expect to hear from you."

The tone on the other end of the line was dry. "I'll just bet you didn't."

Dan knew that Styles had been cleared of involvement in Jess's troubles; certainly he was innocent of the attack on Evan. But still there was something about him that alerted Dan's defensive instincts, and he was on guard. "What can I do for you?"

"I think it's more of a question of what I can do for you."

Here we go, Dan thought. "Oh?" he responded politely. "What's that?"

"First, I want you to know I could care less what happens to the bitch." His voice had sharpened, grown bitter. Dan could well imagine how Jess might have been terrified of him. The man might not be guilty, but he was definitely weird. "In fact, I'm suing her, the police department, and the show for false arrest and malicious prosecution."

There was a smug note to his finish, as though he expected Dan to congratulate him on his cleverness. Dan said nothing.

"You seemed like a pretty smart guy, though. I've got nothing against you. And with all that's going on now, I figured you'd see how to take advantage of a good thing."

"And how is that?"

"My book," Styles said impatiently. "You read it. You've got to see the correlation between it and what's happened now."

Dan wondered if Styles had any idea how many books he read a month in the course of his job, and how difficult it would be to remember all of them. And Styles's book hadn't even been particularly good.

No one had to remind him, however, that antago-
nizing a man like Styles was not a particularly good
idea. He said instead, "Oh . . . yes, of course." And
hoped he sounded thoughtful, not befuddled.

"Now, you should know that other shows have
already called me about doing a spot, so I'm not
promising anything exclusive. But I figured with the
tie we've already got going, not to mention the mile-
age we could get out of the fact that the dumb
broad actually thought *I* was her stalker . . . well,
it's got to add up to nothing but bucks for both of
us, am I right?"

Dan would have wished the man luck and hung
up right then except for one thing: He didn't know
what the hell Styles was talking about. He had too
much curiosity to just let it go, even though instinct
told him this was probably a bigger waste of time
than lunch with Jim would be. But if it wasn't . . .
if Styles did know something . . . if the police had,
after all, let a guilty man go . . .

Dan said, "Yeah, I see the possibilities. So let me
get this straight. What you're saying is that the person who's harassing Ms. Cray has read your book?"
Frantically, he searched his memory for the name
of the damn thing.

"Read it? Been inspired by it is more like it!" Then
his tone grew suspicious. "Hey. You *do* see the correlation, don't you?"

"Of course I do," Dan improvised easily, "but I
have to draw up a proposal for my producer, and
it's best if I use your own words."

"Well, my own words are that if the very elegant
Ms. Cray wants to know who's responsible for her
troubles and why, she ought to read my book!"

Dan sensed he was about to lose him. "Listen, I think we can do something with this. I'd like to meet with you, talk about it. When is good for you?"

When Styles spoke, he sounded grudging. "All right. This afternoon. But I'm not coming to the studio, not until my lawyer talks to your lawyer and we work out some terms."

"I can come to you," Dan said. "But not this afternoon. How about after dinner?"

"All right, nine o'clock. But don't be late. And I'm warning you, screw with me on this and I'm going straight to the highest bidder, and the hell with what happens to your pretty little cohost in the meantime."

If Styles had been in the room, Dan would have quite possibly punched him in the jaw. As it was, he merely copied down the address and promised to see him later.

When he looked up, Bethany was standing at the door. She looked troubled. "Miss Cray buzzed," she said. "She wants you to come to her office when you're free."

"Something wrong?"

"I'm not sure. I think so. That detective was with her; I could hear him talking in the background."

That didn't necessarily mean anything. Candler was spending more time with Jess than without her lately. Still, Dan didn't linger at his desk. He slipped on his suit jacket on the way to the door, saying, "Do you remember the name of that book Jeremy Styles wrote?"

Bethany took a notepad from her pocket and started writing. She was very efficient. "I'll have to look it up."

"Put a copy on my desk, will you?"

And he was gone before she could say, "Yes, sir."

Dan tried to hide his revulsion as he examined the plastic-enclosed paper Candler held up. "Is that what I think it is?"

"If you think it's blood, yes." Holding the plastic bag by the corner, Candler carefully returned it to the manila envelope from which, presumably, it had been taken. "Forensics will probably tell us whose blood, but I think I have a pretty good idea. The newspaper that's dipped in it seems to have the original *Spectator* article in it."

"Do you mean—Freddie Glanbury?"

"That's exactly what I mean."

Candler put the envelope in another, larger plastic envelope, and stripped off his gloves. He tucked the gloves into the inside pocket of his jacket as he glanced at Sylvia. "I'll need a list of everyone who's had access to your desk this morning."

Sylvia was huddled by the door, observing the events that were unfolding like a spectator at a bad traffic accident—too afraid to move closer, too gruesomely compelled to turn away. Now she swallowed hard, her eyes widening.

"Well . . . it's not exactly a private area, you know." She gestured helplessly toward the bullpen, where writers, researchers, spot producers, and technicians all wandered freely and cast their share of curious glances toward Jess Cray's glass-enclosed office.

"I mean," Sylvia went on, obviously struggling, "first, Miss Cray came in, then you, and Dan—I mean Mr. Webber—stopped by, and Carlos from the mailroom, and Betty from the research desk, and Trish wanted to talk to Ms. Cray, but I told her she was in with you. . . ."

Candler said, "Did you leave your desk at any time this morning?

Sylvia looked uncertain. She looked at Dan as though for reassurance, and then at Jess. Then she said, almost defiantly, "I had to go to the bathroom. All right, maybe I stopped by the snack machine, too, but I wasn't gone over five minutes, ten at the outside."

Candler said, "What time was that?"

She looked worried. "A quarter to nine, maybe. But I'd been here since eight o'clock."

"Then you left after the mail delivery?"

"Well . . . yes. Ms. Cray doesn't expect to have her mail opened before 9:30. I had plenty of time."

Candler's lips compressed, and he said nothing.

Jess was sitting behind her desk, her hands folded atop it. Her expression was composed, though her skin was pale beneath the makeup. "Sylvia," she said, "will you do me a favor? Go to the Green Room and make sure our guests have everything they need. Tell them Mr. Webber will be down to say hello in a few minutes."

Sylvia ducked her head and left quickly, as though glad to escape, and Dan thought, *Shit*. In the Green Room were a brace of male strippers and their mothers; it was the kind of show Jess would have loved. Another one down the tubes. How much more of this could the show take?

Jess said to Candler, "Anyone could have been by Sylvia's desk this morning; this is the busiest time of the day in the bullpen. Why did you want to know?"

Candler's face was sober. "There was no postmark on the envelope. It was stamped, but not post-marked, so the casual observer might think it was mailed. But it was hand-delivered, by someone who came in after the regular mail delivery. He probably slipped it into the middle of the stack without any-one noticing. As a matter of fact . . ." He hesitated only slightly. "Only the first couple of letters were mailed. The others were hand-delivered."

Dan saw the muscle of Jess's throat constrict as she swallowed, but her tone was calm. "So . . . I guess that proves it. It's someone I know."

"Or at least someone who had access to the bull-pen, and your secretary's desk," amended Candler carefully. "We're examining the security logs of ev-eryone who had clearance for this floor on the dates you received each of the items in the mail. So far, nothing unusual has shown up."

Dan said, "What about Jeremy Styles?"

Both Jess and Candler looked at him.

He said, "This probably isn't the right time, but I just got a call from Styles. He claims he knows who's responsible for terrorizing Jess—and why, I believe he said. He wants to meet with me tonight."

Jess said horrified, "The man is crazy!"

And Candler said at the same time, "You're not going to do it, I hope."

Dan felt suddenly defensive. "Agreed, the guy is a nut. But I don't think we can afford to ignore any lead at this point. And he claims to know something. I'm starting to wonder if the police didn't let him go a little too soon."

Candler's voice was cold. "I think you'd better let us worry about that, Mr. Webber. And I strongly

advise you to stay away from Styles. Just because
we weren't able to hold him in the stalking case
doesn't mean he's not a dangerous personality. Just
exactly what did he say?"

Dan looked at Jess, then at Candler. He was
aware that the resentment he felt was childish, but
knowing that did nothing to mitigate it. He said,
"Nothing. The ravings of a lunatic, mostly. Like I
said, he's a nut."

The look Candler gave him was long and hard.
Dan ignored it, nodding toward the envelope on the
desk. "So I guess this is it, then. A definite link
between Glanbury's murder and Jess's stalker."

Jess looked stunned, as though the connection
hadn't occurred to her before. Candler didn't answer, but he didn't have to.

Dan sighed. "Well," he said, "at least the six
o'clock news will have something to report."

Jeremy Styles lived in a thirty-year-old, middle-
class neighborhood that had undergone just enough
gentrification to make it stylish. At one end of the
street were two-hundred-thousand-dollar homes, at
the other small clapboard bungalows with neatly
kept lawns and ten-year-old economy cars in the
driveways.

Styles's house was somewhere in the middle, the
kind of thing a man who lived alone might buy for
an investment. Ten-foot-high hemlock hedges separated it from its neighbors, and giant boxwoods
shadowed the front stoop, almost concealing the
front part of the house completely. The first thing
Dan thought when he saw it was, *Perfect target
for burglars.*

Later, he would remember that and feel ill.

He parked in the driveway and went up the walk. A motion sensor spotlight went on when he passed, illuminating his way. That was how he noticed the front door was open.

He should have stopped right there. In retrospect, and given the circumstances, any sensible person would have turned back then. But the door was open only a few inches, as though the last person to enter had not pulled it closed tightly enough, or as though the home's occupant, having been alerted by the light, had opened the door a crack to see who was there.

Dan went up the steps. He called, "Styles?" He knocked on the door frame, just to be sure he was heard. "It's Dan Webber."

He put his hand on the door and pushed it open. He saw the blood spattered on the wall adjacent to him, but he didn't have time to register what it meant. The shot that struck him sounded like thunder.

Chapter 20

Talk-Show Host Becomes Target. Webber Injured in an Attempt to Expose Stalker. Risking His Life for His Partner.

One by one Trish tossed the papers on Dan's desk. Not all the headlines were front page, of course, and none were above the fold, but it was clear that Dan Webber had done his part to give the media something new to report that day.

"They make you sound like a goddamned hero," Trish fumed, glaring at him, "instead of the idiot you are. How dare you take such a chance! Don't you know you could have been killed? Don't you even care? By the way, CNN called."

Dan mumbled dryly, "With a job offer, I hope."

"Damn it, Dan," Jess cried, "how can you joke? Didn't Candler specifically tell you to stay away from him? Didn't I? What were you thinking?"

The two women paced and circled him like jackals coming in for the kill, crisscrossing one another's path, pausing only long enough to fling out their accusations at him before resuming their tight, agitated course from the door to the window and back. Trish said, "For God's sake, Dan, this isn't *Sixty*

Minutes! Our liability doesn't cover stars who walk in front of bullets, you know! What if you'd been hit in the face, did you ever think of that? That would've done your career a hell of a lot of good, wouldn't it? What if you'd been crippled, paralyzed?"

"Jesus," Dan groaned, "I should have let them keep me in the hospital."

That brought instant remorse from both women. Jess came quickly to him, resting one hand lightly on his shoulder. Trish paused before the desk, biting her thumb and looking anxious. She had forgotten her cigarettes.

Jess said, "I'm sorry, Dan. I know you did it for me. It's just . . ."

Trish finished gruffly, "It's just that you scared the hell out of us, that's all. You are *not* expendable, Webber, you got that?"

Dan managed a lopsided smile. "Tell that to the cops, will you? I got the distinct impression that the only thing that was keeping me out of jail last night was this bullet wound. And if they could have figured out how I could have shot myself in the neck and done so little damage, I'd be talking to a lawyer right now, not a couple of mother hens."

The bullet wound over which everyone was making such a fuss was hardly a wound at all; it hadn't even required stitches. The bullet had apparently been fired from around a corner of the room and in a hurry, grazing the side of Dan's neck closer to the shoulder than the ear. The bulky bandage that covered it was more troublesome than the injury itself. Police speculated that the assailant had either been aiming for the head and missed, or had fired blindly and gotten lucky. Neither scenario was particularly reassuring to Dan.

At the scene they had found the letters "SHA" scrawled on a mirrored display cabinet beside the chair in which Jeremy Styles had been shot. The lipstick—Maybelline's Plum Rose—with which those letters had been written was found on the floor, where it had apparently been dropped when Dan interrupted the writer. Most of the blood had soaked into the upholstered chair in which Styles had been sitting, making it too difficult for the assailant to write the word in blood as he had done at Even's attack.

Thinking about how close he had come gave Dan the chills even now. He did not need Jess or Trish to remind him.

Jess said, glancing at Trish, "Does anyone know how Styles is doing?"

Dan answered wearily, "As of eight forty-five he was still in Recovery. The surgery went okay, I guess, but it's going to be touch and go for a while—and a pretty good bet he won't be telling anybody anything about what happened for a good long time."

Jess pressed her fingers to her face, shaking her head. "I don't understand. Why would the stalker want to hurt Styles? Styles hated me. They were on the same side, for God's sake—both of them tormenting me. Why would anybody do this?"

Dan said, "Styles said he knew who the stalker was, remember? And he also said I wasn't the first person he'd told. I guess one of them was the wrong person. Or maybe . . . hell, I hate to admit it, but maybe Candler is right. Maybe the killer thought he was protecting you."

Jess looked haunted and turned away.

Trish said sickly, "Jesus."

The silence grew heavy with horror, enfolding the room like a shroud. Dan knew what they were thinking, because it was the same thing he was thinking. *Who's next?* How could any of them sleep easy in their beds with this thing stalking the streets? How much further could it go?

He said loudly, and with wry, forced lightness, "But hey, enough about me. We've got a show to do. Who's on?"

They protested at the same time, "No way, buster!" and "Not a chance!"

"Jess can carry the show today," Trish said firmly. "You look like hell. You go out there and you'll just scare the audience and the guests, too."

Dan knew she was right; he was in no shape to go on. He'd had three hours sleep, and that had been thanks only to the painkiller they'd given him at the hospital. He hadn't shaved or even dressed for work. The truth was that he had come in more out of habit than anything else this morning . . . or perhaps it was that, after all that had happened, he couldn't stand to have Jess out of his sight any longer than necessary.

Still he felt compelled to put up a fight. "Come on, I didn't get out of bed this morning for my health, you know. I haven't missed a day in five years."

"Go home," Trish said. "Go to bed. I'll bring you hot chicken soup from Servo's for lunch."

He grinned. "Tempting as that sounds, I'm not

the chicken soup type. The least I can do is hang around off camera in case Jess gets into trouble."

He was glad to see that inspired Jess to make a face at him, halfhearted though it was.

He added to Trish, "I can go on. I've got to admit I'm not particularly prepared but—"

Trish cut him off with a sharp shake of her head. Her tone was precise, her expression speculative. She was a producer. "No, it's better this way, builds suspense. Twice as many people will watch tomorrow just to see if you make it back. So spend today getting better and giving interviews." The smile she gave him was only superficially abashed. "Okay, so it's hell. But you've got to admit, it's great for ratings."

Jess glared after her as she left. "If she weren't such a good producer . . ."

"Then neither one of us would have jobs," Dan finished.

Jess turned to him. The effort it had taken for him to get this far was evident now; the strain was showing in his voice and in the lines of his face. And when Jess saw the padded gauze bandage that protruded from the open collar of his shirt, her stomached clenched with a wave of remorse so powerful it was almost nauseating.

"Oh, God, Dan, none of this would have happened if it wasn't for me. I am so sorry—"

Dan lifted an impatient hand to silence her. "Don't start believing what you read in the papers. Trish was right, I was an idiot. I went out there because I was curious—and stupid—and I got what I deserved. I was lucky it wasn't worse."

"You couldn't have known—"

"I knew Styles was unstable. No, I wouldn't have guessed that he'd be a target for the stalker, but common sense should have told me to be careful."

He looked at her then, and all attempts to keep up the brave front drained away. "I'll tell you one thing. It was damn terrifying—enough to make me remember not to ever be that foolish again." His voice was flat and stripped of emotion, his eyes haunted.

Jess said, "But—you didn't see anything?"

"Oh, I saw plenty." Now his voice tightened, and she could see his shoulders tense with the memory. "I opened the door, and I saw the blood on the wall, and there was a second—maybe half a second—when I knew what it was, but I thought, Oh no, this can't be real. And then I heard the gunshot. It doesn't hurt at first, you know. I didn't know I'd been hit. I just kind of staggered back with surprise, and I never knew where the gunshot came from or who fired it. My ears were ringing so I couldn't even hear whoever it was getting away. You wouldn't believe how loud a gunshot is unless you're that close to it. And then I kind of grabbed the door frame and started back in—I was beginning to figure out what was happening, but I think my brain was running mostly on adrenaline, I really wasn't thinking at all—and then I saw it."

Jess wanted to tell him he didn't have to go on, she didn't need to hear, but she could tell he needed to talk about it. And in a gruesomely compelling way, Jess needed to hear it.

His eyes were tortured, looking back. He said, "He was right there, just a foot or so from where I was standing, collapsed down in this chair beside

the door. It was kind of a taupe color, and the blood
had soaked into the arm where his head was and
made the upholstery look black. So much blood. I
thought he was dead. How could he not be dead?
I guess the killer thought so too. The police said he
was shot from the back at pretty close range. The
bullet should have taken out his brain stem, but I
guess it was deflected somehow. Anyway, there's not
much doubt the shot was intended to be deadly.
And you know what's really strange? Seeing him
there, blood soaking into that chair and dripping on
the rug and splattered on the wall—you'd think that
would be the worst part, but it wasn't. It was when
I looked up and saw what was written on that mirrored cabinet behind him. It was like one of those
strobing close-ups they do in low-budget movies,
you know? I looked at it, and everything froze, and
that's when I thought *My God, this is real.* I mean,
the police say Styles was shot within minutes of the
time I got there. The shooter was probably scared
away when I called out. He could have just as easily
stayed and shot me point-blank."

He fell silent again, and Jess felt his memories go
through her like an icy chill. It could have been
Dan instead of Styles lying in a hospital bed, hooked
to life-support equipment right now. It could have
been both of them. Or Dan might have been killed.
At this moment her life might be empty of him. . . .

He said quietly, "The thing is, from the minute
it all started I thought I understood what it was
like for you. But I didn't, I couldn't. No one can
understand what it's like to be that scared until
you've stared your own vulnerability in the face . . .

and once you've done that, your life is never the same again."

He said the last with a sad kind of wonder that tore at Jess's heart. Her throat was too tight to speak, which was probably just as well, because she didn't know what to say. Or perhaps she didn't really need to say anything. Perhaps, for the first time in her life she understood—and was understood by—another person completely.

Dan took a deep, long breath and seemed to pull himself out of the dark reverie with a conscious effort. He said, "Right now, I think the thing that's bothering me most is that I might never know what it was he wanted to tell me—what he was almost killed for. He said it had something to do with his book. I had a chance to skim over the book last evening after work, but I swear nothing rang a bell. I couldn't see any similarities at all."

"His book?" She had almost forgotten, in all else that Styles had become to her over the past weeks, that he was also an author. "What was it about?"

"It was supposed to be based on the Silk Scarf killings, remember? Only in his version, the last three killings were done by a copycat, and the police actually arrested the wrong man. It was the defense attorney I think who was actually doing the killings, and he was doing it to promote his career."

Jess stared at him. "Was he saying it was some lawyer out there stalking me?"

Dan chuckled. The movement caused a twinge in his neck, and he winced a little. "Who knows what he was saying? The man was probably delusional on top of everything else. He sure didn't write a very good book. That plot had holes in it big enough to drive a truck through, and his logic probably isn't much better."

Jess said gently, "You should go home, Dan. You look awful."

He waved away her concerns. "No, I want to see you up close and personal in your one and only chance to be the real star of this show. You'd better take advantage of it, too, because I don't plan on getting shot again."

She tried to laugh. "I'm glad to know you're the type of man who can always see the bright side in his own personal tragedy."

"Just don't do *too* good a job, huh?"

"And you just try not to make yourself sound too important when you're giving interviews to CNN."

He looked at her for a moment, his expression tender and vague. Then he said, "Last night, at the emergency room, when they asked if there was anyone I wanted them to call—I almost said you. Isn't that funny? You're not a relative or anything . . . but the only person I could think of was you."

"You should have called," she said quietly and came over to him. Taking his hand in her, she wrapped her fingers around it and held it silently for a moment. The moment between them was quiet and gentle, and then she met his eyes, and her fingers tightened around his as the horror of what might have been swept over her once again.

"This can't go on, Dan," she said quietly at last, "I'm going to put a stop to it. I don't know how yet . . . but I am. I promise."

At nine forty-five Dan taped an interview for WSBN. They were tough; he could see Jim's fine hand behind the questions asked by the pretty-boy noon anchor, and behind that the very fine hand of Lt. Lyle Candler.

No, he told them, as far as he knew he wasn't himself a suspect in the shooting. He had had an appointment with Styles to discuss what Styles claimed was some information he had about who was behind several incidents that had disrupted the show in the past few weeks. Yes, his partner, Jess, had been the primary focus of those incidents. All of this was part of the police report and what the papers had already.

They asked what relationship Styles had to the case, and exactly how the attack on Jess's brother and the death of Glanbury tied in, and he referred them to the police. Inwardly, he winced at how the facts would be scrambled by this time tomorrow, but he knew if he tried to put his own spin on the situation, Candler would be on him like a cat on a mouse. He couldn't stop Dan from talking to the press, but he could make his life miserable while he did so. And after last night Dan had had enough of the police for a good long while.

He had had enough of it all.

He gave them a nice quote, though, and repeated it for CNN. "I think all of us who are in the public eye are aware of the potential for becoming a target by an obsessive personality. But I don't ever want to reach a point where this kind of behavior is so common it's almost expected . . . where being a target is part of the job description."

The anchor thanked him and, before he left, pulled out a manila envelope which, he said, was from Jim. The Freddie Glanbury file.

Dan turned on the monitor in his office to watch the taping while he flipped through the file. Some of it looked familiar, and then he realized that what he was looking at were photocopies of the very same papers Styles had shown Jess when he claimed he was writing a book about her. He had glanced through them only briefly that night Styles was arrested, but they were obviously the same. Some neatly typed notes, a credit report, some bank statements—Dan remembered wondering how the son of a bitch had gotten that and who was safe in this computerized world anymore—a resumé that Styles had composed listing all of Jess's beauty titles, educational history, former jobs . . . Yes, it was all the same. Dan wondered how Glanbury had gotten it.

Then the theme music started to play, and Dan settled back to watch Jess. She looked competent and composed, and as gorgeous as ever in an emerald suit and a multicolored scarf that picked up the colors of her eyes as she turned to Camera Two and said, "I'm Jessamine Cray and welcome to *Speaking of Which*. My cohost, Dan Webber, is feeling a little under the weather today. Hurry back, Dan."

Warm and natural, her charm practically sang through the wires. Dan murmured, "Go baby, go," and he wondered whether he had given up his place on the show today a little too easily. He wasn't sure he had ever seen Jess perform solo before. She was captivating.

Camera One. "Today we're going to be talking about a very serious subject. Eating disorders affect over two million people around the world, most of them young women. Models, athletes, even the Princess of Wales have all been victims of life-threatening eating disorders such as bulimia and anorexia nervosa. But would you know how to recognize the symptoms of these diseases in someone you love? Today we have with us Dr. Karen Tracy of the Windham Recovery Center, who specializes in the treatment of these diseases." Camera Two. "And these are diseases, aren't they, Doctor?"

Dan lowered the volume on the monitor and tried to divide his attention between Jess and the file before him. He was tired and his head ached; it was hard to concentrate. He wondered if Candler knew Freddie had had a copy of this file. He wondered if it mattered.

Then the phone rang, and it was *A Current Affair*. Dan put the folder aside and didn't think about it the rest of the day.

Chapter 21

Captain Roger Lamb of the Major Crimes Division looked at the three files arranged across Candler's desk. "So this is your shortlist."

Candler glanced at his watch. "As of nine forty-six P.M. Ask me at nine forty-eight and it'll be different."

He sat back and went on, "Witnesses claim they saw a tall woman—or a man—leave the back door of Styles's house shortly after the second shot was fired. He—or she—got into a dark sedan—or light-colored sports coupe—that was parked on Persimmon Drive, which runs parallel to Willow Street right behind Styles's house. He or she had to cross two lawns to get there. One resident reports her dog barking around that time, the other house is empty. About the only thing we know for sure is that Styles probably knew his assailant and invited him—or her—in. The lock definitely hadn't been forced. Of course . . ." He jerked his head toward the fanned-out folders. "That's far from a complete list of people Styles knew, or even people who wanted him dead. But those are the strongest links I can come up with between Styles and Jess Cray."

The captain picked up a file. "I don't suppose anybody you talked to was missing a lipstick."

"One of them doesn't even wear lipstick. Trish Palmer. Man, talk about a hardcase. That woman can wither your balls with a look. She does own a handgun though, complete with permit to carry. A nine-mill, which she surrendered voluntarily."

"And?"

"And nothing, of course. I returned her gun as fast as I was physically able. That's one woman whose shit list I do *not* want to be on."

"But she's still on yours."

"You got it."

The captain picked up another file.

"Sylvia Graham, the secretary. She was very nice about giving us permission to search—after she stopped bawling. We found six different lipsticks, none of which match in color or brand name. We did not find a weapon of any sort."

"What about Webber?"

"The only place we found his prints was exactly where he said we would—on the door and door frame. As far as we can tell, he didn't step more than a foot over the threshold. Lucky for him— or maybe for us, I'm not even sure anymore—the neighbor who heard the shots got there in time to get him away from the house before he corrupted the crime scene completely."

"How's Styles doing?"

Candler shook his head. "Still in a coma. They don't know if he'll ever come out of it, or if he does, whether he'll have any memory of the night."

"But ballistics definitely matches the weapon used in Styles's case to Glanbury's murder."

"Right. Except for one little detail—the missing gun—we'd have this case wrapped up."

Thoughtfully, the captain picked up a file from a different stack. "What about this one, the photographer? He works with models, has access to cosmetics."

"Yeah, he looked good. But there's no link to Styles, and he's alibied for the first confrontation with Jess and the attack on her brother. And let's face it, anybody can go into the drugstore and pick up a tube of lipstick."

"True. But not everybody's going to do that unless they're planning on using it."

"Yeah, I know it."

The captain flipped open another file at random. "Casey Darnell?"

"She was on the first list that Jess gave me. Come to think of it, maybe it was Webber who brought her name up. She works at the news department of WSBN, the same building with *Speaking of Which*. Seems there was some sort of rivalry for Jess's job, and she certainly had access and opportunity. She looked good for a while, but she took a job in Cincinnati a week after all this started. At the time Styles was shot, she was on the air, live, being beamed into the homes of some 80,000 television viewers."

"Which doesn't necessarily mean she's not involved."

"Exactly. The Cincinnati police are cooperating, but she's an on-air personality up there, and they want to be discreet. It may take a day or two to get enough information to keep her on our list—or take her off it."

The other man's expression was sober. "The media's starting to like this a little too much. And the more they like it, the harder it's going to be for us to do our jobs."

"Big surprise. A cute thing like Jess Cray, a big-shot like Webber, Styles the almost-bestselling author, even that poor shit Glanbury—it's got all the makings of a TV movie right now."

"Not to mention you."

Candler looked surprised. "Huh?"

"I mean you've gotten your share of the celebrity draw this past year. The papers are starting to love you."

Candler flushed dully. "Listen, Captain, if you think for one minute that my being on the case is doing anything to jeopardize the investigation . . ."

The captain waved a dismissing hand. "I don't mean anything. Just make sure the *real* media babies don't try to overplay their hands. I'm not going to have anybody turn one of our cases into a miniseries, not when lives are at stake. And if this perp thrives on attention the way most of these sickos do, they need to understand that's exactly what they're doing every time they give him air time— putting somebody's life at stake."

"I think Jess understands that," Candler said. "She's been pretty low profile. About Webber, I'm not so sure."

The phone rang. Candler picked it up. "Candler here."

"Look, I don't want to sound paranoid," she said, "but—you don't have anyone watching my house, do you?"

"No. Why? Are you in trouble?"

"No," she said quickly. "No, it's just that—there's a car parked across the street from my place, and if it was anyone who lived here, they would have a parking space. There's a man inside, I saw a silhouette earlier, but the car's parked away from a streetlight so I really can't tell anything else about it. It's been there for over an hour, and no one's gotten out."

Candler glanced at his captain. His adrenaline was pumping. He said, "I'll send a car by to check it out. It's probably nothing, but—check your windows and doors, will you? And don't let anyone in until I call you back."

Now she sounded frightened. "Okay. But you don't think . ."

"As I said, it's probably nothing. It'll take about fifteen minutes. Stay by the phone."

Jess stood by the window, within easy reach of the telephone, and tried not to descend into paranoia. Through a crack in the draperies she could see the car, its color neutral in the darkness, its make indistinguishable. But the silhouette of a man's profile was still visible. She could feel his eyes on her, just as though he could see through the draperies. She shivered.

It had been two days since Dan had been shot, a flurry of television reporters and news reporters and chaos at the office. Trish was outraged because the police had taken her gun. Sylvia had come in this morning in hysterics and threatened to quit because the police had searched her house. Both women would have been a lot harder to soothe if a team of policemen and women had not searched the desks of every employee on the show. In the end, Trish was more excited by the attention the show was getting than she was insulted by the police, but Jess had a feeling her relationship with Sylvia would never be the same. And she wasn't sure she wanted it to be. After all, the police didn't investigate people for no reason.

And that was perhaps what she hated most about all of it. Dan was right. After this, nothing would ever be the same. She couldn't trust her friends. People she thought she knew might be terrorizing her. Someone close to her could be a killer.

No, after this, nothing would ever be the same. Not even Jess.

The phone rang, and Jess jumped. She stepped away from the curtain quickly, her throat dry, and stared at the telephone. It rang again before she could make herself pick it up.

"Jess." It was Candler. "The car is registered to Dan Webber."

She went weak with relief. "Thank God."

The silence on the other end went on a little too long. "Yeah. I guess."

"Damn it, though. He scared me half to death." She parted the curtain again. He was still there. It was hard to feel as annoyed as she sounded. "I told him he's not my personal guardian. I'm going to go straighten him out right now."

"Jess, maybe you should—"

"What?"

Another hesitance. "Nothing. Just be careful, okay?"

When he had disconnected, Jess stood there for a moment, scowling at the receiver in her hand. She glanced out the window again, at the car in the shadows, waiting, watching. An uneasiness settled in the pit of her stomach, and she hated herself for it. She pulled the curtain closed and replaced the receiver.

She wondered if she'd ever get her life back.

Dan saw her leave the house and start down the walk. He popped the lock when she reached the passenger door, and she got in, slamming the door behind her.

"What the hell do you think you're doing?"

Her voice was tight and angry, her eyes flashing in the dimness. He could see the gooseflesh forming on her arms from the chill air, and it gave her an oddly vulnerable look.

He said, "Obsessing on your loveliness, of course."

She rubbed her arms, warming them. "Haven't you had enough of being the hero, Webber?"

Dan leaned back against the headrest, silent for a time. Then he said, "I've been thinking. We're going about this the wrong way. Trying to figure why I was shot, why Styles was shot, what the hell Glanbury had to do with any of it. We have to go back to the beginning. The day the notes started. Why that day and not another? If Candler's right, and this fellow has been watching you, stalking you for years, something had to happen to set him off, bring him out in the open. So we've got to go back to the beginning."

Jess said a little dryly, "We could have had this conversation over the phone. Better yet, you could have had it with Candler."

"I'm serious. Think about it. What made that day different from any other?"

She was thoughtful for a moment. "Well, it was my birthday."

"True, but that happens every year."

"The new markets," she said suddenly. She turned in her seat to look at him, excitement escalating. "Dan, that could be it! We got four new markets that day. Someone saw us who'd never seen us before—*that's* the new element in the equation! That's what was different about that day; it was the first time this crazy person had ever seen me."

But Dan was shaking his head before she finished. "I thought about that. But the stalker is local, and the markets were in the Midwest. Plus, you got the first note before that day's show even aired—on the new markets, or anywhere else."

Jess sank back in her seat. The leather was soft and crinkly and smelled like Dan. She thought it would be nice to just close her eyes and stay there for a while, safe, surrounded by him.

"Styles," she said after a time, tiredly. "That was the day he was on the show. It's got to be him; he's the only one who makes sense."

"Yeah," agreed Dan, "it just about has to be him. But it can't be." Absently, he touched the small bandage on his neck, which had replaced the bulky one applied in the emergency room and which was now concealed beneath a turtleneck. "Not unless he's got some kind of telekinetic power that allows him to attack your brother twenty-five miles away from inside a jail cell, and shoot me while he's lying comatose only a few feet away."

Jess shivered again, though not entirely from cold this time. She said, "The police are investigating Trish."

"No more than anyone else you work with, are social with, or have ever nodded to on the street."

"But *Trish*, for God's sake."

Dan shrugged. His profile was complacent in the dark, leaning back against the headrest, eyes pointed toward nothing much at all. "Could be. She'd do anything for the show. Or maybe she's secretly in love with you."

Jess sank lower into her seat. "How can you joke about it?"

"I'm not sure I was."

"And Sylvia," Jess added morosely. "God, my own secretary. She was so upset that the police came to her house, she said they looked in all her drawers and even her refrigerator. But they don't search somebody's house for nothing, do they? And she's always been kind of—sullen. And she has access to all my personal records; maybe she was helping Styles somehow or . . ." She glanced at Dan anxiously. "Maybe it was some kind of conspiracy to get money or something. I should have accepted her resignation, but it felt like kicking her when she was down. But I'll never be comfortable with her in the office again."

Dan shook his head slowly. "It's not a woman. I've always said that."

"I think . . ." The next was hard to say. She couldn't quite make herself look at him. "Candler may suspect you."

But Dan was unsurprised. "Now that makes more sense," he said comfortably. "I had plenty of opportunity. As for motive . . . well, it's been great for my career. I got twelve seconds on CNN with footage. Of course, you got thirty, but who's counting?"

Jess smiled. "And to think, only two weeks ago you were ready to leave."

"I was never ready to leave."

Jess turned her head, looking out the side window. It felt good just being here with him, wrapped in the anonymous bubble of his car. She was almost relaxed for the first time in weeks. And what an odd thing that until now she had not even noticed how tense she had been. Her muscles ached with the burden of stress being slowly released.

She said thoughtfully, "I think the way the police have invaded my life is worse than the way the stalker has. I don't know whom to trust anymore. And I never wanted to hear my name on the news— unless I was anchoring it. Anymore than you did."

Dan said, "There's something not right about this. Something that doesn't make sense. Go back to the beginning, that's what I keep thinking. The notes. What are you ashamed of? What does that make you think?"

She shook her head slowly against the seat cushion. She could feel the dread gripping her shoulders again, tightening the back of her neck. "God, I don't want to go through all that again. Do we have to?"

But Dan insisted thoughtfully, "No, I mean . . . he asks a question. It makes you think he's going to answer it. And he never does."

Jess closed her eyes. "Sometimes," she said softly, "I wake in the morning, and for a second it's like everything is normal, none of this ever happened. And then it comes crashing down on me, a big black weight, and I think it'll never be over. Nothing will ever be normal again."

With a soft rustling of leather and fabric, Dan

shifted his position, looking at her. "Jess," he said quietly. "It's going to be over. We're going to catch this guy and put him behind bars, and this whole thing is going to be like a bad dream."

She shook her head slowly and deliberately, squeezing her eyes very tightly against the hot wetness that backed up behind her lids. "No," she said thickly in a moment. "Some things are so bad that— they stain your soul, and nothing is ever the same after that."

Dan didn't answer. He slid his hand across the distance between them and gently cupped the back of her neck.

After a time Jess drew in a breath and released it slowly. She opened her eyes, leaning her weight back into the comfort of his hand. She said, "I really don't want to talk about this anymore. We shouldn't be trying to do the police's job anyway."

"Maybe someone should."

She slanted a glance at him. "You don't like Candler, do you?"

"What? Just because the guy accuses me of murder?" He added casually, "He's got a crush on you, you know."

Jess tilted her head toward him, smiling. "He's not the one sitting outside my house at ten o'clock at night."

"So I noticed."

Jess reached up and removed his hand from her neck, threading her fingers through his. She looked at their entwined fingers for a moment, then said gently, "I don't need a bodyguard, Dan."

He was silent for a time. His eyes dropped to their joined hands, too. When he spoke, his tone was quiet and matter-of-fact. "When I was a young man in the big city, I was dating this girl—actually, I went out with her only once, and we didn't have a very good time at that. That's probably why, when I brought her home, she declined my offer to walk her to her door. Probably why I didn't insist. So I just dropped her off in front of her apartment and drove off, and there was a man waiting in the bushes who beat her up and raped her. I've never stopped blaming myself for that. And I always see my dates to their doors now."

Jess swallowed a sudden mistiness in her throat. He was truly an extraordinary man. Why had she never noticed that before?

She leaned across the console and touched his face, sliding her fingers into his hair. She kissed his lips tenderly, lightly. "Walk me to my door, Dan," she invited softly.

He met her eyes, and in the gentle darkness understanding passed, and quiet welcome. They went up the walk with their arms around one another's waists.

Jess opened the door in a haze of nervousness and excitement and anticipation, the fuzzy glow of being poised on the edge of discovery, of being promised a gift she wasn't sure she deserved. For a moment, for just that moment, it might be possible to step out of this horror and capture something wonderful. And then it wasn't.

Dan pushed the door closed. She half turned to him. And then she saw something, a shadow or a movement or a simple sense of *presence* coming from the dining room. She stepped back quickly, clutching his arm, staring. Her voice was hoarse. "What was that?"

His face had that same fuzzy, warm expression she had been feeling only seconds before. His eyes crinkled with a smile, and he didn't understand immediately. "You're setting me up, right?"

"No." She stepped away from him, her heart beating hard. "I saw something move, a shadow—Oh God, Dan, I think someone's in here!"

And then it was gone, the moment that was too good to be true, and in its place was cold, ugly reality again. Dan's face grew hard, and his touch was firm as he moved her aside. Already his eyes were moving away from her, searching the space behind her.

"Stay here."

He moved quickly but warily out of the room, as he had done once before—methodically, carefully, but, Jess suspected, with a great deal more trepidation, to search the house. She stood there with her heart pounding and her palms sweaty and a cold sickness in the pit of her stomach, knowing that at any moment a shot could ring out, a cry could sound, blood could splash.

She called hoarsely, "Be careful!"

A light went on in the bedroom. She heard doors opening. She couldn't stand it any longer. She went quickly to her purse.

Dan said, coming in from the bedroom, "Everything looks clear to me. It was probably a shadow from outside that you saw. I can't believe you left the front door unlocked—"

She turned around and he broke off, staring at the gun in her hand.

"Jesus, Jess." His voice sounded sick. He didn't take his eyes off the gun.

Jess dropped her own gaze to the weapon, then released a shaky breath. She turned to return the gun to her purse. "I didn't mean to scare you."

"You told Candler you didn't have a gun."

"For heaven's sake, Dan, you heard him. He practically offered to sell me one from the back of a van. After that, I'd be stupid *not* to buy a gun, wouldn't I?"

She put her purse away in the closet and turned back to Dan, pressing her hands together nervously. She felt foolish for over-reacting and being defensive about the gun. And there was an odd look on Dan's face that she didn't quite like.

He said, "That's a .38, isn't it?"

"How would you know that?" She walked over to the bar, mostly to give herself something to do.

"Saturday night special," he responded impatiently. "Cheap, easy to get, easy to fire. Jesus, we did a show, don't you remember?"

She picked up a bottle at random. "Do you want something to drink?"

He was silent for a time. She felt what might have happened disappearing like wisps of fog through her closed fingers.

He said, a little awkwardly, "Listen, maybe this was a bad idea. I'd probably better just go."

She turned around then, bracing her hands against the back of the bar. "Do you know what the trouble with society is?"

He had turned toward the door, but now glanced back with a smile that was weak and humorless.

"We can't order pizza because we're afraid of getting shot?"

"No one knows how to make a commitment anymore. Even little commitments, like trusting someone's judgment or sticking by a friend or staying instead of going."

"Jess . . ."

There was a question in his voice, and he was no longer turned toward the door.

She answered him with a question of her own. "Are you going to let him take this from us, too?"

He came to her, and picked up both her hands, and drew them against his chest. He said softly, "This could be a big mistake."

She held his gaze. "Which is why we've waited five years to make it."

He kissed her. She wrapped her arms around him, letting his passion invade her, letting her own surprise her. And then she pressed her face against the hard, hot beating of his heart and held him tightly, wrapped in him, safe in him.

He said, close to her ear, "Jess . . . before this goes any further, you should know that I'm probably in love with you."

She whispered, "I'm so glad." And, lifting her face to his, lost herself in him once again.

Chapter 22

Dan awoke to a dim far-off noise and a burning sensation in his throat. He coughed and tasted something foul. It was hard to breathe. He felt drugged. That noise . . . He flung out an arm, reaching for Jess, but the gesture was in slow motion, and before it was completed, he had forgotten what he was reaching for. He coughed again, dragging in more polluted air, and he realized what he tasted was smoke. And the faraway screeching noise, growing louder and closer as he struggled to consciousness, was the smoke alarm.

Jess. He couldn't find her. Foggy-headed, he thought maybe he'd dreamed it all, that she had never been here. He swung his feet onto the floor, found his pants tangled in the bedclothes at the foot of the bed, and pulled them on. He stumbled toward the bathroom for wet towels, but the bathroom wasn't where it should have been, and he bumped into a piece of furniture. He wasn't in his own apartment. Smoke clouded the darkness, and he couldn't see, couldn't breathe.

"Jess!" he called hoarsely.

Where was she?

Using the bed as a guide, holding on its edges,

he circled toward the area he thought the door should be. His foot encountered something soft and firm, and he dropped to his knees. "Jess!"

He turned her over, lifting her off the floor, and she moaned. He tried to talk to her, but he couldn't draw a breath. He shook her a little, and she started to cough, clutching at his sleeve. He managed to get her to her knees.

Together they crawled toward the door, Dan half dragging Jess beside him. In the distance he heard sirens. The smoke was so thick he had to keep his eyes closed as he moved across the floor. His lungs were bursting, filled with fire and ash. His shoulder bumped the wall, and he started sweeping his hands along the baseboard, searching for the door frame. His fingers encountered fabric, and he grabbed it, following the flow of draperies upward until he felt the window frame. He was disoriented and light-headed with lack of oxygen. He focused desperately, searching for the latch, finding it, pushing upward. His head swam. The window wouldn't move. He gasped in a huge lungful of toxic air and coughed until he saw stars, and still he couldn't breathe. He collapsed against the wall, holding onto conscious-ness with nothing more than determination.

He heard a crash beside him and dimly saw Jess flinging herself against the window. She had some-thing in her hand, the heavy base of a lamp, and when she swung it at the window again, glass shat-tered and billows of cool, clean air tumbled in.

Dan grabbed the lamp base and helped her break out the remaining panes. He jerked down the drap-ery and wrapped it around her to protect her from cuts as he helped her through the window. When he turned to follow her, a fireman grabbed his arms, helping him out.

"Miss Cray, do you think this is the work of the mysterious stalker?"

"Did you have any warning something like this might happen?"

"Dan, were you here when the fire broke out?"

"Jess, where will you go now?"

"Are you lovers?"

Dan turned and grabbed the shirtfront of the reporter who had fired out the last question. If he had been able to see better, he would have grabbed his throat. "Listen you little shit, stay away from me with that camera, have you got that? And stay away from Jess. Jesus, are you people insane? Don't you know what's happened here? Someone's life just went up in smoke, do you have any conception of what that means? This is not a goddamn stage set!"

He was raving out of control; with every sentence his grip tightened on the little man's shirtfront, and he gave him a shake. People were gathering, bright lights through the smoke haze, cameras rolling. Then a heavy hand dropped on his shoulder and stayed there.

"Let it go, Dan," Candler said.

Dan sucked in his breath, and released the reporter with a snap. He knew he'd acted like a fool. He knew someone had jotted down every obscene word he'd said, and someone else had recorded it on film. He didn't care.

He tried to shake off Candler's hand, but couldn't, not until they were away from the crowd of reporters. Dan pressed the back of his arm to his eyes briefly, which wouldn't stop watering and hurt so badly they felt like they were bleeding. He didn't think he would ever get the taste of smoke out of his lungs. Blue and red lights flashed through a fog of smoke. Radios crackled. Camera lights blazed. A knot of people in bathrobes and slippers mumbled among themselves.

Someone had hustled Jess into the back of an ambulance. They both had received copious amounts of oxygen, but were otherwise unharmed. The paramedics wanted them to be checked out at the hospital, but Jess refused. The attention they were getting now was nothing compared to what would happen if they showed up at the hospital. And at the hospital there would be no place to hide.

Dan climbed in beside her. She was wearing a blanket taken from an ambulance cot, and beneath it a smudged and water-splotched nightshirt that was too short and too thin. Dan wondered if that was what he hated most, the fact that the cameras were focusing on her naked legs and his bare chest. They were fallen idols. He felt vulnerable, exposed, invaded. Which was, of course, how Jess had felt from the beginning.

He covered her hand with his. She was shaking. She said, "Somehow I have a feeling the homeowners' association will be glad to see me go. There've been more emergency vehicles and reporters here in the past two weeks than there have been in the past five years all put together."

Dan admired her feeble attempt at humor, although her voice was so hoarse and broken her words were difficult to understand. But she was alive. When he had found her collapsed on the floor, he hadn't thought so.

It occurred to him that, in all his life, he had never known fear until that moment.

Candler stood at the open door to the ambulance. He said, "The fire captain said it's mostly smoke and water damage. You should be able to get back in as soon as it's cleaned up. A week or so."

He hesitated, then went on with no visible change of expression, "It was a homemade fuse, using a cigarette and a matchbook. Any teenager knows how to make one. The cigarette burns down, the matches catch, by that time whoever planted it is long gone. They put it between the sofa cushions. Those foam cushions don't flame easily, but the smoke they produce is toxic."

Jess said, "So it was arson."

Her eyes looked enormous in her smoke-smeared face, dark and haunted. Candler didn't answer. He didn't have to. His eyes went toward the front of the building, where firemen were winding up their hoses, making final inspections of the property.

The front door was covered with a dark tarp, taped irregularly around the edges. Loose ends snapped occasionally in the breeze. Candler had given the order to cover the door as soon as the first officer to arrive on the scene reported the situation to him by phone. Beneath the tarp, scrawled with black marker on the honey-stained door, was the word "Shame."

As far as they could determine, the reporters had been too involved with the fire—and with Jess and Dan—to notice the indictment on the door.

Candler said, looking at Jess, "Where will you go tonight?"

Dan responded, "My place."

Candler glanced at him, then at Jess, giving her a chance to disagree. She was looking at the broken window to the bedroom, and she said, "I need to get my things. Do you think they'll let me get my things?"

Dan's hand tightened on hers. Candler said, "I'd feel better if you were in a hotel."

"She's staying with me." Dan had no more energy to sound angry. But he was angry. He just wanted to take Jess away from here, to feel safe again. He wondered if either of them would ever feel safe again.

Candler looked long and hard at Dan. Dan returned his gaze without emotion. Then Candler said to Jess, "It's important that you not tell anyone where you're staying. Not your mailman, not your neighbor, not your producer. Not even your mother. Do you understand?"

Jess dragged her gaze away from the ruins of her condo and back to him. She nodded wearily. "Yes."

"Tell them they can get a message to you through Dan or through me. But don't let anyone guess where you are. And I would suggest that you not stay there more than a day or two."

Jess looked up at Dan. "Do you think my mother will see this on the news? Should I call her?"

"Tomorrow," Dan said. "We'll call her tomorrow."

Candler looked at her for another long moment. He said, "I know this is hard on you, Jess. I'm sorry. But this guy is getting bolder. It's more important now than ever that you stay alert."

She whispered, "I know." And her eyes went back to the building.

Dan said, "The smoke detector."

Candler looked at him. "What?"

"The smoke detector, that's what woke me up. If he wanted to kill us, why didn't he disable the smoke detector?"

Candler didn't answer. He said after a moment, "I'll be in touch." And he walked away.

The fire marshal let them in, then stood at the door while Jess walked through the rooms. The once white carpet was a sea of mud and soot that squished under her feet. The sofa was overturned and ripped apart. Draperies were piled in a sodden heap in the center of the room. Lamps were broken. In the strobing red lights from the window she could see sooty columns crawling up the walls, water dripping from picture frames. The flat dead smell of ashes made her want to gag.

Dan said, "Jess, maybe we'd better do this tomorrow."

She shook her head. For a moment she couldn't speak. Then, with an effort she made her voice work. It felt as though the ligaments were being torn from her throat. "No. I need my purse. Money, ID. And clothes. Underwear."

Dan said, "I don't think anything that's left is dry."

He was looking around, too, with an expression of subdued horror at the place that had almost been their funeral pyre. He did not want to go farther into the room. Jess didn't blame him.

She picked her way carefully across the living-room floor toward the set of shelves that held her books. Most of them had been tossed on the floor, their spines broken, their pages swollen. She knelt on the floor, picked up a sodden volume, and let it fall again.

Her beautiful home. All her lovely things. He had taken it all. The bastard had ruined it all.

She went into the bedroom. She saw the broken window, the smoke-smeared walls, the rumpled bed. Now the sheets were soaked, the mattress ruined. Only hours ago she had lain with Dan, their limbs entwined in ecstasy and discovery, and it had been sweet, so sweet, one little island of shining wonder snatched from the nightmare her life had become. But he had taken that, too.

Dan stood beside her. She said in a shaky voice, "Do you think . . . he was here, hiding, waiting . . . listening, while we . . ."

She couldn't finish, and he couldn't answer. He touched her lightly on the back, a gesture that was meant to be comforting, but she walked away.

She went to the dresser and picked up one of the high-school yearbooks she had brought home from her mother's house. The pages weren't too wet. She flipped through them, though it was too dark to see anything.

Dan said, "What's that?"

"A high-school annual. I thought . . . I had this crazy idea that there might be a clue here. Something I did back then that . . . I don't know, might explain it all."

After a moment she picked up both albums and hugged them to her chest. Then she turned to Dan.

"So," she said, "twice now you've almost died because of me."

He said, "Come on, Jess. Let's get out of here."

In the background water was dripping. Outside was the sound of the engines on the big pumper trucks, the crackle of voices of the radio.

She said, with difficulty, "He knew we were together. What he wrote on the door . . ." She took a breath. "Maybe Candler was right. I should go to a hotel."

"Don't let him do this, Jess."

She shook her head. Tears ached in her throat, exploded in her chest that already felt battered and raw. "He already has. He made it . . . dirty, and wrong . . ."

He came to her then and put his arm around her shoulders in a firm, possessive embrace. "You're coming home with me," he said quietly. "You're going to have a shower and wash the smell of smoke out of your hair, and then you're coming to bed, and I'm going to hold you for the rest of the night and all through the morning, and we'll talk if you want to, or be quiet if you want to, or make love if you want to. I can't make it go away, but I can make it better. I promise you that."

Jess turned to him, pressing her face against his chest, and let the tears spill over.

Chapter 23

Trish said with careful constraint, "I don't think you realize what programming concessions we've made to you already, Jess. We've postponed shows and rejected shows. It took us three months to set up the remote from state prison, and who knows if we'll ever get back in. But we didn't want to take the chance of bringing you to the attention of yet another criminal now, did we? Children and weapons—too violent. Women married to cross-dressers—attracts too strange an audience. Men married to cross-dressers, ditto. For God's sake, what's left?"

Dan interjected dryly, "Cross-dressers and their pets?" And at the cold look Trish gave him, he said impatiently, "For Christ's sake, Trish, what are you whining about? I wouldn't say any of these so-called programming concessions have adversely affected ratings, now have they? Wouldn't you even say ratings have been stronger than ever?"

"That has nothing to do with—"

"Oh, don't give me that crap! That's *all* it has to do with, and you know it!"

Jess held up both hands in a plea for silence or peace. They were in Trish's office, and, in contrast to their usual positions, it was Dan who was pacing restlessly from window to desk to door, and Jess who sat calmly in front of Trish's desk.

Jess said, "I know you've made changes to keep from upsetting me or—endangering me since this all began, and I appreciate it. Just to show you how much, I'm going to give you the show of a lifetime."

Dan cast her a dark look and muttered, "This is crazy."

Trish tapped ashes into the whirring electronic ashtray, a look of grudging interest mitigating the resentment and discontent in her face. She said, "Oh, yeah?"

"Yeah." Jess didn't flinch. "I want him on the show."

Trish looked confused. "What?"

"I want the son of a bitch on the show. The topic: Have you ever done anything you're ashamed of? The guest—get me a psychiatrist, any psychiatrist. He'll be there, in the audience, hanging around downstairs, calling in."

As she spoke, Trish's eyes slowly began to light with possibilities. She stared at Jess with the cigarette poised between her fingers above the ashtray, all but forgotten, while possibilities ran through her head. "Good God," she said softly. "Of course."

Dan glared at her.

Jess's fingers tightened in her lap, but only the slightest tension of her voice betrayed her determination. It was as though she had rehearsed this many times, perfecting the words and the intonation—which of course she had.

"We'll tape the promos today, start airing them tonight. We've pulled in enough of the market over the last few weeks to earn us some extra spots locally, so let's use up our budget for the rest of the season. And let's get it in the trades, on the news. We can do the show Wednesday; that should give us plenty of buildup. It's no good if he doesn't watch, and if he knows about it, he'll watch. He'll be there, how can he resist? And if he can't get to the studio, he'll call me, I just know it. This is what he's been waiting for—*his* chance to be a celebrity."

A voice said behind them, "I'm afraid I can't let you do that."

The excitement in Trish's eyes turned to flashing annoyance as they shot toward the door. "Damn it, Lieutenant, who—"

"Your secretary said you were in here." There might have been a hint of apology in his tone, but not much. "The door was open."

In fact, the door was only half open; he pushed it the rest of the way with his body as he came in. The set of his jaw was similar to the stubbornness in Dan's as he said, "I didn't mean to eavesdrop, but I'm glad I did. Jess, this is a bad idea. The last thing you want is a confrontation."

Jess turned in her chair to look at him. She was wearing jeans and a long sweater, her makeup flawless, her hair perfect. The only signs of stress were in her posture and her eyes. Her eyes were like ice.

She said plainly, "No. The last thing I want is to go on like this. We've had the tool all along—the show—and I've been too stupid to see it. It's like he's been waiting for us to figure it out."

"So you oblige him?" Candler demanded. And he gave a sharp shake of his head. "I can't you let you put yourself in danger like that."

Trish tossed the smoldering stub of her cigarette into the smokeless ashtray and lit another with sharp impatient movements. Her gaze and her tone were cold. "I hardly think you can dictate programming to us, Lieutenant. Now if you'll excuse us, we're in the middle of a meeting here."

"Just wait one damn minute," Dan said. He pushed a hand through his hair in one brief tense motion, then turned his full attention to Trish and to Jess. "Just look at this thing logically for a minute, will you do that? Okay." He took a breath. "The way I see it, two things have been accomplished by this guy. The first is, of course, that a celebrity has been terrorized, assaulted emotionally if not physically, brought down to the level of the common man. If we're dealing with a psychotic, the agenda is plain. He started with an element common to everyone—the guilt or shame we all feel for things that most of the time we can't control—and he used it to bring you down to his level. I've been doing some research, and history tells us that the most distinguishing factor in these celebrity-obsession cases is that once the celebrity is brought down to the stalker's level, he perceives that fall as a betrayal, and he reacts with anger—sometimes deadly anger. I'm sorry Jess, but that's scenario number one: You provoke a confrontation, you make him mad."

Jess swallowed hard, but her voice remained steady. "All right. What's scenario number two?"

Candler was looking at Dan with a frown that did not disguise his interest. Dan ignored him. He said, "This guy's already gotten a hell of a lot of publicity. Maybe that's what he feeds on. Maybe giving him the show is *exactly* what he wants . . . and the last thing you want."

Trish drew sharply on the cigarette, tapping the ashes. "So let me guess. You're against the idea."

Candler said, "For once, Webber, you and I are in agreement. But you left out a couple of other important things the stalker has accomplished, and I don't think now's the time to overlook the obvious."

"What?"

Candler's gaze was steady. "Two people are dead, another left for dead."

"All of whom might have exposed his identity."

"Maybe." Candler turned his attention to Jess. "Maybe there's another connection. Why don't you just let us do our job—"

Jess gave an adamant shake of her head and stood abruptly. "No," she said. "No, you've had your chance. You've had your chance, and now I'm homeless and my brother has been terrorized and Jeremy Styles is in a coma and a reporter I don't even know is dead and . . ." She caught her breath and darted a quick glance at Dan. "Someone I care about was almost killed, so now we're doing it my way, do you understand that?"

Candler's lips tightened. Trish looked coolly triumphant.

"All right," Candler said, "so he shows up. Then what? Do you expect him to just turn himself in? What will it accomplish?"

"For one thing," Trish drawled, tapping ashes, "we'll have him on tape. We can keep one camera trained on the audience the whole time, and later Jess can review the tape frame by frame for anyone who looks familiar—past or present."

Jess tossed her a grateful look. "That's more than we have now, isn't it? And that's only the worst case scenario. I think he'll give himself away. I don't think he'll be able to stop himself from stepping into his own trap."

"I disagree," Dan said harshly. "Even if he doesn't see right through your plan—and who wouldn't— it's too risky. Suppose the guy brings a gun—"

"We install a metal detector."

"Suppose he plants a bomb?" Candler said. "He's already shown a talent for arson, among other things. How can I protect you from this maniac? I can't let you do this, Jess. It's insane."

"You can't make me go on living like this." She backed up against Trish's desk, facing down the two men. "We're doing the show."

Trish drew on the cigarette and exhaled slowly, turning a cool, supercilious smile on Candler. "Did you have a particular purpose for coming here, Lieutenant, or is this just general harassment?"

Again the detective's jaw knotted, but only briefly. He said in his most pleasant tone, "Actually, I was hoping to have a word with Mr. Webber."

Dan said distractedly, "Not now. I don't have time. Jess—"

Jess said, "You have time." And then, with quiet deliberation, "It's settled, Dan. With or without you, the show is on."

He lifted an eyebrow. She meant the remark to sound careless, but it didn't quite come out that way. "So. You carry off one show by yourself, and all of a sudden you're a prima donna."

Trish flipped a page on her appointment book. "I can get you studio time at two to film the promos."

And Jess held his gaze. "With or without you."

Dan looked at her for a long moment, the debate

clear in his eyes. Then he said, in a low, harsh exclamation of simple frustration, "Damn it." And he left the office.

Candler followed.

When they were gone, the silence in the room was, for a moment, awkward. Then Jess looked at Trish and managed a smile. It was tired and strained, but it was the best she could do.

"Thanks," she said.

Trish shrugged and stubbed out the cigarette, avoiding her eyes. "It's good television. That's my job."

It would have been safe to talk about the show. Jess could not quite bring herself to do that. She said, "I, um, guess we haven't had too much time to talk since . . . lately."

"No." A single word as heavy as lead.

It hung between them, a curtain of things unsaid, suspicions unvoiced, resentments teeming below the surface. The police had questioned Trish. They had searched her house and taken her gun, stripped her of her privacy and her dignity, and it was all Jess's fault. They should talk about that. Neither knew where to begin.

Then Trish looked at her and pushed a hand through her spiky short hair with a smile that was almost rueful. "Sorry times, huh, kid?" she said.

Jess nodded wordlessly.

Trish grew serious. "Listen, I'm sorry as hell about your place. Did you lose much?"

Jess dragged in a breath and pushed it out. Too often over the past few days she had had to remind herself to do that: Breathe in, breathe out. The weekend had been spent frantically trying to avoid the pain that came with thinking about what she had lost—and not just in the fire, but in other places, in other ways, since the nightmare had invaded her life. Making love with a frenzied desperation and clinging to Dan in what was not so much an affirmation of life but an escape from it. Driving herself, and him, into exhaustion and then sleeping in restless, uneasy snatches and waking to turn to him again. Using him, needing him, making him into a surrogate for all that she couldn't articulate . . . and Dan, perfectly aware of it all but never complaining. She loved him, she had realized, if for nothing more than that.

She said, "I, uh, really haven't been back . . . except that night. The furniture's ruined, and the books. Most of my clothes . . ." She smiled wanly. "Which only gives me an excuse to go shopping, I guess."

"That's the spirit."

Trish lit another cigarette. Jess couldn't help staring at her, couldn't help remembering the cigarette and the matches tucked between the sofa cushions.

Trish said, inhaling, "So where are you staying?"

Jess quickly looked away. "Look, I need to get going. I want to talk to the copywriter about those promos—"

"Jess?"

Jess glanced back uncomfortably. Trish was leaning forward, her arms crossed on her desk, her expression curious and concerned. Jess was miserable.

She said, "Trish . . . Look, I'm not supposed to say where I'm staying, okay?"

Something went out of Trish's face. Even her voice was flat. "I thought we were friends."

Jess glanced away. It was a cowardly, disrespectful thing to do, and she hated herself for it, but at
that moment she seemed to have absolutely no control over her body language. "We are. Of course we
are. It's just that—"

"Bull shit." Two distinct words that concealed a
chasm of hurt and anger. Trish sat back, her eyes
like small coals. "The fucking police have me on
their list of top ten suspects, and for all I know
you put me there! Jesus Christ, Jess." Now her eyes
betrayed contempt, even pity. "Who the hell are
you? What have you become?"

Jess swallowed hard, then raised her chin. "A victim," she said, and she hated the sound of the word
as much as she had ever hated anything in her life.
"Just like you."

She turned and left the office, marking down one
more thing the stalker had taken from her.

Candler walked with Dan to the elevators, and
they rode down together. Dan said with no patience
and very little expression of interest, "Are you here
to arrest me?"

"For what? Overdue parking tickets? Because, try
as I might, that's the most I can find against you.

"I'm surprised you didn't try to prosecute."

"The D.A. kicked it."

"So what're you doing here?"

"Relax, Webber, I'm on your side. Or didn't you
notice just now?"

The elevator door opened at the lobby. Dan held
the button, his expression uninviting. "I'm going to
lunch. Where are you going?"

"You still owe me a drink. I feel like collecting."

Dan looked at him for a moment suspiciously. Then he released the door and stepped out of the elevator. "There's a place across the street, Charlie's. You can look like you're working and maybe get on the evening news at the same time."

"Sounds perfect."

They walked out of the building and onto the street, melting into the ebb and flow of lunchtime traffic. They waited at the corner for the light to change, and Dan said, "Do you know what I think? I think you're jealous."

"Of you? Maybe. You've got a great life, Webber. Good looks, top job, personal fame, beautiful woman. You've also got more trouble than you know."

"So you are here to arrest me."

"You might be better off."

Dan looked at him then, actually curious, but the light changed, and they joined the flow of traffic across the street.

The day was dim and cloudy, the interior of Charlie's even dimmer, yet somehow warmer. It might have been the noise, the energy level, the crowd. Charlie's at lunch was an entirely different experience than Charlie's after work. Dan was glad to be away from the office. And he was glad, because she had tried his patience to the limit, to be away from Jess.

The realization shamed him, and to cover it he said brusquely, "There's a table. I don't eat at the bar."

A reporter noticed them as they moved across the room, and then another, and then several. Dan shouldered past, knowing it was not the best way to engender the goodwill of his colleagues, but lacking the energy to do anything else. He caught the eye of the bartender, and in a moment the crowd around them dispersed, albeit with a great deal of grumbling and a few derisive remarks.

"It's like being out with a rock star," commented Candler.

Dan shot him a cutting look. "I noticed your name in the paper once or twice in the past few weeks, too. If there's anything worse than a celebrity talk-show host, it's got to be a celebrity cop."

To his surprise Candler actually smiled. "Well, you've got me there."

They sat down, and the waitress brought water glasses within seconds. There were some advantages to this newfound fame, and Dan would be the last to deny it.

Candler ordered a beer, and Dan, thinking of the promos he had to shoot in less than two hours, ordered a grilled tuna sandwich and coffee—not with very good grace either.

He then folded his arms and stared at Candler. "All right. Let's have it."

Candler said quietly, "Don't let her do that show, Webber."

"Yeah, well, you might have noticed my vote doesn't count for much in there." But he was curious. "If you had an argument, you should have made it."

"I couldn't, exactly."

"Why the hell not?"

"You're not going to like this."

The waitress brought his beer and Dan's coffee. "That's supposed to surprise me?"

Candler waited until the waitress was gone to answer. He spoke while looking into his beer. "Jess has been staying with you, what? Two days now? And since she moved in—since she's been with you practically twenty-four hours a day, things have been awfully quiet, haven't they?"

"Oh for Christ's sake, Candler, I'm getting sick and tired of these insinuations. Either charge me with something so I can pound your ass to a pulp in court, or shut the hell up."

Candler sipped his beer. "You still don't get it, do you? You're not a suspect in this case, Webber; you haven't been for a while now. It's not you we're after. It's Jess."

For a moment Dan's face displayed no reaction at all. Then he smiled and leaned back in his chair. "This," he said, "I can't wait to hear."

"Let me ask you something. When you woke up to the fire, where was Jess?"

Dan tensed, wishing he had ordered something stronger than coffee after all. "I always did think you were a little too interested in my sex life. Is there something you'd like to tell me, Lieutenant?"

Candler repeated, "Where was she?"

Dan pushed at his hair, glancing around the room. He didn't want to think about that night, didn't want to bring back the smoke and the terror, didn't want, most of all, to bring back the vulnerability.

But he started talking, and he didn't know why. "I couldn't find her at first. I was disoriented . . . I didn't know the apartment, where the doors were or the windows. I couldn't find her." His voice started to thicken, and he was embarrassed. He cleared his throat and reached for the coffee mug. "She was on the floor by the bed. I thought she was unconscious, but she came around when I was trying to get the window open." He looked at Candler. "I told this to the officers on the scene."

Candler nodded. "Didn't you wonder why she wasn't in bed?"

He hadn't. "I figured she'd been overcome by the smoke, like I almost was."

"Without trying to wake you first?"

Dan frowned. "What are you getting at?"

But the waitress came again with Dan's sandwich. She took too long fussing around, asking if they needed anything, offering to freshen the coffee Dan hadn't even touched. When she finally left, the tension at the table was thick enough to cut.

But Candler's next statement was disappointing. "You don't know anything about Jess's early life, do you?"

Dan put together the two parts of his sandwich. "I think we've been through this before—cheerleader, beauty queen, weather girl . . . why?"

"I mean her home life."

"I know it was kind of rough on her, with her brother and all. I guess her parents expected her to make up for what they considered their failure with Evan, so she became an overachiever. Apparently, her father was one of those tyrannical SOB's who made himself feel bigger by putting down everyone else around him. A lot of verbal abuse that wouldn't pass today's talk-show child-rearing standards, but she survived it. We all survived parents who didn't know how to raise kids, so what?"

"I would say a mother who locks a child in a

closet with a sign around her neck that says Shame could be guilty of more than just 'not knowing how to raise kids,' wouldn't you?"

Dan felt the color drain from his face. He put the sandwich down slowly. "My God."

He remembered Jess's uneasiness in the dark, and her only comment about the incident on the stairwell was, "I don't do well with dark places."

He stared at Candler. "How do you know this? Who told you that? Jess?"

Candler went on, "Did you know she was a suspect in Brett Casto's murder?"

For a moment Dan didn't know who he was talking about. "Brett . . . do you mean her college lover? But that was suicide."

"It was ruled suicide because the police couldn't prove anything else. But I talked to the investigating officer, and he was convinced that it was murder. He was shot with Jess's gun, you know . . . which, coincidentally, is the same kind of weapon that was used on Glanbury and Styles—and you."

"This is insane." He stared at the sandwich on the plate before him, but he was thinking about the gun in Jess's purse. How could he not think about it? The gun she wasn't supposed to have, a .38, the same kind of gun she had owned so long ago, the gun she had told Dan that an old boyfriend used to kill himself. *Insane . . .*

Candler caught his arm as he started to rise, and Dan had not even realized that, in his anger, he had pushed up from the table.

"That's exactly what it is," Candler said quietly. "Insane."

Dan sat back down slowly.

"Think about it. If my theory is correct, and this has been going on most of Jess's life, and if the attacks have been motivated to protect her from people and things that would embarrass or hurt her—who would be more motivated than Jess herself? Who would know more about what she's ashamed of—and strike out to eradicate it—than Jess?"

"But . . . her brother . . ."

"Her brother, a prom date, her first live-in boyfriend . . . all of them in one way or another humiliated and betrayed her. There may be more that we don't know about. And the notes . . . I figure the guilt got to be too much for her; she was calling out for help. Hell, I don't know. I'm not a psychiatrist. But it keeps coming back to this. Who would know better than anyone else in the world what Jess is ashamed of? And who else could have followed her from state to state, job to job, knowing all her secrets and private guilts, for almost twenty years?"

Dan had begun shaking his head midway through Candler's last speech. His voice was hoarse, his throat felt raw. His head was starting to hurt, as though the words and images that were filling his brain were toxic. "I don't know. Somebody . . . I don't know. That's your job, not mine."

"And I'm trying to do my job."

With all his might, Dan struggled to hold on to the reality he thought he knew. "You seriously expect me to believe that Jess is on your list of suspects now? Hell, why not?" He gave a short, harsh laugh. "It's no crazier than anything else you've come up with."

"No one's ever heard the phone calls," Candler

reminded him. "The only identifiable prints on the notes were Jesse's."

"For the love of Christ, are you serious? Of course her prints were on the notes—so were her secretary's and everyone's in the mail room and those of a couple of dozen people in the post office as well. Isn't that how you explained to me that prints taken from the notes were useless?"

"As far as we can determine, she was alone on that stairwell," Candler went on implacably. "And it's a forty-five minute drive from her apartment to the Shepherd's Village nursing home—something she could easily accomplish unobserved."

Dan swore and pushed his plate away in disgust. "Why the hell are you telling me this?"

"Because," Candler replied simply, "if you'll notice, it's never Jess who gets hurt. The pattern is that it's those close to Jess, not Jess herself, who always seem to end up dead, and you've already had two close calls."

Dan felt himself growing cold. He tried not to think; he couldn't help thinking. Styles. God, it was too obvious. And Glanbury, he had written the article that exposed her secrets to the world. But Dan . . . what had he done to her? It was crazy. Crazy.

Still, he heard himself saying, "Do you mean— are you saying Jess set fire to her own place? But she was trapped, too."

Candler said, "The association between sexuality and pyromania is well established. My guess is she was trying to punish herself that time as well as you, and that's what worries me. This thing is escalating beyond the point of self-protection."

She hadn't been in bed when the fire started.

What was she doing up? Trying to call the fire department, looking for the phone, disoriented by smoke, half-unconscious . . . it could happen. It was likely. Or she could be returning from having set the fire.

"No." Dan gripped the table firmly, a symbolic gesture that was really nothing more than a desperate attempt once again to hold on to a fast disintegrating reality. But what was reality in the life of a talk-show host? "I'm not buying any of this. She's doing her best to catch this maniac, for God's sake, which is something that wouldn't be necessary if you'd do your goddamn job instead of—"

"Have you ever heard of disassociative personality disorder?"

Dan thought. *Oh, God.* It was as though he had been waiting for those words. "Heard of it? Hell, we've done two shows on it this year alone."

"Then you know that the victim of such a disorder may not have any conscious recollection of what she does in that state—or even any intention of performing those acts. Often when confronted with evidence of what they have done, the victims of the disorder are unable to believe it was them. I'm not saying Jess did any of this on purpose—in fact, I'm convinced she doesn't have the first idea what she's doing. I think you're right." His eyes darkened a little with intensity as he leaned forward. "I think she *is* trying to stop this, and I think she's asking for our help."

"No." Dan started to rise. "No, this is crazy and you've wasted enough of my time. Why aren't you out there trying to catch the real criminal instead of persecuting the victim?"

"She is the victim, I'm not denying that. But she's also the criminal. Face it, Dan, a series of murders or attempted murders spanning fifteen years . . . all centering on the same person and using the same weapon. Who else could have followed her from Jackson, Mississippi, to Athens, Georgia, to Philadelphia, Pennsylvania? Answer me those questions, and you'll have a suspect. I already do."

Dan said, "She was with me the night Glanbury was killed. I know that."

"Do you?" Candler's gaze was steady. "Can you be absolutely certain she didn't leave your apartment while you were asleep and return before morning? She's the only one with a motive for killing Glanbury. The only one."

Dan desperately searched for an answer. He couldn't find one. He wondered if he should tell Candler about the gun. But how could he?

Candler went on, "You told her Styles knew who the stalker was. She had to kill him, don't you see? She didn't expect you to be there. She made you promise not to keep the appointment. I don't think she meant to kill you, but she couldn't let you see her, could she? Even in a disassociative state, people know enough to defend themselves, and she had an agenda."

"Jesus," Dan said. It was sick, it was crazy . . . but was that any reason for not believing it? He heard sicker things two or three times a week from the perpetrators themselves.

But Jess. God, not Jess.

"All right," Candler said calmly. "Suppose I'm wrong. Suppose it's some outside source, and Jess is a completely innocent victim—you know as well as I do it's dangerous to do that show. And if it's her—if the enemy is inside her . . . don't you see what she's doing? She's trying to warn us; she's on a timetable and the final confrontation is Wednesday. Don't let her do the show, Dan. Give me some time to prove my theory, get her some help."

Dan pushed up from the table. It was actually an effort to do so. "I've had enough."

"One more thing."

Dan couldn't help it. He turned back.

"Did Jess ever tell you how her brother became brain damaged in the first place?"

Dan didn't answer. He couldn't move. He wanted to walk away, he didn't want to hear, but he was as helpless as the thousands of voyeurs who tuned into the show every day to experience the most bizarre, to believe the most unbelievable, to witness the most horrific. He had never really understood the compulsion before. Now, with dim and detached fascination, he did.

Candler said very quietly, very steadily, "When Evan was three months old, his older sister stood over his bassinet and held a pillow over his head until he stopped breathing. The paramedics were able to resuscitate, but the brain damage was severe. Jess won't tell you that; she's blocked it out. Her mother won't tell you; the parents always denied it. But hospital records don't lie. Jessamine Cray tried to kill her brother when he was an infant, and *that's* what she's ashamed of."

Dan turned and walked out.

Chapter 24

Dan lay beside her at night, awake while she slept, haunted by the swirling images that darted through his head. He hadn't been able to make love to her. He'd barely been able to touch her. For two days he had looked at her and found himself looking at a woman he didn't know.

It was insanity. It was impossible. Yet . . . they dealt in the impossible every day. Insanity was their stock and trade. How could he not consider it? How could he not, perhaps, be seduced by it?

Glanbury. Styles. A bullet in the dark. Not meant to kill, perhaps, fired out of panic or surprise . . . Evan, God. The dead nurse. It was sick, the whole fucking world was sick, and the sickest thing of all was that he wasn't nearly as shocked as he should have been, he wasn't even *surprised*.

She lay beside him so sweetly, so trustingly—vulnerable in her sleep, innocent, helpless. From the beginning all he had wanted to do was protect her. And now . . .

Have you ever done anything you're ashamed of?

Yes, he was ashamed of himself, but what was he supposed to do? How was he supposed to find out the truth? Her mother? If what Candler said was true, her mother had been lying for years. Any woman who could do to a child what Candler claimed she had done could not be trusted, and Dan had always thought Jess's mother was a little strange, that the whole family was if it came to that. Hospital records on her brother? According to Candler, that's how he had gotten his information; Candler had access to court orders. For an ordinary citizen like Dan it would not be so easy.

He remembered the last time he had done that kind of research on Jess's behalf, tracking down that job application. He had found out that no one had requested a copy, at least not recently. But Jess could very easily have kept a copy from all those years ago.

God, what if Candler was right. What if she was setting herself up for something with the show tomorrow? A suicide, or another killing . . .

Dan couldn't lie beside her anymore, half believing she was a monster, knowing that he was for thinking such things. He got up and pulled on his clothes, closing the door softly behind him as he went into the living room.

Why was it so easy for him to believe? Damn it, why did it make so much sense? Had society reached a point where the bizarre was easier to believe than the commonplace, where the outrageous made more sense than the straightforward? Was that his legacy, as part of the talk-show phenomenon: It's only true if it makes a good sound bite?

He knew he would not be going back to bed tonight. He put on a pot of coffee and sat down to read. The book he picked up was *Dead Love*.

*   *   *

Dan awoke smelling ashes.

He sat up with a start. The book fell to the floor. Jess, who was curled up in the chair opposite him with a cup of coffee, smiled tiredly. "Morning," she said.

Then he identified the source of the burned smell. Jess had one of the charred and water-swollen high-school yearbooks in her lap and was slowly turning pages.

He ran a hand over his face and pushed aside the blanket Jess had placed over his knees. Even as he did so, the ugliness and dread with which he had gone to sleep returned like a bad taste.

He said, "I hope I didn't wake you."

She shook her head, turning another page. "Too nervous to sleep. God, we're both going to look great for the big day, huh?"

Dan went into the kitchen to pour a cup of coffee. "What are you doing?"

She shook her head, turning another page. "It's stupid. I keep thinking about what Candler said—a teacher, a coach, a bus driver, someone I wouldn't necessarily remember—and I think if I keep looking at these pictures, reading the names, something will look familiar or trigger a memory. I know it's a long shot. But even though I didn't want to believe it at first, it's got to be someone who knew me in high school. And maybe—just maybe—he had his picture taken for the yearbook."

Who else could have followed her from Jackson, Mississippi, to Athens, Georgia, to Philadelphia, Pennsylvania, Dan? Who?

He leaned against the dividing bar and sipped his

coffee, watching her. Her head was bent over the book, her hair finger-combed and limp. One slender leg was tucked beneath her, her bare arms so thin they looked like a child's. She was wearing one of his T-shirts, and it hung on her. He could see the shape of her ribs through the material, and the notch of her hipbones. That alarmed him.

He said, "You've lost weight."

She glanced up with a half shrug. "You know what they say. You can't be too thin or too . . . Funny, I can't remember the rest."

He came over and stood behind her, watching her turn the pages. He didn't know why. As though being close could make up for what he was thinking. For the betrayal.

"You were a cheerleader," he said suddenly, staring at a photograph of a pony-tailed, pom-pommed Jess atop a human pyramid.

"You knew that."

"Yeah, I guess I did." His voice was thoughtful. "I just never thought about it before."

She turned a page. "Should you?"

He rubbed the bridge of his nose, trying to ease away a frown. "No, I guess not. It's just—I was reading that book last night, the one Styles wrote. All the girls in it were cheerleaders."

"What?"

"Just as in the Silk Scarf killings, cheerleaders."

"The first two weren't cheerleaders," she reminded him. "The pattern didn't come till later."

"Yes," he agreed slowly. Something tickled the back of his mind, but he couldn't quite put his finger on it. Then he smiled. "And I thought you never did your research."

Jess closed the book and looked up at him, her expression gentle. "We're doing okay, aren't we, Dan?"

What could he say to her? What could he?

"I mean, most couples have sex at least twice before they move in together, and I've been here almost a week and you haven't kicked me out yet."

He managed a smile. "Under the circumstance, it was the least I could do."

She reached up and looped her fingers through his. Her voice grew sober. "Listen, I know that—emotional decisions made under stress usually can't be relied upon, and that there's a lot more mixed up in what we feel for one another right now than there probably should be. But . . . I guess what I'm trying to say is that we both took a big chance, changing our relationship the way we did, getting involved with someone we work with . . . God, I'm not doing this very well, am I?" She looked to him for help. "You'd think a talk-show host would be more articulate."

He smiled at her encouragingly. "Are you trying to say that when everything calms down, we should have a talk about our relationship?"

She shook her head. Her eyes were so clear, so big. So honest.

"I'm trying to say that I don't regret it," she replied. "And I hope you don't either."

He leaned down and kissed her lips. God, it was so easy. "Your turn to shower first," he said.

She stood up. "See? Any couple who can live together for a week without fighting over the bathroom has got to be made for one another."

She stopped and then looked back. "It could be over today, Dan," she said. "It really could."

All he could do was nod.

When she was gone, he went over and picked up the fallen copy of *Dead Love*. Was that what Jeremy Styles had been trying to tell him, then? The cheerleader connection. The notes had started the day Styles was on the show. Maybe he *was* the connection, but not in the way they had imagined. Maybe he had just triggered something else.

God, it was crazy.

He looked at the smoky, swollen high-school yearbook, and he almost opened it and looked for himself. Then he started thinking about the other things Jess had brought with her from her apartment that night.

She had bought a new purse—the other one smelled like smoke—but the contents were virtually the same. Feeling like the lowest kind of criminal, Dan opened it.

There it was. The .38.

Carefully, Dan lifted it out. It was odd, what the feel of a gun in the hand could do. It made him feel empowered . . . and guilty. Justified . . . and wrong. He wondered if that was how Jess felt when she held it.

He almost put it back, then stopped. Hating himself, expecting any moment to hear Jess's voice, hurt and outraged, asking what he was doing and knowing that he deserved whatever she might think of him, Dan began to remove the ammunition.

Chapter 25

Sylvia leapt up to meet them when they arrived at the office, and even as she was speaking, others were crowding around. "Miss Cray, your mother has called twice this morning, and you had three messages from her already—"

"I'll call her after the show," Jess said, taking the messages.

"You and Dan have a magazine interview at noon, and *Hard Copy* called. Trish said to schedule an interview, so I did at three o'clock. But they've got cameras here this morning; they're going to film behind scenes—"

"Jess, for God's sake call your mother," Dan said. "She's got to be going crazy with all the stuff that's been on the news—"

Bethany was at his elbow. "Dan, you've got an interview at two, and we need to coordinate with Jess and Trish for an ET segment. Lieutenant Candler has been asking for you and—"

Trish said, "I need ten minutes with both of you before the show. The police are keeping a list of every person who comes through the studio door, and they've got one of those portable metal detectors to sweep everyone who comes in. It's not that they think you're that important, hon"—she tossed a glance in Jess's direction—"but it would look like shit for a national celebrity to be executed on television, and the police department has enough P.R. problems as it is—"

Dan said, "Jesus, Trish . . ."

"Also, they've got a trace on the phone lines in case anyone truly weird calls in, but in a city this size it's still going to take a few minutes to—"

Gertrude said, "God, Jess, what have you done to your hair? And look at those circles under your eyes." She turned a narrow glance on Dan. "You ain't looking so hot yourself, stud. I'm thinking a Number Five pancake—"

Everyone wanted a piece of them.

Dan wanted to get to the Green Room early, to spend a few minutes with the guest psychiatrist Trish had found. What he would say to her he wasn't sure, but he hoped at the last minute inspiration would come—or perhaps just courage—to ask the questions that would help him find the truth. But his schedule was turned upside down; he didn't leave his office until ten minutes before taping, and then he found Jim Brockett outside his door, preparing to knock.

"Yeah, I know, it's a bad time," Jim said, walking with him, "but I thought I'd let you know we have cameras set up, just in case—"

And at Dan's sharp look, he defended, "Come on, Dan, you don't think anybody's guessing what this show is really about, do you? I mean, metal detectors, for Christ's sake. You're expecting the stalker to show up. Maybe you've got reason to believe he's always in the audience, I don't know, but I can tell you one thing—before this day is out, I'll find out."

"I'm in a big hurry, Jim."

"Listen, Dan, what I want to know—and I'm only asking because I know you'll tell me straight—that first show with Candler, it was a setup, right?"

"What are you talking about?"

"I mean, he and Jess being old friends, it couldn't be just a coincidence. What I don't understand is why you didn't play it up more, especially with all that—"

Dan stopped walking. "What?"

Jim stared at him. "What, are you kidding me? Is this on the level?"

"I'm in no mood for jokes, Brockett. What the hell are you talking about?"

"Didn't you read the Glanbury file? So you really didn't know?"

"What are you telling me? Jess and Candler—it's crazy. They never met before he came on the show. What's this about?"

"Jesus Christ, that son of a bitch! He made it up. Let me tell you something, Dan, if anybody wants to know—this is exactly why nobody listened to that sleaze, not to speak ill of the dead. Okay, thanks, that's what I wanted to know."

He veered off, and Dan was left frowning after him.

By the time he reached the Green Room, the guest psychiatrist was not alone. Jess was with her, and Dan made neutral conversation with them—or at least as neutral as was possible under the circumstances—until it was time to go warm up the audience.

*   *   *

"Have you ever done anything you're ashamed of?" Jess, Camera One, sober and sincere. "Has America lost its moral conscience? These are the questions we asked you, our viewing audience, and today we're here with the answers." Camera Two. "Hello, I'm Jessamine Cray."

"And I'm Dan Webber, and this is *Speaking of Which*. Today we have with us psychiatrist Karen Cramer, expert on the effects of shame—or guilt, I suppose we should say—on the human psyche. Dr. Cramer, let me ask you first, is shame necessarily such a bad thing?"

"Actually, Dan, shame is one of the healthiest human emotions we have. . . ."

The first break came five minutes into the show. It was the longest five minutes Dan had ever lived through. He kept scanning the audience, wondering if a maniac occupied one of the seats . . . wondering if one didn't. He spotted Candler near the back of the room, but as soon as the "taping" light went off, he slipped out the door. The plainclothes officers he left behind stood out like a collection of sore thumbs.

As soon as they were clear, Gertrude was all over Jess with a makeup brush and hair spray, the floor director was pressing a glass of water on her, Trish was saying something in a loud, strident voice about a change in the lineup, and several of the undercover officers moved forward. It took Dan a few minutes to get to Jess.

"You okay?" he asked when he was close enough to keep his voice low.

On camera she had seemed as calm and compe-

tent as ever; now it was clear the stress was taking
its toll. Her hairline was damp with perspiration and
her eyes dark with worry. "God, you were right,"
she whispered, "this was a bad idea. What if he's
out there, watching me? What if he's not even here,
but sees it on television later today—or even tomorrow, or the next day. I wanted it to be over, but it
could go on for weeks. I don't know if I can stand
it if it goes on for weeks." She took a sip of water
and cast an anxious eye over the audience. "But
it's not a bad show, is it? I mean, the audience is
responding, aren't they? Do you think it's going
okay?"

The "taping" light started to blink. Twenty seconds. Dan said, "Listen, Jess, tell me something.
You didn't know Candler before he came on the
show that first time, did you?"

She looked at him blankly. "What?"

"Nothing, never mind." He touched her arm
briefly. "You're doing fine. Nothing's going to happen. I don't think he's in the audience, and I don't
think he's going to call, but it's a great show. And
we're really going to get them stirred up with the
next segment."

Trish had put together a dynamite show that con-
sisted of their most outrageous guests from the past
two years—mothers who had stolen their daughters'
husbands, men who had left their wives for other
men, the woman who had claimed to have found a
condom in an apple tart and had cost a fast-food
company millions of dollars in lost revenues before
she was proven to be a hoaxster—these and other
ghosts of the past stepped in front of the cameras

to put a new slant on their stories: confessing or denying remorse, being analyzed by the psychiatrist, and grilled by an enthusiastic audience, the guests played up their second fifteen minutes of fame for all it was worth. And as, one by one, they recapped their bizarre stories and the motives behind them, Dan was struck by two things: First, that no one person should know as many disturbed people as he did; and second, that he had never seen so little genuine shame demonstrated by a group that had so very much to be ashamed of.

The show was so fast-paced and volatile that Dan sometimes forgot, for long minutes at a time, what its purpose was. People cried. People yelled at each other. He felt like a line sprinter as he rushed back and forth between the rows with a microphone so that indignant audience members could grab their own thirty seconds on camera. At the half-hour break he managed to get close to Jess again.

Her eyes were dark with stress, and she looked as dazed by all this as Dan felt. He said. "We are in one weird business, you know that?"

She turned her face to the stroke of Gertrude's makeup brush. "You just noticed?"

He said, "Aside from the usual . . ."

And she finished for him, "Nothing." She let Gertrude fluff her hair with two strokes of a brush, then turned back to him. Her expression was a little rueful. "You were right. Nothing's going to happen. This was a waste of time. I suppose I should be grateful, but . . ."

"Yeah, I know." He was disappointed, too, and frustrated, though perhaps for slightly different reasons than she. If anything had happened, anything at all, while she was in front of the camera, at least his questions would have been answered. Jess would have been eliminated as a suspect in his mind and in Candler's . . . But the fact that nothing had happened only made it worse.

He didn't believe Jess was behind her own stalking. He didn't. But the more he listened to what passed for normalcy in their own studio audience, the less ridiculous it seemed, and every once in a while another doubt would slip through.

The last fifteen minutes were devoted to the audience. The question was directed to them: Have you ever done anything you're ashamed of? Trish had prescreened some of the more interesting stories, and Jess and Dan were directed to them first. But not everyone was prescreened, and Jess had insisted they leave time for random members of the audience to stand up and speak, on the slim chance— and it was becoming very slim by now—that the stalker might actually want to see himself on camera.

Eight minutes before the end of taping, she got her wish.

He was an unpretentious-looking man in the third row from the back, left. Twenty-six or twenty-seven, wearing a sweatshirt and jeans, with a ponytail and a stubble of beard, there wasn't a great deal to set him apart from anyone else who walked through the doors to the studio. But when he spoke, it suddenly seemed obvious, more than obvious, that he never should have been allowed within a hundred yards of Jess, that he was the most suspicious-looking character who had ever come through those doors, that the meager security precautions they had taken were woefully inadequate, laughable.

He leaned into the microphone Dan held up to him and said, "This question is for Jess."

Jess, who was lining up the next speaker, separated from them by an aisle and six rows, looked around.

He said, "Have *you* ever done anything you're ashamed of?"

Time seemed to freeze in place. Jess's face went very still; Dan's heart stopped beating. In almost surrealistic contrast, activity spun at the edge of his vision—Trish on her feet in the sound booth, leaning forward anxiously as she barked instruction to the floor director, cameramen swinging around to focus, an undercover detective speaking rapidly into his radio, others shifting their positions subtly, moving toward them. Dan stared at Jess. Jess stared back.

After what seemed like several hours, she answered. Her voice was composed, her manner only a little stiffer than it had been moments before. She said, "I think that if there's one thing we have proven in the past hour, it's that we've all done things we're ashamed of. It's how we deal with those things that's important."

The young man leaned forward again and put his hand around the microphone, as though afraid Dan would pull it away. That was the last thing Dan intended to do. He was aware of his heart beating with hard hammer strokes, but otherwise his mind was, for those few short seconds, a perfect blank.

Looking straight at Jess from his hunched-over position, the speaker said, "But you've done something in particular, haven't you? Or at least someone thinks you have."

Dan thought, *What?* and with a kind of lurching freneticism his brain switched back on again. The show, the stalker, eight minutes to fill, Jess, a killer within his reach—or not. Nothing made sense, and not one concept stood out with more importance than the other, so it was the talk-show host in him that took over.

He said with one of his friendly, camera-wise glances at Jess, "I'm afraid you're going to have to be more specific than that. If Jess is like the rest of us, she has a list."

He said, "I could, but I don't think you want me to be on national TV."

Dan thought, *Jesus, who is this guy? How did he get in here?* And he tried to picture the man on the other end of the microphone lying in wait for him in the dark and firing a bullet at his head; stealing through Jess's apartment and tucking a lighted cigarette and matches between the sofa cushions. He tried to . . . but he couldn't.

He glanced again at Jess. Her face looked pinched beneath the makeup. But she was in the talk-show mode, too. She said, "This show really isn't about me, sir." She turned to the woman at her microphone. "What would you like to say?"

Dan started to move away. The young man shouted, "What about this?" and reached for something in his back pocket.

Chaos erupted. A phalanx of plainclothes policemen surged forward; someone screamed; one of the officers cried, "Freeze! Police!" Dan instinctively stepped back and was surrounded by audience members jumping to their feet, crying out, shoving and tripping over each other. He expected the next sound he heard to be the thunder of gunfire, and it could have been, *should* have been.

Instead, one voice rose above the others: "What the hell is wrong with you people? My name is Beringer—from the *Post*! Are you insane?"

Dan thought, *Christ.* It was Styles all over again, only this time cameras were rolling—and at least two of them weren't theirs.

He started making his way through the crowd, keeping his tone calm as he said, "Take your seats, please. No cause for alarm. Just a misunderstanding. Take your seat ma'am." He tried to gently guide people back into their seats.

Of course only seconds had passed, but by the time he got a clear view of the action again, Candler was in charge. No weapons were visible. The indignant—and by this time, very frightened—young man was waving in his hand, not a gun or a knife, but a notebook. "All I wanted to do was ask a few questions! That's what you do here, isn't it? Ask questions?"

Candler said, "Yes sir, I understand. I wonder if we could talk about it outside?"

"What about the threatening fan mail? What about the fire in your apartment, the phone calls, the attempt on your brother's life? According to your secretary all the notes said . . ."

"Sir," repeated Candler firmly, "I'm afraid I must insist you come with me."

"I didn't do anything!"

"Yes, sir. Mind your step there."

Careful not to touch him or make any other

threatening move, Candler and two of the other policemen escorted the man toward the exit.

Dan looked around for Jess. She hadn't moved an
inch from her last position, microphone in hand,
eyes a dark smudge of shock. Trish was out of the
booth, moving quickly toward her. Security guards
were trying to calm people down. The alarm on the
door buzzed raucously as Candler opened it, followed by news crews with their handheld cameras.
The "taping" light blinked.

Dan blotted the dampness from his face with the
back of his hand. He couldn't find his microphone.

Then Jess spoke up. With the aid of a sound boost
her voice sounded clear and calm over the confusion of the crowd. "Ladies and gentleman?" She allowed her Southern accent to show. "Ladies and
gentlemen, please? Could we all settle down?"

Gradually, the attention turned to her. Dan simply stared.

She said, "I apologize. As you see, we've had some
security problems here on the set, but nothing that
should alarm you."

She smiled. It was the most incredible thing Dan
had ever seen.

"Now if everyone's okay, we still have a few more
minutes of taping left, and I want to make sure
everyone gets a chance to speak. Shall we take
our seats?"

And they did.

Chapter 26

"The word from the police is that his story checks out," Trish told them as they walked toward their offices. They kept a tight group and a fast pace—Jess, Dan, Trish, and two Security guards—with reporters a few steps behind, being "managed" by a rep from the P.R. department. "Apparently, they didn't do as good a job as we'd thought of keeping the shame angle under wraps. One of the firefighters let it slip about what was written on Jess's door the night of the fire, and he picked up a few other tidbits here and there." She cast Jess a meaningful look. "That secretary of yours could use a few words on discretion, Jess. Anyway, they say they'll continue to watch him, but chances are there's nothing to worry about."

"Where's Candler?" demanded Dan. "Why doesn't he tell us this himself?"

"What am I, everybody's keeper? I've got enough on my plate with damage control."

She was tense, excited; her steps were fast and her words clipped, but there was a greedy gleam in her eyes. She kept patting her pockets for cigarettes, even though she knew better than to light up in the hall. She thrived on this, and why shouldn't she?

This kind of high-stakes drama was their daily bread.

She went on, "Gloria from P.R. will send down an official statement about the incident during the taping. That's your position—your *only* position on the whole situation until you hear differently. The *Hard Copy* people are really going to love this, and they've got footage. I'll talk to them first and try to get them to give us a favorable slant—Jess as the victim instead of a panic-stricken prima donna who goes around accusing innocent reporters and writers of stalking her . . . Jesus, what a mess. And are we all going to look pretty on the news tonight?"

Dan said, "Jess, are you all right?"

She glanced across Trish as though she did not, for a moment, even know who he was. Then she gave a brief shake of her head. "No, I'm a wreck. I can't even think straight. God knows what I'm going to say at those interviews."

"Don't even think of canceling," Trish warned.

Jess smiled thinly. "Don't worry. I know this is the chance of a lifetime."

They reached the bullpen, and Trish turned toward the elevator. "Don't talk to anyone who hasn't been approved through P.R.," she said, stabbing the button.

Jess and Dan veered off toward their offices. Dan said, without looking at her, "You weren't surprised."

"What?"

"That it wasn't him. That it was just a reporter." Now he made himself look at her.

She returned his gaze with eyes that were weary and worn, and broke his heart. "Oh Dan," she said tiredly, "nothing surprises me anymore. Nothing at all."

He knew he should say something to her, but he didn't know what.

She went into her office, followed closely by her secretary with a handful of message slips. Dan watched until she went behind her desk and sat down, and he couldn't see her face anymore.

Then he went to his own office and opened a file.

Sylvia's words buzzed around Jess's head like so many hornets gathering to swarm. She dutifully turned over one message slip after another, but none of them made sense. It was an effort to keep her head from sagging onto the desk. How was she ever going to make those interviews?

She had thought it would be over today. She really had.

She said, "Sylvia, have you been talking to reporters about what has been going on in this office?"

From the way Sylvia stared, Jess knew she had cut the other woman off in midsentence. She didn't care.

Sylvia's complexion pinkened. "Well, no. I mean, not exactly—"

"Didn't the police specifically warn you not to say anything about the contents of the notes I'd received?"

"Well, yes, but when the man asked me a direct question, just to say yes or no—"

Jess's phone rang. Sylvia sprang forward quickly to answer it, but Jess held up a staying hand and lifted the receiver herself. It was her intercom line.

"Jess Cray."

A moment's silence, then the voice—hoarse and whispery. "I'm ashamed of you, Jess," it said, "for trying to trick me."

Jess felt all the heat leave her upper body. She tightened her grip on the receiver, afraid that if she did not, she would drop it.

She said, speaking each word with care, "I expected to see you today."

Sylvia was staring at her, Jess could feel it. Jess didn't look back, she didn't move. She concentrated every ounce of her energy on the voice that returned to her over the phone.

"You did." A sound, low and breathy, like a laugh. "I was there."

"Where?" She could barely make her voice whisper. "Where were you?"

"Do you want to know me, Jess?" The voice was harsh now, angry. "You want to meet me? I think it's time. Come to the roof of your building. I'll be there in ten minutes."

Jess listened to the dial tone for five full seconds before she could make herself replace the receiver. Her intercom line. The roof. *He was in the building.*

Suddenly galvanized into action, she looked up at Sylvia. "Is Lieutenant Candler still in the building?"

Sylvia's eyes were wide. "I think so—I saw him in the hall just before you came in. Was that—"

Jess jerked open her desk drawer and began to rummage through it. "Find him," she demanded hoarsely. "Now."

Dan stared at the page of poorly typed biographical statistics and tried to make sense of what he was reading. He flipped to the front pages again;

they were exactly the same as the pages Styles had shown to Jess. He had assumed Glanbury had merely obtained a copy and was trying to peddle them for whatever could be made of them, but there was more. Styles's notes on Jess were only the first part of Glanbury's file. The second part concerned Candler.

There were a great many clippings on the Silk Scarf case, a rough chronology of Candler's career with the police department, some notes on some of his previous cases. Until then, Dan had been merely skimming, more annoyed than puzzled. That was when he spotted something odd.

Newbury High, Jackson, Mississippi. Someone had underlined it—probably Glanbury—along with the year. Just to make sure, Dan flipped back to the biographical data Styles had compiled on Jess. There were two underlinings under Jess's educational history. The first was Newbury High, Jackson, Mississippi.

Jess and Candler had gone to high school together.

The second underlining on Jess's bio was college. Dan had skipped over it the first time, assuming it had something to do with the falsified job application. He flipped to the back of the file, looking for a corresponding underlining on Candler's bio. He found it, not under education, but under early job experience.

Lyle Candler had worked in Security at the University of Georgia during Jess's junior year there.

Coincidence? Not likely. But if Jess did know him, why had she lied? What in the hell was going on here?

*   *   *

"Got him." Sylvia held up the telephone receiver, and Jess snatched it from her.

"Lieutenant Candler." Her voice was excited and breathless. "He just called. He's in the building. It worked, damn it, I knew it would! He wants to meet me. He's going to be on the roof in ten minutes."

"Jess, listen to me. Under no circumstances—do you hear me—*no circumstances* are you to go up there."

"I'm not going alone. You're going to be there, along with every officer you can find."

"You leave it to us. If he's up there, we'll get him. You stay where you are."

"You won't have a chance to get him if I'm not there! Damn it, he was in the audience today, just as I said he would be, and did you see him? Did you get him then? No." She shook her head forcefully, then had to push back the strands of hair that caught on her face. "We're doing it his way."

"Don't you see that—"

"Look," she said, trying to inject a note of reason to her voice, "he won't hurt me. You said yourself he's trying to protect me. He said ten minutes and that was five minutes ago."

"Jess, just listen to me—"

"You can't stop me. But if you do what I say, you may be able to stop him."

She hung up the phone.

Sylvia looked at her, eyes wide with horror. "Jess, you're not going to—"

"Don't say a word."

She took a step toward the elevator, then abruptly turned back and went into her office.

Sylvia cried after her, "But you have an interview in thirty minutes! What am I going to tell—"

Jess emerged from her office with her purse over her shoulder, holding it close to her body as she took the few running steps toward the elevator.

Sylvia let her unfinished sentence fall into empty air, looking after her in dismay.

Dan snatched up the telephone on the second buzz. "Bethany, I told you no calls."

"I know, and I'm sorry. But it's Mrs. Cray and she says it's urgent."

"Jess?" His finger was poised over the connect button.

"No, her mother."

"Well, for God's sake, transfer her to Jess."

Bethany sounded a little impatient. "She said she's tried that. I even tried that, and Jess isn't at her desk."

Dan frowned. "She's not?"

"The woman asked to speak with you."

Dan's frown grew deeper with preoccupation as he glanced back at the array of papers spread over his desk—the contents of the Glanbury file. "Yeah, okay, I'll talk to her. And keep trying Jess, will you? Ask her to come to my office."

He pushed the connect button. "Mrs. Cray, it's Dan Webber. How are you doing?"

"Not so blessed well, if you want to know the truth. Where is my daughter? Is she all right? What is this I hear about some maniac burning down her house, and aren't you supposed to be shot? But I see you both every day on television, and you look okay to me—except that one day last week when you weren't on—why are the news people saying such things? Where is Jess and why doesn't she ever answer her phone?"

Dan felt a stab of remorse and then a surge of resentment. She was Jess's mother, and she was worried. He had talked to his own mother every day, since the shooting. Why did he have to deal with this, too?

And then he was ashamed of himself for feeling that way. He knew why.

He said gently, "First of all, Mrs. Cray, those are news magazines you've been watching, and sometimes they make things sound worse than they are, just to get people to watch."

"Do you think I don't know that, young man?" she returned tartly. "Don't I have a daughter who's a television star?"

Dan smiled in spite of himself. "Yes ma'am."

"So she's all right? Why won't she return my calls? And her phone at home has been out of order for almost a week."

Dan said carefully, "We have had some trouble here, but it's all part of being a celebrity. It's nothing we can't handle."

"Did they burn down her house or not?"

"No." It was impossible to put anything past her. "There was a small fire, and Jess had to move out for a while, but no one was hurt."

"And what about you? Was it all lies about you being shot trying to protect her?"

"Barely a nick," Dan assured her.

"Good Lord in heaven, what kind of place do you people live in? First that horrible business out at the home . . ."

It took Dan a moment to realize she was referring to Evan.

"And now this. Is everybody up there crazy? Don't you know anything but shooting and killing?"

"Mrs. Cray," Dan said abruptly, "how did Even become brain-damaged?"

The silence that followed was as sharp as a knife's edge, and Dan winced at the bite of it. He wished he could retract the question and phrase it more tactfully, but the damage was done now. He was surprised that she responded at all.

"Why do you ask?" The voice was very cold.

"Please," he said, "it's important."

The silence went on, and in it Dan could hear his heartbeat. He didn't dare to breathe until she began to speak.

And she told him.

The elevator stopped at the tenth floor. From there a staircase with a fire door led to the roof. There were offices on the tenth floor, but they were not visible from the small lobby into which the elevator opened. The entire floor appeared to be deserted.

For the first time since the phone call, the adrenaline rush faded enough for Jess to feel fear. The hall was so quiet, so empty. Where was Candler? Why weren't there officers everywhere?

Why was everything so quiet?

Jess moved toward the door that led to the staircase, her steps making not a sound on the carpeted floor. Maybe Candler hadn't arrived yet. Maybe she was all alone here. Maybe she should wait.

But then she realized that the last thing any of

them wanted was a large, noisy police presence. Candler wouldn't be obvious. He was probably hiding on the roof, waiting to take the stalker as soon as he made himself known.

She shouldn't have come. This was insane. But what else could she do? How much longer could she go on like this?

No longer, she decided. Not one minute longer. Whatever happened . . . at least it would be over.

The fire door opened with a metallic scrape and closed behind her with a clang. The sound reminded her of that terrifying night she had been trapped on the staircase. The difference was that time she had been running away. This time she was moving toward the danger, deliberately and with her eyes wide open.

Gripping the handrail tightly, she ascended the steps one at a time.

He won't hurt me, she kept telling herself. *He won't.* But she knew in her heart that was a fallacy invented by men to comfort her. If Candler was right, and this maniac was under some misguided impression he was protecting her, that mission was over now. She had tried to expose him, she had brought their secret out for all the world to see, and he would be angry. She was a fallen idol now. He had said he was ashamed of her.

He could be setting her up for anything.

At the top of the staircase she paused with her hand on the door bar. Suddenly, she knew, quite clearly, that this was stupidity. A maniac was waiting on the other side of the door. He had already killed two people and maybe more. He could have a gun or a knife. He could grab her as soon as she opened the door and push her off the roof. Or he could rape her, torture her, punish her for the imaginary crimes she had committed. This was insane. She couldn't do this.

Where was Candler?

And suddenly it occurred to Jess that she could spend her entire life poised at the top of that staircase with her hand on the door, afraid to go forward, afraid to go back. Afraid.

It could be over, she thought. *Just let it be over.* Whatever was on the other side of that door, she could deal with it. But not knowing would kill her.

With a clatter that sounded like an explosion, she pushed open the door and stepped out onto the roof.

The sun was bright, reflecting off the white gravel surface with a force that was momentarily blinding. Jess blinked several times and rubbed her arms against the cool breeze that constantly undercut the reflected heat from the sun.

Jess had never been up here before. She had expected a solid, flat surface, and was somewhat confused by the jutting walls and half walls that intersected at odd angles and created deep pools of shadow where there should have been none. The noise, too, was unsettling. Traffic noise and wind were funneled upward by the surrounding buildings, creating an unsettling sensory deprivation that made her feel isolated and defenseless.

Swallowing hard on a dry throat, Jess placed her hand inside her purse and took a cautious step away from the door—but not so far that she couldn't run back to the staircase for safety if she had to. The gravel crunched under feet. When she glanced

down, she noticed the roof was littered with cigarette butts. She stared.

"So, Jess." The voice came from behind her. "I
don't know about you, but I'm ready for this to be
over."

Jess turned around slowly. A cold, sick certainty
rose from the pit of her stomach as she lifted her
eyes to the speaker.

"Trish," she said.

Chapter 27

Dan picked up a pencil and began to doodle absently, gazing at the papers on his desk without seeing them as he spoke into the receiver. "So," he said, "Evan's condition is the result of a birth defect." Tension closed at the back of his neck, twisting down through his shoulders and back. Nothing made sense. Nothing.

The voice on the other end of the line sounded weary and old. "It's my fault, I guess. But we didn't know then what they know today about smoking and nutrition and whatnot. Not that I ever smoked, not once in my life, or drank either, but I took medicines, you know, for morning sickness and headaches, and when a doctor gives you a prescription you just take it, don't you?" She sighed. "I know it's my fault. But we just didn't know back then. There weren't any talk shows, you know. We didn't know."

The strokes the pencil made became bolder and blacker, underlining one word over and over again. "Mrs. Cray," he said slowly, "when Jess was in high school . . . I don't suppose you ever recall her mentioning a boy by the name of Lyle Candler."

Jess's mother was thoughtful for a time. "No, I

can't say that I do. And I remember every detail
about Jess's growing-up, you can believe that, probably more than she does. I have a whole scrapbook
on her, everything she ever did since she started to
walk, all the pageants she won, and it's so thick I
have to tie it with a string. She was our special
girl, so good at everything, so perfect—like God was
saying he didn't hold it against us too much for
Evan, you know."

Dan barely repressed a sigh. "Yes, ma'am, I know.
Listen, Mrs. Cray, thank you for talking to me about
Evan. I know Jess will be sorry she missed your
call, but she wouldn't want you to worry. Everything
is—"

"Wait a minute. I knew that name sounded
familiar."

Dan's attention quickened.

"Candler. Yes, I remember now. It happened the
year Jess was first runner-up in the Miss Newbury
High contest. She should have won. She had this
most beautiful pink taffeta dress, I remember, with
rosettes at the back—"

An icicle stabbed through Dan's chest.

"Of course she won the next year, but it really
wasn't the same. And I never will forget how disappointed she was, looking like a fairy princess in her
pink dress, smiling so pretty . . ."

Dan said hoarsely, "What happened? What happened that year?"

"Oh. Well, this family named Candler—not really
a family, just a mother and her children, trailer park
trash, you know—well, it made all the papers. It
was toward the end of the school year, I do remember that, and the older boy *did* go to Newbury, I

remember because it was really scary, to think of Jess associating with people like that. But she didn't know him, I don't think he was even in her class."

Dan demanded, as calmly as possible, "Was the boy's name Lyle?"

"It could have been. I remember it was something strange, not Jack or Will or Tom. Yes, it could have been Lyle."

Dan said, with as much restraint as possible, "Please, Mrs. Cray—*what happened?*"

Trish tossed away the cigarette butt and ground it under her heel. "So you found my hideout," she said. "I just had to get away from the craziness, even if it was only for a minute." She glanced around ruefully. "Wish I'd stashed a fifth of vodka up here."

Jess just stared.

Trish walked toward her. Jess's fingers tightened on the handle of the revolver inside her purse, but she could make no other muscle move, not even her legs, to back away.

Trish said, "So what's up?"

Jess said nothing. She couldn't even swallow.

Trish frowned in the sunlight. "You were looking for me, right? So here I am. What's wrong?"

As if from a distance, Jess heard her own voice. "Didn't you . . . call me?"

The frown deepened. "No. I left a message I'd meet you on the set for the interview, but there's no hurry. Did that secretary of yours screw it up again? Honestly Jess, the things you put up with."

For one slow, wild moment sky and rooftop tilted and turned. Jess extended a hand backward to steady herself against the wall, and then Trish was saying sharply, "Are you all right? What's wrong with you?"

Jess drew a deep unsteady breath. "Yes. I mean, nothing. Nothing's wrong. You . . . didn't call me."

"I said no, didn't I? Listen, you look rough. I know it's been a hell of a morning, but the worst is over. Come on, I'll buy you a cup of coffee. Who knows, I might even find a stash of vodka somewhere." She opened the door, waiting for Jess.

Jess shook her head. She was afraid if she moved, even one step, her legs would buckle under her.

"No, I um . . ." She cleared her throat. "I just need to be alone for a while. I'll stay."

Concern deepened the lines between Trish's brows. "You're sure? 'Cause I don't like leaving you."

Jess nodded. She even managed a tight smile.

"You won't forget the interview?"

"I'll be down in fifteen minutes." Her voice sounded almost normal. "I . . . just need some air."

Trish mumbled, "Well, I guess I can understand that." She glanced at her watch. "Look, I've got to get back to the office. Fifteen minutes, okay?"

Jess nodded, and the door clanged shut behind Trish. She was alone.

Jess gazed at the litter of cigarette butts across the gravel roof, and she didn't know whether to laugh or cry. Smoking. That's what Trish was doing here. That's what *everyone* did here. They came to the roof to smoke.

She felt foolish and relieved and disappointed and ridiculous. Another wild-goose chase. If ever the stalker had been here, he was gone now. If ever he had intended to meet her here, he wouldn't come now. Trish had scared him off—Trish or some other smoker.

A little shakily, Jess made her way over to the knee-high wall that surrounded the roof and sat down. There was still a chance that Candler could apprehend the stalker on his way to the roof, but it was unlikely. How would he even recognize him? How would any of them ever know who it was now?

Damn you, Trish, Jess thought. *So close* . . .

From the deep shadows formed by two intersecting walls, a voice spoke, patient and amused. "You didn't really think it was her, did you?"

Jess's mother said, with just a tinge of exasperation, "Well, that's what I'm *trying* to tell you, aren't I? What happened was that this trashy mother—I never did know if she was divorced or just never married, you know—she was arrested!"

Dan said sharply, "Lyle Candler's mother was arrested?"

"For murdering her own baby boy," declared the voice on the other end triumphantly. "Smothered the poor little thing in its crib. I remember it clear as day—why, that kind of thing just didn't happen back then, not like it does today. And the worst part—the absolute worst part—was when they came to take her away, they found the other boy, the teenager you call Lyle, they found him tied up in a closet with a sign around his neck that said—"

"Shame," Dan whispered.

A startled silence. "Why, yes. How did you know?"

But Dan didn't hear her. He was staring at the

paper before him and the one word on Jess's bio that he had underlined over and over.

Cheerleader.

Jess started to rise, her heart thundering, then she sank back down as she recognized the figure that detached itself from the shadows and moved toward her.

"I don't know what to think anymore," she said tiredly, "who to trust, what to believe . . . and maybe that's the most important thing this maniac has taken from me. My judgment."

He came into the light, moving with slow, easy steps across the roof toward her. "Come on, Jess," he said gently, "it's time to stop playing the game. You know who the stalker is. We both do."

He stood before her, so close that his shadow completely engulfed her, and Jess had to tilt her head back at an uncomfortable angle to look at him. For a moment his face was lost in the sun.

"What?" she asked. Her heart speeded a little. "What are you talking about?"

"Jess," he said sadly, shaking his head. "I'm ashamed of you."

Dan slammed open the door of Jess's office, sweeping his gaze around it wildly, even though he had already determined from the outside that it was empty. "Where is she?" he demanded of her secretary, turning so quickly that he almost knocked her down. "Tell me!"

"Mr. Webber, I'm so glad you're here!" Sylvia gasped. "I didn't know what to do, who to call! She told me not to say anything—"

Dan grabbed her shoulders. "Where is she?" His voice was loud enough to make heads turn. He didn't care. "Candler didn't take her, did he? She didn't go with him?"

Big-eyed, Sylvia shook her head. "She . . . she got a phone call. I think from, you know, him, the guy who . . . the guy. And she made me call Candler, and she said something about meeting him on the roof . . . I didn't know, I thought it was all right, she was with the police—how could I stop her? Who was I supposed to call?"

Dan released her with a snap. His face went cold; everything inside him drained cold but already he was running toward the door. "Call the police!" he shouted over his shoulder harshly, "Get them to the roof, now!"

Jess asked hoarsely, "What did you say?"

Candler's smile was thin and humorless. "Come on, Jess, what more do you want from me? I've given you every chance. I've done everything but spell it out for you."

Her throat felt dry; it was hard to speak. "I . . . don't understand."

"Think back. Newbury High, 1981, the year you should have won the Miss Newbury High Pageant. You wore your pink dress for the contest. I was there, Jess."

She stared at him. "You . . . I went to school with you?"

His smile remained quiet and pleasant, his tone conversational. "You don't remember, do you?"

"I don't understand." Her neck hurt from bending backward to look up at him. Her mind felt slow and ponderous, laboring to put the pieces together, and still it didn't make sense. "All this time—why didn't you say anything?"

His expression softened, grew reminiscent. "You were a star even then. There's no reason you should remember me. No reason you should have even noticed me . . . but you did. I was what the counselor used to call from a troubled home. The fact is, my mother was a drunk. Did I tell you that? I didn't have any friends because I was too embarrassed to bring them home, never had the right clothes, and hell, I guess my personal grooming habits weren't all that great . . . little things like that are easy to forget when every day's a fight for survival. I was weird and dorky, two things you do not want to be in highschool. Of course, the other kids tormented me . . . everyone except you. One day you dropped a book, and I picked it up, and you actually smiled and said thank you. You were wearing this pink sweater and a short little pink wool skirt with big pleats. Real wool. You were the classiest thing I had ever seen, even back then, and you smiled at me. Crazy, huh? But you can't imagine what it meant to someone like me to actually be noticed by a girl like you. And afterward, whenever I'd see you in the hall, I'd smile and you never looked away, you always smiled back and said 'Hi.' I know it sound like nothing to you, but you made me feel like somebody for the first time in my life. I'll never forget you for that. But like I said, there's no reason you should remember."

Pain stabbed through Jess's neck. Something was wrong, terribly wrong. She felt nauseated. "But . .

the yearbooks. I looked, I would have recognized you . . ."

"I never had my pictures taken," he told her matter-of-factly. "I was absent a lot that year, and then there was the trouble and . . . well, I didn't exactly graduate from dear old Newbury."

A horrible, sickening picture was beginning to form. It actually made her head swim. Slowly, Jess got to her feet. Candler's eyes narrowed, but he didn't try to stop her.

She said, carefully, "Trouble?"

He seemed amused then. "God, you really don't remember, do you? I don't know whether to be insulted or relieved."

His expression grew distant again, vague and sober in memory. There was nothing threatening in his voice or posture, but even if there had been, Jess probably would not have run. It was a long and twisted trail whose end was in sight, and she would not have missed it, couldn't make herself miss it. She watched him and listened to him, mesmerized.

"Funny," he said, "the things we remember. The things we don't. Do you want to know something I remember, Jess? From high school again. I told you I was absent a lot. I may not have mentioned I was a skinny, clumsy kid, or maybe you gathered that. Anyway, I wasn't exactly the gym coach's favorite student. There was always a group of us—the goofs and homos, in other words, everybody who wasn't on some kind of team or another—who were in trouble. And when you're in trouble in gym class, you run laps. Hell, I should have been a long-distance runner, for all the laps I took. Anyway, there was this one day, here we were, five or six of us, loping around the track during fifth period, and the cheerleaders were practicing. Can you picture it? A bunch of dorky, skinny, pimply-faced kids in gym shorts and sweaty T-shirts that were too big, and the most beautiful girls in school all on the same field? And to make it worse, a bunch of football players were kind of hanging around the bleachers, catching you practice, throwing catcalls at us.

"It had been raining earlier in the day, and there were puddles on the track. So here I am, skinny legs pumping, sweat running into my eyes, just sure as hell everybody on that field is watching me, pretty girls, football players, everybody—and in another minute, everybody was. I slipped on a puddle and took a header into the mud.

"You never heard such laughter. The football players, sure. The other guys on the track—laughing at somebody else made them feel they weren't so laughable, I guess. And the cheerleaders . . . well. I guess I did look pretty funny. I picked myself up and tried to get the mud off my glasses and out of my mouth, and when I looked up, there you were in your short little red-and-blue cheerleader's skirt, big yellow pom-poms in your hands, laughing with all the rest. The only person who ever made me feel I was worth anything . . . laughing at me. I couldn't believe it. No, the worst was, I didn't blame you. I knew that later, after you thought about it, you'd be ashamed of yourself."

Jess whispered, "Oh God." And finally she understood. Finally, she believed it. "Oh dear God."

His expression was pained and sympathetic. "I am disappointed. I expected more of you. I'll bet you don't remember me from college either. I used to

smile at you every time you came through the gate—
to kind of repay the favor, you know, for when you
used to smile at me back in high school."

The wind that brushed through her hair seemed
suddenly icy and it made her shiver. Below her, just
against her back, toy cars scurried and toy traffic
lights changed and nothing protected her from the
street except a knee-high concrete wall. She
couldn't think. She tried to make sense of it, but
she couldn't think.

Jess said, "But . . . you couldn't have been in Athens at the same time I was at UGA. Why would you
have been?"

And he simply smiled. "I thought you needed protecting. Turns out I was right, doesn't it?"

"What do you mean?"

"That fellow you were with. That Brett. He didn't
deserve you, he didn't even know what he had. And
then when he threw you out, when he made you a
laughingstock . . . well, he deserved what he got,
didn't he?"

Jess felt her face go cold as the blood drained out
of it. "My God," she whispered. He had killed Brett.
He had killed him. All those years ago . . .

"You've followed me since high school?" she said
hoarsely. "Everything I've done, everywhere I've
been . . ."

"Of course not." His tone was impatient. "I have
a life. I've done pretty well for myself, too, haven't
I? Kind of ironic, isn't it, that after all those years
I'd finally do something big enough to impress you
. . . and you'd end up needing me?"

Jess's purse felt heavy against her hip. The sun
burned her head, causing prickles of perspiration to

gather on her neck, but her limbs were cold. She tried not to glance down.

She swallowed hard, trying to think, just *think* . . .

She said, "The Silk Scarf killings . . ."

He shrugged. "Part of my job."

"That's what brought us together."

"But that's not what kept us together, was it?"

"No." She licked her lips, taking a step, a small one, sideways, and away from the wall. "It was the notes, the stalker."

And he smiled. "Ingenious. Of course, you were never in any danger. The only people who were ever hurt were those who tried to hurt or humiliate you."

"Yes. You said that . . . before." Another step. He didn't try to stop her. "Roger Dill, all those years ago, who stood me up for the prom . . ." *Oh God,* she thought, *don't let it be true, how can this be true?*

"He didn't really stand you up," Candler pointed out. "He couldn't help it if he was hurt. But it felt just like being stood up, didn't it. It was just as embarrassing. And he didn't think how much *you* might be hurt."

"And Evan . . ."

"He was such a blight on your life. He embarrassed you, embarrassed your whole family. I would have taken care of him for you years ago if only I'd known."

"That nurse. You killed her."

He shrugged lightly, almost imperceptibly. "She was nothing. A complication. But she did stop me from helping you. She deserved to die."

Jess was in the clear now, away from the wall. The door to the stairway was in sight, and she knew if she did not bolt now, she would never get the courage to do it, she would never escape.

She took one running step, and suddenly the door crashed open. Jess cried out involuntarily, and Candler whirled, grabbing her, drawing her back against him with his arm across her throat, holding her like a shield. Dan burst through the door, his hair tousled and his breathing ragged, as though he had run all the way. Jess cried desperately, "Dan, run! It's him, it was Candler all the time! Run!"

But it was too late. Candler had his service revolver out and pointed at Dan, who took in the entire situation with a single glance. He said, breathing hard, "I know."

"Well, well." Candler's voice was stiff now, edged with steel beneath the amusement. "The cavalry. I hope you're not expecting reinforcements because I sent all my men back to the station. They wouldn't believe you anyway."

Dan said, "No, I guess they wouldn't." He was controlling his breathing with an effort, his fists clenched at his sides and the muscles of his neck straining with the attempt to hold his position. "You've got them convinced Jess is making the whole thing up, that *she's* the stalker. Just as you almost convinced me."

Jess's eyes flew to him in horror and disbelief. Dan deliberately did not meet her gaze.

"So what do you have planned for her now?" he went on. "A dramatic plunge off the roof to atone for her sins? Maybe a plaintive suicide note? And no one left but you to solve an otherwise unsolvable case. How else could it end, really?"

Candler's arm was hard under her chin, threatening to cut off her breath. Jess's instinct was to claw at it with both hands, but she deliberately did not. She kept her hands close to her purse, one hand steadying the strap, the other resting on the flap.

Candler said, "Not bad, Webber. I always did think you had potential."

Dan said, "Did you tell her the part about how you killed your own baby brother yet? It was you, wasn't it, Candler? Your mother took the rap for you and went to prison, but it was you all the time."

The muscles in Candler's forearm tightened. Jess had to part her lips to breathe.

He said, "She was a worthless bitch. She didn't deserve to have children. She died in prison. I was glad."

Dan said, his tone gentling, "It's pretty impressive, what you managed to accomplish with the start you had. What happened to you after they arrested your mother?"

For a moment the pressure against Jess's throat relaxed. She could breathe.

Candler said. "The county home. It wasn't so bad. I got my high school diploma. And I got to stay in town, keeping up with things. I read about Jess in the paper, always something about Jess. She won some big pageant; she got a scholarship to the University of Georgia. I decided law enforcement was the career for me. I was good at taking care of things. So I went to Georgia, got a job at the university working Security, went to school at night. So you see, Jess . . ." He bent his head toward her. His breath smelled of wintergreen. "I really owe all that I am to you."

Jess looked at Dan, pleading. His face was pale

and beaded with sweat, but his eyes were calm, steady. She could be calm. She could be strong.

She said with an effort to make her words intelligible, "But that reporter . . . you killed him. You said . . . the message on my machine was 'This one's for you.' Why did you do that?"

Candler replied simply, "He dragged out all your secrets for the world to see. He deserved to die, so I shot him."

Dan said harshly, "Don't be so goddamned pompous, Candler. The least you can do is tell her the truth. You killed Glanbury because he had the file— Jeremy Styles's file. He knew about Jess, and he knew about you. You killed him, and you stole his file, but what you didn't know was that he had made copies. And those copies are with every major news organization in this city."

Candler's arm suddenly dug into Jess's throat. She gasped with pain and fear. He said, "You lying son of a bitch. I ought to shoot you now."

"And Jeremy Styles," Dan went on, loud and steady. "You must have gone back and read his book. You thought he had put it together, that he knew it was you who was stalking Jess. But all he knew was that it was the Silk Scarf killer. He always maintained you had arrested the wrong man. He just didn't know *how* wrong."

He looked like an oak in the wind, eyes steady, hair tossed, muscles tense. Jess loved him then, with all her heart.

Candler said, "You shouldn't have kept that appointment, Webber. You said you wouldn't. I hadn't planned on killing you, not then, but you almost forced me to. That would have been messy."

Jess's hand crept slowly under the flap of her purse, fingers stretching, straining. "The fire," she said. It was hard to get the air to form the words; her voice was scratchy and soft. "It was never meant for me at all. It was meant to hurt Dan. But why? What did he do?"

Once again, for just an instant, the pressure on her throat eased. "Why don't *you* tell *me*? He had threatened to leave the show, hadn't he, without even telling you? That had to be humiliating. And he was sleeping with you, all the time planning to ruin you personally and professionally. He was using you. He deserved to die."

"But . . . I was there. The fire could have killed me, too."

He merely smiled. "Perhaps you shouldn't have been in bed with him, now should you?"

Jess shivered. Insane, she thought hopelessly. He's completely insane.

Dan said quietly, "It was you, wasn't it? You were the Silk Scarf killer."

Candler said, "We got the right guy. He did the first two. But those girls I interviewed, the cheerleaders . . . they deserved to die. They weren't nearly as nice as you, Jess. So I killed them."

Jess felt sick.

Dan said, "Don't do this, Candler. Don't destroy the last thing you love."

And Candler replied simply, "I have to, don't you see that? I have to."

Jess held Dan's gaze, focused on him, tried to take strength from him. Dan's eyes were strong and blue, as blue as an autumn sky. She could die looking at those eyes . . . but she didn't want to die.

Her fingers crept inside her purse. She managed to say, almost steadily, "What have you done that you're ashamed of, Lyle?"

Lyle. It was the first time she had called him that. She knew it; he knew it. The pressure against her throat almost disappeared. Jess saw relief, cautious and guarded, flicker across Dan's eyes.

Candler said, "Me? My whole life is a litany of shame. Remember the drunk mother? She was real big on shame. As though having her for a mother wasn't enough to be ashamed of. Her idea of discipline was to lock a kid in a closet with a sign around his neck. It didn't matter whether what he did was his fault or not. Didn't matter that he was only a kid." And he looked at her. "Can you imagine how that must have felt, Jess? Can you?"

"No," she whispered. "I can't."

Jess thought, *He's going to kill me.*

She thrust her hand into her purse, throwing her weight sideways to break Candler's grip. She saw horror streak across Dan's face; he shouted, "Jess!" and lunged for her.

Gunfire exploded. Dan slammed into Jess, throwing her against the wall. Candler lurched with her, grabbing for her. Jess saw his arm extended for her, alarm on his face, and she realized he thought she was going to fall. She screamed and flung out an arm for him, but the momentum of his weight carried him past her.

Dan caught her against him, and Jess buried her face in his chest as Candler went over the wall.

Chapter 28

"I'm Barbara Harvey and we're live outside the WSBN studios where a police officer has apparently fallen to his death from the roof of this building only moments ago. The officer has now been identified as Lieutenant Lyle Candler of the Major Crimes Division of the Philadelphia Police Department. Few details are available at this time, but we do know that Lieutenant Candler was in charge of the Jessamine Cray stalking case at the time of his death."

Jess turned away from the television on the desk and walked to the door of the Security office, looking through the small window into the lobby. It was chaos outside. The police had cordoned off the lobby, but reporters were pressing the barrier; cameramen jostled for position and lights glared. Office workers huddled curiously near the elevators, and uniformed policemen strode quickly back and forth, ignoring the questions newspeople shouted at them. Red and blue lights pulsed silently in the street in front of the building.

"—is that correct, Ms. Cray?"

Jess turned around slowly, focusing on one of the two detectives who was interviewing them. She had given a statement already, though she couldn't remember what she had said. They had taken Dan to another room to question him separately; now they had brought them together in the Security office and were asking the same questions over again. Dan sat in a folding metal chair, looking rumpled and exhausted. Every now and then he would cast a concerned glance in her direction. One detective perched on the desk across from him, and another, younger one, moved around the room, examining objects and putting them down again, adjusting the volume on the television set, watching Jess.

Jess asked, "It wasn't my gun? That's not what killed him?"

They had taken her gun earlier, and her purse. The purse had a ragged hole burned through the side from the force of the bullet, but she did not know whether or not the bullet had struck a target.

The craggy face of the detective who sat on the edge of the desk hardened briefly and grew unreadable. Then he said, "There were no bullet wounds in the body, no."

Jess turned back to the little window, wondering if the emotion she felt was relief and, if so, whether she had any right to feel it.

The younger detective said, "Miss Cray, we need your attention, please. I know this is trying for you, but you and Mr. Webber were the only people on that roof, and—"

"And you're asking us to believe some cock-and-bull story about one of the best officers in the department—" put in the craggy-faced one.

"And," the younger one said in a deliberately smooth tone, "we need you to corroborate—or correct, if necessary—Mr. Webber's story. Now we know that whatever actually happened up there, it must have been a high-tension situation, and there are going to be some details that are a little fuzzy in your head. Things you thought you heard that didn't really—"

"Like this shit about the Silk Scarf case," interrupted the other, harshly. "What the hell is that all about? What kind of twisted—"

"I told you," Dan said wearily, "he admitted it all. That was why he tried to kill Styles—Styles's book was about a copy-cat killer, and that's exactly what Candler was. Hell, maybe he's done similar things before—committed a crime, then solved it, to build his career. I don't know. All I know is that when Styles started bragging that the identity of the stalker would be clear to anyone who read his book, Candler panicked. The only thing that puzzled me was why he let Styles live that long but now I think Candler must not have read his book. He didn't know. The thing is, it was the cheerleader angle that gave him away, and he never guessed that. Styles put it together right away—the Silk Scarf killer and Jess's stalker were the same person."

"Hmm." The detective sounded impatient and skeptical. "Interesting theory, Mr. Webber but—"

"But you know if you weren't such a pair of high-profile personalities we'd be having the conversation down at the station, and we wouldn't be doing it so nicely either. As a matter of fact, it may end up there yet so—"

Jess said, "I have it on tape."

She turned around, unfastening the Art Deco brooch from her lapel. Comprehension slowly dawned on Dan's face as she pushed the spring clasp on the back and removed the microcassette. But the detective was impatient when she handed it to him.

"What the hell is this?" he demanded.

"It's a tape recording of everything that happened on the roof. I turned it on when I saw Trish—when I thought it was her." Jess's voice fell momentarily as she remembered. "Later . . . I forgot to turn it off. There's supposed to be two hours' worth of tape. It should have recorded everything."

The craggy-faced detective turned the small tape over in his hand. His partner came to look over his shoulder. "Where did you get something like this?" he asked.

Jess answered simply, "We did a show."

Scowling, the detective thrust the tape at his partner. "See if you can find something to play this on."

The younger man left the room, but the door hadn't closed behind him before a uniformed officer stuck his head inside. "Detective? Could you step outside for a minute?"

The older man gave them a wary look, then left them alone.

Dan pushed a hand through his hair. "Jesus, they think we killed him. The man stalks you for years, holds you hostage on top of a building, and we get treated to the third degree. Is this some great country or what?"

Jess said quietly, "He was reaching for me. He thought I was going to fall and . . . even then, he was trying to protect me."

Dan got to his feet, his eyes dark and his face tight. "Oh, no. No, you're not doing that. You're not

making him the victim here. He was a killer. He
enjoyed killing, and what he used as an excuse
doesn't matter."

Jess rubbed her throat in an absent, soothing gesture. He had never held her hard enough to hurt,
but the ghost of the pressure of his arm against her
throat still lingered, no matter how hard she tried
to push it away. "He was . . . disturbed," she said.
"Tormented. All these years, so many people dead
. . . and I never knew any of it."

Dan was silent. There was no response, and they
both knew that. The knowledge of Candler's crimes
for her sake was something she would have to live
with and learn to come to terms with in her own
way.

Then she looked at him. Her eyes were wounded
and anxious, pleading for something even she didn't
understand. "But he never hurt me. I tried to shoot
him; I would have killed him if I could have, but
he never did anything to me. He was trying to *protect* me."

A moment's indecision was poised in Dan's eyes,
then his face hardened. "No, Jess. That's what he
told himself he was doing, but he had another
agenda. God, haven't you interviewed enough of
these psychos by now to see through them? They
play by their own rules, and their rules are the only
things that matter—and the worst part is they've got
people like us convincing the rest of the world to
feel sorry for them!"

He took a step toward her. "Jess, listen to me.
Candler was toying with you. He was the cat and
you were the mouse with the broken leg, and he
was enjoying every minute of it. But torturing you

wasn't enough—he was setting you up to take the fall for Glanbury and Styles and Nurse Richman, too, all those people he had to kill because they got in the way of the game he was playing with you. He . . ."

And there Dan paused and thrust his hand through his hair again. He looked haggard and worn, and as broken as Jess felt inside. Dan met her eyes, and he said, "Jesus, Jess, he even had me believing it for a while, that you were crazy, that you had killed those people and that it was you, stalking yourself."

Her eyes widened, but she said nothing.

He went on, "I know it's no excuse, but Christ, I was an easy mark. We see crazier things every week, we learn to believe anything . . ." And he took a breath. "I even—Jess, I was afraid you'd hurt yourself, so this morning I even took the bullets out of your gun."

She stared at him. "But—"

He gave an impatient shake of his head. "I couldn't do it. I put them back. At the last minute I just couldn't leave you vulnerable, I couldn't be responsible . . . So anyway," he finished tiredly, "before you blame yourself for any of this, think about this. If I had followed through with my original plan, your gun would have been empty, and maybe we'd both be dead now. But I lost my nerve, and a killer is dead. Should I be sorry? Are we supposed to think any of it makes sense?"

Jess whispered, "I don't know."

And for the longest time they simply looked at one another, the width of the room between them, but more than that separating them.

The door opened, and they turned. A man they had not met before, dressed in a suit and tie like the other detectives, came inside. His expression was grave. "Mr. Webber, Ms. Cray, I'm Captain Roger Lamb of Major Crimes. I wanted to let you know we took your tape to headquarters and are playing it back now. We expect it to confirm everything you've told us. We'll want you to come down to the station in a day or two to sign your statements, but for now you're free to go."

Dan looked wary. "A minute ago we were practically under arrest," he said. "What's going on?"

For a moment it appeared the captain wouldn't answer. Then he said, "We searched Candler's apartment. We found certain evidence that links him to the shootings associated with Ms. Cray's case, as well as indications of a . . . criminal involvement in other cases, including the Silk Scarf killings."

"The gun," Dan said. "He must have had a personal weapon—a .38—aside from his service revolver. You found it."

The captain looked at him for another moment before answering. "Among other things, yes."

Jess released a shaky breath.

The captain glanced toward the door. "It's a circus out there. I believe your producer has arranged a press conference. We'd prefer she didn't do that, of course, but she has agreed to coordinate her press release with our department. In the meantime, though, we can't stop you from answering questions. We would appreciate your discretion until we have more details."

Jess said, "I hope you're not asking us to cover anything up."

The captain's gaze was steady. "No. We're asking that, as much as possible, you not sensationalize. Of course, I realize that, in your business, that will be difficult."

"Yes," Dan said. "It will."

The babble of excitement from the lobby outside flooded the room briefly as he opened the door, then grew muffled again when he closed it behind him. Dan and Jess simply stood there for a time.

"He kept asking me what I was ashamed of," Jess said quietly. "Now I know."

"Jess, don't."

"You don't understand." She looked up at him. "The worst part is—I still don't remember him. Even after all this, I don't remember him."

Dan met her gaze in gentle sympathy, but there was nothing he could say. It would take time, for both of them.

"Nothing will ever be the same," she said.

"No," he agreed quietly. "But then—I don't think I'd want it to be."

He came over to her, standing close but not touching her. His eyes were tired and quiet and years older than they had been yesterday . . . as old as Jess felt inside.

He said, "I need to ask you something, Jess. This morning—you said you didn't regret what had happened between us. But now . . . so much has happened. Changed. Do you regret it now?"

Jess looked at him intently for a moment, searching his eyes. She said, "It's true. Everything's different. And emotional decisions should never be made under this kind of stress."

Dan dropped his gaze.

Jess reached for his hand. "I can't make any promises, Dan," she said softly. "I won't be able to for a long time. But for right now, for just this moment . . . Finding you, and loving you, is the one thing in the world I don't regret."

Her fingers closed around his, and she felt his answering response. They leaned against one another quietly for a few moments, taking strength in one another. But the world outside clamored, and could not be denied.

Together they went out to meet the crowd.